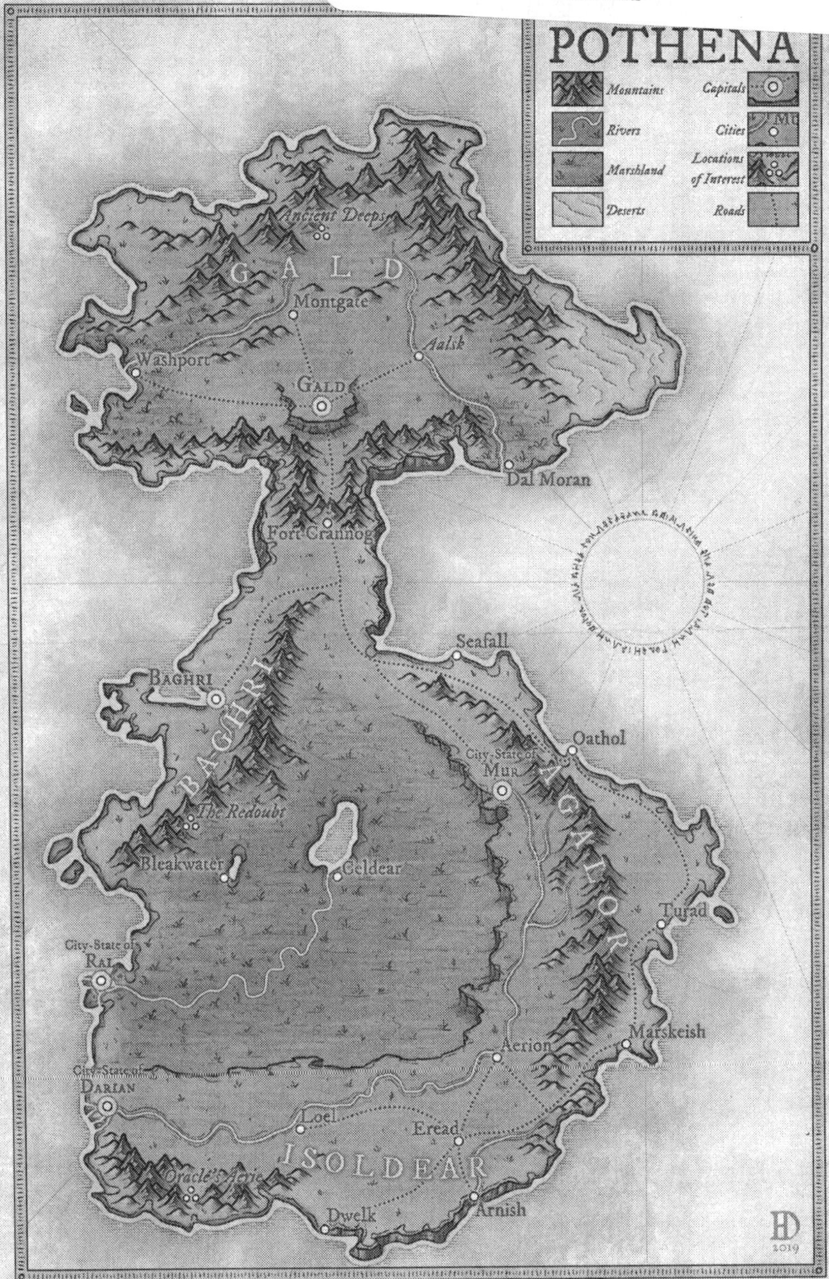

POTHENA

Mountains · Capitals
Rivers · Cities
Marshland · Locations of Interest
Deserts · Roads

Ancient Deeps

G A L D

Montgate

Aalsh

Washport

GALD

Dal Moran

Fort Grannog

Seafall

BAGHRI

Oathol

City-State of
MUR

The Redoubt

Celdear

GATOR

Bleakwater

Turad

City-State of
RAL

Marskeish

Aerion

City-State of
DARIAN

Loel

5 SOLDEAR

Ered

Oracle's Aerie

Dwelk

Arnish

HD
1019

QAPIRA AWAKENING

Dragon Ally

Dragon Revival

Dragon Peril

Ava Richardson is a pen name created by Relay Publishing for co-authored Fantasy projects. Relay Publishing works with incredible teams of writers and editors to collaboratively create the very best stories for our readers.

Cover Design by Joemel Requeza

www.relaypub.com

AVA RICHARDSON

DRAGON REVIVAL

QAPIRA AWAKENING BOOK TWO
DRACWYN PART: III

BLURB

Del will protect his new friends at any cost…

Street rat Del used to only rely on himself, but since being stranded on a desert island with Lathan, Etenia, and a pair of newly hatched dragons, he's learned about the importance of friendship. Which is why he'll do anything to prevent them from being hurt, even if it means leaving his homeland Pothena vulnerable to a threat that lurks deep off the coast; something even deadlier than a kraken.

Etenia insists that Pothena needs the warning, and they are the only ones who can deliver it. Without dragons, Pothena has no defenses against this deadly new foe. But the days of dragon-riding in the kingdom are long gone. To stand a chance, they'll need to somehow revive the dragon-riding academy that has lain dormant for two and a half centuries.

Del will need to find the balance between protecting his friends and defending Pothena as the danger around them grows. The Qapirans have only begun to wake, and if they aren't stopped they will rain down havoc on Pothena and beyond.

MAILING LIST

Thank you for purchasing 'Dragon Revival'
(Qapira Awakening Book Two)

If you would like to hear more about what I am up to, or continue to follow the stories set in this world with these characters—then please take a look at:

AvaRichardsonBooks.com

You can also find me on me on
www.facebook.com/AvaRichardsonBooks

Or sign up to my mailing list:
AvaRichardsonBooks.com/mailing-list

CONTENTS

CHAPTER 1

F our, five, six wingbeats and then they glided on the wind, weightless in the endless blue realm of a cloudless sky. Del held tight around his dragon Searsha's neck with his knees and spread his arms wide, letting the wind whip past him—the roaring sound of freedom coming to an end.

It was cold up where they were, but Del didn't mind at all. His white shirt was sleeveless and torn half to shreds, and his trousers were threadbare and stopped at his knees, but the near-freezing temperatures were almost a relief after the weeks he'd been marooned on the tiny island he and Searsha had left behind. He'd spent more than enough time in the crippling heat, desperate for shade; up here, the sun made no difference. Just another amber disc in the sky, like Searsha's eyes, waiting to see what he'd do next.

Searsha was curious what he'd do next, though she was being uncharacteristically coy about it. Usually, she would be needling him about the emotions she could feel him trying to hide and drawing his secret worries out into the light. But as they finally closed the last few miles of their journey, she hadn't said a word to him at all. Like she could feel his trepidation and knew better than to make it worse.

She was something to behold: a fiery red, armored scales glimmering in the sunlight like embers in a fire. She had grown in the days since they'd left the desert island; she could carry him with ease now, and her confidence in the air was palpable. She moved with purpose, tweaking her wings this way and that to keep the perfect speed, perfect altitude, perfect focus on her destination.

Their destination.

Del felt the pit of his stomach twist yet again—as it did regularly these days—as he stared off into the distance at the land mass approaching below.

He wanted to turn back. He didn't know how he'd rationalize it, or what the reaction would be, but he—

It is too late to turn back, said Searsha, sensing his thoughts with expert precision.

"I think I forgot something back in Jiffra," said Del.

That is odd, because you have no belongings to forget.

"Are you seriously picking on a homeless orphan?"

No, I am picking on a bad liar. You did not forget anything in Jiffra. You are looking for excuses to go back on your word.

Del stared ahead at the landmass. His stomach twisted some more.

"I shouldn't have agreed to this in the first place. It's a bad idea. It's going to go so wrong."

It will not.

"But it will. You don't understand. These people hate me. They see me coming, and they call for help. I'm a threat to them. I always have been.

A bad omen, sleeping in the street outside their windows. What do you think they'll say when I swoop in from the sky and land in their streets again?"

Oh my, what a majestic dragon?

Del laughed. "You're probably right. But if you're wrong...."

If I am wrong, they will still need you to save them from the war that is coming, Del. Do not forget that. The Kraken's masters will not rest until they have their dragon eggs, and when they find them, we will be the only hope Pothena has of survival. This is not a popularity contest. It is a matter of life and death.

She was right, as usual. They had battled the Kraken—the terrifying sea monster that seemed more myth than reality—on that wretched desert island, and won. Barely. The Kraken had outright destroyed the kingdom of Sivarna in search of dragon eggs to steal, and had fought a relentless war against Del and Searsha and their friends in a bid to claim its prize. But Del had learned—through a psychic link between himself and the Kraken—that there was more to the story than simply a sea demon hoping to devour some magical eggs. The Kraken was part of an army from an underwater civilization that was hellbent on stealing the eggs for themselves. They needed them, somehow. He wasn't sure why, but he could feel the desperation in their actions.

They wouldn't stop trying until they had what they wanted.

Which meant the battle had only just begun.

Searsha must have sensed his concern and wanted to distract him, because she tucked her wings in and dove down, passing beneath and then around Cember, the blue dragon, flapping his wings to stay steady and true on his way to their destination. Cember was a stubborn dragon, and prideful, which is why he had volunteered to carry two riders on the last, longer leg of their journey. From the prime position on his back, Etenia Browder, his bonded rider, held tight to his spine, eyes locked on their destination like it was all that mattered.

Her clothes were shredded like Del's, the orange fabric looking like a peasant's hand-me-downs instead of the majestic outfit she'd started off with. She'd braided her hair before leaving Jiffra, Del noticed, probably in an attempt to hide how ragged she looked after so many weeks on that island. It worked, too: she seemed like a wealthy merchant's daughter who was role-playing poverty for the afternoon. The closer she got to home, the more noble she appeared. It made Del even more uneasy, just seeing it.

Behind her was Lathan Phrac, an older gentleman with gray hair and the remnants of a sleek black uniform. Lathan was a dragon trainer from Sivarna, and he was the keeper of the eggs the Kraken had hunted, and had helped—albeit grudgingly, at first—Del and Etenia learn to properly bond with their dragons. His home was in ruins, and his future entirely dependent on a pair of seventeen-year-old dragon rider novices...but for some strange reason, he seemed to be getting more calm the longer they spent together. Like he could sense how this adventure would end, and it somehow didn't worry him at all. Del wished he had that level of confidence. Any confidence at all, really.

Etenia noticed Del and Searsha and broke her stare at the distant lands ahead. "So? How does it look from up there?" she called to them.

"How does what look?" Del replied, before realizing she meant Pothena, their destination. "Oh, it's...you know. Land."

"I've never seen it from the air before," she said, her smile widening at the thought of it. "I suppose no one has seen it from the air in generations!"

She had a point: while Sivarna had a vibrant dragon riding culture going back centuries, Pothena had absolutely none. Even magic was basically absent from their society, so there was really no way for any

Pothenian to have seen what they were seeing since...whenever it was the last Pothenian dragon rider lived.

Etenia's smile faded when she noticed Del's expression. Cember, sensing her need, inched closer to Searsha. "Are you alright, Del?" asked Etenia.

He tried to shrug it off, but he knew he was doing a bad job of it. "Yeah, everything's fine. Why wouldn't it be?"

"Because you swore you'd never go back to Pothena again, and now you are?" suggested Etenia. "But don't worry, Del. Things will be different this time."

"Because I'm on a dragon?" he asked.

Majestic dragon, corrected Searsha.

"No," said Etenia. "Because you're with me, and Browders protect their own."

It was hard for Del to express how that didn't make him feel any better at all. Etenia came from the upper crust of Pothenian society, where statements of loyalty and kinship were like true currency beneath their power. He had no doubt the Browder family would stand firm against anyone who dared insult them. The only trick was: Del wasn't really one of them. He was the kind of person the Browders stood firm against. And as much as Etenia believed the words she was saying, Del had a very strong suspicion he would be shunned the second he landed.

He wanted to believe Etenia wouldn't abandon him too, but a lifetime of betrayal suggested he was in for a very bad day indeed. His stomach twisted even more, just thinking about it. His heart, too.

Etenia was waiting for him to say something back, he realized, so he gave her a shrug and said: "Let's hope you're right."

It was the closest he could come to optimism.

5

"Was it cold up there?" called Lathan, squinting across the way. "The eggs look frosty."

Del had forgotten about the eggs. They were bundled up in a net and tied around one of Searsha's hind legs for safekeeping. It was impossible for Del to see them from where he was, but he was fairly certain they weren't really coated with frost. Lathan was just very protective of the eggs, and prone to a little bit of paranoia along the way.

"Don't worry," said Del. "Pretty soon they'll be baking in the sun."

"Very soon," said Etenia, and Del looked forward again and saw Pothena coming up fast.

Etenia had been right: it was amazing, seeing it from this vantage. Del saw the harbor first, spread out in a giant crescent and packed with a huge array of ships that, from this distance, just looked like beads of color mashed all together. They came from all around the world for a chance to do business in Pothena, buying and selling whatever exotic treasures their homelands could produce to an eager populace. Pothena wasn't just a major commercial hub; it was the commercial hub, where everything of value changed hands before finding its rightful home. It was a city that valued value—and ruthlessly dismissed all else.

That harbor, like a rainbow mosaic, was where Del had gone his last day there, to escape. And here it was again, welcoming him back.

His stomach twisted even more.

Up from the harbor was a long slope that led straight into the heart of the city. He could see little patches of red—the market tents along the sides of the boulevard. From here, they seemed almost beautiful, and dazzling to behold. Up close, they were a place where angry shopkeepers beat anyone who didn't smell of money, and weaker children died in the streets.

6

The sandstone buildings that towered above the market, where Etenia and her kin lived, were casting an ominous shadow on the rest of the town. They'd always felt dominating and scary, but seeing them from here, like this? It made so many of Del's childhood fears—of faceless men with brutal minds, lurking just out of view—make so much more sense.

Childhood fears. Adult traumas.

"Where should we land?" Etenia asked.

He drew in a sharp breath and scanned the horizon, then pointed a bit to the west of Pothena's main harbor. "How about there?" he asked. "We can land there."

Etenia followed his gaze and frowned. "Seafall? Oh! Good idea!"

The issue with being an impoverished orphan in Pothena was that there were a lot of places you simply couldn't go: the functional area of the city was the market and its surrounding homes, and the harbor itself—the original settlement, surrounded by ancient walls. Originally, the walls were meant to keep invaders out, but over time they'd taken on a new function: to keep the lower-class citizens out of the merchant villas built all around the outside of them. Del was a nimble thief and quick on his feet, but he'd never come close to getting past the heavily guarded gates at the north, east, and west of the market quarter. And certainly not the one leading to Seafall.

When he'd suggested landing there, he hadn't really known where he was pointing, except that it seemed less populated, and therefore with fewer obstacles to overcome. But the second she said "Seafall," he knew he'd made a mistake: this was the suburb for Pothena, where only the richest of the rich merchants lived. Built on a natural bay, it had once been an important shipping hub in its own right. That is, until its citizens got so wealthy they reserved the port for their yachts, tore down most of the housing for their mansions, and evicted all the poorer folk back inside the walls. Nestled between beautiful beaches on the one side, and an imposing mountain on the other, it seemed like a little slice of heaven—if you were rich.

Del had somehow made his worst nightmare even worse.

"They'll be so excited to see us," said Etenia, her smile so wide it was almost infectious. Almost.

Cember, possibly sensing Etenia's excitement, flew suddenly faster, closing the distance as quickly as possible. Searsha paused for a moment, though, before following suit.

You will be fine, she said. *Everything will be fine.*

"I really hope you're right," Del sighed, and held tight as she sped up, straight into the heart of his worst nightmare.

CHAPTER 2

A t first, it looked like they were headed for rocky shores. It reminded Del of the island again, with the dark and dangerous formations that had shielded the Kraken from them for a time. But the closer they got, the clearer the picture became: these rocks were moving, and filling up the beaches all along the Seafall bay. They were people, by the hundreds.

Ahead of them, Cember turned off to the left, wings spread wide as he made a gentle arc in toward the town. At first Del thought it was a question of being cautious and checking for danger—but then he saw Etenia waving at the people below, and he realized she and Cember were just assuming everything was good and fine and safe. It made Del even more uneasy. Searsha beat her wings a little faster to catch up, probably in an attempt to ease his worries. But all that accomplished was to make his inevitable collision with Pothena come up even faster.

Searsha followed Cember's arc, swooping along the beaches, tipped just enough sideways that Del could see down clearly at the people assembled there. They were screaming at him, yelling things he couldn't make out, but just the volume of it and the way they were bunched so close together created a panic inside him he couldn't handle anymore. He squeezed with his heels, trying to guide Searsha away.

"We have to get out of here," he said.

Why? she asked, though she did as he requested and tightened her turn to head back out to sea.

"They're angry," he said, as the sounds faded.

They are cheering, she said. *Can you not hear it?*

"Cheering?" he asked, looking back toward the crowds. "For Etenia?"

For all of us, she said. *Come, listen.*

Del was about to argue when Searsha did a twist and a loop backward, back toward the shore. It was a fancy trick she'd been working on since they first left the island, and she was getting very good at it—and Del was getting good at not losing his grip, too. The second it was complete, though, something odd happened: the people below cheered even louder, their voices rising into a deafening roar all around him.

They were happy to see them.

For now, anyway.

Cember's circles grew tighter and tighter as he zeroed in on a spot to land, and the crowds cleared a spot big enough for both dragons. Etenia glanced over her shoulder and caught sight of Del for just an instant, and then Cember looped back to pace Searsha again.

"It'll be all right, Del," Etenia said to him, over the sounds of the cheering.

"Easy for you to say," said Del. "Those are your people down there."

Her face changed from happiness to solemnity in a heartbeat. "We'll only stay a few minutes," she said. "We'll say hello, and then head straight for the council chambers."

Del winced involuntarily. "You really think the council is going to listen to us? That they'll take us seriously?"

"How can they not?" she asked with a wink. "We're on dragons."

And with that, Cember made his last turn down, straight toward the clearing on the beach, where he made a gentle landing, with perfect form.

Are you ready? Searsha asked Del.

"Not at all," he sighed. "But let's do it anyway."

She tucked her wings in tight, then dove down toward the crowd, corkscrewing as she approached. The people on the beach scrambled back, screaming, because to anyone watching (and Del, too) it seemed like she was about to crash headlong into them.

But then, at the last moment, she spread her wings wide to brake her descent, and with an impressive twist of her body, landed softly on the sand next to Cember, finally settling down on all fours with her head held high.

For a second, no one made a sound.

Then the crowd erupted in cheers.

Majestic, said Searsha, pleased with herself.

Del had imagined that, when confronted with a massive and almost mythical beast like a dragon, the people of Pothena would be scared a little, keep their distance, watch with a wary eye the way they did when he strolled through the market. But the second they saw the two dragons had settled, the crowd began to shift. The nicer-dressed men dragged their wives and children closer, reaching out greedy hands to touch, to pet, to claim the historic moment they were at the forefront to see. Meanwhile, Del noticed, the poorer Pothenians held back, watching with curiosity and intrigue, but knowing not to crowd their betters. Things were quickly getting out of hand as it was, with people pushing and shoving each other to get closer. Cember flinched at first, but settled into a reluctant kind of acceptance. Searsha, meanwhile, openly preened at the attention, looking as imposing as she could. She was enjoying the attention, Del could tell—even without their bond telling him so.

Lathan lowered himself off Cember's back and hurried to the net holding the eggs, shielding them from the curious onlookers who were quickly getting too close. One woman, wearing a dress more expensive than all the things Del had ever stolen in his life, reached to touch one of the eggs that was peeking through the rope and Lathan flinched away, trying to keep her fingers at a distance. The woman snorted angrily at him.

"Do you know who I am?" she sneered, stepping closer to pin Lathan against Searsha's side, so there would be nowhere to run. Lathan didn't look intimidated, exactly, but he was clearly more concerned with the status of the dragon eggs than anything else, and was not prepared to fight a battle on two fronts at once.

The woman reached a hand out to touch the eggs again, and Del had had enough. He slid off Searsha's back and landed right next to Lathan.

"No touching," he warned her.

The woman, a highborn lady of Pothenian society, was not used to being told no. More than that, she wasn't used to being told no by someone who looked like the beggars she tried not to see out her window. And she certainly wasn't used to being touched by one of them. Her eyes widened at the sight of Del, and when he grabbed the woman by the wrist and pushed her hand away, it was a wonder they didn't pop right out.

"How dare you touch me!" she sneered, pulling free and getting a look on her face that Del knew all too well: the look of a merchant about to call down fury upon his head. His heart started racing involuntarily, his eyes darting for exit routes, for some way of escaping. He'd killed the Kraken, but this woman was somehow scaring him just as much. "I'll have your head for this," she said. It was happening, Del thought. Exactly how he'd known it would. He was still just as much—nay, more—an outcast than ever before.

Before Del could react, Searsha turned her head around and bared her teeth at the woman with a low and booming growl from deep inside. *Try it,* she said.

The woman blanched at the face-off and stumbled back, pushing her way into the crowd, whimpering loudly about respect and decorum and the insolence of the underclass. Searsha gave Del a wink, and he did his best not to laugh—maybe she was right. Maybe the difference between his old life and this new one would come down to having a towering red ally on his side.

He checked on Lathan, who was still searching through the bundle of eggs, checking for cracks and dents and other damage. "Everything all right?" Del asked him.

Lathan nodded, too distracted to look away. "A little scuffed here and there, but they're fine, I think. Though I would really like to get them into a proper crate as soon as possible. The temperature variances they've endured these last weeks can't have been good for the dragons."

Del had no idea if temperature variances really mattered to the eggs, but he was fairly certain they'd suffered harsher conditions in the Kraken's care than being carried by Searsha. Still, any excuse to get off this beach to someplace more isolated was a welcome idea. He turned back to Etenia, who was still perched atop Cember, and cupped a hand to his mouth to call—

"Etenia!" came a voice from the crowd, and she flinched at the sound of it. She and Del both searched for the source, though with her better vantage she spotted it far more easily. Her face ran through a bundle of emotions in a single heartbeat, from joy to worry to fear to hopefulness, and then straight back to worry again. Intense, overpowering worry.

Del didn't need to see who it was to know what was coming. It was Arretal Browder, her father. The one who'd treated her like an unwanted consolation prize her whole life. Every time she'd worked hard for something, he'd given it to some stranger—some man—who had neither the talent nor vision to pull off what she'd imagined. The whole reason she'd been on the ship the Kraken had attacked was because she was trying to prove to her father that she was worthy of his trust and respect. And then that ship had gone down, along with all its cargo...and now she was wondering, Del knew, whether her father would scold her for failing, or just wish she had had the guts to go down with the ship.

She glanced down at Del, and he could see the same fear in her eyes that he'd felt on their approach. The trick was: there was nothing Cember could do to fix her situation like Searsha had his.

She took a bracing breath and then dismounted, landing on the ground near Del. She squeezed her hands together tightly, like she was trying to summon courage she wasn't sure she had. The crowd ahead of her started to move as her father approached; even the highborn knew who their superior was, and knew how to treat him with respect.

When the last of them finally parted and Del saw the famous Arretal Browder, he had a hard time not sharing Etenia's worry. He was a formidable man: tall, broad-shouldered and muscular, with a hint of gray in his hair, and in the well-kept beard that graced his strong jaw. His eyes were a stunning color, like a harbor filled with fog. And they were locked on Etenia, wide open, trying to process what he was going to do next.

Del turned himself, subtly, ready to stand between the two of them. He wouldn't be able to stop him from hurting her, but he could make sure he didn't lay a finger on her.

"Etenia..." said Arretal, looking her up and down—at her tattered state —as his jaw tensed.

"Father," she said, with a flawless curtsy. She kept her head bowed, possibly out of respect, and possibly to avoid his gaze any longer.

"The ship..." he said, voice nearly a whisper. "They said the ship went down, and—"

"I apologize, Father," she said. "It was my responsibility and I—"

He strode forward so fast Del didn't have a chance to react before Arretal wrapped his arms around Etenia and held her tight. "I thought you were dead. I thought I'd lost you. I..."

She was so stunned, it took her a moment to return the embrace. Del could see, on her face, just how surprised she was by this show of affection. "I'm sorry for scaring you," she said.

He laughed, kissing her forehead and then hugging her again. "Don't be silly, girl. You've nothing to apologize for. I just thank the gods you've come back to me in one piece." A thought came to him. "Where have you been all this time?"

"We were shipwrecked," she said. "A secluded island, not far from Jiffra."

"Jiffra!" exclaimed Arretal. "We were searching in the wrong place after all."

"You...you were searching?"

He held her by the shoulders, looking straight into her eyes; his own were tearing up. "Of course I was searching. I would search to the ends of the earth to get you back. To the ends of the earth. And I—" He frowned. "You were shipwrecked. You said 'we were shipwrecked.' Who is 'we'?"

It was the moment Del had most dreaded: the one where Etenia would have to see how, despite her own open-mindedness, the rest of her merchant kin would never accept someone like him in their world. The moment where Arretal Browder gave him a reluctant nod, tossed him a coin, and sent him on his way. He held his breath, ready for the blow to land—

But Arretal Browder hugged him instead. "I will forever be in your debt, sir," he said, voice trembling with emotion. "Thank you for saving my daughter."

"She mostly saved herself," said Del, flashing Etenia a grin. "She's a tough one."

"That she is," said Arretal, taking a step back. "She very much is. And I imagine you both have tales to tell about your adventures, so why don't we—" His face changed as he saw Lathan step out from behind Del, carrying the bundle of dragon eggs with great difficulty. The second he saw the shredded uniform, his mouth dropped open. "So it's true. Sivarna has fallen."

Lathan winced at the words, but nodded. "I beg your mercy, Mr. Browder, on behalf of the—"

"No, come now," said Arretal, stepping forward to help Lathan with his load—but Lathan instinctively pulled away to keep them safe. It took a moment for Arretal's face to register understanding...and then he gave Etenia a stern nod. "We'd best retire to the villa."

The Browder estate was even more luxurious than Del had imagined— and he'd imagined quite a lot of luxury in all his years on the street outside. The sandstone walls that had seemed so ominous to him from the outside were adorned with intricate mosaics mimicking beautiful oases and incredible vistas straight out of the ancient myths. The grounds themselves were made up of lush gardens and winding stone paths; towering fountains and little wading pools where exotic fish meandered about.

The main house was made of imported white marble with gold leaf etchings up and down the walls. Del couldn't read any of the writing—though at least he knew now that he couldn't read for a reason other than illiteracy, thanks to Etenia's teaching—but just the sight of it was impressive to behold.

The main dining area opened out onto a courtyard near one of the foun-tains, where Cember was drinking his fill with a bemused look on his face. The two dragons fit comfortably there, taking a well-earned rest after far too long in the air. Searsha stayed closer to the humans, like she was eavesdropping on their conversation rather than lending Del the courage he needed to stay put a little longer.

Etenia seemed out of sorts, Del noticed. It was like her years of living in luxury had somehow dissolved away in those weeks on the island, leaving a version of herself that was off-balance and wary in the place she called home. Del could understand why: every story she'd ever told about her father had had the same general theme: he distrusted her, he overlooked her, and he thought she'd never measure up. And with that hug—in public no less!—he had turned her entire world upside-down. Del could tell she was struggling to make sense of it, still.

The servants came back out with another round of food and wine, circling the Browders and their guests with expert coordination. Del felt incredibly uneasy, having someone else bring him things and ask if he wanted anything else. These were the same kinds of people who had spat on him in the market and called for his arrest. In fact, Del knew one of the servants well: a bald-headed man with a big bulbous nose and angry little eyes. He'd beaten Del with a stick more than a few times, for no reason at all—which was saying something, because Del very regularly deserved at least some of the abuse he took.

The bulbous-nosed man, whose name was Makom, it turned out, was doing his best not to look Del in the eye, or acknowledge their long-standing enmity. It made being here in the Browder's estate, being treated as an equal even more awkward than it already was.

"I still can't believe it," said Arretal, leaning back into his well-cushioned seat. "All our friends—the Braitmans especially—will be so relieved you're back. The Braitmans even sent out a ship to look for you the moment they heard. Speaking of which, we should send for them at once and—"

"Maybe not quite yet," said Etenia, like she was afraid of saying the wrong thing. "I mean…it's been quite a long day for us."

Arretal took a moment before he seemed to understand what she meant. "Ah, yes," he said. "I imagine that would be a difficult journey. On dragons! Dragons! I still can't believe it. You're a dragon rider now. My daughter, a dragon rider."

"It came as a shock to me too." Etenia smiled, but if she was trying her best to seem at ease, she was failing horribly. She made eye contact with Del, like she wanted his opinion on the whole dynamic. He shrugged slightly, which did nothing for her at all. "Lathan has been teaching us, but as you can imagine, it's a lot to take in, and under difficult circumstances."

"Well, that difficulty is over now," said Arretal. "Now that you're back in Pothena, you shall want for nothing. You have my word. Your days of strife are over."

Del and Etenia exchanged nervous glances. "Actually, Father, I fear they're just beginning."

Arretal sat forward, a frown on his face. "How so? I thought you said you killed the Kraken. What else—"

"A lot else," said Del. "A whole army is coming. For them." He pointed at the dragon eggs Lathan had set out on a silk sheet in the shade.

"What army?" asked Arretal. "The same one that attacked Sivarna? Which kingdom are they from? Maybe I can find other ways to pressure them into peace, and—"

"You can't," said Del. "There's no bargaining with them, either. They're coming, and they'll keep coming until they get what they want."

"But coming from where?" insisted Arretal.

Del wasn't sure how to say it except to just come out and say it: "The bottom of the ocean. They have a huge city, easily twice the size of Pothena."

"Do they have a name?"

Del had hoped his nightmares or visions or whatever they were would die with the Kraken, but he had had more dreams of these enemies in the days since the Kraken had died. One particularly terrifying nightmare, in Jiffra, had given him a sound he hadn't quite understood, but just the sound of it in his mind haunted him. His voice croaked as he tried to speak it: "I think they call themselves the Epyr. The Army of Epyr."

Arretal's mind was working furiously, trying to make sense of it. "Hmm. Doesn't ring a bell. They might be aligned with Wystrom. Sounds like a Wystrom word, epyr."

"No, Father," said Etenia, delicately. "You don't understand. These aren't humans. They actually live at the bottom of the ocean."

The confusion was palpable. "Then how do you know anything about them? How do you know what they're called?"

"Because I dream of them," said Del, knowing exactly how absurd that sounded. "The Kraken opened a channel into my mind to speak to me, and that channel has stayed open, even after its death, so I...it's like I can eavesdrop on them. Against my will."

"Well, that's one advantage we'll have, at least," said Arretal, seeming to take all of these strange revelations in stride. "And you say they're after the dragon eggs?"

"Urgently," nodded Del. "They seem to need it to repair this...thing...at the core of their civilization."

"Another advantage," nodded Arretal. "They'll be desperate, and desperate people make mistakes."

There was something in the way Arretal was talking—his body language, maybe, or just the tone of his voice—that made Del incredibly uneasy. They were telling him fantastical stories about incredible creatures from the bottom of the sea, and none of it seemed to faze him at all. His only concern was to count off their strategic advantages? It made no sense.

Unless it was a scam, Del realized. That was the bedrock of a good con: take an impossible situation and spin it to your advantage. Arretal Browder would be working on a whole other level than Del was used to, but if he was right, Etenia was in for a crushing betrayal.

"Mistakes, yes," she said, nodding to herself. "Exactly what I was thinking." Her father looked at her with surprise and admiration, which suddenly took on a sinister tone, if this was all just part of a scheme, if Arretal was just putting on an act. "If we work fast enough and hard enough, we can ready Pothena for the invasion and deal the Epyr a blow so severe they won't dare come back again. Now, it will take coordination on many fronts, from clearing the harbor to staging defensive positions all throughout the city, but if we—"

"Etenia..." said Arretal, gently as he could. "I know you've figured this all out, but—"

Her face flushed red. "If you say you're going to give it to some boy to handle, I'll—"

"No," he said, taking her hands in his. "Not that. Never again. I know you can handle yourself. But the thing is: it's not just up to you. It's a matter to be put before the—"

"The council, yes," said Etenia. "And I'm ready. We're all ready to make our case."

"And I'm sure you'll do a fine job," said Arretal, his patience starting to fray. "But the thing is: the two elements you need most right now, as you say, are to work fast and hard. And neither of those qualities, I'm afraid, are to be found in our council. They move carefully, deliberately, and slowly, for even the simplest of ventures. For this? For mobilizing all of Pothena to fend off an attack from a—and no disrespect, Del, when I say this—but an invasion from sea-people? I'm afraid that will be a hard sell, at best."

A hard sell for the council, but not him? Del was even more convinced something was amiss. He just couldn't quite figure out what.

Etenia stood. Stood tall. Del watched her eyes narrow, and knew the look well: she was digging in her heels, ready for a fight. And she would not give up until she won. "Let me plead our case," she said. "I know I can make them see reason. There are too many Pothenian lives at stake for them to say no. Their first duty is to protect the lives of their citizens. They have to say yes."

Arretal watched her for a moment, then smiled in a way that felt shockingly foreign to Del: it was the look of someone proud of their kin. Win or lose, he was proud of his daughter. He nodded to her, returning her confidence in spades. "All right," he said. "I'll send messengers straightaway, call a meeting for this afternoon. Rest up 'til then."

He headed out, the servants rushing to follow him as he started barking orders that seemed at odds with the jovial, friendly host he'd been this whole time, and with the description Etenia had given of him, back on the island.

Del and Lathan joined Etenia, who was shaking a little, like she was finally getting a chance to relax after an extremely arduous task.

"Are you all right?" Lathan asked her, voice quiet.

"I think so," she said. "It's just so strange, being back. I think maybe I'm just nervous about presenting to the council."

"Don't be," said Del. "They're going to say no."

Etenia and Lathan both stared at him like he'd slapped them in the face. "Why would you say that?" said Etenia. "They haven't even—"

"You heard him," said Del, pointing after her father. "They find any excuse to not make decisions. They'll do it for this, for sure."

"But so many innocent lives will be lost!" she said.

Del stared at her for a moment before saying: "I'm not going to laugh at you for saying that, but just be aware that I really should. You think the council cares about innocent lives? Trust me, as a former innocent life myself, I can tell you with absolute certainty that they don't care about anyone but themselves at all. The only thing the council will do, once you warn them of the danger, is to get themselves into a safer location, so no one important gets hurt."

Etenia looked truly shocked by his words. "I forgot how cynical you can be."

"And I forgot how blind you can be," said Del. "But hey, I hope I'm wrong. I hope you can convince them, and everything turns out fine." He headed out to the fountain, where Cember was still drinking, and muttered to himself: "And when it doesn't, we'll come up with the real plan."

CHAPTER 3

They'd been told to rest up, but after what they'd been through—and what they still had to face—Del, Etenia and Lathan were in no mood for sitting around. If her father hadn't warned her the council would be more receptive to well-groomed applicants, Etenia wouldn't have even let herself be bathed. She had been hurried away in the care of her servants, while Del and Lathan had both been shown to their own rooms, and Del had found a tub full of warm water—and an attendant —waiting for him.

Del had never had a bath before. Not formally, anyway. He'd jumped into more than a few fountains and private pools over the years, but never to clean himself, and never for very long. He was vaguely aware there would be soap involved, and scrubbing, but he wasn't sure how to make it happen. Worse yet, it seemed the Browders had their servants do the scrubbing for them, which was simply out of the question. He shooed the servant out of the room and locked the door, then stared down at the bath like it was as terrifying as the Kraken itself, and ready to devour him whole.

He didn't have much in the way of clothing to begin with, and after the beating it took on the island, it wasn't exactly "clothing" at all—but when he pulled off his shirt and set it on the bed and saw it clearly against the vibrant patterns of the luxurious sheets…

He felt so alien. So alone.

He set out his trousers, arranging them neatly as if to make a point, and then turned to the bath. The water was scented, faintly, and just warm enough to be pleasant. Del settled at the bottom of the marble tub and rested his arms at the sides, leaning back like he was on a very unorthodox throne. His heart kept racing, though, like he was still under threat. He didn't know how to fix that, or if it would ever stop. He felt like he had snuck into a rich person's home and was pushing his luck, taking a moment to relax. That was usually when something horrible happened and he ended up dragged away in shackles.

He closed his eyes, tried to calm himself. It was like casting a spell, the way Lathan had taught him: clear your mind of everything but the thing you most wanted to see, and let the world fade away. He took long, even breaths, and felt his heart race slow, slow, slow, and he—

He was there again, in the courtyard beneath the waves, as the massive Epyrian army hurried about, checking spears and shields and all manner of weaponry. And there, shouting orders in words Del couldn't quite make out, was a commander of some kind; tall and lithe with black hair and grayish skin, he was clad all in shining golden armor like a prince. He finished calling to his troops, glancing over his shoulder toward Del—and then did a double take. He raced over, putting his hands on either side of Del's face, and spoke urgently, determinedly, to whoever's eyes it was Del was seeing through. He felt himself say something in return, and the prince's eyes opened wide: "Pothena."

Del tried to scream, but his lungs were full of water. He flailed madly until he caught the edges of the marble tub and pulled himself out into the air again, coughing up the scented water and gasping to catch his breath.

What is it? asked Searsha, from afar, sensing his panic. *What is wrong?*

Del's eyes looked out the window, out toward the harbor below and the massive blue ocean spread out beyond, and felt a wave of dread crash over him.

"They know we're here."

It took Del five tries before he finally found Etenia's room. He didn't knock, just threw the door open far enough to see if she was inside, and then stormed right in. Her servants were midway through putting on her dress and gasped in horror at the stranger in their midst—especially a man, soaking wet and shirtless, heading straight for their mistress. They formed a protective shield around her, warning Del off with their glares.

"If you recall the book we read, back on the island," Etenia said, checking her hair in the mirror, "it had an entire chapter on the proper etiquette for entering a room without..." Her voice trailed off as she turned and saw the expression on Del's face.

She waved the servants away. "That will be all."

"They're back," said Del, pacing back and forth. "I was afraid this would happen, and I was right. The connection still goes both ways."

"The Epyr?" Etenia asked. "They know we're here?"

"They know we're here," nodded Del. "And the army they've assembled...they'll run straight over Pothena without blinking. There's no way we can—"

"Del," said Etenia, catching him by the arm and holding him still. He paused his fretting long enough to look into her eyes and see the confidence there. She was different than she'd been on the island—or on the ship, for that matter. Her hair was brushed and styled to perfection, the makeup around her eyes applied with skill, her clothes the most elegant thing he had ever seen. She seemed very much like the daughter of the most powerful man in Pothena. He felt intensely uncomfortable being in her presence.

"Del," she repeated, making sure he saw her. "We can do this."

"You don't know that," he said. "You didn't see what I—"

"Del," she said, with a slight smirk on her face, and in a flash she was the same Etenia from the island again, beneath all that artifice. "We fought the Kraken and won. We can handle anything."

He felt a little better, but not by much. "You remember how it almost killed us, right? Multiple times?"

"Yes, but that was when it was just the five of us, half-starved on a hostile island. Cember and Searsha didn't know how to breathe fire, or to fly, and we barely knew any magic at all. This time we have all of Pothena on our side."

"And they have a massive army on theirs. Are you really so sure Pothena's up to the challenge?"

She put a hand on his shoulder and nodded solemnly. "I do. So long as you're here with me, I know we can overcome anything."

His heart stopped racing, and his urge to run subsided. He looked into her eyes—the eyes from the island, dressed up like a Browder—and drew on the confidence she was projecting. This was how she'd gotten control of a ship and earned Captain Qallo's respect: by being the person the moment required, no matter how daunting. It had been annoying to him at first, but now...now it was the only thing keeping him from hopping on Searsha and running for cover.

"I should put some clothes on," he said, suddenly realizing he'd only put on his trousers, after tumbling out of the bath. "And, uh, sorry for barging in."

He made his way back to his room, passing Etenia's scandalized servants on the way, and closed the door behind him. He had an outfit laid out on the bed for him. It hadn't been there before, he was sure. Someone had laid it out for him while he was gone, and then disappeared without a trace. It only contributed to his unease.

The clothes were just as fine as Etenia's, but decidedly more reserved, like they were trying to ensure he didn't outshine her. If anything, he'd have liked it to be more reserved, so he could disappear a little. By the time he got the gold-laced burgundy vest on, he felt well and truly absurd.

When he stepped out of his room, Lathan was standing there in a fine replica of his old Sivarnan robes, with a wheeled crate behind him that must have held the dragon eggs. He'd never let them out of his sight again, Del realized. In a place like Pothena, that would be harder than he expected.

"You look well," said Lathan, nodding to Del's new clothes.

"I feel like a jester," grumbled Del.

"Richest jester I've ever seen. Now stand taller, please. A skulking prince makes men nervous."

Del realized he had reverted to his old self, who had been most comfortable hiding in shadows, trying not to be seen. Lathan's observation was exactly right: poor people could do that all they wanted, because no one really paid them any mind; rich people skulking, though? That was a sign they were up to no good.

"Where'd they get the Sivarnan clothes?" Del asked him, noticing the fine stitching up the sleeves.

"Mr. Browder had them made for me when we arrived," said Lathan.

"From scratch?" Del gasped.

Lathan nodded. "It seems nothing is beyond him, if he wills it so." His face lit up as he saw Etenia coming down the hall, the rest of her outfit now in place. She had a translucent orange veil over her face and wore a tiara covered in jewels. She looked magnificent, and regal. And, upon seeing Del and Lathan, just the tiniest bit nervous.

"My dear," said Lathan, taking her hands in his. "You look stunning."

"How about competent?" she asked. "Because what we need are votes, not compliments."

"Stunning and competent," said Lathan. "Don't you agree, Del?"

Del's eyes met hers, and he gave her the same confident nod she'd given him, earlier letter her know that she will do great. She smiled, faintly.

"I want a tiara too," he joked, trying to break the tension a little.

"You'd just pawn it," she laughed.

He shrugged. "Can't deny it. But I'd look fabulous in the meantime. Here, let me try on yours..." He reached for it, and she slapped his hand away, laughing even more.

The joking continued out into the courtyard, and then through the gates to the Browder estate, and out into the streets of Seafall. They had to leave the dragons behind—they would cause a crippling commotion wherever they went—so they were able to take the narrower side streets and laneways through the gilded utopia of Etenia's hometown.

Every wall, every gate, every window or vine was carefully sculpted by the finest minds in the kingdom, so that no matter where you looked, you were dazzled by the beauty of the place. Del read the name plaques at the front of some of the estates: people he knew from his past—all nemeses—and some he had mistaken for long-gone kings from the days of old. Apparently some of the richest members of Pothenian society were so rich they never had to venture outside Seafall at all.

Etenia's nervousness burned away the more time she spent on the perfectly landscaped streets. She pointed out landmarks to them, like the spot where the fifth king of Pothena had declared all men free; or the ancient wall that had been cracked by a falling meteor and helped crack the code of physics; or the spot where Briggs Browder—Etenia's ancestor—had plotted the first trade routes across the treacherous seas.

"He designed his ships to outrun storms," she said, face alight with pride. "So we would reach places no one else could. Velos, Wystrom, Jiffra..."

"Too bad they didn't have dragons back then," said Del. "They could've just flown there."

"They did have dragons," said Lathan, and Del and Etenia turned to see his face wracked with consternation. "Pothena was a great dragon society in those days. Even more so than Sivarna is now."

"Really?" asked Etenia. "I always thought the dragons disappeared from Pothena thousands of years ago..."

"No," said Lathan. "It was much more recent than that. But I find it strange that in all the things you've shown us here, in all the landmarks, there's not a single mention of dragons, or magic, or anything not crafted by humans themselves."

Etenia looked around like she'd been put on the spot, having to defend her home against unexpected criticism. "I...I suppose it's just to focus on science, and not supersti—" She caught herself, realizing how offensive it would be to call dragons like Searsha and Cember "superstitions". She cleared her throat and corrected to: "The old ways."

"The old ways," said Lathan, like the words were really no better than "superstition" at all. "The old ways kept the world safe for a millennia. There's value in that heritage."

"Well yes, but..." said Etenia, and then seemed to give up on being delicate, and outright said: "But the old ways were limiting, weren't they? Out of a million people, how many could be dragon riders? A dozen? Two dozen?"

"Yes, but—"

"And how were they chosen?" she persisted. "Not by skill or capability, but by bonding with an unknowable creature, with no oversight and no standards to be set, or met. A society based on science rewards ingenuity and intelligence, so that those deserving of greatness can achieve it, regardless of where they come from."

Del cleared his throat and raised his hand. "Um, hi there."

Etenia's face went red when she realized what she'd said, and what it meant to him. She raised her hands to signal a truce and spoke more compassionately for a change: "Obviously, not everything turned out the way it should. But my point is: even the poorest Pothenian could make his fortune in this new society, but if a dragon didn't choose him, he would never be a rider. And that is why we likely gave up on dragons altogether."

Del glanced over at Lathan, who seemed just as nonplussed by this argument as Del was. "Well," said Del, "I suppose it's good you're getting all the insulting stuff out of your system now, instead of saying it at the council."

He finished his statement with a grin, and after a moment Etenia laughed. Lathan did, too, and the tension between them dissipated into the air. They'd been through too much together for a little argument like that to do much damage—but still, it made Del wonder if she was right about why Pothena had given up on dragons. Maybe not for the noble reasons she'd assumed, either: if dragons bonded with whomever they chose, and those dragon riders were not from the upper class, it would create a power dynamic that the upper-born would find incredibly disagreeable. What if they'd shunned dragons and magic because they saw them as existential threats to their dominance over Pothena?

What would they say to a pair of dragon riders—one, a homeless orphan—suddenly trying to take control of their city, to fight a foe none of them had even heard of before?

He had a terrible feeling they were headed into a disaster, but he wasn't sure how to tell Etenia. If he questioned her strategy, he'd fall right into the role her father used to play: the doubter, who never believed in her. But if he didn't warn her and she failed…

No, he had to do it. Their relationship was built on brutal honesty. She'd understand.

"Etenia," he said, and she turned, smiling at him so genuinely it twisted his stomach in a knot.

"Yes?" she asked, looking amused at the long pause he was taking to answer.

"I…" he said, then sighed and muttered: "Nothing. You'll do great."

Her brow crinkled a little, like she could sense there was something wrong with him…but then she turned away and led them down the lane. "Come on! We don't want to be late!"

The city council chambers were outside of Seafall, in Pothena proper, so they had to cross through the Seafall gates. There were guards there in immaculate and shining armor, their swords sheathed out of deference for the rich citizens they were there to protect. One of them caught

Del's eyes and wouldn't look away, like he recognized him and was trying to figure out what kind of a con was being played just now. Del huddled a little closer to Etenia and waited impatiently for the gates to be opened for them.

The second they crossed through, it was like Del was back in a memory again. The sandy streets, angling down toward the harbor below, and the smell of the sweetfruit in the air, and the shopkeepers all yelling out to anyone who would hear them to "buy this treat! try this fish! feel this silk!" It was bittersweet, coming back like this. The place he'd fought to escape, and now he was right back where he started—except, he thought, looking down at his clothes—he wasn't the same person any more.

The moment they stepped into the main boulevard, Lathan froze, entranced by the view. They were standing at the point, at the peak of the market, where the entire city opened up around them. The market stalls were buzzing with commotion, packed with people straight down the side of the mountain and into the harbor, where the ships they'd seen earlier were more distinct, but still just as chaotic. It was insanity. It was home. And it was going to be impossible to defend against the Epyr.

"How are we ever going to fortify a place like this?" Del sighed. "Look at it: there's barely anywhere for a dragon to land. Once the enemy gets on land, there's nothing to stop them from running straight up the middle. And half these people live in the line of fire—where are they going to go when the fighting starts?"

Lathan squinted, then nodded. "Del's right. This will be a challenge, even with Searsha and Cember at our side."

Etenia, though, was undeterred. "It's a big job," she said. "And it won't be easy. But if there's one thing I know about Pothenians, it's that we always rise to the occasion. Working together, we can overcome any obstacle at all."

CHAPTER 4

"Y ou must be joking," laughed the council chairman. "Pothena, under siege? Impossible."

Etenia adjusted her stance, standing a little taller, chin high, as the old men all around her scowled and studied her with obvious suspicion. The council chambers were a massive room in an ancient building, its roof decorated with elaborate paintings of Pothena's golden age, with giant golden chandeliers looming at key points around the room, as if their only purpose was to intimidate those who came to speak.

The council sat a long, curved bench, wrapping around the speaker's dais, and elevated so that witnesses and petitioners would be questioned from on high—and from all directions. It didn't help that Etenia, Del, and Lathan barely fit on the stand together, but what was truly agitating her, Del could tell, was that these men didn't seem to give her family name the slightest bit of deference. To them, she might have well been some girl off the street, wasting their time.

She cleared her throat and tried her pitch anew: "It's not impossible, my lords. It's true. And it's coming. The Epyrian army—"

"Epyrian?" scoffed one of the men with a long, white beard. "There's no such place as Epyria."

"Epyr, actually," corrected Etenia, which only made things worse for her, as a rotund, red-faced man got to his feet and slammed his fist down on the table.

"You dare tell Master Mirra the shape of the world, girl? This man has visited every continent in the world, he has!"

The other council members pounded their fists on the table in agreement, drowning out Etenia's protests for the first few times she tried replying. "I apologize, my lords, but the kingdom of Epyr is not on the continents. It's below. In the sea."

This earned her a bemused frown from Mirra. "The sea, you say? So: an army of fish, is it?"

"Not exactly," said Etenia, looking to Del for affirmation before heading into what was sure to be a difficult part of her pitch: "Epyrians are apparently human-like, though they live underwater, and—"

The laughter from around the room drowned her out before she could get much farther. She shrank a little, her confidence shaken. Del wasn't sure what she expected would happen when she told these old men her tale, but it clearly wasn't this. A reaction closer to her father's, he guessed. If he and Etenia didn't turn things around soon, they'd be laughed right out of the room.

"It's true!" he said, stepping forward and projecting his voice powerfully. "I've seen them, and they are no joke. They have more soldiers than the population of Etenia, and they—"

"How have you seen them?" called a councilman, from somewhere to Del's right.

"Yes," said the rotund one. "How have you seen them, if they live beneath the waves?"

Del hesitated, because he knew exactly what he was walking into. "I...I have visions."

The council burst into laughter. A few of them stood up and walked away, straight out of the building, as if they had far more important things to do. Those that remained made the most of their bemusement, going out of their way to make Del feel as foolish as they could. It didn't bother him, really, any more than all the other cruelties they'd inflicted upon him over the years. But what stung was how much this was hurting Etenia. She thought they were better than this..and now she was seeing how wrong she was.

"Tell me, boy," laughed Mirra. "What else do you have visions of, hmm? Would it require a large donation of gold to ensure our survival perchance? Is that what this is about?"

"No, I—"

"I thought he looked familiar!" gasped another councilman. "He's that brat from the market! The one who cuts pockets and purses!"

"Moving up in the world, aren't you!" said another.

"Bigger and better scams every day!" said another.

"Tell us," said Mirra. "Tell us what happens if we don't do as you say."

Lathan stepped forward, his voice trembling with rage. "Ruin, my lords. Ruin, death, and destruction to you and your kin. That is what happens if you ignore these warnings."

The Sivarnan robes and the silvery hair set the council back a little. Whether they believed Lathan or not, he seemed to be owed at least a hint of respect. The chamber quieted, and when Mirra spoke next, it was like he was speaking to an equal: "Dire words, Mr—?"

"*General* Phrac," said Lathan, earning him a wide-eyed stare from both Del and Etenia, who had never heard his full title before. "General

Lathan Phrac, Royal Master Dragon Trainer and First Minister to the Kingdom of Sivarna. At your service, my lords." He bowed deeply and came up only as Mirra began to speak next.

"Welcome, General Phrac. You are most welcome in Pothena. And, if I may speak for the whole council: our deepest condolences on the disaster that befell your nation."

Lathan's eyes narrowed. "It was no disaster, my lords. It was the Epyrian army that felled Sivarna. And if you don't listen to our pleas, I can all but guarantee the same fate will befall Pothena, too."

This elicited quiet chatter all around the room. Lathan continued:

"Sivarna was attacked, without warning, by a terrifying sea monster known as the Kraken."

Mirra chortled despite himself: "An old fisherman's tale!"

"A tale that cost me everything I loved," said Lathan, and Mirra went quiet again. "It was very real, my lord, and very deadly. It wrecked the capital, killed countless dragons and their riders, and sank the Sivarnan navy. The entire Sivarnan navy. It was only by sheer luck that my ship escaped the carnage and, by chance, intercepted Ms Browder's ship. She offered her help, but sadly the Kraken caught up with us, and—"

"With all due respect, General," said the rotund one. "All we know of you is that you're a man dressed in Sivarnan robes, speaking with what I'd say is a dubious Sivarnan accent, at best—putting a fantastical spin on what is well known to be the earthquake that decimated Sivarna a few months back. So I ask you, General—and let's assume you are a general—how can we believe a word you're saying? How can we be sure you're not just another con artist from the market, spinning a tale to fleece us of our money?"

"Do con artists have dragons?" asked Del, forcefully.

The rotund councilor shrugged. "I'm no expert in the ethics of dragonkind."

Mirra interjected before Del and Lathan both lost their tempers. "Let us assume you are telling the truth, all of you. What would you have us do? Shut the port? Fortify the city? Dig trenches and build ramparts in the streets? Send the citizenry into the mountains, and hire an army to defend our shores?"

Etenia gave a meek shrug—a piece of old Etenia, Del realized, coming back from the dead to take her subservient role in the shadows of Great Men. She cleared her throat and spoke softly: "Yes. Essentially that."

Mirra laughed, and it was a cruel, condescending laugh. "You've your father's vision, my dear," he said, "but not his mind. Do you have any idea how much it would cost to do even half of those things?"

"But the people—"

"The people will never stand for a rise in taxes. Not on that scale. We'd have a rebellion on our hands, never mind your imaginary threat from the sea."

Etenia nearly staggered back; Del caught her before she could show how much the words had hurt her. It was no surprise to Del that the council would respond this way. It was what he had predicted. But that didn't stop him from being aghast at witnessing his prediction coming true. Here they were, pleading for a way to save the lives of everyone in the city, and the council was concerned with paying their fair share. Because that is what it would all come down to: the shopkeepers, sailors, and fishermen held so little wealth that the council could tax all their income and still not be able to pay for the things Etenia was describing. To properly secure Pothena, the citizens of Seafall would have to foot the bill—and that was clearly something they were not going to do. Del understood that dynamic on a very deep level, but for

Etenia, it was like a slap in the face. Her entire worldview had been wrong, and she was only just finding out.

Mirra saw the look in her eyes and softened a little, possibly out of pity. Probably out of concern what her father would do if he didn't smooth things over, at least a little.

"Truthfully, my dear, your plan is valiant, and brave. But if these sea monsters could flatten Sivarna so easily—Sivarna, which was built like a fortress—how could we possibly stand a chance against them in Pothena, built to be open and free as we are?"

And there it was: the same doubt Del had, put into words. Even if they cleared the harbor, and even if they fortified the city, and equipped every last citizen with a sword and shield and taught them to fight—there was no way Pothena could withstand the onslaught of the army he'd seen in his visions. Sivarna had a well-trained professional army, and dragons, and they'd still fallen prey to the Epyrians. As much as he hated to admit it, the council was right: there was no way Etenia's plan would work. As long as the dragon eggs were in Pothena, the city and everyone in it was in danger.

He turned Etenia around, and Lathan, too, and brought them into a huddle: "They're not going to help us," he whispered. "So there's only one thing to do. We have to get the eggs out of here."

"But where?" asked Lathan. "Searsha and Cember could barely fly us this far. Asking any more of them might put their lives in danger."

"And escaping by boat is too dangerous," said Etenia. "We have no idea where the Epyr are coming from, so we might sail right into them."

"I know," said Del. "So we go somewhere they can't follow. Up through the mountains."

Lathan was uncertain, but Etenia was dead set against it. Del could see it in the way her shoulders squared and her nostrils flared. She was not backing down. "No," she said. "No, that won't work. Think of it, Del: yes, we'd escape with the eggs, and maybe they couldn't follow. But they'd still raze Pothena to the ground in our absence."

He gave the council a sideways glance. "Maybe they deserve it."

Now she was angry. She turned away from him, facing the council once more. She pulled the veil off her face and stood taller, more direct than before. She wanted to be sure they all saw her. Saw how serious she was.

"My lords," she said. "Whether you believe us or not, the Epyr are real, and they are coming for the Sivarnan dragon eggs in our care. They will not negotiate, they will not back down. They will tear all of Pothena apart to get them—even if we left with them today. Whether you like it or not—whether you can afford it or not—the enemy is on its way. Del and I can only do so much on our dragons, so we will need support. Your support. But it needs to be now. If you say no to us now, and Pothena falls, history will judge you for your inaction...if anyone remembers Pothena at all."

The men around the table shifted uncomfortably, looking to each other for a sense of how to react. The rotund one seemed especially displeased, like he greatly resented having someone threaten his legacy —even if he didn't believe it was at risk in the first place.

Mirra pounded a fist on the table: once, twice, three times, and sat a little taller.

"Miss Browder," he said. "I do not doubt your love of your country, and the people therein. But planning a war is an expensive matter, and not one to be undertaken without evidence. To do so would be a great sin against the population of Pothena, and the survival of our people. And yet, as you so eloquently put it, it is also our duty to protect those citizens from dangers seen and unseen. Your fish monsters may be imaginary, they may be a con, or they may be real. But if they do show up at our shores, trust me when I say Pothena is equal to the challenge."

He waved a hand in the air and one of the heavily armored guards from the back of the room strode forward, standing beside Del, Etenia and Lathan. He had in his hands a long metal tube, decorated with intricate designs that led to a glowing blue base. A handle was mounted on the side of it, which he used to hoist the tube up, taking aim across the chambers at another guard, who was standing at attention.

Etenia and Lathan were confused, but Del knew exactly what was going to happen.

"Captain, if you please," said Mirra, and the guard twisted the handle and suddenly the tube vibrated violently, and a crackling blue pulse shot out of the end—emitting a deafening crack—and tore across the room in half a heartbeat. It hit the other guard in the chest, throwing him into the wall so hard he tumbled to the ground, unconscious.

"Pacifiers," said Mirra. "Already in circulation within the central quarter, they are more than capable."

Lathan was stunned by what he'd seen; not just the technology, but the fact that Pothenians would demonstrate weapons on their own so recklessly. "If you think some fireworks will stop the Epyr, my lords, you're—"

"Don't worry, General," said Mirra. "With a few adjustments to the energy source, our pacifiers can go from a warning shot to a lethal blow, killing a man in one shot."

"Or a child," said Del, fists tight at his sides. "Because they do, already, don't they? I've seen these things before, out in the market. Guards taking cheap shots at the poor kids for fun. Knocks a grown man off his feet, but stops the heart of a five-year-old."

41

The council's discomfort was palpable, but not because they were appalled that children had died at their command—because someone was saying it aloud.

"And don't call them 'pacifiers'," said Del. "They're called Snappers."

The rotund one seemed taken with that name. "Because of the sound they make when they fire..." he said, a smile growing on his face.

"Because of what they do to the five-year-old's neck," said Del, and silence reigned again.

Lathan stepped between Del and the council before something even worse broke out. "My lords, your technology is truly impressive, I will admit. But speaking as a soldier, I can say even with the best of weapons, the defense of a city is—"

"Not something we would leave up to a pair of children and their wild animals," scoffed Mirra. "Honestly, General, would you put your faith in a duo such as this?"

Lathan worked hard not to snarl, and failed: "If they were my only chance of survival, without hesitation."

Just then, the back doors opened and a familiar voice called out: "My lords, I apologize for the interruption," said Arretal, coming in to stand next to his daughter. "I know I am not a member of council, and so have no standing in this meeting, but I've been listening to the proceedings from outside, I just wanted to come in and say—" He smiled at Etenia, gave her an affirming nod. "I wanted to say I believe my daughter, and I trust in her plans and her abilities. If she says danger is coming, then danger is coming. And if she says we need to prepare...I will be the first to pour my fortune into the work to be done. For whatever it's worth, my lords, Etenia has my unconditional support."

Etenia smiled back at him, and then met Del's eyes, and he had a hard time not smiling back. For almost the entire time he'd known her, she'd believed her father distrusted her, thought she was second-best. So much of her personality seemed based on that notion—so now that he was actively praising her, it was like a dam had broken, and pent-up emotions were flooding out.

Del gave her a look that said: "how's that for a surprise?"

Mirra whispered to the councilman next to him, and then turned to face them all once more. "Eloquent words, Master Browder, and moving, truly. And it is certainly your right to believe in, and even fund your daughter's fantasies. But this council has greater loyalties to consider, and far greater consequences. Fortify the Browder estate if you like— and the Braitmans', too, I expect—but you are hereby forbidden to turn Pothena city into your own little war games." He slammed his fist down on the table and called out: "The council has spoken!"

And with those four words, Del realized, Pothena had sealed its fate.

CHAPTER 5

The second they were outside the council chambers, Etenia's pace quickened to an almost breakneck speed. She threaded her way through the petitioners waiting in the courtyard, oblivious to the fact that Del and Lathan were being left behind—and once she got to the gates back into Seafall, Del was pretty sure he wouldn't be able to follow at all. He was forced to act as a go-between, trying to call her back, while not letting Lathan get lost in the crowd.

He couldn't see her clearly, but every so often he caught sight of her shoulders, tense and high, and knew she was angry. He didn't blame her one bit. It was a good thing he hadn't been the focus of that inquisition, or he'd have let the frumpy old councilors have it.

Do you need help? asked Searsha, straight into his mind.

"No," he said under his breath, struggling to keep track of Etenia. "We'll manage."

Cember senses despair, and Etenia is not answering him, said Searsha. *And from you, I sense distress. Are you certain you do not need someone set on fire?*

"I'm pretty sure that would make things worse," said Del. "I'll handle it. But thanks."

Until she'd said it, Del hadn't been able to identify how he was feeling, but "distress" was exactly right. Etenia was hurting, and he couldn't do anything to stop it. In the past, if someone had come to him with a sad story about their life, he would have told them to toughen up and quit whining. But here, with Etenia—suffering from nothing more than a verbal lashing—he felt as ill as if someone had stabbed him in the gut. He wanted to help her so badly...

"Etenia!" he called out, but she didn't hear him—or didn't want to hear him—and kept pushing on. "Etenia!" he yelled, louder, and the people around them stopped to stare. Still, she kept going, and this time he knew she was filtering him out.

He ran a little faster, hopping up onto the edge of a fountain, and cupped a hand to his mouth and shouted: "Hey! Princess! This is no time for crying!"

That did the trick, just as he suspected it would. She stopped cold, fists tight at her sides, and then spun around, glaring at him like he was the reincarnation of the Kraken. The look on her face gave him chills, but he didn't dare change the cocky smirk on his face. He needed her to be angry so she'd slow down.

She stormed back through the crowd, walking straight through people until she was close enough to bellow: "Crying? You think I'm crying?"

"Oh dear," said Lathan, from Del's side. "Are you—"

"Shh," said Del, and then called back to Etenia: "It didn't go the way you wanted. Boo-hoo! Maybe daddy can buy you a pony to make it better and—"

She finally arrived, but didn't slow down at all. Instead, she shoved him off the ledge, sending him crashing into the pool at the base of the fountain. He was so shocked he couldn't even save himself; he landed with a splash, getting a mouthful of water as he went completely under. He coughed and choked as he came back up, keenly aware that everyone nearby was watching every second of it.

"I'm not sad, Del, I'm angry," she said. "Angry and disappointed and angry some more and yes, I'm also sad. For Pothena. For..." She stopped herself, as if only just now realizing exactly how public a space they were in. "I don't need a pony. I need a plan."

Del was still mostly submerged, watching her warily. "Like pushing your friends into fountains?"

She grumbled a bit, avoiding his gaze. "I'm sorry. I lost my temper." She held out a hand to him, to help him out. "Truce?"

He smiled, nodded, and took her hand. "Truce." And then he pulled her into the fountain too. She screamed, thrashing to stay out of the water, but it was no use. She was soaked. She came up, gasping and laughing at once, her perfect makeup streaming down her face, and splashed water in Del's face.

"You're awful," she said.

"We're awful together," he corrected. "Now let's figure out what kind of awful we'll be."

They sat in the veranda of the Browder villa, still wearing their wet clothes as the servants poured them drinks and frowned at their generally wretched appearance. Lathan, still as sleek and proper as ever, sipped wine, lost in thought. And not happy thoughts, from the expression on his face.

"So here's my plan," said Etenia, pausing like she was putting her thoughts in order. "We'll go back to council with firsthand accounts of—"

"No," said Del. "Waste of time. Won't work."

"What?" she said, incredulous. "You don't even know what—"

"They said no, Etenia. They made fun of us. They're not going to change their minds, no matter what you say."

"But maybe—"

"What do you think, Lathan? Is there hope?"

Lathan finished sipping his wine, then set down his glass and thought a moment before answering: "I'm sorry, Etenia, but Del is right. Whatever their reasons—and I would hope their reasons are not as crass and selfish as they seem—they will never understand the dangers they face. The attack on Sivarna was sudden and swift, but I admit there were signs leading up to that fateful day. But the leadership refused to see it. I refused to see it. And by the time we did...it was far too late."

If Etenia had expected an easy time in this planning session, she was quickly realizing it wouldn't be going according to plan. She frowned deeply and leaned forward like she was about to leap out of her chair. "I can't just do nothing. The Epyr are coming to destroy my home."

"So we leave," said Del, like it was so simple it was obvious. And it was. It was the only answer at all.

"Leave to where?" asked Lathan. "Whatever kingdom we land in will be in danger, too."

"Not to mention," said Etenia, "how do we know the Epyr won't ransack Pothena anyway? How do we know they'll even know we've gone to a new city?"

"Who said we're going to a new city?" asked Del with a grin, and then pointed up, out the back of the villa, to the mountain behind Pothena. "Fish people probably aren't the best rock climbers."

"But wait," said Etenia. "How—"

"We get the dragons to fly us up there," he said. "Someplace really inaccessible. Then I send a vision of our location to the Epyr—"

"Can you do that? On command?" asked Lathan.

Del looked a little sheepish. "Well, not on command, but—"

"And what if they try anyway?" asked Etenia. "They'd end up using Pothena as a staging ground for their assault on the mountain. That would almost be worse than—"

"But we'll be safe!" said Del. "Even the Kraken couldn't reach that far into the island. If we go someplace you can't reach without wings, the Epyr won't stand a chance."

"No, Del," said Etenia, forcefully, "the people of Pothena won't stand a chance."

He couldn't tell if she was being intentionally dense, or if he was being overly cruel, but: "They don't want our help, Etenia. You heard them. 'A pair of children and their wild animals' is what they called us. We offered nicely, and they said no. Whatever happens next is their own fault, but it won't be our fault."

"But it's not just about us, Del!"

"I know!" he said, and pointed to the collection of dragon eggs nearby. "It's about them. We have an obligation to those eggs. We didn't keep them safe all this time, against impossible odds, only to give up now. The council only cares about themselves. It's always the same. It'll never change. But just because they're committing suicide doesn't mean we should let them take us with them."

48

Etenia's anger and hurt were on full display. Her face was red, her teeth were gritted and her eyes were just on the verge of tearing up—she looked like she was going to throw something, or curl into a ball and sob. It was like she was having trouble deciding what kind of upset she was going to be. She looked to Lathan for support. "What do you think?"

Lathan sighed, staring down into his hands while he thought. When he spoke, his words had weight to them, and sorrow. "We do have an obligation to the eggs," he said. "Or at least I do, officially. The Epyr are not coming here for Pothena or Pothenians; they are coming for the eggs. My—our first priority must be to ensure their survival."

He glanced at the eggs, lost in thought a while longer before continuing.

"But the role of a dragon rider is to protect the weak and save the defenseless. Your dragons may be Sivarnan in body, but they are now Pothenian in spirit, and it would be a grave dishonor for them to run from a fight for the survival of their adopted home." He shrugged to Del. "I'm sorry, but we can't run. Pothena needs its dragons."

Etenia's eyes widened in an instant. "That's it!" she said. "That's exactly it!"

"It's not going to work," said Del. "Two dragons against a massive invading force of—"

"No, not two dragons," said Etenia, and looked over at the eggs again.

Del and Lathan took a moment to catch on, and when they did, Lathan took a sharp breath: "Etenia, you can't—"

"You train dragon riders, Lathan—"

"*Sivarnan* dragon riders, Etenia," he said. "On Sivarnan dragons. In Sivarna."

"But there is no Sivarna anymore," she said, then winced at her callousness. "I'm sorry, but it's true. Sivarna is in ruins. It could take generations to find enough Sivarnan candidates for all these eggs—assuming there will still be eggs left to bond with. But Pothena has thousands of citizens, and even if we assume only a tenth of one percent are suited for the job, that's still more than enough—"

"Wait," said Del. "We have thirty-five eggs in there, and only one Lathan. And let's face it, he's pretty old. You really expect he'll be able to train that many—"

"No," said Etenia. "So we'll help."

Lathan laughed so suddenly, it caught Del and Etenia off guard. It wasn't a mean-spirited laugh, but it wasn't kind, either. "I'm sorry, but no. You two are, absolutely, talented. But you are still novice dragon riders yourselves. How do you expect to train someone lacking your natural instincts? Because believe me: just because a dragon bonds with a human, it doesn't mean the human will be easy to teach."

Etenia was knocked down a peg, but by the look on her face, she was not yet ready to quit. "We have to do something."

"Yeah," said Del. "Like flying up into the mountains and surviving."

Lathan rubbed his face with his hands before gesturing toward Del. "We cannot abandon Pothena in its hour of need." And then he gestured toward Etenia. "But we cannot risk our few remaining dragons based on a hopeful fantasy." He clasped his hands together like he was praying. "We need to find a way to defend Pothena with the tools at our disposal."

"Even if we die in the process?" asked Del.

"If that is our fate, then—"

"And the eggs? You'd sacrifice them too?"

Lathan stared at Del for a long moment, and Del could just guess what he was thinking: he was torn between his two pillars of responsibility. On the one hand, he was sworn to protect the dragon eggs at all costs, and was willing to do whatever was necessary to make that happen. But on the other hand, his sense of honor wouldn't allow him to abandon a city full of innocents to certain death.

For Del, it was a much simpler equation to solve: he had an allegiance to the eggs because of Searsha, and he would do what he could to ensure their safety. As for Pothena, it wasn't really a city full of innocents anyway—it was a city full of scoundrels, and if the whole place burned to the ground while acting like scoundrels, then so be it. Del could understand why Etenia was so adamant about fighting: she'd never really spent enough time in actual Pothena, so she still thought they were worth saving. Del knew better. He had the scars to prove it.

Lathan finally came to his answer: "I couldn't live with myself if I ran."

Del got to his feet, letting out a defeated sigh. "And I couldn't live with myself if I stayed. Because I'd be dead, just like everyone else in this godforsaken city."

When he stormed off, no one tried to stop him. And that hurt most of all.

CHAPTER 6

D el needed to be alone, but everywhere he turned, he seemed to run into another group of well-to-do merchants out for a stroll with their families. It didn't help that Seafall was like a maze, constantly sending him in circles, and never very far from the Browder estate. Part of him hoped to see Etenia there, waiting for him, asking him to return and talk it through some more. But when he finally realized that wouldn't happen, his frustration boiled right over.

There were a handful of sweetfruit trees along the edge of the wall dividing Seafall from the rest of the city, where rich young lovers came to promise each other the moon. That made it even more satisfying to Del when he stormed right in, climbed up the branches of one of the tallest trees—shaking a small storm of sweetfruits down on a pair of horrified lovers—and then hopped right over the wall and into the streets beyond.

He landed at the edge of the market so suddenly, shoppers yelped in surprise and scrambled for cover. Even the nearby guards were staring at him in disbelief and confusion—usually, people tried to get into Seafall, not the other way around—until suddenly they gave him polite bows and carried on with their business. That was when Del remembered he wasn't dressed like a penniless orphan anymore.

An elderly woman near him lowered her head to him as a sign of respect, and it made him sick. If he'd pulled this exact same stunt a few months ago, he'd have been swarmed and beaten and spat at, and dragged off to jail. All it took was a nice shirt and trousers, and suddenly he was a better person?

This was why Pothena deserved its fate. It put too much faith in shiny objects and the people who owned them, despite the fact that those people had no interest in protecting anything but their own possessions, and anyone but themselves. Etenia had practically begged them to let her save them, and they'd laughed in her face. It was absurd: why should she beg them to allow her to do something entirely for their benefit? And despite being rejected, and mocked, and disrespected, she was still going to risk everything to try anyway? She was just as entranced by the shiny objects as the rest of Pothena. It was distracting her from the rot underneath.

Del walked into the crowd, his old instincts coming back as he wove this way and that, trying not to be noticed and never walking in a straight line, lest he get trapped. Some people moved out of his way because of the way he looked, while others must have recognized something in the way he moved and instinctively tried to avoid a thief on the prowl. The further he walked, the more at home he felt, until he very nearly pickpocketed a man in a purple tunic who was far too distracted by a cart stocked with pastries. The man was out shopping with his young daughter, holding her up on his shoulder so she could see the higher-up displays, and so lost in that conversation you could have stolen his clothes and he wouldn't have noticed the difference.

Del would have done it, too, in the past. But something about this display—of a father genuinely caring about his daughter, without any hidden agendas—felt too pure to interrupt. He took the man's wallet and moved it to his other pocket, where it would be harder to access, and carried on his way. A few moments later, he heard the poor fool start to panic at his lost money and wondered how long it would take for him to realize the switch.

As he walked, Del became acutely aware of eyes following him: thieves sizing up a mark. They couldn't yet tell that he wasn't carrying any money, and probably assumed he was wearing jewelry somewhere they couldn't see. It would only be a matter of time before one of them took a pass at him. He had to get away before that happened, or he might find himself—

A hand grabbed him by the shoulder and yanked him backward, nearly off his feet. He was dragged into an alley and around a corner, into a little alcove he used to sleep in when he was nine. A pair of men with rotted teeth slammed him into the wall—one pinned him there, elbow to his neck, while the other searched his pockets quickly and efficiently.

"Don't make a sound," said the first one.

"Nothin' here," said the second, rechecking the pockets again. "No wallet. No coins. Nothing."

"I don't have any—" Del said, before the first man smacked him in the face so hard his vision swam.

"I said quiet!" snarled the thief, and pushed Del back against the wall again, this time digging his fingers into Del's throat. He nodded toward his partner. "Check again."

"I'm tellin' you, there's nothing—"

The man didn't get to finish his sentence, because a wooden bat cracked into the side of his head, sending him sprawling. The first thief turned in shock, only to get a whack to the face. He landed on the ground, spitting blood and teeth.

The bat was wielded by a boy of maybe fourteen, flanked by a second younger boy who had a pair of sharpened bones held out like knives. The younger boy let out a primal scream and stomped his feet on the ground, and the two thieves shrieked in horror and ran for their lives. The boy gave chase, wailing like a deranged animal the whole way.

Del's head still stung from being hit, but he couldn't afford to let his guard down. He pushed himself into the corner of the alcove, fists at the ready, trying to think of a way to get past that bat without losing any teeth.

The boy, though, slung the bat under his shoulder and flashed Del a grin. "No worries, sir. You're safe now."

Del's relief was quickly replaced by bitterness as he realized the boy had only saved him because he seemed rich, and a rich man might give a healthy reward for such an act of bravery. He wondered if the two thieves were in on the act, too. Maybe this was their game: stage a mugging, and then collect the reward for thwarting it, too.

"I don't have money," he said, knowing full well it might end with him getting beaten unconscious. "I'm not rich."

"No, you're Del," said the boy, giving him a wink. "Del in nice clothes."

Del laughed, because that was exactly how he felt. Himself, wrapped in fancy fabric. He held out an arm to the boy, who took it in a Pothenian street greeting. Solemn and sincere, and very, very rare.

"Thank you for saving me," he said, trying to place the face. "Have we met before?"

"Womp," said the boy. "They call me Womp."

Del frowned. "It sounds familiar. You ran with Jiri's crew?"

Womp nodded, grimaced. "Until Jiri got himself killed."

"Jiri's dead?" asked Del, incredulous. Jiri had been one of the more formidable gang leaders in Pothena, and far too paranoid to ever fall prey to an assassin's blade. "How?"

Womp pointed at his throat. "Choked on a bone. Real sad. But it's like they say: eat like an animal, die like an animal."

Del was just about to answer when he felt an emotion he knew wasn't his: relief. A heartbeat later, up on the rooftops on either side of the alley, Searsha brought herself down for a graceful landing. She bowed her head down into the opening, breathing a smoky warning to Womp as her full set of teeth were bared.

Womp nearly fell over, eyes open wide, mouth making motions to speak, but no sound came out.

"Speaking of animals," sighed Del.

Did this runt injure you? asked Searsha.

Del held out a hand to calm her down. "No. He saved me. He's a..." He blinked as a realization hit him, and turned to Womp: "Why did you save me?"

"You're good people," said Womp, eyes darting between Del and Searsha, Del and Searsha. "I learned how to survive by watching you. You're like the closest thing I got to family. And we protect our own, yeah?"

It felt wrong to admit it, but Del realized it was true: despite the brutal and cutthroat nature of living on the street, the ones who survived were the ones who understood you do protect your own. Sometimes "your own" was hard to define, and sometimes it felt like there was no one on your side but you, but if you saw someone good in trouble and it wouldn't come back to haunt you, you would take a chance for your friends. That was how Del had ended up with Isham—the stranger who'd raised him, and been the closest thing to family he'd ever had.

Del had grown up alone, but he shared that aloneness with a community—and they really did take care of their own, when it mattered most.

Del sighed, shoulders slumped, and then gave Searsha a sheepish look. "I'm going to need a ride back to the villa."

Lathan had left by the time they returned, and Etenia was deep in conversation with her father, and purposely ignoring the sight of a mighty dragon landing in the courtyard. Del slid off Searsha's back and stormed across the stones as Arretal gave him a nod in greeting and poured him a glass of wine to drink—only to stop when he got a better view of Del's face.

"Your eye could use some ice," he said, and gestured for a servant to fetch some.

"It's fine," said Del, turning his attention to Etenia, who was doing her best to ignore him. "Can I speak with you for a second?"

Etenia was pretending to be fascinated with a flower. "Hmm?" she asked.

Del had forgotten how annoying she could be. "Can you just look at me when I—" She wasn't budging. "Fine. Never mind. I won't agree with you after all."

He turned to go, until she said: "Agree with me?"

"About some of it," said Del. "Not everything."

She touched her father's arm gently, and he took the hint, nodding to Del. "I'll check on that ice." He left them alone, and the servants faded into the background, too.

It was late in the day, and the sun was low, casting long shadows along the courtyard. The dragons' shadows, in particular, were a menacing sight. In any other context, it would have been the perfect scene of peace and tranquility. But all Del could think was that it felt very much like the calm before an especially nasty storm.

Etenia was doing her best at playing coy. She fought with the smile that was overtaking her face. "You agree to training dragon riders?" she asked. "It's a good idea after all?"

"No, it's still a terrible idea," he said, flopping down into a chair. "It's not just a terrible idea, it's a terrible idea that's going to fail, and probably get you killed."

Her smile faded. "This is the worst apology of all time."

"It's not an apology," he said. "I know you. You're going to do this no matter what, running lessons from your patio or whatever."

"Actually, I'm thinking it needs to be more of a school."

Del sighed. "A school. Really."

"If we're going to do this, we should get it right, don't you think? A proper school, with structure and discipline and—"

"You're really making it hard for me right now."

"Nobody said you have to help, Del. I just need you to not fight me."

Del pressed his hands into his eyes to stave off a headache. "Of course I have to help. The only way I can keep you safe is to be there with you."

Etenia's smile was confused, tentative. "Keep me safe?"

"Old habits die hard." He shrugged, thinking back to Womp. "We protect our own, right?"

She nodded to that. "We do. We'll save Pothena—"

"Well...you protect Pothena. I'll protect you. Searsha will protect me."

Presumptuous, said Searsha.

Etenia laughed and offered Del her hand. He took it to shake, but she pulled him up, so he was standing so very close to her. Her makeup was still smeared, and her clothes smelled like a wet dog, but there was that same look in her eyes that was her. Intense and focused, and ready to make the impossible come true.

"We'll need to convince Lathan," she said.

"Good luck with that."

"And we'll need candidates. Good, noble people."

"In Pothena?" winced Del.

"And someplace to train. A building with lots of space, and—"

"Have you actually figured any of this out yet?" asked Del. "Because all I'm hearing are a lot of insurmountable obstacles."

Etenia crossed her arms and frowned at him. "We killed the Kraken. We can do anything if we put our minds to it." Arretal was coming back—they could hear him talking to a servant—and Etenia took a step away from Del and stood a little taller, like she was afraid of what her father might think of her ease around him.

Del was a little confused about that as well. Sometimes it felt like they were the oldest of friends, able to share their deepest secrets without a second thought. Other times, they seemed more likely to tear each other apart than agree on the tiniest detail.

And sometimes—every so often—Del swore he felt a different dynamic at play entirely. Like the way she looked at him—like she was studying him a little more than made sense, with a little more kindness than she'd admit to—when she thought he wouldn't notice. Or vice versa.

This post-island existence was only going to get more exhausting, he could tell.

"Father?" asked Etenia, as Arretal arrived. "Del and I were just discussing the location of the school..."

"Ah, yes," said Arretal, handing Del a chunk of ice wrapped in cloth. "I've been thinking about that. I'd offer the villa, but if even half those eggs hatch, we'd run out of room fast. Space in Seafall is at a premium, but there are some warehouses down by the harbor that we might be able to convert, depending on your needs."

Del raised an eyebrow to Etenia. "What are our needs?"

She sighed and looked back toward the house, face full of worry. "It's time to win over Lathan."

CHAPTER 7

"I already told you no," said Lathan, the moment he opened the door to his room.

"Just hear us out," said Etenia, which made Lathan shift his focus to Del, who was standing behind Etenia and trying to disappear.

"She convinced you?"

It was a lot more complicated than being convinced, but Del didn't know how to explain the situation to Lathan without bringing him on a tour of some seriously twisted logic, so instead he shorthanded it to: "We beat the Kraken."

"The Kraken was not a logistical nightmare," said Lathan, letting them into his room as he paced. "This is beyond complicated. Never mind my concerns about risking the last Sivarnan dragon eggs for your experiment—is it even possible to develop a functional dragon force in time?"

Etenia seemed flummoxed by the question, but Del was catching on to Lathan's train of thought: they had no idea how far away the Epyr were, or how fast they could move. They might show up in a few minutes, or a few days, or weeks, or months. Even if he managed to gain access to another vision, he had no way of knowing where it was taking place. It would make planning extremely difficult.

He didn't want to crush Etenia's spirit immediately, but he had to be honest: "I don't know how long we have until the Epyr show up. And no guaranteed way to find out."

Lathan nodded like Del had confirmed his suspicions. "But even if we did know—even if we knew it would be exactly a month from today—there is the issue of maturation."

Etenia's face showed she knew exactly what that meant, and also that she hadn't considered it before. "A dragon hatched this very instant would not be battle-ready for at least two months. Without fire-breathing, at the very least, they would be nothing more than exotic workhorses. And if you think I would allow young dragons to fly into battle before they're big enough to carry their riders, you are—"

"All right, fine, I understand," said Etenia. "But what if we have more time than we think? What if things actually work out in our favor for a change?"

Del gave her a wry smile. "You must be new here."

Lathan was struggling with diplomacy, it was clear. He clasped his hands together and spoke gently, but with an edge that was unmistakable. "I don't think you understand how the bonding process works. What happened with you and Del on the island, that is not normal. We have thirty-some dragon eggs. In Sivarna, it might take thirty or forty years to find riders for each of those dragons. It's not simply a matter of numbers. In the entire population of Pothena, there might only be one or two—or none!—worthy of that bond."

He pointed to Del. "How big is the Epyrian army?"

Del remembered, with a shiver, the images from that last vision he'd had of the Epyrian army—thousands and thousands of soldiers with gleaming armor and spears. "Too big."

"Best-case scenario," said Lathan. "Best case: we have four, maybe five full-grown dragons in the air when the Epyrians arrive. Sivarna had twenty times that number, and it still fell."

Etenia seemed stunned by these facts. She was staring off into the distance like she was stuck in a trance, not even blinking. Del wanted to say something to reassure her, but what Lathan had laid out was hard to refute. She had a plan—no, not even a plan, a dream of a plan—that was so divorced from reality that there was really no way to save it. The only thing Del could think to do was wait for her to accept it, and pledge to help her when she decided to move on.

Finally, after an incredibly long pause, she took a sharp breath, and nodded to herself.

"Numbers don't lie," she said, and Lathan looked so sad for what she was going through.

"Etenia, I wish—"

"Pothena has five times the population of Sivarna," she said. "How did you test for candidates? Based on merit?"

Lathan was taken aback at the way she was asking. "I...yes? Of course."

"So a fraction of a fraction even stood a chance of being bonded," she said. "On what, a yearly cycle?"

Lathan muttered: "Four years."

"Four years?" she said.

"There are steps to follow. Pre-selections, selections, aptitude testing, physical testing, then a series of double-blind examinations where—"

"No wonder it took you so long," said Etenia. "No, we'll do it faster."
She hurried to the door, not waiting for them to catch up.

"Where are you going?" called Lathan.

"To change the equation!" she called back, already halfway down the hall.

Del gave Lathan a shrug that said: "well, what did you expect?" Lathan
just sighed in return.

Womp stood at attention, his hands clasped behind his back like an
undersized soldier, clad in rags and a filthy face. He was doing his best
to fit in amongst the decadence of the Browder villa, and only made
himself stand out more in the trying. Del felt absolutely terrible for him
but didn't know how to show it without making everything even more
awkward than it already was—for both of them. How could he explain
his connection to this penniless orphan? Etenia's servants had picked
him off the street like he was nameless and disposable, which grated at
Del's nerves. But doing something about it would only draw attention
to the fact that he didn't belong there, either.

Etenia was writing something on a large sheet of paper, concentrating
so intensely that it was like the rest of them weren't even there. Del felt
bad for Womp: all those times, growing up, when some rich man's
servant had come into the slums and offered two bits for a smart, strong
lad...this was what the other side of that transaction looked like. Del
had never taken the bait, and if it had meant a situation like this, he was
glad he hadn't. Womp had no idea what he had been summoned to do
and was trying to cover his anxiety with an expression and stance that
he thought looked grown up. It didn't. At all.

"There," said Etenia, finishing her writing and letting Lathan get the
first read-through.

He seemed uncertain by what he read. "It's too prone to failure," he said. "Wouldn't you rather create a nominating committee to—"

"No," said Etenia. "That takes time, and we are desperately short on time." She handed the paper over to Womp. "What do you think? Would you say yes?"

Womp took the paper carefully and looked down at it, frowning like he was deep in concentration, before saying: "Yes, ma'am. I would."

Del watched Womp with a suspicious eye as Etenia beamed. "And you understand what's at stake?"

Womp looked at the paper again, and Del recognized the expression immediately, because it was the same one he'd had until a few months ago: he wanted to look confident, but he had no idea what the paper said. And once again, Etenia was completely blind to the notion. She assumed everyone operated at the same level as her, while Del assumed the opposite. The difference between them was intensely frustrating sometimes.

"He can't read, Etenia," Del sighed, then realized what he'd said. Womp was trying not to look upset about it, but Del could see the hurt in his eyes. This was exactly what he hated about the rich—the callous disregard for other people—and he was doing it himself. He cleared his throat. "I mean, probably."

Etenia's expression changed in an instant, because she knew, from their time on the island, that street kids couldn't read, and how defensive they were about it. He gave Womp an apologetic smile and said: "I'm sorry. I didn't mean to offend." He took the paper from Womp to see for himself. "It says—Hold on a second, what?" said Del, reading it over himself. "What is this supposed to be? 'Wanted: Dragon riders'? It's a poster?"

She was on the spot again, and not enjoying it one bit, he could tell. "Master Gafri will make copies, and I'll pay to have them plastered around town and—"

"You're going to scare people," said Del, pointing to the writing at the bottom of the page. "You say Pothena's about to be invaded by a deadly army, and there's no time to lose. Do you want to cause a panic?"

Lathan nodded his agreement. "He's right. People will either assume it's a lie, or that the world is coming to an end."

"But it is," said Etenia. "Unless we do something about it!" She looked to Womp, face tense and serious. "How about you? Would you join the academy? Would you like to be a dragon rider?"

Womp's eyes went wide with excitement and he was nodding so vigorously it was a wonder his head didn't fall off. Apparently being terrorized by Searsha hadn't dampened his enthusiasm at all. "Yes, ma'am. Yes I would. Very much so!"

"He's too young," Lathan muttered to Etenia. "Don't get his hopes up over nothing."

Etenia ignored him and spoke to Womp again: "Your name will be at the top of the list when the school opens. May I have the paper back for a moment?"

Womp handed it over with a crisp gesture, but still couldn't quite mask his giddiness. It was a good thing Searsha and Cember were out of view, or he'd probably have burst into joyful tears and ruined his professionalism entirely.

Etenia took her pen and scratched out the middle part of the poster, mentioning the Epyrian army and the fate of Pothena. She showed it to Lathan and Del. "Better?"

"It's not going to work," said Del.

"Or we will attract nothing but halfwits and scoundrels," said Lathan. "Either way, this will not help."

"Excellent," said Etenia, and pulled free another paper to start a new copy of the poster. "I'll just have to prove you both wrong, then."

Del knew what Lathan's concern was: in a city like Pothena, very few respectable candidates would come forward, if any. The ones they'd attract would be the unserious ones excited at the notion of being around a real-life dragon, and they'd never stop to wonder why they were getting such an incredible opportunity. Del agreed with Etenia that the Sivarnan process was painfully drawn out to the point of absurdity, but she was taking things too far in the other direction. Or, well, that was Lathan's point of view.

To Del, there was a different issue altogether: if she put these posters up around the market, she might indeed find a small assortment of young men and women eager to become dragon riders—but they'd all have one thing in common: they'd be able to read the posters in the first place. If Del hadn't been stranded on that island—if he were still just an orphan living on the streets of Pothena—and these posters had gone up around town, he wouldn't have stood a chance of becoming a rider himself. He wouldn't have even known that he was missing out.

Dragons didn't bond with just anyone. They sensed the character and sensibilities of their candidates, and if they found something they liked, they would hatch. Searsha had seen something in Del that no one else had—not even he had seen his worth, at first—and chosen a nobody to be her lifelong companion.

The trouble with Etenia's plan wasn't that it was too broad, it was that it left out a huge part of the population that might actually be better-suited to be dragon riders. The upper classes, like the members of council, couldn't see past their own checkbooks when making decisions. In the face of a crisis, they doubled down on convention. Even if it meant thousands of people would die.

But the kids on the street, like Womp and his friends, they knew how to adapt. If they didn't, they'd die of starvation, or in jail, or from an unexpected block to the back of the head. Etenia's peers would look at a baby dragon and expect it to conform to their wishes; Del's peers would be thinking of ways to use its nature to their advantage.

As Etenia wrote out a new draft of the poster, Del crouched down near Womp and spoke quietly, without making eye contact. It was how street kids passed information without drawing too much attention, and it immediately put Womp at ease.

"You know what's going on?" he asked.

"Mmhmm," said Womp. "Dragons."

"Right. We're looking for smart people to ride dragons. Understand?"

Womp nodded. "Yes, sir. I'll cover all the best spots. Library, tax office, charter—"

"No, you're not hearing me," said Del, and then gave Womp a stern look out of the corner of his eye to really make it land: "We're looking for smart people."

Womp's eyes widened in understanding.

Del grinned. "Spread the word. When it's time, I want to see you at the front of the line, no matter how young you may be. Understand?"

"Yes, sir," nodded Womp. "I'm your man."

Del smiled and stood back up as Etenia returned with the new poster. She handed it to Womp and laid a small sack of coins in his hand. "Give this to Master Gafri. I need as many copies as he can make. Put them all over the city, in all the important areas: the library, tax office, charter bank—"

"He's a smart kid. He can figure it out," said Del, and shooed the lad away. Etenia seemed incredibly proud of herself for finding a way to recruit new dragon riders. Del did, too—for making sure they got a better selection. "I noticed you didn't write where the school was going to be," he said. "That's kind of an important detail, don't you think?"

Before Etenia could answer, Arretal strode in from the garden with a roll of papers under his arm. "I've some news on that front," he said, and set down the biggest of the papers on a table, unrolling it to reveal a map of Pothena, in incredible detail.

He pointed at three large rectangles down near the harbor. "I've asked around, and these are the best candidates for your academy. The Braitmans own one of them, thankfully, and the other two are willing to sell. It won't take long to clear them out, so you'd be able to move in within a week or two.

"A week..." said Etenia, unhappily.

Lathan leaned closer to see the tiny writing along the tops of the rectangles. "What are these sizes? Pothenian yards, or—"

"Standard Imperial," said Arretal. "Why?"

Lathan winced like he hated to be the bearer of bad news—yet again. "These two won't work. They're too small for the number of candidates we're facing." He placed a finger on the third option, near the mouth of the bay. "This one, though..."

"Won't work either," said Del, and everyone looked up in unison. He shook his head at their blindness. "You do remember we're trying to fend off an invasion of sea-people, right? Building our academy on the water's edge may not be the best idea."

Arretal and Lathan looked back at the map, mouths hanging open at having been so blind, but Etenia's mind was already moving on to the next question, he could tell.

"There isn't a lot of land at this scale further up from the shoreline," said Arretal, scanning the rest of the map. "Certainly not something we could buy on short notice, or convert into a school for dragons."

"We don't need to," said Etenia, eyes shining with excitement. "Because there's already a school for dragons in Pothena!"

Del and Lathan had no idea what she was talking about—Lathan being a foreigner, and Del sometimes feeling like a stranger in his own city—but Arretal seemed to know exactly what she meant, and shook his head very seriously. "No, it's not safe."

"You don't know that," she said. "No one knows that."

Del tried to understand: "Wait, where are you—"

"Etenia, I forbid it," said Arretal. "You'll die in the attempt. The dragons of Pothena abandoned that place centuries ago. Don't you think there's a reason why?"

"We have our own dragons, Father. We'll be fine."

"You can't just—"

"Someone please explain what's going on!" shouted Lathan, which quieted everyone down.

Etenia unrolled the very top of the map, off the northern edge of the city, beyond the walls, where there was only mountainside and shadow. She planted her finger below a tiny scrawled label at the top of the tallest peak that said: "RUINS."

"Mount Pothena. The original city of Pothena," she said. "Back when dragons weren't taboo."

Arretal was not giving up on his dissent: "It's a myth."

"It's not a myth, it's real," she said. "I'm not saying it won't be in bad shape, but at least we know for certain that it can accommodate us, because this..." She stabbed at the label on the map with her finger. "This was the Pothenian Dragon Academy."

Arretal made his opinion clear by grunting unhappily and storming off. Lathan kept staring at the map, his face twisted with concern, like he was trying to find a better option in a sea of terrible ideas.

"Del?" asked Etenia. "What do you think?"

Del thought for a moment, running through everything he knew—and everything he knew he didn't know—and what each choice would mean for him, for his friends, for the eggs, and for Pothena at large. In the end, there was only one thing he could say:

"I think we'd better get Searsha and Cember a nice big meal, because it'll take a lot of energy to fly us up there."

CHAPTER 8

L ess than a day after they arrived in Pothena, they took off into the morning sun. Cember carried Etenia and Lathan as before, with Del on Searsha's back, and the eggs in their fancy new crate clutched below her. It was a familiar feeling, taking flight like this—so much so that Del had to remind himself they weren't leaving for good.

Etenia and Arretal had insisted they could leave the dragon eggs behind, to lighten their load, but both Lathan and Del had protested. Lathan, because he was sworn to protect them until his dying breath; Del, because he still didn't quite trust Etenia's father. He had nothing definitive to back up that feeling, but he wouldn't have been surprised if they'd come back to find Arretal had sold the eggs and run away with the money. He couldn't say that to Etenia, though, so he had just shrugged and told her it was best not to rile up Lathan.

Mount Pothena, from which the city took its name, was not a pretty-looking mountain. Ancient earthquakes had shattered it, causing massive shards of rock to slide out of place and re-settle. It looked like a mirror that had been hit with a hammer. That made it next to impossible to traverse by foot, and not exactly fun to survey by air, because for every bit of solid ground they might find, another five such areas were being obscured by ledges or outcroppings or canyons. It was a terrain built to confound and obscure.

The trees didn't help matters much, either. Pothena and Seafall had light and breezy tropical vegetation, much like the island they'd been trapped on. But the further up the mountain they went, the colder the air got, and the thicker the plant life became. Massive trees sprung out of the rock, their pointed tips touching the clouds that moved, lazily, around the middle of the mountain.

Etenia had dug deep into her school notebooks to find the things she half-remembered about the legend of the ancient city of Pothena, which was founded a millennia before. Del had never even really known how old the place was—such things weren't really important when trying to find your next meal—so he listened with intense curiosity.

The city had only housed a few hundred people, and even to its contemporaries seemed more myth than reality—except when the Pothenian dragon riders came swooping in from the sky to lay waste to anyone who dared cross them. Pothena in those days was not an economic superpower, but a collection of highly skilled bandits who rained down terror from above. Etenia clearly thought they'd changed a lot in the last thousand years; Del thought not much had changed, except the targets of their banditry.

According to Etenia, the dragon academy had been the crown jewel in Pothena's empire, a place renowned around the world for its teachings in bonding and warfare. Even Lathan admitted that much of Sivarna's oldest theory was borrowed from Pothena—though of course he phrased it as "Sivarna improved upon the Pothenian techniques."

But somewhere along the way, Pothena fell out of love with dragons, and the last time anyone actually saw the old city was over two hundred and fifty years. There had been expeditions sent out over the years— mostly in search of a rumored treasure that had been locked away in a massive stone vault by the original bandits—but none had found a trace of the city. Some believed the whole thing was just a myth, with no basis in reality; some thought the old cliffside road that led there had crumbled away forever; but some, like Etenia, thought they just hadn't come at the mountain from the right angle yet. To find the home of the bandit dragons, you had to be a dragon.

But after nearly two hours of flying, everyone was starting to wear out a little. Searsha and Cember were struggling to keep their altitude, and Etenia was visibly shivering in the frigid air. After a few more promising sites led to dead ends, Del called for them to land on a nearby platform to regroup.

It was the oddest thing: a meadow as big as the harbor, with trees and grass and flowers blowing in the wind. From the right angle, it seemed like something out of a fantasy of a far-off land—almost exactly the same scene that Del had imagined when he dreamed of dragons soaring through the sky—except it was sandwiched between two massive slabs of stone, a thousand feet above Pothena.

Cember stretched himself out in the grass and took a nap, looking absolutely content with his environment. Searsha, meanwhile, prowled the edge of the cliff, looking down at the world below with a wary squint of her eyes. Del, Etenia and Lathan unpacked their lunch—it was such a novelty, having ample food!—and gathered to figure out their next steps.

"It certainly is beautiful," said Lathan, looking around in awe. "But for the cold, it would be a fine place to live."

"Or hide out from sea monsters," said Del, pointedly.

Etenia glared at him. "Don't start with me."

He shrugged and took a bite of his food, chewing in silence, watching Searsha cock her head side to side as she looked at Seafall, far below. *Tiny little city,* she said. *Tiny little humans.*

"Feels like you could squish them like bugs, doesn't it?" Del asked, remembering their approach to Pothena the day before.

I could do that anyway, said Searsha, and Del laughed.

Etenia had prepared all her food but hadn't taken a bite. She looked too agitated for eating, and when Del finally noticed, she launched into expressing her frustrations: "We're no closer than when we started," she sighed. "I thought we might see some sign of something...but it's all just rocks and trees, rocks and trees. I wish the stories had given us more to go on. Everything is so vague. Up in a mountain? Where in the mountain?"

"Are we sure we're on the right side?" asked Del. "Who's to say the old city was even facing this direction."

Tiny little birds, said Searsha. *Yum. May I—*

"No," said Del. "You're supposed to be resting, remember?"

She sighed and went back to spying.

"You said the old Pothenians used to launch raids out onto the water, right? That means they must have been able to see the water. So that narrows the options down to—"

"An entire side of the mountain," sighed Etenia. "Which we've only managed to cover a small fraction of."

"Perhaps more research is in order," said Lathan. "There must be some books on the subject we could read, and with any luck, we might find—"

Old building, said Searsha.

Del waved her quiet. "We don't need you to announce every single—" He paused when he noticed the difference in her wording: "Tiny old building?"

No, she said. *Just old. Look.*

Del hurried over to the edge, where Searsha was leaning over—and there, down below, he saw it: the ruins of an ancient building, tucked in between two massive slabs of stone, masking it from the outside world to anyone who didn't know exactly where to look.

He gasped, and Etenia and Lathan hurried over to see.

"Do you think that's it?" asked Etenia. "It has no roof."

"It's been two hundred and fifty years," said Del. "It's a miracle it's still standing at all."

It is bathed in magic, said Searsha, craning her head to see better. *Ancient magic. Dragon magic.*

Lathan took a sharp breath. "Guarded magic? Is it booby-trapped?"

Searsha squinted, concentrating on something Del couldn't perceive, though he could feel the contours of the energy she was feeling. It was almost like a taste to him. Copper-ish, and stale. Searsha was probing it more carefully, bathing in the sensation.

I do not sense hostility, she said. *Though there is...sorrow.*

Lathan straightened out, face in a deep frown. "We proceed, but with caution. Dragon magic could still be quite potent, even after all this time. We don't want to get on the wrong side of a spell that no one alive can undo."

They mounted their dragons again and drifted gently down through the air currents, swaying this way and that to avoid coming in too suddenly. Lathan already looked wound so tight he might pop, so they did their best to seem cautious—even though they were all desperate to see this ancient building up close.

It had been hard to judge the scale from above, but as they got closer, it became clear this wasn't just any structure: it was massive. Lathan had been concerned about the scale of the warehouses down by the water, but this building could have fit three such buildings inside it, easily. The walls—more like tightly packed pillars—stretched up so far that they dwarfed the tallest buildings in Pothena.

The roof had indeed collapsed sometime in the past, leaving giant chunks of crumbled stone all over the place. Finding a place to land was a challenge, but they managed, settling down near the center of the structure.

It was surreal, standing there. Del had never felt so small in all his life. It wasn't just the scale of the place, but the way nature had started to retake its domain, with grass and vines and even trees covering every available surface. If they hadn't seen it from the air, they might have mistaken it for a very odd forest. Humans had made this—something this incredible—and then simply disappeared.

"Look," said Lathan, kneeling down and pulling some vegetation out of the way to reveal a long narrow trench, made in stone, running lengthwise down the middle of the building. "It's a fire channel. They had fire channels." His smile faded when he realized neither Del nor Etenia had any idea what he was saying. "It helps focus a dragon's skills. An intermediate test. Done right, they can target their fire into this channel, and have it run straight through to the other side."

Del looked down the length of the building. It would take him an hour to walk it, even if it weren't so cluttered with obstacles. "The other side of this?" he asked.

Lathan nodded, his smile returning. "I'm telling you, there is so much you haven't learned yet. But in a place like this..."

Del surveyed the area again. "Is a place like this even going to work?" he asked. "I mean, I don't want to be negative but it's—"

"Perfect," said Etenia, and when Del saw her face, he knew she was sold, one way or another. This would be their dragon academy. There was no debating it. "What would you call this space, Lathan?"

"The training hall," he said. "Depending on what else we find, it might double as the dragons' sleeping quarters. I'll be interested to see what other features the vegetation is hiding from us."

"Good," said Etenia with a smile. "You investigate here, and Del and I will see what other buildings we can find."

She started off without waiting for Del; he scrambled to catch up. He was so conflicted by their situation: to him, this place was nowhere near ready to use as a school in the timeframe they needed. Not to mention it was completely inaccessible by foot, which meant it would be up to Searsha and Cember to fly recruits back and forth—along with supplies, or they'd all starve to death. If Etenia's posters did the trick and they were swamped with applicants, he had no idea how they'd manage. Not to mention the issue of where that many people would eat and sleep. A roofless stadium was not going to be fun for anyone, especially with temperatures as low as they were.

He wanted to warn Etenia off the idea, but every time she looked back at him, her smile was so intoxicating he couldn't bring himself to say anything. He followed her outside the building and down a long stretch of winding stone steps, into a courtyard at the edge of another cliff, right above a massive waterfall that was cascading down an impossible distance, into the misty nothingness below.

There were more buildings here, carved into the mountainside itself. Some had wooden doors, still intact, while others seemed to have been blown open by a powerful force of some kind. They peered in a few windows, revealing offices and living quarters that hadn't been touched in hundreds of years. They were covered in dust, true, but looked ready for their owners to come back home and pick up where they left off.

Dishes on tables, beds made up with linens, vases whose flowers had long since rotted away.

It was ghostly, and strangely ominous. Copper-like, and musty.

Around a corner, they found a pair of massive doors that were closed tight, and by the way Etenia was marching toward them, it was clear she was keenly interested in what was inside. She grabbed a large metal ring on the left door and started to pull—no such luck. Del joined her, and together they managed to open the thing enough for them to sneak through.

It was a library. Built on the same scale as the training hall, it was lined with wooden bookshelves and thousands upon thousands of tomes. Some had basically disintegrated with age, but there were still more to be found here than in the rest of the Pothena, several times over.

Etenia walked past the closest shelves, her mouth hanging open in shock. There wasn't much light to go by—only what came through the half-opened door—but even in the small distance they covered together, the treasure trove of knowledge made itself well known.

"Dragon riding..." Etenia said, scanning the titles. "Defensive techniques. F-flight formation, I think?"

"An...ana..." said Del, struggling with a word. "Anatomy?"

"Dragon anatomy?" gasped Etenia. "Really? Oh! Anatomy and physiology, and here, saddle constructions, and—"

"Dragon diets," said Del. "Dragon care. *Egg* care we've got that one covered, I think."

"Dragon habits and culture?" said Etenia.

"Dragons have culture?" laughed Del.

I can still hear you, said Searsha.

Etenia gasped loudly and pulled a large book off the shelf. It nearly came apart in her hands, and she scrambled to hold it together. Del raced over and helped her carry it across the room to a table that was luckily in the thin shaft of light coming in through the door.

Etenia opened the book carefully and turned to a page with an intricately designed map...of Pothena. Parts of the paper were so stained with moss and mildew, and the writing wasn't in an alphabet Del recognized at all. It was like being illiterate all over again. But he did recognize the Seafall bay from their approach, and the curve of the harbor area from their flight up the mountain.

"What's this about?" he asked. "I can't read it."

"Neither can I," sighed Etenia. "But if I'm right, these letters here mean 'nest'...which means this might be a map of dragon nesting sites in Pothena."

Del frowned at her. "Nesting sites? You mean—"

"Pothena used to be a powerful dragon-based society," she said. "I always thought the dragons left us, but after what I saw at council yesterday...maybe we're just ignoring them. Maybe Pothena still has dragons, and we just haven't found them yet."

CHAPTER 9

They landed back in Seafall in the early afternoon, but took no time to rest. Etenia was crackling with energy, unable to sit still, gripping the ancient book so tight Del was afraid it might come apart and blow away in the wind.

"What's the plan?" he asked, as she paced back and forth, waiting for Lathan to return from his room.

"I know many of the council elders speak Old Pothenian—at least at ceremonies—but I don't want to alert them to our plans."

"Don't worry," said Del. "I doubt they'd even agree to see us again."

"Which leaves us with one option: the university."

Del shivered at the thought of it: occupying some prime real estate in the center of Pothena, the university was home to some of the most obnoxious people he'd ever seen. Rich people would abuse you and call for your arrest, but the professors and students at the university weren't that wealthy, and they were bitter about it.

They came into the market wearing their ceremonial robes, using words nobody fully understood, and instead of haggling over prices, they subjected farmers to rambling treatises on the history of the agricultural this-and-that until they were given a discount just to shut up. Shipping merchants would look at him like he was a waste of space, but university-dwellers actually said it to his face. And worse yet, they didn't carry enough coin on them to make mugging them worthwhile.

It made sense that Etenia would want to go there to have someone translate the book, but that didn't make it any less unpleasant. Del might have let her go alone, but the way she was carrying that book made it seem like she had a valuable treasure in hand—and that would make her a target.

The second Lathan emerged from his room, they were off: they kept to Seafall as long as they could manage, exiting at the gate closest to the university. The streets were mercifully quiet thanks to the blazing sun right overhead—though Del still spied a few unsavory characters watching them from doorways and shaded alleys. That would have been him, not so long ago. It made him want to move faster.

The main doors to the university campus were guarded, though selectively. Faculty and students were left alone, while anyone who looked "uneducated" would be caught and thrown back outside. Thankfully for Del, the clothes he was wearing masked the truth; the guards gave him a curt nod of acknowledgement and otherwise ignored him.

The campus was incredible: at its center was a green space full of winding stone paths, immaculately maintained trees and wading pools, around which students sat and pondered the fate of the universe. Or at least that's what it looked like they were doing, just staring into the sky. Even on the island, with literally nothing else to do, Del had found better ways to spend his time. He glared at them all. Not that they noticed.

There was a collection of beautiful buildings all around the edge of the green space, looking like the ruins from the mountainside city with modern Pothenian architecture. Each one had words carved into the stone above their entrances, but in a script Del couldn't decipher. Some of the letters seemed to match the writing in the book, so at least they were getting closer to their goal, hopefully.

"Excuse me," Etenia said to a passing student. The young man snapped out of his educated trance and regarded her like she was a talking rodent for having disturbed him so.

"Yes?" he asked, eyeing her cautiously.

"Where would we go to find someone fluent in Old Pothenian?" she asked. "Is there a department or—"

He pointed off to the left, to a towering building with a glimmering marble facade. "History and Letters," he said. "Seek out Professor Holgum. He shall illuminate you."

Etenia's pleasant smile froze, and Del did his best not to laugh. The student turned on his heel and marched away, like he was upset at having conversed with such simpletons at all.

It took a few tries, but they finally located the esteemed Professor Holgum, hunched over a long table at the back of the building, reading from a scroll with a magnifying glass pressed practically to his eyeball. Etenia cleared her throat to get his attention, and he looked up, unhappily sneering at them with one gigantic eye.

"Hmm? Yes?" he grunted, setting down the glass. "Office hours are—"

"We're not students, Professor," said Etenia in her more pleasant voice —Del was starting to realize she could turn the pleasant version of herself on and off at will. "We're actually—"

"Enrollment takes place in the fall," he said. "See the Admissions officer to—"

"No, sir, sorry for the confusion. We're looking for someone to translate some text for us."

His face twisted up like he'd eaten something extremely sour. "Translate, you say? From which to what?"

She gripped the book a little tighter but didn't reveal it yet. "Old Pothenian," she said. "Or at least we think it's Old Pothenian. The script is—"

"The Second Reformation," he said, like something had happened during this Second Reformation that had personally offended him. "They rejected the notion of the old alphabet, you see. Influenced by heretical thinking, so they upended the whole language. It sounds the same, but the words are...are..." He seemed to lose his train of thought. Then he squinted at her. "You look familiar."

"Etenia Browder, sir," she said, giving a small curtsy. "Daughter of—"

"Arretal Browder, of course," he said. "In the eyes. It's apparent in the eyes." He snorted loudly, and spat behind the table, then regarded them all once more. "Most of the so-called ancient texts in circulation are fakes, you know. Just because you found a book with cracked binding at the back of your father's study, doesn't mean—"

"It's not that, Professor," she said. "It's a genuine relic." She carefully laid the book down on the table, just shy of Holgum's scroll, and stepped back so he could see.

His face changed from displeasure to surprise, and then for a second he almost looked like a child getting a shiny bauble. He put the glass back to his eye and leaned in a little closer, trying to focus better, his lips mouthing something inaudible as his hand danced just above the cover and the words written there.

"Where did you find this?" he asked.

Etenia was about to answer truthfully, Del could tell, so he interjected: "Hidden room in the villa. Discovered during renovations."

Etenia glared at him. Apparently lying was frowned upon in her world.

Oh well, she'd get used to it.

"It is incredible..." said Holgum, lifting the cover gently. "I'm sure your father will not mind the university borrowing it for—" He stopped, and his face tightened into a frown. "What is this?"

Etenia didn't get a chance to answer before he dropped the cover and shoved the book back toward her, and almost sent it tumbling off the table. "A book about dragons, hmm? That's what you brought me? Fairy tales?"

Del watched Lathan tense so suddenly, he thought he might take a swing at the aged professor. Etenia was more surprised than offended.

"But it's a genuine artifact that—"

"*This* is the Department of *History*, my dear. We study *fact*. If it's fantasy you're after, seek out Professor Staaf in Literature and Mythology." He looked back at his scroll again, as if they weren't there at all. "Good day."

Etenia gathered up the book and practically stumbled her way out of the building. Everyone around them was staring—they'd either overheard Holgum's outburst, or heard fast-spreading rumors of it—and it made Etenia walk even faster, just to escape it. When they finally got outside, Del could see she wasn't upset about the exchange so much as furious.

"The nerve of that man!" she hissed. "Mythology? Fairy tales?"

"We should have Searsha and Cember pay him a visit," said Del with a grin.

"Del, please, act responsibly," said Lathan. "One dragon is more than enough."

It took them a few minutes to find the building for Literature and Mythology—it was crammed in the back, cast in perpetual shadow where no one would see it. The front door stuck and took both Del and Lathan's help to pull open. Inside, the filthy windows made the entire place dim and dingy, even at midday. The place was deserted, except for a few students passed out at tables with emptied bottles of wine in their hands.

"What exactly are they studying?" asked Del as they walked past, trying to keep as quiet as possible.

There was only one light on in the whole place, so they headed that way directly. Off to the side, amongst rows of dubious bookshelves, was a woman hunched over a table, scribbling notes in a book while reading another. Her graying hair was a mess, and she had ink stains on her fingers and face, but she was possibly the most frenetic person Del had ever seen: she seemed electric in her movements, eyes wide open despite the dark circles under them. She didn't react to the first two times Etenia cleared her throat, so Del tried:

"Professor Staaf?"

The professor suddenly swatted at her face like a fly had landed there. Then she looked at her hand like she wasn't entirely sure why it had just struck her, and only then did she notice the three strangers standing across the table from her.

"How long have you been there?" she asked.

"We just arrived," said Etenia, cautiously. "Professor Staaf, my name is—"

"Bettine, please. No one calls me Professor Staaf. Or Doctor. Or, well, anything. Who are you again?"

"My name is Etenia Browder, and this is Del, and Lathan Phrac of Sivarna, who—"

Bettine's eyes went wide in surprise. "Sivarna! Sivarna, really!" She turned her book around to show them. "You people need to find better illustrators. This textbook on dragon physiology is just...it's an abomination. My eyes hurt from reading it." On the page was a drawing of a dragon—not unlike Cember—but in a cross-section, and highlighting the bone structure. Bettine pointed her pen to a few key areas. "See? Here, here and here. How would that even work? The wings can't connect to the shoulders like that, or they'd never be able to walk!"

Lathan frowned at the illustration, but then doubly so at her. "But...that's how it is."

She laughed like a maniac. "Oh, is it? And how would you know something like that?"

Lathan seemed unsure how to answer, so he tried: "Because I'm the Sivarnan Royal Master Dragon Trainer, and I have lived my entire life in the company of dragons."

She rolled her eyes at him and started gathering up her things. "Right. Sure. Sivarna's Royal Master Dragon Trainer, here in Pothena, nitpicking my work. I believe you completely." She stood up and sneered at them all. "Who put you up to this, hmm? Dillard? It was Dillard, wasn't it. Well, I won't fall for it. You go back and tell him I won't be fooled again. Three times is plenty, thank you, so please leave me be. I have very important work to do, and if you think—"

Etenia put the book down on the table and opened to the cover page. "This isn't a prank," she said. "We need your help."

Bettine scoffed as she leaned over to read the text. "And what makes you think I'll—oh goodness are you kidding me?" She looked up, eyes wide in shock. "This is a Nnsi! A genuine Nnsi! 'Pothena's Dragon By Class and Nature, Fifth Edition'! Where did you find this?"

Del had been intending to lie about the origins of the book a second time—and as many times as it took before they got an answer they could live with—but something about Bettine struck him as different. She was nothing like him, but he still felt a kind of kinship. Maybe it was the way she single-mindedly focused on the task at hand, or the way she didn't seem to have a filter at all. Whatever it was, he couldn't bring himself to tell her a story about where they'd found the book. He had a feeling she'd be more useful with all the facts, anyway.

He pointed in a generally upward direction with his thumb. "The library in the Old City," he said.

Bettine crawled over the table to grab him by the shoulders. "*You found the Old City?*" she said so loudly that the sleeping students woke up, momentarily. "How?"

Etenia turned a few pages deeper into the book, to the map. She set her finger on the text. "Please, Professor," she said. "We need your help to translate this text. What does it say?"

Bettine leaned in a little closer, running her finger along the words until her face broke into a smile and she nodded exuberantly. "I have no idea."

Del did a double take. "Wait, what?"

"You have to understand, at the time this was written, Pothena was under constant attack by outside armies intent on stealing our world-class dragons." Del couldn't help but notice Lathan stifling a chuckle at that. "Nnsi wrote these catalogues in code to prevent their secrets from falling into the wrong hands. I mean, can you imagine what would happen if some barbaric invader"—she gave Lathan a sideways glance —"were to discover the exact location and temperament of all our dragon nests?"

Etenia got ahead of Lathan's scoffing, just in time: "So you're saying the book is useless?"

88

"No, of course not," said Bettine. "If you have the key, translating the code will be simple. Without the key, however, you'll never know if you're walking into an egg cache, or a booby trap. And oh, ancient Pothena so enjoyed their booby traps."

"What does the key look like?" asked Del. "How can we find it?"

Bettine scratched the back of her matted hair as she thought: "It would be another book. Something fairly light, and on a totally different subject, meant to disappear into the background and never be noticed."

Del winced and looked at Etenia: "There's a lot of background in that library. How are we supposed to find just one book?"

"Well," said Bettine, closing up the book and hugging it to her chest like it was her most treasured possession. "Despite all my many pressing deadlines and responsibilities to the student population of the department of Literature and Mythology, I would be willing to accompany you back to the Old City to help you look."

Del was amused enough to agree on the spot, and he could see Etenia was thinking the same thing. But then Lathan cleared his throat and whispered to them both: "A moment, please."

They regrouped a short distance away, where Lathan's expression said very clearly that he was not on board with bringing Bettine with them, or even talking to her further. "This is a mistake," he said. "We should find another way."

"What other way?" asked Del. "Even if we find the key book—which won't be easy—we'll still need to bring it all back here to have her translate it."

"And time is of the essence, Lathan," said Etenia. "If there are Pothenian dragons to be found, wouldn't you rather we start our dragon academy with them, rather than—"

"Dragon academy?" asked Bettine, suddenly far closer that any of them expected. "Sorry, I was just dusting this...thing...and happened to over-hear you talking about a dragon academy of some sort."

Lathan glowered at her. "You're not invited."

The vitriol was so sudden, Del's face turned up in an involuntary grin. Something about Bettine really got under Lathan's skin. It was enter-taining to watch.

"Lathan!" gasped Etenia. "Professor Staaf is a—"

"Professor Staaf is a historian," he said. "No, I'm sorry, she's a mythol-ogist. Her knowledge is theoretical, out of date, and based on scraps of information that other, more advanced cultures threw away." He pointed at the physiology book she had been studying when they came in.

"Excuse me?" she gasped. "I'll have you know this is a—"

"Middle-grade textbook," said Lathan. "For children. Civilian children. And yet they will still know more about the wing structure of a dragon than you evidently do!"

Etenia looked scandalized and horrified by Lathan's outburst, but Del was enjoying it immensely. He'd always suspected Lathan had more fire in him than he let on, but now that it was on full display—and directed at someone else—it was wildly entertaining. He sounded an awful lot like Professor Holgum's protégé, but that only added to the fun.

Bettine turned to Etenia and held her chin up high. "Miss Browder, I formally request to be an advisor at your new dragon academy. You will need someone with experience—"

"Ha!" laughed Lathan.

"—with experience in Pothenian dragons, as they are very different creatures of a nobler pedigree, and require special care that someone steeped in Sivarnan dogma—"

"Dogma?" gasped Lathan. "Are you implying—"

"I imply nothing, sir," she said, scowling at him. "The abuse Sivarna subjects its dragons to is well documented, and honestly despicable."

Lathan was just about to shout something back when, from outside, they heard screams and shouting, and an alarm bell started to ring like mad. Del's heart stopped: The Epyr? Already? He dashed through the building, Etenia, Lathan and Bettine close behind, until they burst out into the sunlight and out toward the courtyard—

—where Cember was sitting in one of the ponds. He glared at the students, who were all scrambling away, shrieking in terror, running to hide inside their pretty stone buildings.

Bettine came to a stop, her mouth hanging open in shock—which then turned to giddiness. "A Laros Blue!" she gasped. "Oh my, he's magnificent! Look at the coloring around the snout, and the eyes!" She started to laugh. "Why is he here?"

Del gave Etenia a sideways smirk. "Yeah, why is he here?" he asked.

She shrugged like nothing much was going on. "I asked him to stop by," she said, nodding across the way as Professor Holgum came rushing out to see what the commotion was about, and came face-to-face with a stunning blue dragon. Cember took one look at the old man, then arched his back like he was about to breathe fire—

—and belched a big cloud of sulphur at Holgum. The old man staggered back, hacking and coughing.

Etenia grinned, satisfied. "How do you like that fairy tale?"

CHAPTER 10

Getting back to the Old City was much simpler, now that they knew where it was. They came in from the front this time, between two giant stony towers that masked the buildings tucked inside. It was a truly magnificent sight, especially in the late afternoon sun. The mountainside seemed to be made up of shards of orange and blue as the light cast rich shadows in the most unexpected ways.

At the front of the city was a large space like a town square, looking out over a steep drop toward the ocean far beyond. There were remnants of a kind of railing along the edge, but some of it had clearly broken off in the last few centuries. It gave a dramatic view of the bay, of Pothena and Seafall. Del wondered if this was the place the ancient dragons had landed when they were coming back from their raids. He imagined the square bustling with dragons of every size and color, milling about in a world where they were commonplace.

All his life, he'd dreamed of a world like that, and it had been right behind him, up in the mountains, the whole time.

Cember landed directly, but Searsha, sensing Del's mood, took a moment to swoop around the area and let the moment breathe a little longer before they, too, landed in the square.

Before they'd left, Bettine had been desperate to see this place, and more specifically the library. But now that she was here, she was easily distracted, running from place to place to gush about the trivia that suddenly made a lot more sense.

"There, here, do you know what this is?" she asked, pointing to an old metal ring embedded in the stone. Del tried to think of what it could be: the thing was about as wide as his torso and as thick as his arm.

"Someplace to tie your dragon?" he asked.

Lathan made a loud noise of intense displeasure, as if Del had greatly offended him. But Bettine clapped her hands, nodding excitedly. "That's right! That building over there must have been for the dentist. They had a kind of muzzle that attached to a rope, and then tied here to keep the dragon from thrashing about during extractions."

"Extractions," sighed Lathan. "Dragons don't need tooth extractions."

"Maybe not Sivarnan dragons," she said. "But Pothenian dragons grew a new set every three years, and if they weren't removed safely, an infection could—"

"Infection!" he said. "Oh, now I've heard everything."

Etenia gave Del a nervous smile, and he took the hint: "The library's this way," he said, and led them on.

Del and Lathan managed to push both of the heavy doors open fully this time, letting in the sun to help them work. Del had been about to light a torch when Etenia pointed out the whole place was brittle and dry, and might go up in flames a little too easily if they weren't careful. They only had an hour or so before it got too dark to read, so they had to move fast.

"So," said Del, as they all gathered back together. "This is where we found the book. We don't have a lot of time, so let's split up and see if we can—"

"Here it is," said Bettine, taking a thin book off the shelf, right next to where the Nnsi one had been.

"Seriously?" asked Del. "It was right there?"

Bettine shrugged. "Nnsi was a genius. The librarian? Less so."

She hurried over to a table and set down the two books, turning to the map on the one hand, and with the key book in the other. She scanned the text, back and forth, muttering things to herself as she worked. Etenia was watching carefully, clearly trying to understand what was happening. Del watched her, amazed at how hard she was willing to work. Whatever the issue, whatever the skill required, she seemed determined to master it. It was constantly bewildering to him, because he always saw the rich and powerful as being too lazy to do anything for themselves. Whatever the issue, they'd hire help to do it. Etenia didn't fit with that image, and he wasn't sure why. Was it their time on the island that changed her, or had she always been special? He wanted to know, but he didn't know how to find out.

"Ah," said Bettine, and turned the book around to show the rest of them. "Yes, well. If you see this marking here..." She pointed to a symbol that looked like a triangle spearing a circle. "That is the root word for 'nest'. Anywhere you see that, Pothena had an established dragon nest."

"Excellent, thank you," said Lathan. "You've been a great help. We'll get you back home immediately." He turned to Del and Etenia. "It's too dark to go out looking tonight, but if we—"

"Excuse me?" said Bettine. "I'm not going home. I'm staying here."

That was unexpected, and not just because the place was a horrifying mess of mold and dust. Del still trusted Bettine more than made sense to him, but his first reaction to her saying she wanted to stay was sounds great! But he could see on Lathan's face that that opinion wasn't universal…

Lathan sighed and glared at her. "This isn't a hotel."

"Funny, I saw lots of rooms."

"Professor Staaf, we greatly appreciate the help you've given us, but I think we can take it from here."

"Oh really? I translated a few words on a map and now you're fine?"

"Yes, I think so."

She pointed at the map. "This is a very old book. Over three hundred years old. The markings on it might not even be accurate anymore, so—"

"Ah, yes," said Lathan. "But as you know, dragons are creatures of habit. Once they establish nests, they won't leave."

She pointed to a portion of the map. "So you expect me to believe there's still a dragon nest here, after three hundred years?"

"Trust me," he said. "I know dragons."

She sighed melodramatically. "Well that's a relief, because I would have assumed the dragons might have abandoned this particular nest after an earthquake a hundred and fifty years ago caused the whole area to break loose and fall into the sea."

There was a long awkward silence.

Lathan turned to Etenia. "She's a distraction."

"She seems helpful to me," said Del, which earned him a stern look. He ignored it and smiled to Bettine. "How would you feel about leaving the university and teaching at a dragon academy instead?"

Her mouth dropped open and she started to tremble with excitement. "I'm glad you said that, because I already resigned and I have nowhere else to go." She shook his hand enthusiastically. "I will do my best to help you discover and train dragons to live in this modern world, in peace and prosperity."

Peace and prosperity? Del had a sudden realization they hadn't explained everything to Bettine yet. "It might not be quite so peaceful," he said. "We're aiming more for a war footing."

Bettine looked taken aback. She looked from Del to Etenia to Lathan, confused. "Who are we invading?" She gasped. "Sivarna?"

Lathan grumbled. "We're not invading anyone. We're protecting against an invasion. And when the Epyrian army climbs out of the water to wreak havoc in Pothena, you won't want to be—"

"Epyrian?" asked Bettine.

Lathan was so frustrated with her every word, he looked ready to snap. "They're an aquatic race that lives at the bottom of the sea, and are—"

"Oh, you mean the *Qapira*. Sorry, I misunderstood—"

Etenia was confused, and didn't bother trying to hide it. "Who are the Qapira? H-how do you—"

"The Qapira are an ancient civilization that, as you say, live at the bottom of the sea. This city we're in now was actually built in response to the threats posed by the Qapiran army, which is why it's up so high, and also why Pothena's earliest heroes were all dragon riders who swooped down to save passing ships from Qapiran marauders."

Del was stunned by the revelation. Etenia's version of the story, about Pothena being a nation of ruthless pirates preying on the weak, had made such obvious sense to him at the time. He could imagine the straight line from that reality to his. But if what Bettine was saying was true, everything he'd believed about Pothenians was wrong.

Pothena had been protecting ships with their dragons? From the Qapira? It was a shocking revelation, because it meant those Pothenians had been noble, and selfless, and heroic. How had things gone so wrong that they had abandoned their dragons, abandoned their city, and started abusing their most vulnerable citizens? There'd been a cruel sort of comfort in the idea that he was just another in a long line of victims under the thumb of the ruling class. The notion that it had been better in the past? That was infuriating.

But there was another angle that jarred him even more: it meant those early Pothenians, dragon riders and masters of the sky, had found the Qapira so terrifying they built their home in a mountain to escape them.

Suddenly, their predicament seemed more terrifying than ever.

Bettine, meanwhile, was stuck on another thought: "You called them, what, Epyrian? What is that?"

Etenia nodded toward Del. "He overheard it. In a vision."

Bettine turned to Del, her mouth hanging open. "You have a psychic link with them? In this era? Oh, that's incredible!"

"It's happened before?" asked Del.

"Three times, in the distant past," she said. "Some of the greatest heroes in Pothenian history have had psychic links to the Qapira. It's a double-edged sword, of course. You can spy on what they're planning, and—"

"They can see through my eyes, too," nodded Del.

Bettine froze. "Oh. Uh. No, I meant about losing your mind and dying young. But yes, that too."

Del could feel Etenia's eyes on him, but he didn't need her worry to make his own worse. Losing his mind? Dying young? All because the Kraken had tried to use him as an agent to steal the dragon eggs? When he'd left Pothena in search of a better life, he had been trying to avoid dying young. And now suddenly he was doomed, with no way to escape his fate at all?

"All right," he said, shaking off the terror deep inside him. "The link only matters if the Qapira are alive to use it. So let's find some dragons and make sure we're ready when the Qapira creep out of the ocean."

"Good idea," nodded Lathan, who, by agreeing with Del, was accepting that Bettine wasn't a complete crackpot. It looked like that fact pained him. And yet, he seemed willing to put the mission first and ignore that conflict for the greater good. "There's lots to prepare," he said. "Both here and in town." He gave Bettine the slightest of nods. "The professor can stay here tonight, and get an early start on reading."

Bettine flashed him a wide grin and patted his arm. "We'll make great partners, Master Phrac."

That pushed Lathan back over the edge. He looked ready to vomit.

Every time Del had a moment to breathe, he kept returning to the idea of losing his mind and dying young. He had so many questions, but was afraid that if Bettine explored his connection to the Qapira any more, she might stumble upon a fact that would make him a liability to their plans. But still, the questions burned inside of him: why would he lose his mind? Was the mind issue related to the dying, or were they separate things that happened regardless? Would he know when it was coming, or would he just snap one day, and never know why? Was his connection to all Qapira, or could he save himself by severing the connection with the one whose eyes he kept seeing through, and—

"All right," said Etenia, snapping him out of his thoughts. "It's been a long day. We'll all stay here for the night and start fresh in the morning. Lathan, we'll drop you back at the villa. I need you to prepare a new poster, telling all those interested in being dragon riders to meet in the northwest square every day at dawn. Cember and Searsha can take turns flying applicants up here, starting next week."

"What's happening between now and next week?" asked Del—there were three days in there unaccounted for.

"A lot," Etenia said, and Del wondered when all these plans had apparently been made. "Professor, can you prepare us a new map on a smaller paper, and only include the nests that could have survived the change in terrain over the years?"

"Of course," said Bettine. "I'll do it right now, while there's light."

"Thank you," said Etenia. "Cember and I will take that map and search for any surviving dragons. Del, you and Searsha can help Professor Staaf clean up the Old City and make it ready to house—"

"No, sorry, that's not going to happen," said Del. "I'm not letting you go dragon hunting alone."

Etenia stood taller, her expression on the edge between confusion and anger. "Everyone has a role to play, Del. Just because you don't want to clean—"

"It's not about the cleaning. It's about the danger," he said. "You're going to be flying into places where nobody has been in centuries. Yes, there might be dragons there, but there might not be, anymore. There might be mountain-Krakens waiting to kill you."

"Del, you're being—"

"And by the way, what's to say Pothenian dragons are friendly? They might eat you on sight! No, we're going as a team."

"You don't even care about Pothena!" Etenia said, a cold edge to her voice. "What would happen if we actually find a dragon out there? What would you say?"

"What, you think I'd sabotage the school because I got kicked a lot as a child?"

Etenia gave him a look that said that was exactly what she was worried about.

"I'm not that dumb," he said. "And if it's your responsibility to fly off into danger, it's my responsibility to protect you."

"No, Del," she said. "Your responsibility is to do your job here at the school. I don't need protecting, especially not when there's so much to do." She took a step back. "Professor, bring me the map as soon as it's ready." She glared at Del before leaving, and said: "And we don't need two copies."

CHAPTER 11

D el woke early, mostly because he'd barely slept. There were rooms in the Old City—sleeping quarters for the ancient residents—and some even had beds in them. But between the dust and the mold and general mustiness, those rooms were quickly rejected as an option. Lathan had suggested retiring to the villa for the night, but Etenia refused to go. She wanted to get Bettine's map at first light, and traveling back and forth would take too long, not to mention tiring Cember out before another potentially arduous flight.

The end result was each of them finding an old office to sleep in, and finding the delicate balance between the choking, dusty air and freezing to death with the doors left open. Del was used to hostile conditions, but even he found it painfully difficult to relax. He was up before the sun rose, sitting in the doorway to his room, watching Etenia's quarters for any sign of movement.

It was a difficult situation he was in, being at war with her. He could understand her anger: he did talk about how awful Pothena had been to him quite a lot. If someone had told him that he would potentially be an ambassador for Pothena on a life-or-death mission, he would probably have laughed himself silly. But he couldn't just abandon her, even if she didn't want a chaperone. Her own issues made it even more complicated, too, given her father's habit of doubting her ability and hijacking her ideas to benefit someone else. When Del told her he was accompanying her on her search for the dragon nests, he had poked every bruise she had at once, and she'd lashed out in anger. She must've thought he was dismissing her planning abilities and treating her like a lesser member of the team. And he was, in a way.

But what she didn't understand—and he didn't quite know how to explain—was that it wasn't her that he doubted. It was the rest of the world. The cardinal rule of living on the streets was to be ready and assume everything—everything—would go wrong. Was a stranger offering you free food? It was probably poisoned. Did you find a stray coin on the ground? Probably a trap. Did someone call you their friend? You were about to get suckered. The only way to survive was to plan for the absolute worst thing that might happen, and be surprised if things went your way.

Etenia's plan to go searching for dragon nests seemed simple enough, but it left no room for disaster. What if she got caught in a rockslide with no one to help? What if the ancient Pothenians' booby traps were still in working order? What if there were dragons in the mountain, and they wanted to stay hidden—and were willing to fight for that right? Her plan assumed things would go right, but Del knew nothing ever went right. But since he couldn't tell her not to go, his only option was to insist he accompany her, to be a second set of eyes to spot the danger coming before it struck.

He trusted her, he did. He was just afraid she trusted fate more than it deserved.

He wanted to go to her room and tell her that, to explain himself as best he could, but the look on her face when she'd gone to bed had been a pretty stern warning to keep his distance. Interrupting her sleep would only make things worse. He had to wait for her to get up, and catch her then.

But as the sun started to rise—faintly, almost imperceptibly at first—a worry crept through Del's mind: Etenia wanted to start early, but she hadn't woken up yet. Maybe the events of the last few days had worn her down, but even fighting the Kraken hadn't slowed her that much. Suddenly he was afraid something bad had happened to her. He hadn't checked her room before she'd shut herself in—maybe there was a wild animal in there that had attacked her in her sleep. Maybe she was dying, while he watched her door, waiting for her to leave.

It would only make things worse, but he had to be sure. He walked across the courtyard to her room and pressed his ear to the thick wooden door. No sounds. No sounds at all. He knocked lightly, then more forcefully. "Etenia?" he called. "It's morning."

No answer. No movement. His jaw tightened as his heart raced. He took the handle and pushed the door in and gasped—

—because the room was empty. Etenia was gone.

He hurried back into the courtyard, trying to tell if he'd just opened the wrong door. But no, that was definitely her room. She'd left in the night, while he'd been trying to sleep. She'd snuck off, which meant...oh no. She'd already gone!

Del raced through the city, skidding and slipping on loose rubble—they really needed to tidy up, and soon—before bursting through the front door of the library, where Bettine was sitting at a tall stack of books, reading in a way that could only be described as intense. Had anyone even tried to sleep last night besides him? She looked up at him as he came in, and he could tell she hadn't slept a wink. She had a small candle off to the side, safely away from anything flammable, that was near the end of its wick.

"The map," he said, out of breath. "You gave her the map?"

She nodded. "As requested," she said. "She came by hours ago so she wouldn't miss a second of daylight."

Del slumped, biting back a curse. She'd outsmarted him. She was so intent on proving her ability that she was racing into danger, and there was nothing he could do to stop her. She'd probably sworn Bettine to secrecy, and without her help, he'd never be able to figure out where to go.

"Professor," he said gently. "About the map..."

"Oh, yes. A fine specimen, if I do say so myself. Very clear. All sites marked in order of likelihood of success. Took forever to get it just right."

Del sighed, feeling even worse. If it had taken Bettine forever to get it right, what hope did he have?

She sorted through a sheaf full of papers. "I mean, look at all these drafts..." She turned a map around for him and gave him a devious smile. "This one has a smudge. Totally unusable, wouldn't you say?"

Del realized what she was saying, and what it meant. He snatched the map from her hand with a wide smile on his face and barely had time to yell: "Thank you, Professor!" before racing out the door toward the broken cliffside railing.

"Searsha!" he shouted, tucking the map into his shirt. "We have to hurry! You ready?"

She must have sensed him getting up, because her answer was instantaneous: *We are chasing Cember and Etenia?*

"You knew they were gone?"

You did not alert me of your plan to defy Etenia's wishes and make her angry. But I am prepared nonetheless.

"Fine. Good," he said. "Then let's go!" And he leapt off the edge of the cliff, arms spread wide like he could fly himself. He expected Searsha to swoop in and catch him, but worryingly, she was nowhere in sight.

Oh, you mean now? she asked.

Del started to panic—but only for a second, before Searsha came soaring out of the clouds and navigated under him with expert precision. He grabbed hold of her and settled himself into his riding posture.

Perhaps next time you might consider advance warning before jumping off cliffs.

"I trust you," he said—and he surprised himself by saying it. What had happened to him that he was willing to throw himself off cliffs and just believe there would be someone to catch him? He did trust her, more than he could express. And it was liberating.

I am honored, she said. *But you are still stupid. Where are we going?*

Del pulled the map from his shirt and studied it long enough to spot the first candidate in Bettine's list. It wasn't far, just a little farther down and to the right. He concentrated on the drawing as hard as he could, and felt Searsha's mind join in, too.

Ah, I see, she said, and dove straight for their target.

The passed through a stretch of clouds before coming out just above a jagged peak that was perfectly replicated on Bettine's map. From what Del could see, the nest across the way from the peak, beneath a heavy overhang. Searsha glided downward with expert precision until they found the overhang—or what was left of it.

"It collapsed," sighed Del, as they circled the scene. The rock had broken loose some time in the last few centuries and crushed or covered whatever had been there before. It was hard to tell if there had ever been a nest there at all, but one thing was for certain: there wasn't one now.

And Etenia wasn't there, either. She'd already moved on.

Del found the second-most likely candidate and barely had time to take hold before Searsha raced into the sky again, wings flapping urgently to make up for lost time. He didn't know if she was on his side or Etenia's in their little fight—she'd claimed ignorance, but he doubted she hadn't figured out his plan on her own. Maybe the bond between dragon and rider didn't cancel out all other relationships. Maybe, if Cember asked her to play dumb, she would. He wanted to ask, but was afraid of the answer. But at the same time, he knew—in ways he couldn't describe—that she felt his urgent worries for Etenia's safety, and wouldn't let him down.

The second spot was around the side of the mountain, and as they approached, there was a flash of something darting against the green and gray slopes of the rockface. Del couldn't quite make it out—it looked blue, like Cember's skin, but it was moving fast, in and out of the misty clouds. Could it be Cember? Or was it some other dragon, guarding its nest? Was he already too late to protect Etenia? Beneath him, Searsha was silent, focused. If she was still in league with Etenia and Cember, or if she was worried about whatever it was they saw, Del couldn't tell.

They moved in carefully, keeping to the shadows as much as possible until it was clear it really was Cember they were approaching. Del felt Searsha's mood shift at the sight of him, like she hadn't been completely sure herself. Cember looked to them as they approached, and subtly nodded toward a cave entrance not too far away. The closer they got, the clearer things became, until they could see the entire area around the cave was carved with intricate designs, and boulders made to look like dragon heads, screaming in the sun. Del hadn't been sure what a dragon nest would look like, but this was definitely it. And Etenia was inside, alone.

Searsha set him down at the edge of the cave, peering inside with narrowed eyes. *She told Cember to wait outside,* she said. *To watch for danger.*

"And he agreed?" asked Del, the accusation thick in his voice.

Cember glared at Del.

"What did he say?" asked Del.

I should not put that into words. You would not like it.

Del felt a tiny bit relieved that at least she was making wise decisions on her otherwise ill-conceived solo mission. The cave was pitch-black near the rear, with no sign of life.

"Is it safe in there?" he asked Searsha.

Use my senses, she said. He closed his eyes and shared her vision, peering through the darkness to see things he never could. The walls were all carved out and smooth, with stone totems cracked and broken on the floor. At the back was a tunnel, leading off to the right, but it was unclear where, or how far it went. There was no sign of Etenia. She had gone deeper than Searsha could see.

Del opened his eyes and felt a shiver run through him.

Would you like me to wait outside, too? asked Searsha.

"Actually, I'd rather keep you close, in case we need to fight."

And by 'we' you mean me.

"Well, yeah."

I am glad you can admit your inadequacy.

"I wouldn't call it an inadequa—"

A cry from the darkness sent them both charging into the cave. Etenia was in trouble, and nothing else mattered. Del scrambled through the rocky debris from memory, frantic to reach Etenia, while Searsha and then Cember rushed around him, hurrying to the source of the alarm. The two dragons quickly outpaced Del, disappearing from sight into the darkness, leaving Del stumbling behind, furious at his slowness. Del had just reached the corner he'd seen when a single thought from Searsha burst into his mind—*no!*—spurring him on even as his heart dropped. If anything had happened to Etenia— but then he was around the corner, and Searsha had breathed fire to light a sequence of lanterns along the wall, and there was Etenia, sprawled on the ground, Searsha and Cember looking down at her. Del stopped, afraid to take a step further, afraid to learn the truth—but then Etenia turned, her eyes glistening in the lantern-light, wide with fright.

It wasn't even a thought. Del shot forward, scrambling faster than he had ever moved in his life, until he was at her side, checking her for injuries. "What is it?" he asked. "What happened?"

She pointed across the room. "That."

He understood her reaction the second he saw it: the skeleton of a warrior, bound up in his decaying armor, a sword just out of reach, head tipped to the side and jaw a short distance away like he was frozen in an endless scream. Behind him was a dragon's skeleton. Its skull, pierced with a dozen spears, was resting on the lower half of the warrior's body, jaws wrapped tight around his waist. His legs and pelvis were down its throat, like it had died in the act of tearing him apart.

Etenia caught her breath and got back to her feet. "I'm sorry," she said. "I didn't see them in the dark and tripped over his head and..." She looked over at Del and frowned. "How did you find me?"

Del pulled the map out of his shirt and grinned. "It's not a copy, it's a draft."

Etenia sneered. "The traitor."

"Listen, I know you wanted to do this on your own, but since we are talking about ancient, booby-trapped dragon nests—" He gestured toward the violent scene behind them. "—with a history of unpleasantness, to say the least—"

"I don't need a babysitter," she warned.

"Don't think of me as one. Think of me as the witness to your tragic death."

She laughed. "Fine. But if we keep finding abandoned nests, will you agree to go back and clean up, as planned? The dust in that room last night was incredible. We can't let anyone else visit until that's sorted."

He offered his hand. "I promise to consider it."

She rolled her eyes and shook his hand. "It's a wonder we got off that island at all."

She headed back to the door with Cember. Del noticed Searsha looking at the dead warrior and dragon. He could feel a sense of concern from her. Uneasiness. "Something wrong?" he asked.

Ancient dragons must have been terrifying creatures, she said. *I would not want to digest armor like that.*

He could tell she was making light of it to change the subject, but he shared her sense of unease. Whatever had happened in this nest, it had been violent and terrifying. A giant dragon, biting a man in two, and only taken down by that many spears to the head? If that weren't bad enough, he was certain he recognized some of the markings on the warrior's armor from the carvings at the university, which meant this was a Pothenian soldier, killed by one of his supposed allies?

If there was some kind of violent falling-out between the humans and dragons of Pothena, their whole mission might be even more doomed than he feared.

He caught up with Etenia just as Cember was about to take off.

"Hold on," he said, and she paused. "Maybe we should let Professor Staaf read a little more about the history of this place before we keep going."

"Del, the Qapira are coming. They've been here before. We don't have time to—"

"I'm just saying maybe we don't want to rush headlong into a situation we don't understand."

"It's been two hundred and fifty years! What kind of situation could there be that—"

Del felt Searsha tense, and Cember quickly scampered back from the edge of the cave mouth, arching his back to shield Etenia, and baring his teeth. Del instinctively called upon defensive magic—a pair of blocking shields—and dashed closer to Searsha, who had a mouthful of fire at the ready.

Before Del could ask why, a massive figure rose up from below them, sending the clouds and mist swirling in the sunlight. It was a dragon, an enormous one. Its wings were longer than Searsha's whole body, nose to tail, and its jaws were heavy enough to snap Cember in two like a twig. Something about it seemed ancient. The texture of its skin, or the horns around its crown, or the way it moved...it was older and more powerful than anything Del had ever seen—including the Kraken. This dragon would have killed that sea monster in a single blow.

Searsha and Cember were ready to fight, but it wasn't a battle they could win.

State your business, it said, and Del realized it was a she. Elegant and stately, and unmistakably female.

Etenia cleared her throat and said: "Greetings from the new city of Pothena. I am—"

You are trespassers, said the dragon. *You are not welcome here. Leave now, or die.*

Del glanced over at Etenia, hoping she would take the very obvious hint and go. But from her body language, he knew she was seeing this as an opportunity to bargain. He hoped his magic would be able withstand a blast of ancient dragonfire.

"I beg your patience, O great dragon—"

Beg all you like. It will not change your fate.

"Our ancestors may have had a falling-out—"

The dragon laughed, but it had a bitter, angry edge to it. *Interesting choice of words.*

Etenia was struggling, Del could see. It was like the council all over again, except this time it wouldn't end in disappointment so much as incineration.

"Pothena is in danger," he said before he even realized he was going to speak, and the ancient dragon's nostrils flared as it turned to look at him. "The Qapiran army is on its way to—"

To kill you all, I hope, said the dragon. *I do hope they still drink the blood of their enemies. That would be most satisfying to watch.*

"P-please," said Etenia. "Please, without your help—"

You are young, and obviously ignorant, so I will grant you some patience, said the dragon, hovering a little higher, so that she was looking down on them all like some kind of empress. *You will get no help from the dragons of this mountain. Not after the way your kind abandoned ours, all those years ago.*

Etenia stammered: "Wait, what did—"

You humans will have to handle your own affairs for a change. If you can.

She flew back a bit, and the clouds around her swirled into a kind of funnel, obscuring her more and more until she was nearly gone. *But be warned, Pothenians: if you trespass again, I will raze your city myself.*

CHAPTER 12

A s they made their final approach toward the Old City, Cember suddenly shifted his wings and flew higher, up onto the grassy meadow they'd found the day before. By the time Searsha caught up with them, Etenia was off Cember's back and stalking into the distance, hands in tight fists at her sides.

Del slid off Searsha and chased after Etenia. Carefully, though. He didn't need a dragon's bond to know she was upset, and angry.

He'd been expecting trouble—disaster, even—on their mission to find the dragon nests, but he hadn't foreseen the way the disaster would unfold. If they'd found a bunch of empty caves filled with skeletal remains, that would have been depressing. If they'd been attacked by savage dragons from a forgotten era, that would have been awful, too. But to be told, matter-of-factly, that they were being abandoned to fight off the Qapira on their own? That was a blow that was devastating. And Del knew it hurt Etenia more, because she had failed to convince the dragon to help them. She was trying to control the disparate elements of a complex situation, and turn chaos into order. It just wasn't working.

And he was worried that she'd wrapped up too much of her own self-worth in a happy outcome.

She stopped a short distance away, staring up at the towering slabs of mountain on their side of the meadow, and let out a long, desperate sigh. Del knew exactly what she was feeling: tiny, in the presence of grandeur. And far out of her depth.

"I've been trying to think of a way forward," she said, without acknowledging he was there. "Some way to turn this around. Something I can offer her that will change her mind."

Del didn't want to upset her more, but he had to speak. "I don't think there's much room for negotiation," he said.

"She said we abandoned them. Humans abandoned the dragons. Whatever we did—whatever our ancestors did—it must have been awful. To know that Pothena faces certain doom and to sit back and do nothing? What kind of monsters would do that?"

Del bit his tongue, literally, to keep himself from saying what was on his mind. What kind of monsters would do that? The kind in Pothena, and especially in Seafall, who already had abandoned their fellow citizens, which was why Del and Etenia had been forced to look for more dragons in the first place. He wanted to explain to her how there were no heroes in this mess, in any direction...but this was the wrong time. He kept his thoughts to himself.

She turned to look at him, tears in her eyes, like she was trying to work out the unworkable, and it pained her to try.

"Without the Pothenian dragons, we are desperately outnumbered, Del. To a degree I can't even...I can't even fathom it."

"You had a plan before we even knew they existed," Del countered. "Don't forget that. We came up here to start a dragon academy with the

Sivarnan eggs, not full-grown dragons. We can still do that. There's no reason—"

"It was a reckless plan," she said. "I mean think about it: simply finding the riders for each egg is a statistical nightmare on its own. How many applicants can we expect, really? A handful, at first?"

"You seemed pretty confident back at the villa," he said. "I don't see why—"

"Because nothing ever goes according to plan, Del. Or haven't you noticed?"

He had noticed. Noticing disaster was what he did best. He just didn't expect that she was noticing, too. Sometimes her stubborn optimism was frightening. Every time they hit a wall, she found a door nearby. But eventually, even the most relentless of optimists had to understand that things weren't working out anymore. Sometimes, that was the difference between surviving, and a sudden, unexpected death.

Etenia closed her eyes, probably imagining all the terrible things they'd endured, all at once. "I mapped out the perfect route for my father's ship," she said. "I knew every detail, every port, ever current we'd encounter. And the ship went down, and so many died."

"That wasn't something you could control," said Del. "And you didn't know to—" He caught himself, waved it off. "Never mind."

"Didn't know to what?" she asked, and he could see she was getting ready to fight. It was clear as day in her eyes. She was going to take her fury out on him.

And he was going to let her.

"You look at everything in terms of likelihood," he said. "This is most likely, that's less likely, that's never going to happen. You mapped out the perfect route thinking the worst that would happen is you get caught in a storm—and you probably knew exactly what to do if that happened."

"Northeasterly detour into the Bay of Cliffport," she said softly, like she was being put on the spot.

"See, that's the problem. You have all the answers, so when something truly unexpected happens—something you couldn't see coming—you freeze. You think your whole plan is wrong, and you fall apart."

"I do not fall apart."

Del spread his arms wide. "You're standing in a meadow, crying about being dismissed by a dragon you didn't even know existed a day ago. That's called falling apart."

She wiped the tears from her eyes and stood taller, which was exactly what Del wanted. He wanted her to remember who she was, and what she was fighting for.

"And I suppose you'd do better?" she said, an unmistakable iciness to her voice.

He laughed. "You know what I'd be doing. I'd have taken the eggs and hidden in the mountains, and waited for the Qapira to get bored and go home."

"You'd have let Pothena die! You'd have let all those people die!" she shouted.

"Yes, because I looked at the situation, and I looked at all our options, and all I saw was disaster, so I did the reasonable thing and chose the option that will keep us safest." He gestured between the two of them, and then to the dragons.

"At the expense of everyone else," she said.

He shrugged. "It's what people do." She was about to argue, but he cut her off: "Council did it, didn't they? They were so concerned about the inconvenience of defending Pothena that they abandoned their own citizens to save a little money. And I bet they're just carrying on a grand legacy of betraying their allies, which is why the dragons are still holding a grudge. Everyone looks out for their own. It's how we survive. We protect the people that matter the most, and the rest...the rest can save themselves, if they want."

She looked at him with hurt in her eyes. "I can't believe you think that."

"It's not what I think, Etenia. It's what the world thinks. You think you know better, prove it. But you won't convince anyone by standing up here and feeling sorry for yourself."

Her jaw tightened and he hoped it was because she realized what he was trying to do—what he was trying to provoke her into doing. If not, he had a feeling she would punch him. But then he saw the telltale signs of her eyes darting back and forth as she formulated a plan, and he knew his words had landed.

"We don't have full-grown dragons," she said, "but we still have the eggs. We'll bring Lathan back down as planned, and let him be in charge of convincing people to sign up."

"He's got those slick Sivarnan robes. People'll love that."

She nodded, and started walking back toward the dragons. "Once we finish clearing up the city, we'll go down and help him with recruiting. Maybe get Cember and Searsha to put on a show."

"They'll love that, too," smiled Del.

I excel at amazement, agreed Searsha.

Etenia was moving faster, her mind finally on a roll: "We'll bring them up as we find them, and have Lathan and Professor Staaf start the training immediately."

"Together? Because I think it might be safer to trespass in some nests..."

She ignored him and continued: "Our goal should be to find fifty candidates by the end of the week, and hatch one dragon. Maybe two, if we're lucky."

"And next week?"

"Do it all over again, until we have what we need...or the Qapira show up."

Del gave her a wary look. "As plans go, it leaves something to be desired."

"I know," said Etenia. "But we'll just have to adapt as things go wrong, won't we?"

He grinned at her, and she grinned back. It felt good being part of a team. He'd never been close enough to someone that he could tear apart their hopes and dreams and reveal their unspoken beliefs and not make them an enemy for life. It was an odd feeling, but satisfying. He hoped they'd survive long enough to see where it went next.

They flew back down to the Old City and found Lathan and Bettine at opposite sides of the library, scouring books. When Bettine saw them come in, she practically fell over a stack of texts as she hurried over.

"Oh, thank goodness you're back! I think you may need to reconsider your outings. I don't know what happened exactly, but it seems like the ancient Pothenians had quite the falling-out with their dragons, and—"

"Yeah, we know," said Del. "I think they like the Qapira more than us."

"Oh dear," said Bettine.

Lathan arrived with a book of his own, open to a page of illustrations. "Shockingly, this library has a number of antique Sivarnan texts that I've never seen before. The language is a little archaic, but I think it describes the genealogical split between the different breeds of dragon, and—" He noticed Etenia's face. How intense her expression was. "What's wrong now?"

"We're bringing you back down to Pothena," she said. "We need to find candidates as fast as possible. Find a book or two to read, and meet us in the courtyard in five minutes."

Lathan didn't even answer; he just scurried to the pile of books and started searching.

Etenia took Bettine aside with Del, and spoke quietly: "With any luck, we'll be sending you a student or two in the next few days," she said. "We need you to initiate them into the world of dragons."

Bettine glared across the room at Lathan. "Won't someone be upset?"

"Maybe, but he won't be here to see it," said Etenia. "So make the most of the time you have."

"Oh," said Del, "and if you could get them to clean up, too, that would be great." Etenia glared at him but he was unapologetic. "What? I can't sleep in one of those rooms another night, and I have actually slept in horse dung before."

Etenia shrugged. "Fair enough. Professor, good luck. Hopefully we can find you a student or two soon."

They met out in the courtyard in less than five minutes and climbed aboard Searsha and Cember at the edge of the broken railing. It was midday and the sun offset the bitter chill they were all feeling, just a little. Lathan, behind Del on Searsha, looked across the way to Etenia, who was just as intent as before. She was obviously trying not to show any uncertainty—which was almost as comforting as actual confidence, in a way.

"What happens if no one volunteers?" he asked under his breath. "What if we get down there and they refuse to try?"

"A northeasterly detour into the Bay of Cliffport," said Del.

"Pardon?"

Del grinned over his shoulder. "She'll figure it out; don't worry."

The ride down was even faster than before, now that the dragons knew the ins and outs of the wind currents in the area. Cember dove directly, which was easier because he only had one rider. Searsha came down in a gentler spiral motion, turning in big, graceful arcs until the city opened up below them, sundrenched and oh so fragile.

As they got closer, though, Del noticed something wrong about the image: the market was emptier than it should have been at this time of the day, and many of the surrounding streets seemed deserted too. It didn't take long for him to realize why: it seemed as if half of Pothena was crammed into the large town square at the northern end of the market. During festivals it might have accommodated a thousand people, maybe more...but now it was packed with bodies, so tight it was a wonder anyone could move.

For a moment, Del worried the Qapira had arrived and this was what a failed evacuation looked like. But there was no smoke in the air, no screams of terror.

"Is that normal in Pothena?" asked Lathan, pointing down at it.

"No," said Del. "Not at all."

Etenia and Cember were heading straight for the square—probably wondering what was happening, too, and whether they could help. Searsha followed close behind. As they came in closer, it was clear there was nowhere they could land on the ground. The people had nowhere to go, and if they tried, it might cause a stampede. Instead, Etenia had Cember land on the roof of a nearby building. Searsha did the same, across the way.

The crowd erupted into cheers as they settled, and doubly so when Del and Etenia climbed off their dragons. Del couldn't quite pick out what they were chanting, but it wasn't hostile, at least.

There was movement below, and then Del saw someone pushing through the crowd on the way to the building he was perched on. After a moment, he saw who: it was Womp. He was climbing the drainpipe, up the side of the building, with the grace of someone who had done it before. When he was within reach, Del held out his hand and hoisted the lad up onto the ledge.

"Hello, sir, hello, ma'am," he said to Del and Etenia, then added a small salute to Lathan: "General, sir."

Del was amused. Somewhere along the way, Womp had heard some gossip about them, and had connected the dots admirably.

"What's all this about?" asked Del. "They just want to see our dragons?"

Womp looked at him like he was insane. "No, sir, not that. These are your riders."

CHAPTER 13

I t took Del a moment to fully appreciate what Womp had told him. It was like there was a disconnect between what he was seeing with his eyes, and what his brain could understand. Here was a massive sea of people from all across Pothena, all gathered together waiting for—not for handouts or food rations or a lottery—but to join their dragon academy. The academy they hadn't even properly started, in a place barely fit for human occupancy.

These were people who believed in the dream he was selling, in the future he was promising, and were eager to sign up. And there were just so many of them. It felt like he was running a scam on an epic scale, but instead of that feeling like a leg up—because imagine the returns from conning this many people at once—he felt a sudden and oppressive sense of doom. These people were going to revolt when they realized the truth—that they didn't have a proper school yet, and there weren't even close to enough dragon eggs to appease this many hopefuls. When they figured that out, they weren't going to target the Browders, they were going to go straight for the player with the least wealth and power to use as protection—him.

He scrambled along the rooftops with Lathan in tow until they reached the spot Etenia was standing, waving to the assembled crowd like she was a newly crowned queen greeting her subjects. To her, this was a happy moment. To him, it had all the makings of a nightmare.

Womp had stayed behind and was reaching out a hand toward Searsha, asking permission to touch her. Del could feel her happiness at being treated so well. She bowed to the boy and soon he was climbing all over her—which only made the people in the square more enthusiastic.

This was headed for a riot. He could feel it. They had to get out.

"What are we going to do?" he asked Etenia, as she stared out at the crowd with the most joyous smile he had ever seen. "Etenia, what are we going to do?"

"What do you mean?" she asked, still not really paying attention to him.

"I mean look at this. Look at them."

"I know," she laughed. "It's amazing! It's—"

"A disaster!" he said, and that snapped her out of her reverie. She frowned at him.

"We needed recruits, and now we've—"

"It's too many," said Lathan. "There must be a thousand out there. There's no way we can screen even a fraction of these. I'm sorry, Etenia, but Del's right. We need to send these people home and try again."

"Try again?" she asked, with an edge to her voice. "No! If we don't use what we have now, we'll never find this many people willing to—"

Lathan gestured out to the crowd. "In all these people, you can expect to find one, maybe two souls who would meet even the most basic standards of being a dragon rider. And that's assuming any of them are able to bond with a dragon at all. We would have to sort through a thousand people to find one or two."

"With a process in place, and the right interview questions—"

"It would take you weeks to interview them all."

"Well then we'll find some other way to sort them!" she said, turning away from the square to avoid anyone seeing her losing her temper. "All that matters is that we have them. We'll get them back to the Old City, and figure out the rest as we go."

Lathan raised an eyebrow at that. Del knew exactly what he was thinking: "How long does it take to fly up to the Old City?" he asked.

"Twenty minutes, give or take."

"Sure. Twenty minutes there, maybe ten minutes back? Sound fair?"

"Yes," she nodded, and he could see she was starting to understand where this was going. "All right, fine, it will take a long time to make the trip."

"No, not just a long time," said Del. "Searsha and Cember can carry maybe two people each, each trip. So that's—"

"Two hundred fifty trips," said Lathan, thankfully, because Del wasn't accustomed to numbers that large.

"Exactly," he said. "And if each one takes thirty minutes—"

"One hundred twenty-five hours," said Lathan.

"Thank you," said Del with a grin. It was nice to have his own personal math wizard on hand. "And let's say we can only do trips during daylight, so that's—"

"Around ten."

"Around ten hours," nodded Del.

"No, ten days," said Lathan. "One hundred twenty-five divided twelve hours a day is—"

"Fine, fine!" said Etenia, and they both fell silent. "This is impossible. The whole plan is impossible. I'm crazy for even considering it." She turned her attention from the crowd to the ocean beyond. To the dark, ominous waters beyond. "But those numbers won't stop the Qapira. They're still coming. We still need to do something. So maybe instead of telling me why we can't succeed, you should try thinking up ways to help us win."

Del and Lathan, properly scolded, fell silent. Del was still overwhelmed by the sight of the crowd. The sound of it was just deafening, and made his ears ring. Etenia was right, of course: if they didn't make the most of this moment, they'd lose most of these people forever. Worse yet, they'd lose them for good, so when the Qapira eventually showed up, it would be even more challenging to raise a defense.

But the numbers didn't lie, and in fact sounded even worse when Lathan spoke them aloud. Ten twelve-hour days, flying up and down, up and down? That didn't even account for breaks along the way, or the very real possibility that Del and Etenia might need their dragons for something other than a taxi service. And even if none of those things were a concern, how would they sort out who went first, and get the others to wait their turn? If there was one thing Del knew for certain, it was that in any queue, the ones that ended up going first were almost never the ones who deserved it. And that meant their school would be jam-packed with obnoxious merchants' sons who thought it was their right to bond with a dragon.

Del really didn't want to be stuck in an ancient city with that kind of people. Regardless of what Etenia and Lathan were after, he wanted the candidates who knew how to work harder, to survive against the odds, and think on their feet. He needed—

"Hey, Etenia," he said, trying to control his enthusiasm until he was sure his idea had merit. "How did people get to the Old City, back in the old days?"

She shook her head. "I don't know. You'd have to ask Dr Staaf."

"They didn't all fly, right? There's no way Pothena had enough dragons for every human that would've lived in that place."

"No," said Etenia. "I suppose not. So either they just never left, or..." Her eyes opened wide, and Del knew she'd arrived at the same thought as him. "There must be a path. A route from here to the Old City."

"Exactly," said Del.

Lathan seemed bothered by both their idea, and their enthusiasm for it. "But if no one's used it in two hundred fifty years," he said, "who knows what state it's in? It might be impassable. Or at the very least dangerous."

"It would take some courage to make the trip," nodded Del.

"Courage and stamina," said Lathan. "And a sharp mind, too, not to mention a dextrous spirit and—" He froze, mouth open in mid-sentence, as he realized. "Ah, I see."

"Anyone who makes it to the Old City will have earned a spot in the academy," said Del. "Whether or not a dragon chooses to bond with them, they'll deserve to be there. We'll have solved all our problems in one."

Lathan nodded his agreement, though Del could tell he was still uncertain about the whole plan. Etenia grinned at Del, and he grinned back—they really did work well together, he realized. They didn't always see eye to eye, but that was one of the best parts of their relationship: they came at the world from wildly different places, but always seemed to be heading in the same direction.

She turned to face the crowd, spreading her arms wide to get their attention as she yelled: "Welcome, one and all!"

No one heard her. The noise was too loud, the gathering too rowdy. She tried again: "Excuse me! I said excuse me!"

Still, no reaction. Womp stopped playing with Searsha and scurried over next to Etenia, putting his fingers in his mouth and delivering a whistle so piercing it silenced the whole square. Every eye turned to Etenia. Womp winked at her and waited to hear what she had to say.

"Welcome, everyone!" she called out. "I am Etenia Browder, head of the new Pothenian Dragon Academy."

The crowd buzzed excitedly at that, though Del couldn't help but feel a tinge of betrayal. Etenia was the head of the Dragon Academy, while he was...what? Her assistant? Just some anonymous other who was lurking in the background, unable to contribute in a meaningful way? The more the words rolled around in his head, the angrier he became. He tried to tell himself he shouldn't care so much—after all, the academy had been Etenia's idea, but still...

"I would like to introduce you to General Lathan Phrac of Sivarna, master dragon trainer and senior advisor to the academy." There was a smattering of applause for Lathan that grew steadily as people got a better look at him. There wasn't a lot of anti-Sivarnan sentiment in Pothena—no one thought about them enough to have an opinion either way—but any stranger inspired a certain amount of distrust. Evidently Lathan's posture and robes gave him enough credibility to overcome those worries.

And yet still: Lathan, the outsider, was given a round of applause, while Del was ignored.

"And you've of course seen them," said Etenia, "but let me properly introduce you to Cember and Searsha!" She waved to the dragons. Cember snorted loudly and let out a terrifying roar which sent the crowd into a frenzy of cheering, while Searsha kept quiet. Del knew in an instant she was planning something spectacular, but when she finally did it, it took his breath away.

She arched her head upward, spread her wings wide and blew a shot of flame straight into the air, which swirled and then burst outward like fireworks, sending little flaming embers tumbling down all around. She sank back down into a coy pose as the crowd cheered wildly.

"Show-off," said Del, some of his irritation at Etenia forgetting him eased, just for a moment, at Searsha's glorious display.

Magnificence is my natural state.

Etenia clapped loudly along with the crowd until the sound died down enough for her to speak again. "I know you're all excited to see a dragon up close, and for the chance to ride a dragon. But I warn you: this is no easy journey. Only a small number of you will be chosen to bond with a dragon."

There were murmurs of displeasure from the crowd—she was being a little too honest. Del really wanted to warn her to ease up, but a large part of him was still upset about being sidelined. She really had forgotten him entirely, it seemed. He took a step closer, trying to decide if he'd be the friend she clearly wasn't, or watch her stumble and fall. Then she continued on, and he lost his chance.

"But being chosen is just the first step of a long and complicated journey that will test you in ways you never thought possible. To be a dragon rider requires skill, tenacity, courage, and intelligence beyond compare. Some of that you will bring with you. And for the rest, you will learn from the best—our Head Dragon Trainer, Del!"

Del was so shocked, he didn't even register that the crowd was cheering for him until Etenia gave his arm a nudge, and he raised it to wave. Womp was jumping up and down, letting out a wild and enthusiastic noise. Searsha even beamed a kind of pride into Del's heart that he couldn't describe. He looked to Etenia, whose smile was too big to be believed, and laughed. It was the oddest sensation he was feeling...happiness, maybe?

"Etenia..." said Lathan, standing between them and speaking as softly as possible. "Naming Del as Head Dragon Trainer is—"

"A really stupid idea," said Del, even though he felt like his heart might explode at the honor.

Lathan shrugged. "I was going to be more diplomatic, but yes, that's fundamentally it. Del is talented, yes, but he's just a student himself."

"Oh, don't worry, either of you," she said, not breaking her smile one bit as she spoke without moving her lips. "Del is a figurehead to put people at ease. People need to see Pothenians in charge of a Pothenian academy, but you will do the actual teaching." She winced at Del. "I hope you're not offended."

"Offended? I'm relieved," said Del, and he truly was, though at the same time he suddenly realized he wanted to be worthy of the title Etenia had bestowed on him. "I thought you'd truly lost your mind."

She laughed, then raised her hands again to quiet the crowd. "I know you're excited to start, but there's one trial you must face first, to gain admission to the academy." She turned and pointed up the mountain, up past the clouds. "The school itself is up there," she said. "In the Old City of Pothena. To attend, you need to reach it."

This elicited a concerned murmur from the crowd, and some louder remarks that, while Del couldn't pick out the exact words, he could tell they weren't happy about it, until someone shouted, "That's insane!"

"How are we s'posed to do that!" asked another, and then people started to move, pushing and shoving their way back home. At a glance, it looked as though a third of the audience was trying to go— and by the looks of it, it was the rich ones they were losing: the ones who stayed behind were wearing more muted clothes instead of the vibrant silks that were heading for the exits. And that suited Del just fine.

"Well, that's one way to lighten the intake," he said.

"It's brilliant," said Lathan. "You've eliminated the pretenders in a single stroke."

Etenia called out one last time: "I look forward to seeing you all at the academy soon. But in the meantime, we would be happy to answer any questions you may have..."

They made their way down to the square, where a crush of bodies was already waiting for them. Womp and some other street kids had formed a protective bubble for them, and were holding the line remarkably well for such small and slight creatures. Etenia nodded to Del, and walked out to meet the chaos head-on.

The questions they were asked covered a huge spectrum from the insightful ("How does a dragon know who to bond with?") to the cynical ("Can I bond with more than one dragon at once?") to the curious ("I'm scared of heights—do we have to fly?") to an over-whelming number of questions along the lines of: "Can I touch your dragon?" Del did his best to answer them all honestly, though occasion-ally he was faced with someone who deserved a punch more than a response.

After over an hour of this, his voice was going hoarse, and he could see Etenia was starting to fade, too. He made his way over and was just about to suggest they wrap up for the day when her face went slack with shock and she took a half-step back.

He turned to see what she was looking at, ready for whatever fight was coming—but all he saw was a handsome young man, a little older than they were, in clothes so fine, they made him feel like a beggar all over again.

"Etenia," said the man. "You're a hard woman to pin down."

"I've been busy..." she said, and Del could hear the worry in her voice. He positioned himself in front of her, to make it clear she was protected. But the stranger didn't seem to notice or care.

"I'm sorry, who are you?" Del asked, arms tensed for a fistfight, if need be.

The stranger chuckled and held out a hand to shake. "Oh, I'm sorry. Finnlay Braitman, at your service."

Braitman. The Braitmans that Arretal was always talking about, who owned the too-small spot for the school, and would be excited to know Etenia was safe. He was theoretically an ally, then—but Del didn't want to shake his hand. He wasn't sure why, but he really didn't want to.

"It's all right, Del," said Etenia, dejectedly, "He's not a threat. He's my fiancé."

CHAPTER 14

"F-fiancé?" asked Del, as Finnlay stepped past him and took Etenia's hands in his own.

"Your father told me about your plan, and I have to say, Tenny, it's brilliant. Just brilliant. Though that's no surprise, is it? You always were something of a genius."

Etenia smiled sweetly and turned her face away like she was bashful, and at that exact moment, Del knew for certain he hated Finnlay. It was a multitude of things, all at once: the cut of his clothes, like his most pressing commitment was lounging in the garden all day; his accent was grating too—the elongated vowels and syrupy rhythm of the upper-upper crust. His perfect, unblemished skin was also a keen source of annoyance, because it showed Finnlay had never been in the sun for even a minute longer than he wanted to. And the way he'd pushed Del aside to see Etenia—*Tenny!*—that was just unforgivable. Oh yes, Del hated him.

He just wasn't sure what to do about it yet.

"I admit, I always expected great things of you, Tenny, but this..." He gestured up at Searsha. "A dragon of your own?"

"That's my dragon," said Del, but Finnlay ignored him.

"And head of a dragon school! Founder of a dragon school!"

"I'm not really the founder," said Etenia, modestly. "It was founded centuries ago. I'm just bringing it back to life."

"Hi, sorry, Del again," said Del, injecting himself into the conversation. "We've really got to get back to important dragon school things, so if you don't mind—"

"I was so worried for your safety," Finnlay said, resting a hand on Etenia's cheek and looking into her eyes. "When I heard your ship went down, I led a rescue mission, with ten of our fastest ships. Yena and I— we looked everywhere, Tenny. Everywhere. And even when they told me there was no hope, that you were gone, I..." He rested his forehead on hers, and Del nearly retched. "I never stopped believing in you," said Finnlay. "I knew you'd survive."

Del pointed up at the mountain. "Dragon school..."

Etenia looked into her fiancé's eyes, so close, and said: "Finnlay, I—"

"Shh," he said, and pulled her into an embrace. "You don't need to relive it. We'll make new memories together. Better memories."

Del sighed, unable to hide his annoyance. "Memories full of fighting the Qapira?"

"The Epyrians, yes!" said Finnlay letting go of Etenia and turning to Del. "Arretal told me all about your dreams! That's why I'm here! To help defeat them!"

Del was fully expecting Finnlay to announce he was the descendant of a mythical hero with a magic sword that could kill Qapirans with a single blow—but he kept that cynicism to himself.

Finnlay nodded seriously to Etenia. "I'm here to help with the school."

Del shook his head far more aggressively than he intended to. "No, no, no. I'm sorry, you can't skip the line. Dragons won't just bond with you because you have—"

"Oh, no, Del," said Finnlay, earnestly. "You misunderstand. You and Tenny are the dragon riders here. I'm just offering logistical support on the ground. I have extensive experience with managing large work-forces, coordinating across sectors to enhance—"

"I don't know what any of that means," said Del. Why was Finnlay being so nice? So slick? Del didn't trust it. He didn't trust anything about this secret fiancé of Etenia's.

Finnlay laughed and nodded. "No, you're right. I apologize. It's time for action, not talking. Here's what I offer: whatever you need built, I can build it. Just tell me where and when, and it will be done."

Etenia positioned herself between them, smiling so artificially it was clear to Del she didn't want him to make a tense situation worse. But he was going to do it anyway. No matter what Del said, no matter what objection he raised, Finnlay seemed to have a smooth way of turning things in his favor, and it was driving Del insane. He was like a silver-tongued con man, except he wasn't after money, he was after—

"Stairs," said Del, a wide grin spreading across his face. "We need stairs." Before Finnlay or Etenia could ask the obvious next question, he pointed up at the mountain. "To get people from here to there."

Etenia's jaw dropped. "But the whole point of the test we announced is that only the most capable—"

"It'll still be hard," Del countered, though he had to admit she was right. "But it shouldn't be deadly. So your, uh, Finnlay here, can build stairs over the most dangerous parts. The places where people will fall and die a lot."

It wasn't as graceful as he'd intended, but it did the trick: give Finnlay a task so unpleasant, he'd find a reason to leave. Odds were, after two hundred fifty years of disuse, the trail would be in really bad shape indeed. The only people who would dream of rehabilitating it would be the stupidly ambitious, or the wildly masochistic. Either Finnlay would take offense and storm off like the spoiled brat he was, or he would begrudgingly accept the offer and end up getting lost in the mountains, possibly forever. Either way, Del wouldn't have to look at him all the time, which was really all he needed. Plus, it would help keep Etenia focused, which would be important in the coming days.

Finnlay looked up the mountain, his mouth hanging open a little. "Up...there...?"

"To the Old City," said Del. "Where the school is."

"Is there a path, or—"

"Maybe, maybe not," said Del. "Either way, we need stairs that go up."

Etenia gave Del a warning glare, but he ignored her. He was far more interested in Finnlay's upcoming meltdown.

Finnlay's eyes darted side to side, side to side, and he looked pained, almost. He sighed, nodded, and turned back toward the crowd.

"All right, you lot!" he shouted. "We're going to build some stairs! I'm hiring scouts, engineers, carpenters, stonemasons and general laborers! Go fetch your working gear and meet me by the Trillo Plaza in one hour!" He looked over his shoulder and winked to Etenia. "We'll get it done. Don't you worry."

And with that, he disappeared into the crowd.

"Well, that's one problem solved," said Del, trying to put a positive spin on things. He frowned at Etenia. "Any of your other secret lovers have special skills we can use?"

Etenia looked at him with such venom, he cringed and took a step back.

"That was childish," she said. "And unnecessary."

"Unnecessary? He's building us a path to the—"

"You know what I mean!" she snapped. "You were trying to pick a fight. Don't deny it, it was clear as day. You wanted to make him angry, so he'd yell at you, and—"

"Oh no, another rich boy yelling at me," deadpanned Del. "Whatever shall I do?"

Etenia glared. "He's not like that."

"No? What's he like, Tenny?"

That pushed a button with her. She turned on her heel and stormed away, back into the building they landed on. Del had half a mind to let her go, but then he realized he wasn't done with her yet. There was still more to say. He chased after, calling up the spiral staircase as she was halfway to the next floor.

"What didn't you tell me?" he asked. "We were stuck on an island for weeks together, and you never said a word about a fiancé."

"How would it have come up?" she said, angrily. "Hmm? We were sitting on a beach, starving to death. How would he have come up?"

"This rockfruit reminds me of Finnlay's skull," said Del, in his best Etenia voice. "Finnlay, the anchor of my soul, the love of my live, who would do anything for me, and—"

"He's not the—" said Etenia, then cut herself short, and kept storming up the stairs.

Del ran after her. "He's not what? What isn't he?"

"Nothing, Del! Find something else to be offended by for no reason!"

He laughed loudly. "For no reason! Oh, I have a reason!" He caught up with her and grabbed her arm. She spun around and looked ready to deck him, but she resisted. His hurt was bubbling close to the surface, and he wasn't sure if he could contain it much longer. "This isn't nothing, Etenia. You kept something from me. Something big. I thought we were friends."

"We are friends," she said.

"Friends tell friends that they're engaged to be married."

She watched him closely. "Why does it matter?"

He paused, trying to think of what to say.

She was watching.

"So I can let Lathan down easy," he said. "He's got a crush. It's a little creepy, but he'll get over you."

The spell was broken. She smiled at his joke, but there was a distance between them again.

"The point is," he said, avoiding her gaze, "we fought the Kraken together. We raised dragons together. For things like this...there shouldn't be secrets anymore."

She nodded, held out her hand to shake. "Agreed. No more secrets."

He shook her hand with a serious nod of his head. "Good. Now, when's the big day?"

She sighed and continued on up the stairs. He walked next to her, reveling in how annoyed she was. He wasn't sure why Finnlay bothered him so much—aside from the obvious issues of him being a rich blowhard who seemed to come out of nowhere, of course—or why teasing Etenia was making him feel better, but so long as it kept his mind off of the crushing stress of building a school to train dragon riders to fight a race of marauding sea monsters, he was going to embrace it.

"There's no date set," she sighed. "It's still being negotiated."

"Negotiated?" laughed Del. "What are you, part of a business deal?"

By the look on her face, Del could tell that was exactly what was going on.

"Oh," he said, suddenly feeling guilty at how much he'd teased her.

"My family controls shipping and commerce, and the Braitmans are engineers and architects. Finnlay's ancestors built the university, amongst other things. The Braitmans are looking for someone from a good background, and my father wants to leave his company to someone capable—"

"And how is that not you?" asked Del.

Etenia stopped, staring at the floor as she thought. "It's not all simple, in Seafall, Del. The marble houses and the silk sheets cost more than coins. The powerful only stay powerful by making the right deals."

"So that's what you are? You're part of a deal? You're marrying Finnlay as part of some kind of business arrangement?"

She nodded. "Pretty much."

Del could see the pain on her face, the sorrow in the words she was speaking. Here was this woman who'd proved her worth, not just by planning a trading mission, but by surviving an attack by the Kraken, defeating it, becoming one of the first Pothenian dragon riders in centuries, and then starting a dragon academy by sheer force of will. All that—and she was still just a pawn in a game played by rich old men.

Arretal's kindness seemed even more suspicious, in light of all this. Why was he supporting her, giving her hope and cheering her on, when he knew he was going to take it all away on her wedding day and give it to Finnlay and the rest of the Braitmans? Was her father really that cruel, or just oblivious to how much it hurt her? She was going to go from Etenia Browder, cunning hero, to Etenia Braitman, whose father once ran a powerful shipping empire.

The way she'd been reacting to Finnlay suddenly made sense. Del couldn't deny that to all appearances Finnlay seemed to be in love with her, but she couldn't get past what that love meant: the end of her sense of self.

Del wished he hadn't pushed so hard.

"Aren't marriages supposed to be about love?" he asked. "Or is that just a poor person thing?"

She shrugged slightly. "Love can be built," she said. "That's what his father says. Love built on a solid foundation lasts longer. And it's not like he's a bad person. And he's easy to look at."

Del cringed. "I mean if you like chiseled statues with nice hair, maybe."

"It's fine," she said. "It's not as if I have to stop being a dragon rider just because I get married. I'm sure his father would let me continue at the academy if we had enough—"

"Whoa, hold on," said Del, stepping in front of her and frowning deeply. "You need permission from his father?"

She gave a weak shrug. "He's the head of the family."

"And you have a dragon!" said Del. "Nobody should be telling you what to do!"

"Like I said," she sighed, and stepped past him on her way up the stairs. "My life costs more than just coins."

Del watched her go, anger and disgust welling up in his stomach. He hadn't liked Finnlay before, but now he was nursing a hatred of the entire Braitman clan, top to bottom. And Arretal, too! What kind of father treated his daughter like that? Suddenly her entire history made so much more sense: Arretal had kept passing her over because she was never meant to inherit anything at all. She was meant to be sold off and become someone else's problem. The thought of it made Del tremble with rage. They already had enough to worry about, with the school and the thousand candidates and the Qapira—but he was going to find a way to fix this problem for Etenia, one way or another. For her sake.

As he chased after her, he said a little prayer that the path up the mountainside would be long and treacherous and slow—and maybe they wouldn't see Finnlay again for a very long time.

CHAPTER 15

Del grumbled as Finnlay gaped at the sight of the Old City's ruins. "Incredible..." Finnlay said, turning in a circle to take it all in. "It's just...majestic." When he smiled at Etenia, he actually had tears in his eyes. "I had no idea we lived so close to such beauty. Thank you for showing me, Tenny."

Del, arms crossed over his chest and hiding his displeasure badly, waited until Finnlay had wandered off before muttering to Etenia: "Explain again why he had to come up here?"

"He's an engineer, Del," she sighed. "He works better when he can see the whole picture. And there aren't many places with a better vantage point than up here."

She followed Finnlay, leaving Del to be frustrated on his own. It had been three days since he'd met the glorious Mr. Braitman, and he had yet to spend more than a few hours without seeing him, or hearing about his exploits. Del had been hoping to focus on repairing the Old City and welcoming their first candidates, but somehow, every topic related back to Finnlay. Yes, Arretal was bankrolling their project, but when it came to using that money in a sensible way, Etenia seemed to think Finnlay was the one and only choice. It was like, now that Finnlay had returned from searching for his "lost love," she was surrendering her autonomy already—and it was driving Del up the wall.

They weren't close, exactly. Finnlay was given to touching her hands and her face, or hugging her unexpectedly, whenever they met—but it was a chaste sort of affection. Etenia seemed content to stay a few feet away from him at all times…but then they'd go on walks together, like they were right now, and Del could almost imagine them as husband and wife on a stroll by the seaside, talking about shipping routes and building stadiums and other rich people things.

It was making him grumpy. Searsha had even said so—indelicately, of course—which only amplified his crankiness. He had to get Finnlay out of the Old City. Fast. Otherwise he was going to lose his temper or do something stupid that he really didn't want to do.

"So, Finnlay," he said, hurrying to catch up and purposely placing himself between the two of them. "How is the construction going? Still trying to find the old path?"

"Actually, no!" said Finnlay with a broad and welcoming smile. "We lucked upon it on the first day. A stream had diverted sometime over the last century and turned it into a waterfall. If you didn't know what you were looking for, you'd never have guessed. But there it was, clear as day!"

"Great," said Del unhappily. "But won't the waterfall slow you down?"

"Oh, no, don't worry about that," said Finnlay. "We built our own staircase for that portion, connecting up to a path above. It's safer that way, and it also gives a wonderful view of the heritage of the area. You can really immerse yourself in the history of the journey as you're taking it."

To his dismay, Del found himself wanting to see that for himself. He shook the thought away and persevered: "So how long until the path is ready, do you think? Weeks, months—?"

"A week, I'd say," said Finnlay. "Truthfully, most of it seems to be in excellent shape already. We're just bridging a few gaps here and there, and adding safety features where necessary. That's a big part of why I came up here today: to get a sense of the finish line, and make sure this end is ready when we get here." He stopped short and his mouth dropped open in awe. "By the gods...look at that!"

They were near the entrance to the library, and he was seeing inside for the first time. Del and Searsha had managed to find and remove the shutters that covered the windows along the sides of the building—which had been blocking the light and making the place so dark and dreary—and now the interior was filled with crystalline patterns through the stained glass artwork. Even to Del, it was an astonishing sight—but he still distrusted Finnlay's enthusiasm.

Bettine was outside the doors, reading a book, as Del, Etenia and Finnlay arrived. She looked up briefly, and then really looked up, with a giddy smile spreading across her face.

"Hello, who's this?" she asked.

She got a bow in reply. "Finnlay Braitman III," he said—to which Del gave Etenia a wide-eyed stare that said the third? "At your service, madam."

Bettine blushed, but then she gasped in surprise: "Braitman! You're a Braitman!"

"Yes, madam," he said. "My family—"

"Your family built this library!" she said, pointing back at it like he might not have noticed it was there. "I was just reading the history of the city, and they said a Valder Braitman worked his whole life to finish this structure before he died, and he's actually buried in a crypt near the back!"

Finnlay laughed with amazement. "I always knew my forefathers had done great things, but I never imagined it was so...glorious."

Del was really, truly struggling to keep his cool. The whole point of having Finnlay build the path up to the Old City was so that he would be indisposed for an extended period of time, to allow Etenia to focus on the challenges of starting up a dragon rider Academy and fight off an invading horde—not so that he could show up at random and wow everyone with his multigenerational excellence. Now, every time he saw the library, he would think of Finnlay and end up in a bad mood.

Before he could interrupt their little cult of self-adoration, Lathan came around the corner, carrying a trio of dragon eggs in his arms with some difficulty. "Professor," he said, not yet noticing they had company, "have you seen my blue notebook? I need to record the—" He paused at the sight of Finnlay, and then Etenia, and then especially Del's reaction to the other two. Del knew him well enough to know he was amused by what he saw.

"Apologies," said Lathan, shifting the eggs around to a more comfortable arrangement. "You must be Mr Braitman. Thank you for your generous assistance in the rebuilding of our school."

"No, sir, General Phrac," said Finnlay, stepping forward and giving Lathan a deep and respectful bow. "Thank you for saving my Etenia, and keeping her safe on that desert island for so long. I am forever in your debt, sir. When Sivarna is ready to rebuild, I pledge the Braitmans will lead the effort, and do you proud."

To Del's displeasure, Lathan seemed genuinely touched. "Thank you, Mr Braitman. That means a great deal."

He tried to rearrange the eggs to shake Finnlay's hand, but it was proving difficult. Finnlay stepped forward, though, to help: "Here, let me help you with that. May I?" Maybe it was the manners, or maybe the wealth oozing out of Finnlay's pores, but for some reason Lathan actually let him take one of the eggs. Once both men were settled, he shook Lathan's hand with more passion than average. "Whatever you need, General, just ask."

"Please, call me Lathan. Oh, and don't worry too much about the dragon egg. That one's got a thick shell, so it can take a little jostling."

Finnlay looked down at the egg in amazement. "Dragon egg? Is that what this is?" Del did his best not to scowl. Of course it was a dragon egg, and of course Finnlay knew that. All this fakery was nauseating. Finnlay laughed to himself. "I feel so blessed to be surrounded by so many incredible sights."

Del cleared his throat: "Speaking of which, the incredible staircase could probably use some—"

Before he could finish, Finnlay gasped—because the egg he was holding was starting to crack! The thick shell—much thicker than Searsha's had been—broke open near the top and fell down, revealing a tiny gold-skinned dragon with pitch-black eyes and miniature curled horns. It blinked at the bright sunlight, then looked up at Finnlay and made a gentle coo sound.

"Oh come on!" said Del. "Really?"

Etenia rushed to Finnlay's side and leaned over to greet the new baby dragon. "She's so adorable! Look at those eyes! What's her name?"

For a second, Finnlay seemed confused by the question. But Del and Etenia both knew what was happening in that moment: the dragon was speaking straight into his mind, forging a connection that would last their entire lives.

"She says her name is Garra," said Finnlay, tears in his eyes. "And… and I'm to be her rider!"

Lathan smiled a bittersweet smile and nodded. "She deemed you worthy. A good choice, by any standard."

Del couldn't help remember how upset Lathan had been that Searsha had bonded with him. How he'd tried to talk her out of it. Either he was getting less protective of his eggs—unlikely—or Del had yet another reason to be resentful of Finnlay's existence.

"Garra, I am Finnlay Braitman III, your most humble servant. Whatever you decide, wherever you go, I will be your most ardent supporter."

Garra stared at him, unblinking, for a long, long second. Del wondered if she, too, found his dramatic statements irritating. Maybe she was trying to think of how to get back in her shell. That would be embarrassing. And hilarious.

But no. Finnlay gasped and told them: "She said we are bound, now and forever."

Etenia laughed and hugged Finnlay from the side, gushing over the newest addition to their dragon family. She was clearly overjoyed, but Del couldn't figure out why. Yes, this meant they had another dragon on their side, but it meant Finnlay would be even more tied to them. If she was bothered by his presence, how would this make things any better? He'd be around all the time.

Del gasped as he realized this meant Finnlay was technically his first student, meaning they'd be spending even more time together. He wanted to scream, but given how happy everyone was, that seemed like it might draw attention.

"Sir!" came a voice from behind, and they turned to see Womp racing across the stones toward them. He was slick with sweat, which was no small feat given the low temperature and brisk winds that swept through the Old City. He must have been running for some time to be in such a state—but if he was tired, he didn't show it. Instead, he stopped short, eyes wide as he saw Garra for the first time.

"Is...is that...?" he stammered.

"A baby dragon," said Finnlay, beaming with pride like a new parent. "Here, come see."

Del caught Womp before he could get that far. "Hold on, before we do that: how did you get up here? I didn't know the path was even fully mapped yet..."

"It's not, sir," said Womp with a little shrug. "But a few gaps in the road never slowed us down much before, right?" He flashed a grin and Del couldn't help but laugh. That was exactly right: for street kids, imperfections were a nuisance, not an obstacle. Others might demand a sturdy bridge to cross a chasm, but to someone like Del or Womp, the only thing they saw was: *yeah, I could jump that.*

"I had to move fast, sir, on account of the messages," said Womp. "They said it was important, and to hurry." He pulled three letters from his pocket and held them out to Etenia with a bow that he seemed to think was required. He kept that pose until she accepted them, at which point he went back to ogling the baby dragon.

Etenia checked the writing on each, handed one to Bettine, and then opened one of the others and unfolded it. She started scanning it, and very quickly her expression changed. The joy of seeing a new baby dragon faded away, replaced with concern and anger.

"What is it?" asked Del. "What's going on?"

"It's an official letter from the council," she said. "They're saying...it's a lot of words, but they're angry because so many people are trying to join the academy, and they're worried..." She flipped to the second page, which seemed packed with lettering. "I think they're mostly angry because some of the council members' sons and grandsons are planning to join. They're saying it's a waste of a future generation—"

"Dragon riding, a waste?" scoffed Lathan. "Ha!"

Etenia kept reading: "Because we won't listen to reason—"

"When have they ever been reasonable?" said Del.

"—they are..." Etenia gasped. "They're condemning us. The academy is condemned."

Del looked from Etenia to Bettine and then Lathan, trying to understand. "What does that mean? Why do we care?"

"We care because it's against the law," said Finnlay, face ashen and serious. "Anyone who signs up—who even tries to reach this place—will be defying the wishes of the council."

"We're running an unlicensed personal fighting force," said Etenia, turning yet another page. "That's the excuse they're giving."

Bettine laughed, bitterly. "Oh, that's rich. The personal fighting force rules were put in place because, a hundred years ago, the Seafall merchants kept hiring mercenaries to raid their competitors' ships. It was a well-funded gang war that nearly burned the city down, until the old council established restrictions and compelled each family to contribute toward a single, unified police force that would work independently for the good of the people."

"Some of the people, anyway," muttered Del.

"Rightly or wrongly, that's what they're charging us with," said Etenia, finishing the letter and shoving it into her pocket. "We're running an unlicensed force, so we'll be hit with escalating fines until we stop."

Del rolled his eyes at that. "If they want to fine us, they'll have to climb up here and do it in person."

"That won't be the issue," said Finnlay. "They'll fine the school, yes, but they'll also target the students. Especially the wealthy ones. Targeting them will be much easier—and profitable—and cause many applicants to stay away."

Del gave him a sideways glare. "How about you? You're rich."

Finnlay frowned defiantly, and held Garra a little closer. "I am bonded."

Etenia had opened the second letter and started reading. She suddenly let out a gasp and sank to her knees. Del raced to her side, trying to support her as she finished reading.

"What now?" he asked. "What did they say this time?"

"It's not the council," she whispered, seeming genuinely pained now. "It's...it's my father."

Del prepared himself for what was coming, because he knew it would be bad. "Is he...?" he asked, as if he was worried about Arretal's well-being, instead of waiting for the betrayal to hit.

"He received a warning from council," she said. "The fines are significant, but he...he's more concerned with the optics of our situation. That's what he called it: 'your situation'. He's afraid he'll lose access to trade routes, ports, infrastructure if he—" She set the paper down, lowering her head like she was fading off into the afterlife. "He's pulling his support. He won't give us any more money, and he's telling me to come home and apologize."

"Apologize for what?" asked Del. "You're trying to save Pothena!"

"Apparently bravery requires council's approval. And I have to apologize formally to the council for my insolence."

Del shook his head defiantly. "We'll do it without them. Without council or your father. We still have dragons, and not everyone will be scared off by fines—"

"Without my father's money, Del, we can't afford to repair the school. We don't have money to buy supplies, or to feed the candidates, or even finish building the path up here."

"She's right," said Finnlay. "There's a lot we can do without money, but basic survival requires funding. I would say my family might help, but if even Arretal Browder has folded, there's no way my father will stand up to council."

Lathan, as always, was the calm voice of reason in the storm: "It's a setback, but one we can manage. Let them think they won. Wind down the public face of the school, but build up our capacity in secret. Find supplies, food, and people without letting council know, and then—"

"I don't think we have that much time anymore," said Bettine, rereading her own letter urgently. "The Qapira are on their way."

"The Epyrians," corrected Finnlay, and got an angry glare from Bettine.

"What do you mean?" asked Lathan. "How do you know?"

"This is a letter from a colleague at the university in Yancey. Our mutual friends were traveling by ship to another port city—Varum, it seems—but they never arrived. Their ship never arrived."

"That could be anything," said Lathan. "A bad storm, or a detour, or—"

"It's not," said Bettine. "And I'm certain of that because of three facts: one, the ship they took was a Pothenian build, which has a distinctive shape when seen from below. Two, if you draw a straight line from here to Varum, and Yancey, you will see they're all in a row. And if you follow that line further, it goes into the darkest part of the ocean, where legends say the Qapira live."

Del felt a shiver run through him, because just the words "darkest part of the ocean" felt exactly like the images he'd seen while connected to the Qapira. If they were on the move, that was a terrifying thought—

even more terrifying than facing the Kraken with nothing but his wits and a handful of spells.

But Bettine wasn't done yet: "Thirdly," she said, "We know the Qapira are hunting eggs for some kind of ritual that I suspect involves draining the magical qualities from the eggs for their own purposes."

Del remembered, in the visions of the Qapira, how they placed the eggs near their cracked stone, and it...it was like it healed, almost. What Bettine was saying felt true, though he couldn't explain how he knew that so certainly.

"I don't think they're limited to draining magic from eggs," said Bettine. "Because my friends—the ones who never made it to Varum—they were mages. Powerful mages."

Lathan gasped. "If the Qapira are taking people, too—"

"They're either really weakened," said Etenia. "Or preparing for a very big war."

Del looked out past the mountain's peaks and beyond the city below, off into the distance where the blue ocean glistened with sunlight and the promise of something better. That was the image that had beckoned him away in the first place, and now it was full of doom and death.

"Weak or angry, it doesn't really matter," he said. "The result is the same. We may not have money, and we may not have allies, but we need to start training new dragon riders. Fast."

CHAPTER 16

T he next morning, at their regular meeting to start the day with Lathan and Bettine, Etenia let everyone else speak before stepping forward. She looked nervous about something. Worried about something. And not just the impending arrival of the Qapira—this was something more immediate.

"Make a list," she said softly, then cleared her throat and tried again: "If everyone could make a list of things they need for the running of the school, and get it to me by this afternoon, that would be...um...good."

Bettine nodded and started jotting down what appeared to be a list of things to get. Lathan was contemplating, by the crinkle in his brow, but Del had already picked up on the detail Etenia had been trying to bury:

"Why would we do that?" he asked. "We have no money to buy anything."

"I'm working on—"

"Listen," sad Del. "I know you think you can convince your father to change his mind. And maybe you can. But it will take time we don't have, and we need you—"

"It's not my father," she said. "I'm not asking my father."

Del frowned at her. "Finnlay's family?"

"No," she said. "Well, not exactly. It's the trust my father set up when I was little. It's not as much money as he has, obviously, but it should be enough to buy food and basic supplies for the school."

Bettine set down her pen, a look of worry on her face. "But that's your money, dear. That's the money you'll need to—" Bettine stopped, looked at Del, then back at Etenia. "If you spend that—"

"I think it's a solid plan," said Lathan. "Everyone needs to make sacrifices, and though I know it's hard, it will make a significant difference to—"

"But it's her money," said Bettine. "If she spends it all on the school, her future will be limited and—"

"If she doesn't spend it on the school, she may have no future at all."

Del interrupted with the question that most bothered him: "How do you get at it?" he asked. "Because if it were easy, you wouldn't be talking about doing it, it would be done."

He'd found the sore spot. Etenia shrank a little, looking uncharacteristically uncertain. "It's a dowry. A fund for my husband, to help take care of me. It's..." She shook her head like she wanted to stop explaining things, but knew she had no choice. "The funds are unlocked once we set the wedding date."

Del's heart stopped, and he didn't like it one bit. "Th-the wedding date?"

"The money is meant to help pay for the ceremony, so if we set a date and make it official, the money is mine—"

"Finnlay's, you mean."

"Finnlay agrees with me," she said. "He said he'll funnel the money straight to the school."

Del was doing his best to contain his anger, and his deep suspicion that Finnlay would do no such thing, but it was not going well. "Whose idea was this, really? Yours, or his?"

Etenia looked at him, her eyes full of sorrow. "This is the only way, Del. If we don't have money for food, no one will sign up. And those who do won't stay. We need this. It's the only way. So...let me make this sacrifice."

Del didn't like it for a multitude of reasons—chief amongst them the fact that they were going to be entirely at Finnlay's mercy when it came to the basics of survival—but he knew there was nothing he could do to stop her, in the end. When she made up her mind about something, that was it.

"Fine," he said. "But let's look over the lists we made again. Let's cut out anything we don't absolutely need. We need to keep things as cheap as possible. Lean and efficient, that's the goal."

At first, everything was fine. But as the candidates trickled in—after Finnlay finished making the pathway secure—they quickly realized they were welcoming a large group of people with their hearts set on being dragon riders who were never going to be dragon riders, purely because of the numbers of eggs available to be claimed. The tension was palpable some days, and it was turning into sporadic fistfights that were hard to police, given how busy everyone was.

"This is a scam," grumbled one of the poorer applicants as he carted chunks of stone out of the half-opened dormitories. "They said we're here to train, but we're just doin' chores without pay."

It was a common refrain that was hard to counter. They did have some success on the hatching front: three more Sivarnan eggs bonded with Pothenian candidates—one of Etenia's peers and two street kids who Del strongly suspected had been intending to steal eggs and had been interrupted by the unexpected hatchings. Lathan had been so certain they might find, at most, two dragon riders out of the thousand they'd seen in the square that day, but they were already up to six.

But that only made things worse on other fronts. Some applicants were bitter they hadn't been chosen, and didn't understand why. Some thought they hadn't been given a fair chance at bonding, and kept trying to break into Lathan's quarters to manhandle the eggs and inspire them to open. One morning, Lathan had awoken to a teenage girl pounding at an egg with a rock, trying to break it apart. She was the first pupil expelled from the school. But after only a couple of weeks, she was joined by several others, for a variety of incidents.

"We need to find something to distract them with," said Lathan one morning, looking nearer to death than he had while starving on the island. "If we don't keep them busy, they'll tear each other apart."

"No more construction projects," said Del. "They're not even trying anymore, and it's getting dangerous. I almost got crushed by a collapsing wall yesterday. We need something else that's less deadly."

Lathan winced when he said: "I was thinking of teaching them magic."

Del and Etenia both gave him concerned frowns. "Magic?" asked Del. "Are you insane?"

"They already get into fights enough as it is," said Etenia. "Imagine what will happen when they can cast spells, too."

"Magic has a way of focusing the mind," said Lathan. "With the right guidance, I think we can solve our two biggest problems in one go."

"Keeping the applicants occupied is number one," said Del. "What's number two?"

Lathan looked out at the ocean as he said: "Expanding our fighting force so we don't die all at once."

It was hard to argue with that, so that same afternoon, Lathan started training students the basics of magic. He offered it as a special course for anyone who might be interested, but soon found himself inundated, trying to schedule as many classes as he could throughout the day. It got so busy, the school had to make a rule that said you couldn't attend a magic class until you'd finished your chores for the day. Suddenly, the school started looking cleaner, safer, and more polished than ever before. A bunch of students even rebuilt an old amphitheater to make it easier for Lathan to teach more students more easily. It could also double as a command center for when the Qapira attacked, Del thought, but didn't say aloud. It felt like bad luck.

One day, as Lathan was taking a well-needed break between sessions, a pair of white-haired young women peeked in the library, which was the de facto head office for the school. They seemed shy, and a little in awe of where they were. Del watched them out of the corner of his eye; they were new to the school. He couldn't wait for them to see a dragon for the first time.

"Excuse me, Professor?" they asked, and Bettine looked up from her work, nearly knocking her candle over in the process.

"Yes, my dears?" she said

The taller of the two women put her hands together as if begging for mercy. "Oh, no, we're sorry. We meant Professor Phrac."

"It's General Phrac," said Lathan, lying on the floor with a book tented over his face to block the light. "And class doesn't start for another twenty minutes, so—"

"We aren't students, General," said the shorter one. "We'd like to help."

Lathan sighed. "Help with what, exactly?"

They exchanged tiny nods, and then turned their palms upward, and suddenly in the air above the bookcases, a thousand tiny pinpricks of light flickered into being, illuminating the entire library in a way none of them had ever seen before. Bettine let out an excited gasp, and even Del found himself gaping at the beauty of it.

Lathan pulled the book off his face and then his eyes went wide in horror. "No!" he snapped. "No, no! Take them away! The books are too dry! You'll start a fire and—"

"Don't worry, General," smiled the taller woman.

The shorter one held up her hand, and one of the pinpricks drifted downward, landing in her palm. She closed her fingers around it, and opened them again. "They generate no heat. Very safe."

"And very useful!" said Bettine, reaching out to touch the spark. The woman "poured" it into Bettine's hand with a polite nod.

Lathan hurried over and checked it over, too. "How did you do this?" he asked. "I haven't—"

"We are mages," said the taller one. "From Mykos. I am Taria, and this is my sister Wen. We were visiting Pothena when we heard about your school, and decided to come see for ourselves."

"It is very wonderful," said Wen.

"But you are one man teaching a thousand souls to use magic," continued Taria. "In Mykos, classes are ten to a professor, at most. It is safer that way, and better for the students."

Wen nodded her agreement. "Fewer accidents."

"We would like to help you teach," said Taria. "So you can help more people."

"And have fewer accidents," said Wen.

And so the dragon academy became a magic academy, also featuring some dragons. Lathan struggled with relinquishing control to his assistant professors at first, not knowing if they could be truly trusted, but over time seemed to really enjoy having them around—they even taught him a spell or two.

Every day that passed, the school was becoming more and more impressive to behold. They had long since used up all of Etenia's dowry and had no money to pay for things, but all the crumbling buildings had been repaired, and the pathway was getting such heavy use that Finnlay's patchwork fixes had been replaced by more permanent solutions.

The Qapira still hadn't attacked, which felt like a blessing and a curse, because it made Council seem wiser than they were, and made Etenia's standing in Pothena even more tenuous. She wasn't just a disrespectful brat, she was a delusional brat. Her father's letters had slowed to a trickle, like he was embarrassed to communicate with her, even in private. She tried to hide how much it hurt her, but Del could see it clearly. Every time a courier arrived, he got involuntarily cranky.

"Another fine," said Etenia, slapping a paper down on the library table. "They're charging us so much money, it would even bankrupt my father." Except, of course, her father had essentially disavowed her and the academy. Especially since she'd never gone to apologize, as he'd demanded. Del had no idea how the Braitmans hadn't called off the wedding already. Surely they must have been as much of a target as the Browders. He couldn't tell if things were worse than Finnlay was letting on, or if the Braitmans just had no idea what he was doing. Either way, he was lying to someone…and hopefully the lies wouldn't come back to haunt them.

"Forget about the Council," said Del, scanning through a book on dragon armor. "They can't do anything about it. It's just words on a page."

"Actually, they can do something about it," said Etenia. "They've started fining anyone who gives us food."

"What? That's just—"

"Petty? Yes. But it's going to hurt soon if we don't find a way around it. Finnlay says there's only a little money left in the wedding fund, and we only have enough food to last the students several months. With six growing dragons to feed, I don't know how that can work."

She was right. Searsha and Cember still weren't full-grown, but even their appetites seemed to pale in comparison to the new crop. Garra ate more in a day than Searsha had the entire time they'd been on the island, and Del had a strong suspicion she'd gladly eat more if they offered. If they didn't maintain their nutrition, their entire dragon force might be undersized and less effective in battle.

"Do you have any ideas of how to work around this?" he asked Etenia.

"No," she said, shaking her head like it was a question that had been plaguing her for some time. "I wish I did, but I don't."

"Neither do I," said Del. "But leave it with me. Finding food is what I do best."

Working with Womp, Del started hunting for other black market sources of food. It turned out the most reliable way to feed the dragons was with seafood, straight from the fishermens' ships. Every morning before dawn, Searsha and Cember took off, flying down around the western edge of the bay where a small collection of boats were waiting for them with giant nets of fish ready for transport. The captains took payment without reporting it to the authorities, and everyone got fed.

You are unhappy again, said Searsha one morning, after returning with the day's catch. *Do you not like the smell of fish?*

Del sighed, slumping down next to her. "It's not the fish. It's the sea. It's what else comes from the sea."

The Qapira are late, she said. *I had noticed that, too.*

"I don't know how far they're coming from, but how are they not here by now? It's been weeks. Months, even! Why aren't they attacking?"

Perhaps they are slow swimmers.

"Or maybe they're preparing for a serious battle. One that we can't hope to fend off."

Searsha watched as Cember tried to control the younger dragons' feeding frenzy, and mostly failed. *We will be ready, whenever they arrive. We may not win, but we will not go easy.*

That didn't make Del feel any better. He wished there were some way to increase their forces—to convince the Pothenian dragons to join them. But that was a lost cause, and he couldn't blame them for not trusting the Pothenians.

Instead, Del had been working hard to truly become as expert as his title of Head Dragon Trainer implied he was, studying every dragon riding-related book he could find. There was a lot that he already knew, instinctively, but he learned a handful of tricks that made flying even more seamless between himself and Searsha. She kept growing, too, which allowed them to try new techniques that had been too unwieldy when she was smaller.

Bettine, too, was churning through the books, creating a new set of documents to better prepare the next generation of dragon riders for the challenges ahead. She had originally been writing directly into a fresh book, but every time she finished a page, Lathan would wander over and explain to her how her methodology was antiquated, and no one did things like that anymore. She would snap back about Pothenian superiority, and then he would note the Pothenian dragon riders had gone extinct, and then Del would find someplace else to be.

Lathan and Bettine had each other—for better or worse. Etenia was in charge of managing the school, and in her free time, managing Finnlay, who never seemed to have much to say about the troubles down in Pothena, and was always quick with an optimistic take on every situation. That left Del more or less on his own—so he dove into his work, teaching the new dragon riders—including the ever-present Finnlay—everything he knew about the journey they were just embarking on.

He told them the basics, about how you could close your eyes and live through your dragon's senses. He told them to pay close attention to their dragon's emotions, because sometimes that was the clearest way to know when something was wrong. They learned how to let a dragon boost their magical potency, and how to communicate with each other through their dragons.

And then one day, very unexpectedly, Del realized the new dragons were large enough to carry riders. For him, that moment had been a matter of desperation: the Kraken had been escaping, and he needed to give chase. But with no sign of the Qapira anywhere, Del realized these new riders, they were going to get to experience their first flights without it being a matter of life or death. They were going to get to enjoy themselves.

He was jealous, he realized. And proud. It was the oddest feeling, because just a few weeks ago, these four students had been absolute strangers—not to mention one of them was Finnlay—and now they were some of the best friends he had ever had.

He spent the morning reviewing the techniques with them. He called in Bettine and Lathan to explain the methodology behind every second of dragon riding. They had their up-to-date manuals, with large, detailed diagrams they both seemed happy with, and they talked for a solid hour about how to ride a dragon the proper way.

They stood side-by-side, Del noticed, and were finishing each other's sentences.

He wondered if Etenia would be around to see the newbies take flight.

Of course she would, he realized. Finnlay was one of the newbies.

Again, you are displeased, said Searsha, as the four new dragons and their riders got ready, near the edge of the broken-edged plaza. *What is it about happy moments that you dislike?*

"It's not the moment," said Del. "It's...it's hard to explain. But I am happy for them. I just hope I prepared them for what's coming."

Searsha looked out at the preparations and sighed. *Pochok will drop like a rock,* she said, referring to the youngest of the dragons with dark gray skin and stout little legs. *He seems to believe flying is a psychic skill, not a physical one.*

"Has anyone told Biri?" said Del, suddenly panicked for Pochok's rider.

No, said Searsha pleasantly. *Cember and I agree the only way to truly convince Pochok he is wrong is for him to realize his stubbornness could, if left unchecked, result in Biri's death.*

"And what happens if Biri actually dies?" Del asked.

Searsha looked out at the riders for a long moment.

Yes, perhaps you should warn her beforehand. That seems wise.

Del hurried over, ducking underneath the flexing dragon wings before stopping at Pochok's side. Biri was already in place, holding on tight with her face locked in serious concentration. Del tapped her boot to get her attention, and for a second, she didn't seem to understand what was happening because she was so focused on what was coming. But then she looked down at him and smiled.

"Am I ready, Professor?" she asked, and Del felt the oddest sensation, deep in his chest. Pride and happiness and worry and all kinds of emotions tangled up together, swelling so strong he felt like he might cry. No matter what happened next, he knew, these two would be all right. He'd taught them how to work together to overcome any obstacle.

That was when he realized this was what he was meant to be: a dragon rider. A teacher. A trusted voice.

"Yes you are," he said with a smile. "Have fun out there."

CHAPTER 17

I t was a constant battle, every day, between confidence and terror.

The training was going exceptionally well. Finnlay and the other riders had been well-prepared by their theory lessons and were progressing so quickly Del had to spend his evenings working with Lathan to figure out what else to teach them. Most days, their dragons went soaring out over Pothena, performing incredible acrobatics and mock battles that shocked and amazed. It was mostly out of necessity—they needed space to maneuver, after all, and better to practice in the spot the battle would actually take place—but it had the added benefit of irritating the council into a frothy mess. They kept sending ever-larger fines up the mountain, which Etenia used as kindling for her fires.

She hadn't had much time to fly, herself, thanks to the mountain of other responsibilities she'd taken on. At first, it seemed like only Finnlay could drag her away from her desk, but soon even he was left behind too, as she worked late into the nights, trying to keep the whole enterprise from collapsing. The Council had truly made it their mission to attack the academy from as many angles as possible, so every time

Etenia smoothed over a conflict with one supplier, or one student's family, someone else would come running to her with a fresh crisis.

Despite that, they had no shortage of fresh recruits: some, like Taria and Wen, were from the world beyond, and had been so inspired by the dragon school that they insisted on joining. Most kingdoms were like Sivarna, to some degree—their schools were reserved for the chosen few, and shrouded in secrecy. This new Pothenian school was open to anyone, and very much in the public eye. That alone drew crowds.

And from the crowds came students. Lathan, Taria and Wen were soon overwhelmed by the interest in learning magic, and had to deputize their top students to become instructors as well. The results were incredible to behold, as hundreds of mages-in-training, standing side-by-side in the Old City square, performed their spells in perfect unison, like an army without swords.

The eggs, meanwhile, kept hatching. Sometimes in batches, and some-times none for several days in a row, but the trend was clear: by the end of the month, they'd bonded nearly thirty dragons. Lathan was at a loss to explain it—it wasn't just that Sivarnan dragons were bonding with outsiders, it was that for his entire life, the bonding of a dragon to its rider was a momentous occasion, and something that happened very, very rarely. Bettine had theories about how this moment of crisis was helping the dragons see beyond their usual constraints and choosing people they might not have considered otherwise. Lathan took comfort in that, it seemed; he occasionally called the new students "exceptions" —which he quickly corrected to "exceptional" to save face.

The influx of humans and dragons put an incredible strain on the school's resources. Etenia's deal with Finnlay had unlocked funds, but not nearly enough. Even with the six oldest dragons making their runs to the fishing boats every morning, they were falling behind, because there simply wasn't enough supply to feed everyone. Searsha and Cember volunteered to do without—they had experience with starving, after all—and Garra routinely claimed to be full when she'd barely touched her food. It was a group effort, but one with a dark undercurrent.

Del and Searsha went out most mornings before anyone else was awake. She flew him up to the meadow between the peaks and practiced her swoops and swirls while he ran laps through the grass. It helped him focus, not just because of the blood pumping through his body, but because being surrounded by so many people for so much of the day was truly exhausting to him. He was so used to being invisible, but everywhere he went, students would wave and say hello, or ask him a question about bonding, or just want to chat about their lives back home.

He was always afraid someone would ask him about his family, and that he'd answer honestly. No one really cared about his past anymore, but he knew it was only a matter of time before the truth changed how people saw him.

One morning, Searsha dropped him off at the library before continuing on for the fishing run; Del had expected to be the only one there, but the doors were open, and he could see Bettine studying something intently.

"You're up early," he said as he came inside.

"I haven't slept," she said, and looked it. She rubbed her eyes and kept tracing lines along what appeared to be a map of Pothena and the surrounding areas. "I don't think I will, either."

Bettine had a habit of saying outlandish things, but this was different. "How do you mean?" he asked. "What's wrong?"

She pointed to the map where she had made a series of markings in red. They were all in the water, and all a good distance away. But there was something very distinctive about them: "It's a circle," she said. "Like a barrier."

166

"What is?" asked Del, trying to make sense of it.

"Ever since the downing of the ship between Yancey and Varum, I have been plotting incidents in the seas. Missing ships, mysterious storms, sudden detours. The placements aren't exact, but you can see a pattern. And then there's this: I've been tracking the origins of all our students, as they come in. Do you want to know what they all have in common?"

Del didn't know, and his face showed it.

Bettine drew a circle within the circle of red markings. "They all come from inside this barrier. In fact, I would be surprised if Pothena has hosted a single ship from outside this circle in months."

"The Qapira..." he said. "But why? Why aren't they attacking?"

"That's what I couldn't figure out, until last night. I was fretting about the lack of fresh fish for the dragons—a lack of nutrition can have strongly adverse effects if it goes on too long—"

"Yeah, I heard that somewhere," said Del.

"And then it hit me," she said, setting another map down on top of the first. It was the same general area, but with streams of blue markings in the water, and clusters in certain areas, like lakes and rivers within the sea. "Fishing grounds."

"What?" asked Del, studying the map a little closer. "They're fishing?"

"No, Del," she said, and drew the circle on this new map in red—leaving all the largest fishing grounds outside the barrier. "They're trying to starve us. That's why the boats can't keep up. The fish that would be coming to Pothena are being diverted by the Qapira, and anyone that might warn us—or bring us outside supplies—is being scared away."

"Or killed," said Del.

Bettine nodded. "Have you had any visions lately? You haven't mentioned any..."

"No," said Del, thinking back to the last one he remembered, weeks earlier. "Not recently, anyway."

"Maybe they're trying to hide their strategy."

"How do you mean?"

"Well, I was wondering why they hadn't attacked yet, but then I realized: they have been attacking. Just not directly."

Del turned and looked out the door, out past the peaks and at the distant ocean. The rising sun cast a brilliant light across the surface, like a beam of fire through the void.

"Do you think we'll ever be ready?" he asked. "I know we're training for a battle, and we've gotten farther than we really have any business to...but sometimes I wonder if it's enough."

Bettine thought a moment before answering. "Dragons and mages are some of the most powerful creatures the world has to offer. And we have them in spades."

That only made things worse. "We had three mages and two dragons on the island," he said. "Against one enemy. One Qapiran. And we very nearly lost that battle. The army I saw in my vision—and I don't know how many I didn't see—is enormous. We have thirty dragons and maybe two hundred mages. Even if they were all at the top of their game, those are still steep odds."

Bettine smiled weakly. "I read a quote the other day that seems apt: 'the second fatal blow is irrelevant; all that matters is how your body lies.'"

Del thought for a moment, and then a moment more, and then turned and frowned at Bettine. "How is that helpful?"

She grimaced. "I think it loses something in translation. The original Patí is really quite elegant."

The sun was momentarily blocked by a dark shadow, and a second after, Cember landed by the doors and lowered himself so Etenia could disembark. She said a quick goodbye and hurried inside, clutching a letter in her hand. The look on her face said it was bad news. She had so many letters from so many places lately, and they were all bad news. Either direct from Council, or from friends or brave allies around Pothena.

"What's wrong?" asked Del. "A bigger fine?"

"No," she said, setting it down on the table. "It's—what's that?" She pointed at the fishing map with the red circle on it.

"The Qapira," said Del.

"They're boxing us in," said Bettine. "Trying to starve us, cut us off from the outside world."

"We think so, anyway," added Del. "It would explain why they haven't attacked yet."

"But they have," said Etenia, and unfolded her letter. "Cliffport was besieged."

Del's world, historically, consisted of Pothena's market area, the harbor, and a few alleys in the industrial district. It had expanded significantly to include a desert island and Jiffra, but beyond that, he knew next to nothing about what was where, and how far away that meant it was. Cliffport was a name he had never heard before, but it sounded like a place founded by Pothenian merchants.

"Where is Cliffport?" he asked, and Etenia and Bettine both put their fingers on the map at the same time, pointing to a city not quite halfway between Pothena and the red circle.

"This is Cliffport," said Etenia. "Or was, anyway. It's gone. Razed to the ground."

"If that is the Qapira," said Bettine, "then they may be trying to tighten the noose."

Etenia sat down in a chair and exhaled like she'd been holding onto an incredible tension for far too long. Del knew the feeling all too well.

"A handful of survivors made it to the harbor last evening," she said. "They were interrogated by the council all night, because the council is interrogating everyone that shows up in Pothena these days. Trying to stop students from reaching the Old City. But these people were different: they said Cliffport was attacked by an enemy that came out of nowhere. There were no ships off the shore, and no troops at the city walls, but suddenly they had invaders on the streets, killing without mercy."

Del could imagine the terror that would have brought. Even just the fragmented images he'd had of the Qapira made him shiver, but to actually face one down when you didn't even know they were coming? That must have been a waking nightmare.

"They came in from the sea," he said. "Nobody would have expected the enemy to walk directly out of the water. They didn't stand a chance."

Bettine's voice wavered when she spoke: "Does council believe us now? Do they understand the threat?"

"No," said Etenia, and rested her head in her hands. "The opposite. They arrested the refugees for spreading lies. They said Cliffport hasn't fallen, or if it has, it was because of traitors inside the gates who let the enemy through. They insist Pothena is safe—aside from us, of course."

"A dangerous time to know the truth," whispered Bettine. "I'll...I'll keep looking for references to the Qapira. There must be something, somewhere."

She wandered off into the back, bumping into shelves as she fought off exhaustion.

Del looked to Etenia; she seemed so exhausted, it was heartbreaking. Between running the school and teaching students, and then managing their dwindling funds while being threatened by the council on a daily basis...she was taking the brunt of the stress. Del could go up to the meadow and run to relieve his street, but Etenia's spare time was reserved for Finnlay, so she never really had a moment to herself.

He felt like he should leave her alone, even as he wished he could help her hash out a strategy like they had in the old days, before everything got so complicated. But neither of those options would work, given the circumstances. He had to be a different kind of friend.

"Are you all right?" he asked, gently.

She shook her head and took a halting breath. "I don't remember what being all right is like."

"You can take a break, you know. You don't have to be doing this all day, every day."

"If I don't..." she said, looking into his eyes. "If I don't, and we fail, I'll know it was my fault."

Del gave her a smile. "If we fail, you'll probably be dead, so I wouldn't worry too much about that."

She laughed, wiped her eyes and sat taller again. She was back to being Etenia Browder, Solver of Everything. She glanced at the map again, and then marked Cliffport with a black X.

"You know what? I will take a day off. I'm going to Cliffport."

"Ah, yes, a nice vacation," laughed Del, and then realized she was being serious. "Wait, you're not joking? Why would you possibly—"

"Look at it, Del," she said, tracing the red circle. "They've got this perfect arc around us, equidistant from Pothena in all directions. And yet they attack Cliffport, a little nothing town that's actually out of the way. I mean...that's not closing in, that's a diversion."

Del could see it: Cliffport was an odd spot to attack, if you were trying to move closer to Pothena. It was closer, but not efficiently so.

"Why did they choose Cliffport?" she asked. "What were they after?"

"Maybe just picking an easy target to practice on?" asked Del, but even to him, that sounded wrong.

"I have to go see," she said, standing up again. "Maybe there's something to Cliffport that will help us survive."

"Or maybe the fact that it's a diversion is a clue we shouldn't go," he said.

Etenia paused, and he could tell she was about to start a fight. She had that look in her eye that said *I am fully aware that what I am about to say will annoy you, and I will do it anyway.*

"We aren't going. You've got to stay here," she said. "I'll go alone."

"Uh, no you won't," said Del. "The Qapira just leveled Cliffport. Who knows if they left troops behind? You're not flying into an unknown situation like that. Not alone. No way."

"Del, we have a responsibility to the students—"

"Yes we do! Both of us! So why is it that you get to take off on dangerous outings while I have to stay at home and babysit a bunch of—"

"You know you're the better instructor. They need you more than they need me. This place can survive just fine without me."

"But I can't—" said Del, but cut himself off before he said something stupid to Tenny, fiancée to Finnlay Braitman.

If Etenia noticed, she hid it well.

"Cember will take care of me. We'll be fine. I promise."

Del let her go without saying another word. He knew better than to argue with her about things she believed so passionately. Sometimes you had to know when to stay quiet.

Searsha flapped her wings harder until they punched through the clouds, up into the coldest air Del had ever felt—colder than the Old City's, by far.

Tell me when you realize how foolish this is, and I will dive, she said.

"I'm fine," he said, though he wasn't entirely sure he was. "Just make sure you don't lose sight of them."

She will be quite angry when she discovers what you are doing, said Searsha. *I am looking forward to witnessing your excuses.*

"She won't discover what we're doing," he said. "And even if she does, it's not like it's bad that I want to make sure she's safe."

Protecting one's friends is a noble pursuit, said Searsha.

"Exactly," said Del.

Offset, of course, by the stalking aspect.

"I'm not stalking her. I'm just...watching her. From a distance. Without her knowing."

Searsha said nothing to that.

"And anyway," said Del, "I'm not following her to spy on her. I'm following her in case Cliffport really is dangerous, and she gets into trouble, and needs help."

She has Cember, if you recall. I do not suspect you will add much to the equation.

"Me and you," said Del.

Hmm. You make a compelling argument.

"The point is: keep a safe distance, keep an eye out, and if we see any signs of trouble, we'll—"

"What are you doing?" shouted Etenia, from behind him. He twisted around to discover Cember had come up through the clouds without their noticing, and was flying close behind. The stalkers had been stalked.

Del had been expecting to have to explain himself, but not while flying. He stammered to explain himself: "W-we're just...I mean I'm only..." He grumbled to Searsha: "Why didn't you warn me?"

Cember is a sneaky creature. I did not realize until it was too late.

"Yeah, well—"

"Del!" shouted Etenia, as Cember pulled up alongside Searsha. "I'm serious. What do you think you're doing? We talked about this. I'm doing this alone."

"I know that's what you decided," he said, "but I can't just ignore how dangerous—"

"I can take care of myself!" she yelled.

"I know you can!" he said. "Until you can't, and then—"

"You don't trust me!" she said, incredulous.

"Don't be stupid. Of course I trust you!"

"You don't trust that I can make good decisions," she said. "You think I can't handle it, when things get too messy. You think this is all my fault."

"What is all your fault?" he said. "Cliffport? How does that make any—"

Etenia wasn't just upset, she was angry. And not in the same way he'd seen countless times since the island. There was something to this rage that went far beyond anything Del had seen before.

"I messed up with the council," she said. "You tried to warn me, and I didn't listen, and now everything has gone wrong, and we're headed for a disaster, and it's all my—"

"First of all, I didn't warn you about the council—"

"You wanted to! I could see it on your face!"

Del couldn't really argue with that, because he had been suspicious of their pitch to the council. But not because of Etenia—because he didn't trust the old men she was trying to sway. If anything, he'd come out of the meeting believing in her more. But none of that mattered at the moment, because he was starting to get offended by her accusations, despite himself.

"What's done is done, Etenia!" he shouted. "The council said no, and we adapted. That's what you do. I don't see why you need to make yourself responsible for every bad thing that's happened since we got back."

"I don't," she said. "You do. Every time I suggest something, you and the others always find a way to knock me down. Because you don't trust me. And that's why you're following me, after I specifically asked you not to. Because you think I'm going to make a mess of this, just like I make a mess of everything else."

"I never said—"

"I don't know why I'm surprised," she said. "This is how it always works. They tell you you're special, that you're different, that you're worthy...and they give you a taste of freedom, of independence. And then they use your mistakes as an excuse to take it all away and say you're better off doing as you're told."

"Etenia, I—"

"I know I'm not perfect, Del. But I wish you'd stop reminding me of that fact every chance you get." Cember pulled ahead, forcing Searsha to move out of his way.

Del sat there, mouth agape. All he could think was that he barely even saw Etenia anymore. How could she think that he didn't think she was perfect? She was a real pain sometimes, but—

"Leave me alone!" Etenia shouted over the wind.

"Fine," said Del. "We won't go to—"

"No," she said, turning back to glare at him with tears in her eyes. "Leave me alone. For good."

And with that, Cember dove back down through the clouds, leaving Del shivering from the cold, and stunned by the sudden loss of his only real friend.

CHAPTER 18

The first hint of trouble, as Del and Searsha swept in for a landing, was when a young mage in a yellow tunic was blasted clear across the square, landing in a heap outside the mess hall. Even from a distance, Del could see the residual effects of a spell at work, and knew bigger trouble was sure to follow. As he ran to the scene, he could hear angry voices yelling over one another, and saw a group of students in the midst of a wildly undisciplined brawl.

"Stop it!" he shouted as he closed in. "Everyone, stop it!"

The students either didn't hear him or didn't care to listen. He noticed a few of them with their eyes closed, winding up to use magic against their peers. If it ended up anything like the poor fool who'd been tossed like a rag doll, things would quickly get even more out of hand. Del had to act.

He drew from his memories of the island, when they'd been fighting the Kraken. The moment when he'd created a shield around Lathan and Etenia to protect them from harm—that exact moment wasn't just the fuel for his magic, it was the inspiration, too. He created a new bubble at the center of the brawl, nice and tiny, and then with a twist of his hand, grew it exponentially. The force of the movement was so sudden and so powerful, it blasted all the students out and into the air, scattering them along the cobblestones like petals on a flower.

They were stunned, confused, and winded, which is when Del marched toward the scene, yelling: "What do you think you're doing? Who started this? Who's responsible?"

"It's rigged," said one of the students, a tall man named Lufien. He was getting back to his feet, but checking his fine silk shirt for rips and damage. "The whole thing is rigged."

"What's rigged?" asked Del, but he had a strong feeling he already knew: Lufien had been trying to bond with an egg for weeks, every day since he arrived, with no success. Some of the other students Del knew well, because they were in his dragon riding class. This was a fight between the chosen few and the neglected majority. Any other day, he might have been willing to talk it out. Any other day he might have helped them understand. But today, after his fight with Etenia, he was done with stupid arguments. He was in a foul mood and he knew it. These kids were about to take the brunt of it, and he didn't care.

Lufien pointed an accusing finger at Kinto, one of the more recognizable dragon riders, thanks to her half-shaved, half-braided hairstyle and her patchwork clothes. "They're not meant to be dragon riders," said Lufien.

Kinto rolled up her sleeves and got ready to charge: "Say that again, you big polished turd—"

Del cast a quick spell that knocked Kinto's feet out from under her, sending her crashing back to the ground. His temper was boiling right over. "Everyone stop!" he shouted. "You think they're not meant to be here? You're supposed to be learning to fight the enemy, not each other. You know what? From here on out, anyone caught using magic against their peers is getting expelled on sight. No second chances. Got it?"

The students, mostly back on their feet now, nodded unhappily. The tension was mostly gone, but there was still something bugging Del. Something he'd only half-noticed in the moment: there was more than one difference between Lufien and Kinto. Yes, Kinto was a dragon rider, and yes, Lufien was jealous of that fact—but Del couldn't help but notice the differences in their backgrounds, all the way down to the clothes they wore.

The anger he'd just about spent came roaring back. "What did you mean, 'they're not meant to be dragon riders'?" he asked Lufien.

If Lufien had had any sense, he would have bowed out, found some excuse, explained it away. But he was clearly still very bitter about being passed over so often, and thought he had nothing else to lose. "My father is an admiral in the Royal Navy," he said. "Like his father before him, and his father before him. I have been training on sea and on shore since I was five years old. My marks in school were perfect, I was accepted to the Royal Academy before I even finished—"

Kinto made things worse by yawning loudly, which prompted a portion of the students to laugh. Not all were dragon riders, Del noticed. And not all dragon riders laughed.

"Watch yourself, girl," snarled Lufien.

"Don't need to," said Kinto. "My dragon watches for me."

Up above, Kinto's dragon circled the scene. He wasn't full-grown, but he was big enough to maim on command.

Del glared at Kinto and she took a step back out of respect for his authority. That was the street kid in her: do what you must to survive, but when there's someone you respect telling you what's what, do as you're told. Even if just for a minute.

"Lufien, we've talked about this," said Del. "The dragons bond with whatever rider they choose. It's not a question of your academic record, it's—"

"The marks aren't it, Professor," pleaded Lufien. "But they are a good indicator of what kind of a man you are. You don't get accepted into the Royal Academy by chance. Only the best of the best are chosen. So if I can get in there, how does it make any sense that I'm denied my dragon here, while someone who can't even read is flying around all day?"

Del was having a very hard time not blasting Lufien with a spell himself. He was so angry, his heart was pounding in his ears. For the last few months, he'd almost forgotten what life had been like in Pothena for him. The rich treating the poor like disposable slaves to be kicked and belittled for sport. All this time, he stupidly believed maybe the class system that had crushed his spirit for so long might not have survived the trek up the mountain. Maybe up here, none of that would matter anymore.

And here it was: the same old troubles, all over again, and just when it felt like the Qapira were tightening the noose.

"What you're worth has nothing to do with your family or your school or the places you visited on vacation," said Del, slapping his chest. "The dragons see who you are, in here. If you're worthy. If you're not. It doesn't matter where you come from. It's about where you could go."

Lufien's face changed from anger to confusion, and then to acceptance. He clearly felt foolish for losing his temper, and was finally looking for a way to smooth things over. "I'm sorry, Professor. It's just so frustrating sometimes."

"I know," said Del, trying to let his own anger go, too.

"I'm just so used to things making sense," he said. "There's no logic to this stuff. I'm not saying she's not a good person...she's just not like us, you know?"

Del froze, because he realized that when Lufien said "us", he meant himself and Del. And that's when it hit him: he was wearing the clothes the Browders had provided him, he spent most of his time in the library, hanging out with Etenia and Lathan—a Sivarnan general—and had arrived in Seafall like it was a place he was meant to be. When Del looked around at the students assembled there, the wealthy ones were looking at him like he belonged to them. Like he was one of them, and understood them in a way he really couldn't fathom.

"She's not like us?" he asked, voice trembling with anger. "She's not like us? Well that's true. But then again, neither am I."

Lufien frowned at that. "I...I don't—"

"I lived my life begging for scraps in the Pothena market," said Del. "Most days, I had so little to eat, I could barely move. I was the top of my class at pickpocketing, but not much else. I only learned to read a few months ago, when I was stranded on a desert island—and shockingly, that desert island was less terrible than my life had been up until that point."

The rich students were looking at him like he'd suddenly peeled off his skin to reveal a Qapiran monster underneath. The poor students were nodding in silent agreement.

Del pointed at one of the rich kids. "You, I actually remember from back then. You spat sweetfruit seeds at me like you didn't know I was there. Every time you visited the market. You were a world-class jerk. Who knows, maybe you still are. But here's the thing: it's not up to me to decide that. It's up to the dragons. If they're not choosing you, Lufien, there's probably a reason."

He pointed into the air, at Kinto's dragon. "Got a problem with that, try complaining and see how it goes."

The students took the hint. Heads lowered, they started to back away, trying to avoid eye contact with one another, but especially with Del.

He'd been pretty controlled over the last few months—at least when he was working—but now they were seeing his true self. The other part of himself. The part that mattered most. Evidently, it scared them a little.

Lufien joined his posh friends as they started back toward the dormitories. "I knew he smelled funny..." he said under his breath. But not quietly enough.

"What did you just say?" shouted Del, shoving up his sleeves and digging up the meatiest memory he could find. "Hey! You have something to tell me, tell it to my face!"

Lufien turned, tight fists at his sides, as Del wound back and—

"Del, no!" said Finnlay, grabbing him under the arms and pulling him backward. Del fought and twisted to get free, but Finnlay had a solid grip, and wasn't letting go. "Del! It's me! Just—"

Del swung his elbow back and caught Finnlay in the ribs, then got loose and turned to face his new opponent. Finnlay looked more shocked than anything. He held out a hand like he was begging for peace. As if he would ever beg for anything from Del.

"Del, just calm down."

"Don't tell me to calm down," snarled Del. "Tell your friends to learn some respect."

Finnlay glanced over at Lufien and his comrades, who were quickly leaving the scene before things got any worse for them. "My friends?" asked Finnlay. "I don't—"

"You think just because I don't have money, I'm not worthy?" said Del.

"Of course you're worthy!" said Finnlay. "Searsha chose you!"

"Not her!" Del snapped, shocked by what he'd said, and what it meant. Etenia was engaged to Finnlay, and there was never any question that she would end up with someone rich, like her. But until now, Del hadn't even realized how much it hurt him to be so unworthy of even the chance to be...to be...

Suddenly, he felt a surge of panic strike him, broadcast from Searsha.

Del! Be careful!

"Don't worry. I can handle him."

Not Finnlay, she said. *Them!*

He didn't have to ask what she meant, because a moment later, a trio of full-grown dragons came swooping in from above, their massive wings casting dark shadows across the square. Kinto's dragon just barely got out of the way before the three strangers lowered themselves down onto the cobblestones, blocking Del and the others from the shelter—the only place they had to run was back toward the ledge, and certain death.

The other students scrambled closer to Del, as if he could defend them against...whatever was going to happen. He wasn't sure, but he strongly suspected these were Pothenian dragons. Not the same ones as before, but there was something about the look of them, and the magic aura he could feel off them—it was foreign, but familiar. The only question was why they were here. Their only other interaction had made it very clear that if Del and the others didn't leave them alone, things would get very bloody, very fast. Were they angry the Old City had been revived? Were they here to follow through on their threats?

He held out his hands to calm the situation. "We don't want any trouble," he said.

I am not opposed to trouble, said Searsha, landing behind Del and filling her mouth with flames. Garra did, too, and Kinto's dragon landed and growled menacingly. These Pothenian dragons were twice the size of even Searsha, and the plating to their skin looked like it could withstand a thousand times more punishment, too. But that wouldn't stop Searsha and the others from trying. Del felt a swell of pride as they faced down death together.

"We haven't broken the rules," he said. "We kept away from the nests like you asked."

Yes, you have, said the central dragon, a green one with long, sharp tusks protruding from its jaw. *That was surprising. Discipline was never one of your strong suits.*

"My—?"

Your kind. Your race. Pothenians, said the dragon. *You break everything you touch, and then go looking for more.*

Del felt Searsha's anxiety building. She expected a trap. They were talking to keep Del and the others distracted while they moved other dragons into position. It was an unfortunate side effect of bonding so closely to him: she was starting to be as cynical as he was.

"State your business," said Del, eyes darting around, trying to spot the second wave. "Because if it's a fight you want—"

It is a fight we want, said the dragon, and Del's panic spiraled higher and higher and— *But not against you.*

Del and Searsha's confusion collided so suddenly, all he could manage to say was: "Huh?"

The lead dragon bowed its head. *I am Ragir, hunter of the Parryen Range. My rider was Utann Innsfar, General of the Pothenian fleet and the hero of Kaspir Gorge. I stood witness when Pothena lost its way. I hope to be there when it finds its way back.*

The other two dragons lowered their heads too, and then Searsha and the Sivarnan dragons followed suit. Del didn't know what else to do: he bowed, too.

"It's an honor to meet you," he said. "But I still have no idea what's going on right now."

Ragir grinned. *Humans. Slow as always.* He turned his head up toward the edge of the meadow, far above. *We have been watching you. At first, our hunters wanted to eat you, leave your bones as a warning to others. But then we saw...this.*

He meant the school. The people and the dragons. Del could feel an emotion from him that was hard to pin down, but it felt like pride.

This is how it was, before the fall, said Ragir. *Dragons and humans working together as one. Striving for a better existence. Using these bonds for good, against all those who would threaten the peace.*

Del remembered the revelation about the Pothenians and their dragons flying out to save ships in danger from the Qapira. He wondered how that had started—and more importantly, why it had stopped.

"So you're not angry with us?" he asked.

No, said Ragir. *We are here to help.*

Del felt Searsha's shock before he saw it himself, but suddenly the sky was full of dragons swooping in from above, from the east and west, from wherever at once. Dozens of them, blocking out the sun as they circled overhead. It was majestic and terrifying at once. Del was so glad they didn't pick a fight with these dragons. And he was sad Etenia wasn't here to witness it.

The Qapira are coming for you, Del of Pothena, said Ragir. *You killed their hero, and they will have their revenge. But after they defeat you and take your dragons, their hunger will turn toward us. We cannot let that happen.*

"How do you know that?" asked Del. "Are you spying on them too?"

Ragir tipped his head, betraying the slightest smile. *Empress Lomasi has been trying to use your eyes against you,* he said. *We have intercepted her attempts and stifled them.*

At first, Del didn't understand. But then he remembered he hadn't had any dreams about the Qapira for the last few months—shortly after meeting that first Pothenian dragon outside the nest. Somehow, Ragir had been blocking that bond from a distance, giving him a break from the waking nightmare. But a thought occurred to him: "What do you mean by 'intercepted'?"

Ragir smiled very clearly this time. *I can see why she fears you. But yes, we are able to catch glimpses of their preparations—which is why we are here. You would not survive the assault without us.*

Del couldn't help but smile back. "So that means...you'll fight with us?"

Fight, yes. And where appropriate, we will bond with your riders.

Del's feeling of joy was perfectly captured by one of Lufien's comrades, standing nearby. He suddenly saw his chances of being a dragon rider increase exponentially. Del was happy for him, too, even if he was wary about the kind of dragon that would bond with someone so shallow.

"You'd be willing to do that for us?" asked Del. "After what our ancestors did to you?" He still didn't know what it was, but it seemed like a bad time to bring up such a sore subject in great detail.

We have spied many worthy candidates amongst you, said Ragir. *For instance, her.*

He was looking at Kinto. Kinto's dragon growled in return. Lufien's friend sighed dejectedly.

We will supplement your eggs with our own, said Ragir. *And teach you how to be proper riders. None of this Sivarnan nonsense.*

Del was less sure about that. He liked the way they ran things, and the insights Lathan brought to the table. Besides, most of their dragons were Sivarnan. "I don't know if—"

It is not a discussion, Del of Pothena, said Ragir. *The Qapira are coming. They slaughter their enemies without mercy, until they get what they want. And then, after they've won, they kill all the rest.* Del shivered because he knew, deep in his bones, how true that was. And because Etenia was out there, at Cliffport, alone. Unprotected. *This is not a fight for your survival anymore. It is a fight none of us can afford to lose.*

CHAPTER 19

D el wasn't sure how to integrate Ragir and the Pothenian dragons into their school—or if the Pothenian dragons even had any interest in being involved as dragons to be ridden at all. The way they acted around the humans suggested they saw themselves as beyond a bonded relationship, even though they didn't explicitly reject the idea. Rider candidates kept trying to suck up to the dragons, only to be rejected with a dismissive snort. Whatever boost they might have brought to the school's morale was quickly overpowered by their general pricklishness. Lathan was no help, either, constantly deferring to the "Pothenian Master", meaning Del—who was trying to keep their little experiment from collapsing under its own weight.

The dragons were so hard to read, always cocking their heads to the side and playing dumb when asked a question, and never saying anything in a straightforward manner, that Del really had no idea what to do with them. When he asked Ragir about just about anything, she replied: "That is not how we do things in Pothena," without actually saying *what they did do* in Pothena.

What he needed most of all was to pair up riders with dragons, so they'd have time to get to know each other. But how? He'd tried "presenting" his leading candidates to the dragons to see if anyone was interested, but they scoffed at the gesture like it was a joke. Was it because the candidates were too old? Too set in their ways? Or offensive in some other way he hadn't thought of? Should he try pairing the dragons with the newest riders who'd only just arrived at the school? Or should he try to find the most capable candidates—other capable candidates—through rigorous testing? Or was the real issue that Del was taking the choice away from the dragons at all? Were they offended by his attempts at matchmaking? He didn't want to be the one who lost the Pothenian dragons because he'd said the wrong thing—but he wasn't good enough at diplomacy to know what the right thing was in the first place. All he knew for sure was they'd probably tell him he'd gotten it wrong.

That crushing insecurity only made Del feel Etenia's absence even more. She'd been gone for hours now, and as the sun started to set, his anxiety started to manifest in unfortunate ways, like snapping at Womp and rolling his eyes at Ragir. It got so bad even he saw what he was doing, and had to pull himself out of the mix before he made a really terrible mistake. He told everyone he had to go make important preparations before nightfall, and stormed off before someone asked him if he needed help.

He hurried straight to the back of the library, tucked in a dark corner where no one would think to look for him, and he could let his heart beat a little slower. It felt good, being alone again. As much as he liked being a teacher, sometimes he really needed to have some time to himself, where he could work through his own thoughts without distraction.

"Hiding, are we?" said Bettine, peeking around a bookcase with a smile.

Del sighed. "I'm researching," he said unhappily, wishing she'd go away.

"Ah, researching what?" asked Bettine, standing opposite him, looking down at the completely empty table he was seated at.

"How not to offend Pothenian dragons," he said. "These are all the books I could find on the subject."

She laughed. "Well, if you're ever looking for ways to offend them, I have quite the collection. And not just the dragons. It seems as though ancient Pothena had a very bad habit of picking fights with their allies. Nations like Hidexi, Chamenos, Lakseom...there's even a Sivarnan curse with roots in the old Pothenian word for 'soul mate' that I think Lathan would appreciate, given—"

Just then, they heard heavy footsteps rushing through the front of the library. "Professor?" called Finnlay. "Professor!"

Del waved her closer, out of sight. He held a finger to his lips to tell her to keep quiet. The last thing he needed was to have Finnlay inject himself into yet another situation. He just hoped Finnlay would give up looking before he spotted them.

"Professor!" called another voice—Etenia's!—and Del burst off his chair, stumbling past Bettine and skidding into the light.

Etenia was there, with Finnlay and Lathan behind her. Her hair was windswept and there was soot on her face, but she seemed fine. Physically fine. But the look in her eyes as she saw Del was the exact opposite: worry, verging on terror. Worse than he'd seen since the island, when they'd been battling the Kraken. Something terrible had happened in Cliffport. Something truly awful.

"What is it?" he asked, hurrying over. "Are you all right?"

He found himself about to check her head for injuries, about to touch her face—but Finnlay was right there, watching him intently, and stopped himself. He kept a respectful distance, crossing his arms across his chest to give them something to do.

"I'm fine," she said, though her expression suggested she really wasn't. "And Cliffport is...it's—"

"Destroyed?" asked Lathan, voice hollow.

"No," said Etenia. "That's what's strange."

"The Qapira didn't attack?" asked Del, trying to figure out why she looked so upset—and why she had soot on her face.

"They did, but not the town," she said. "It turns out Cliffport had a magic school. Very few people knew about it until the Qapira showed up, but they...they seemed to be targeting the school, and nothing else."

"They're trying to eliminate anyone who might help us," said Lathan. "Decimate our allies so we're all alone."

"Maybe," said Etenia. "But there was something else, too: from what I heard, they weren't trying to kill the mages. They were dragging them into the water."

"To drown them?" gasped Finnlay.

"No," said Del. "There's got to be something else to it. Why go to all the trouble of dragging them to the water just to kill them?"

"Maybe they're hostages?" asked Etenia.

"Maybe," said Del. "I mean, the Kraken did take you and Lathan when it was trying to get me to—" Del's heart froze when he realized: "They're not hostages. That's not what they're after at all."

He could tell by the expressions on their faces that the others didn't understand what he meant. He really wasn't in the mood to have to play teacher yet again, but they weren't going to figure it out on their own, he could tell.

"The Qapira are hunting the eggs because they need the magic inside them, right? Somehow the magic connects with that glowing stone I keep seeing, and does...something. But the Kraken didn't just steal the eggs, it stole Searsha and Cember, and you and Lathan. We always assumed you were just hostages, but... what if you could also be used to power that stone? I mean, think of it: back when the Kraken first attacked the ships, did it kill those Sivarnan mages? No, it pulled them under. It kept a hold of them."

Etenia's face darkened. Del imagined that day was burned into her memory the same way it was his, but now the images took on a more sinister tone as they realized the Sivarnans hadn't just been casualties in a battle, but targets from the very beginning.

Lathan looked horrified by the memory, too, but Del could see he didn't doubt the theory. "The Qapira use magic to power their stone. To what end?"

Del shrugged. "That, I can't tell. Every time I saw it, it looked like it was breaking. Like it was in bad shape. So whatever it used to be—"

"A weapon," said Bettine, voice grim. "It's a weapon." Before anyone could ask, she hurried to her desk and grabbed a handful of scrolls. She started to unroll them, but then seemed to notice it was too dark in the fading light, and motioned for the others to join her outside.

She set down the first scroll and held it flat with Finnlay's help. It showed a map of Pothena and the surrounding seas—crudely rendered, but still recognizable—with dense lettering around the margins.

"Del, remember when I said Pothena made a lot of enemies? Well, this map is from right before that period started. Back when we all had a common enemy..." She pointed at some letters in the middle of the ocean, and even though he couldn't read it, Del knew exactly what it said.

"The Qapira," he gasped.

Bettine nodded. She traced her finger around a set of lines drawn in the waters, all around the area. "Anything look familiar?" she asked.

It was Etenia's turn to gasp. "The boundaries! It's the same as on the fishing charts! What did—"

"Their territory," said Bettine. "Back then, humans knew not to cross these lines, or else risk angering the monsters of the deep. It looks like they're reclaiming their old territory."

Not the Qapira's territory, said a voice from nearby, and Ragir swooped in and landed next to them, making the earth rumble beneath them.

Etenia gaped at the dragon—she'd been gone when they arrived and pledged themselves to the fight—but Del didn't have time to explain. He stood up and did his best to sound respectful when he said: "Wait, what do you mean it's not the Qapira's territory? Whose is it?"

The Balikkan, said Ragir. *Mortal enemies of the Qapira. I have never seen them myself, but my grandmother spoke of the wars between the sea peoples, and how the suffering spread and spread. The Balikkan ruled these waters, until the Qapira launched a hundred years' war, and turned the seas red with their blood.*

"And then what happened?" asked Bettine, trying to reconcile her map with Ragir's story.

The human world rallied to help the Balikkan defeat the Qapira. Dragons from Pothena, Chamenos, Sivarna and elsewhere joined in the battle. When Chamenos found itself besieged, Pothena rode to its rescue, forging a bond in blood they said would never die. Over the years, there were many casualties, many tragedies. And then sudden-ly...it ended.

"We won?" asked Del.

No, said Ragir. *The Qapira vanished without warning. No one knew why, so no one was willing to let down their guard. There were so many kingdoms with so many armies ready to strike. So eventually, they did. Against each other.*

"Sivarna," said Bettine, connecting the dots. "Chamenos—"

Sivarna retreated and built walls like the cowards they are, said Ragir, eyeing Lathan for a reaction, which he wisely did not give. *Chamenos —our allies, our brothers—they fought until the price was too great, and went back home to lick their wounds. And then Pothena turned against its own dragons instead.*

Silence fell. Etenia looked ashamed by her peoples' past; Finnlay seemed to be muttering a silent prayer out of respect; Lathan and Bettine were subdued too. Which left it to Del to respond to the delicate situation they all faced:

"How far away is Chamenos?"

Everyone blinked in confusion, but no one more so than Ragir.

Pardon me?

"You said it yourself, Pothena rode to the rescue when the Qapira attacked. It's time for them to return the favor."

I feel as though you did not listen to the full story—

"I heard you just fine," said Del. "But here's the issue: maybe the reason the Qapira gave up the fight was because their super weapon was damaged, and they had to retreat. And now they're trying to fix it again, by attacking us. If they succeed—and let's face it, we've got about thirty baby Sivarnan dragons, and give or take twenty creaky old Pothenian dragons on our side—they'll be unstoppable. And where do you think they'll go next?"

Ragir glared at him. He could feel the animosity, but ultimately, Del decided he didn't have the luxury of worrying about the Pothenian dragons' feelings. They were either going to be steadfast partners in this war, or liabilities. The sooner they made up their mind which ones they were, the better.

Del glared right back at Ragir, who took a moment before answering.

What do you propose, dragon trainer?

"Send one of your dragons to Chamenos to ask for help. Explain the situation, and tell them we're calling in the favor."

They will refuse.

"Knockabout brothers," said Del.

Ragir couldn't mask her confusion. *I do not—*

"I couldn't put it into words before, but when you..." He chuckled. "We protect our own. That's what Womp said to me. Out on the streets, we take care of our friends. And I've been trying to think, all this time, of how we know who those friends are. It's not because of their bank accounts, or their nice clothes." He did his best not to look at Finnlay when he said that, but he suspected everyone knew who he meant anyway. "And it's not because of titles or history or who we're supposed to respect." This time, he did his best not to look at Lathan. "Our friends are the ones we bleed with. The ones who get kicked by the same boot, and crawl back to the same hole. Our knockabout brothers."

Ragir sat motionless for a moment, then took a deep breath and said: *A bond forged in blood.*

"I don't have a lot in common with historical Pothena," said Del. "But that part, I definitely understand. We fought for Chamenos. It's time they fought for us, too."

Ragir straightened up and spread her wings to take flight. *I will find a negotiator at once,* she said. *I only pray the Chamenos have retained the same code of honor as you, dragon trainer.*

She took off, leaving Del to face the uncomfortable silence of his human allies. Especially Etenia. She was avoiding eye contact with him, and for a second he couldn't understand why—until he remembered their fight. She might still be his ally, but she wasn't his friend anymore. Really, none of these people were. The thing about knockabout brothers—that Del did his best not to dwell on—was that they were all about loyalty, not friendship. You could defend your ally while still hating their guts. He wondered how many of his allies felt that way about him.

Finnlay excused himself awkwardly and ambled off in silence. Lathan and Bettine rolled up the maps and went back into the library.

Del expected Etenia to make an excuse to leave, too, but instead she got that determined-to-be-nitpicky look on her face and said: "But how are we going to stop them?"

Del sighed, because he had that same concern. "We have more dragons now," he said.

"Yes, I saw that. But if ancient Pothena struggled fighting the Qapira with what sounds like an entire society based around warfare, how—"

"By taking away their advantage," said Del. "Their secret weapon."

Etenia frowned at him. "You do recall how it's deep underwater, right?"

Del looked out toward the ocean. "Yeah. Another impossible task to add to my list, I guess."

CHAPTER 20

There was a trick Del used when he was little, when there were coins at the bottom of the fountain near the north end of the market. The older kids could just reach in and grab them, but the water was too deep for Del to wade in, so he had to find another way to claim the change before someone else did. After many failed attempts that nearly ended with him drowning, Isham, his guardian-ish mentor, taught him a trick: take a brick or a big enough rock, and throw it into the fountain near the coins. The surrounding water would, for a very brief moment, be displaced away from your prize—and if you were quick enough, you could reach in and grab it.

It rarely worked, of course. But it did soak quite a few wealthy merchants in the process, so it wasn't a complete waste of time.

But there was something to that memory that Del couldn't get out of his mind, as he tried to think of a way to steal the Qapira's magic stone. Maybe, with enough dragons working in concert, they could carry a giant boulder, or a column from the broken parts of the school, and carry it up high enough in the sky, and drop it like a stone in the fountain...

It might work. Though he had no idea how big of a splash it would make, or if it was even possible to get to the bottom of the sea, grab the stone, and escape before the waters came rushing back in. Maybe magic could be used to hold it off a little? So he'd need a handful of dragons, a handful of mages, and also a general idea of where the Qapira actually kept their stone. That might be tricky. Tricky, or impossible.

He was so caught up in his theories that he barely slept, forgot to eat in the morning, and was largely sleepwalking through his classes. When it came time to practice flight tactics—simulating aerial attacks on dragonback—he was so distracted he very nearly agreed to sending up a pair of novices to try a complex duck-and-dive maneuver.

"Del," said Finnlay, concern written across his face. "Are you sure you're all right?"

"Of course I'm all right," snapped Del. "I'm just a little busy."

"If you say so. I just don't think—"

"You go demonstrate instead," said Del, feeling his anger spiral out of control. What was Finnlay after? Did he want Del's job? Fine, then prove it. Out on the streets, you didn't get the big prizes by needling more-talented thieves about their technique; you got the big prizes by doing better. If Finnlay wanted to take over even more, he should prove he could.

"Me?" said Finnlay. "B-but Garra and I have never—"

"Finnlay, if you can't handle yourself up there, what are you even doing here? We need dragon riders, not play actors. Now can you do it, or not?"

Finnlay looked properly scolded. He took a step back, bowing respectfully. "I can do it. I'm sorry for intruding."

Finnlay took off, leaving Del to contemplate his plan in peace again. Except not really in peace, because he kept feeling incredibly frustrated at Finnlay's continuing presence at the school. The last thing he needed was to be questioned by someone like that—and in front of the other students! Was he all right? Finnlay might be Etenia's fiancé, but he certainly wasn't Del's, and since when had he ever suggested they could be friends? Del was his teacher, and if Finnlay couldn't handle that dynamic, he should—

"Sir!" shouted one of the students, and Del only barely snapped to attention in time to see the student pointing up, and Garra stuck in a spin—

—and Finnlay falling to his death.

Garra was trying to recover fast enough to catch her rider, but there was no way she'd make it in time. The other students were frozen in fear and shock, watching their classmate plummet toward the rockface.

Del leapt into action, racing forward and pulling on all the magic he could muster to create an invisible shield in the air below Finnlay, angled downward so that when he hit it—crash! He hit it hard, and started to tumble. Del used all his energy to help direct Finnlay's path back toward the safety of the school grounds, but couldn't quite manage the feat as well as he wanted. Finnlay bumped off the edge of the shield and then landed on the cobblestone with a crack, lying limp with his right arm bent at an unnatural angle.

Everyone rushed forward to help, but Del stayed behind, stunned by what had happened, and terrified to discover he'd accidentally killed Etenia's one true love. How was he going to tell her why Finnlay was dead? Because he'd lost his temper? Because he'd been in a bad mood and hadn't cared enough about Finnlay's safety? Because he'd casually dismissed his responsibility to his students, because really, deep down, he didn't belong here? He didn't belong in this life? Because he was pretending to be someone he wasn't, and eventually it would get even more people killed?

What was he going to tell her?

"He's breathing!" called one of the students. "He's alive!"

Another student paused on her way to see Finnlay, smiling at Del in amazement and admiration. "You saved him!" she said. "You did it!"

"I did it," said Del, blankly, and walked away.

He could hear Cember coming, so he knew his peace and quiet was about to be ruined. Del didn't sit up to show Etenia where he was lying, amongst the tall grass in the upper meadow, above the school. She'd find him soon enough. There was no point in hurrying the fight that was about to happen.

After a few minutes of listening to her storm around, she finally found him. She stood over him, hands on her hips, face red with anger.

"What were you thinking?" she said, voice trembling with rage. "He could have died!"

"Did he wake up?" asked Del, sheepishly.

"Yes," she said. "And he...he said to thank you for saving his life."

Typical Finnlay. Always so polite, always so perfect. Even now, he was trying to make Del look worse than he was. And he was pretty bad to begin with. He covered his face with his hands.

"Why would you send him up there to do that trick?" she asked. "Not even I can do that trick."

"Well maybe if you practiced more, instead of—"

She kicked his leg. Hard. It shocked him so much, he actually yelped. "Hey!"

"Are you seriously going to suggest I don't do enough around here?" she said. "If it weren't for me, we wouldn't have food, or building supplies, or—"

"Finnlay?" said Del, and Etenia's eyes opened wide.

"Please tell me you didn't do this on purpose."

He scowled at her. "Why would I hurt one of my students on purpose?"

"Finnlay's just not any student, Del," she said, and he gasped at how blunt she was being. Was she really going to address the tension between them? Between all three of them? And if so, how was he supposed to react? She got a look on her face like she was scolding a small child. "You can't treat him badly just because he's rich."

Rich? "I—"

"I know it hasn't been easy for you, working with so many of the people who used to treat you so badly, but Finnlay isn't like that. He's good. He cares about Pothena, and all its citizens."

"I didn't—"

"And furthermore, your whole outlook makes no sense, because if you hated all rich people, how are we friends?"

Del gaped. "W...we're still friends?"

Etenia raised an eyebrow like she couldn't tell if he was joking. "Why would we not be friends?"

"Because..." He waved his hand into the air, in the general direction of Cliffport. "Because I followed you and you yelled me and—"

"I always yell at you!" she yelled.

"No, you don't always yell at me to leave you alone! Trust me, I'd remember that!"

She quieted for a moment. "Maybe not," she said. "But that doesn't mean we stop being friends. How do you not know that?"

"They don't teach us about friendships in street school," he said, dryly.

"Yes they do." She sat down in the grass next to him. "You said it yourself: knockabout brothers. That's us. We bled together, so we're bonded for life. We can fight all day, every day, but we'll never stop being friends. Get it now?"

Del grumbled a bit to himself. "I kind of glossed over the fact that knockabout brothers tend to stab each other in the back a lot."

She winced. "Probably best you left that part out."

"Didn't want to give Ragir any ideas."

They laughed together, and almost instantly, Del felt better. Like all his worries had been washed away, and life would be smooth sailing from now on. He knew, in the back of his mind, that wasn't true—but he let himself be fooled just a little longer.

Etenia lay down in the grass next to him, staring up at the sky as he tried not to stare at her. He imagined Finnlay showing up, seeing them there, together, and his genial personality shattering into a fit of jealousy. Del knew he shouldn't be here, like this, with Etenia...but he couldn't bring himself to move.

"I'm sorry for following you," he said, after a while. "I didn't mean to offend you. I know you're capable. But I just..." He shrugged. "Friends stick together, right?"

She turned her head and smiled at him, and he felt so good, and so guilty all at once. "You didn't offend me," she said. "I shouldn't have yelled. I'm just so used to everyone second-guessing my ideas, I lost my temper even though I knew you were only trying to help."

She held out her hand to shake. "We're both idiots?"

He laughed, and shook her hand. "We're both idiots." He paused, then said: "But maybe I can be the bigger idiot."

She frowned at him. "Uh-oh. What did you do now?"

"It's not what I've done," he said. "It's what I want to do."

Etenia's eyes opened wider and her face went blank as she looked at him, at all of him, her eyes ending up focused on his lips. He suddenly realized she thought he was about to kiss her! He didn't know what to do, or what to say—but before he got a chance to decide, she sat up, looking off into the distance, trying to change the subject without saying a word.

"W-what do you want to do?" she finally asked.

Del felt sick to his stomach. He hadn't even been thinking what she thought he'd been thinking, but suddenly he felt hurt that the idea of him kissing her was so offensive that she had to physically escape it.

He pushed that hurt aside as best he could, and tried to focus on more important things. Like surviving the Qapira. He proceeded to explain his "drop a boulder from the sky and use magic to open a portal to the Qapiran city, so they could steal the magic stone" theory. By the time he was done, Etenia's expression was distant—different than before, but no less enchanting—like she was too overwhelmed by all the information to even know how to react.

"So?" he said. "What do you think?"

"I think you are the bigger idiot," she said, a smile returning to her face that made Del nearly giddy with relief. "There are so many problems with that plan, I don't even know where to begin."

"The biggest issue, from what I can tell, is how much weight we can reasonably lift with the dragons we have, because—"

"No, the biggest issue is you don't know where you're trying to do all this," she said. "Think of it: all we know for sure is that the Qapira came from somewhere outside that territorial ring that was drawn on the map. And since it took them so long to get here, they could have come from a long way away."

"Yes, but—"

"You'd have to drop this boulder in the perfect spot to even stand a chance of it working," she said. "Have you seen how big the ocean is? How are you going to find out where to aim? And even if you found out, is there any land nearby, or do you expect the dragons to carry a massive chunk of rock for hundreds of miles before they—"

"All right, all right, all right, I get it," sighed Del. "It's a bad idea. Sorry I brought it up."

"Don't be sorry," she said, lying back down and propping herself up on her elbow to look at him directly. "Bad ideas can spark good ones. It's only when we stop trying that we're truly doomed."

Del smiled at her. At the look on her face as she said that. At how perfect this moment was.

"Sounds wise," he said. "Who said that? Some great Pothenian philosopher?"

"No. Just Finnlay."

Del's mood soured instantly, especially because it seemed like the longer Finnlay hung around, the more Etenia liked him. "How is he, anyway? His arm looked—"

"Broken," she said. "Lathan is working on it now. He said it was lucky you were there, because he never would have thought to break Finnlay's fall the way you did."

Del shrugged. "I didn't really think."

"That's a theme with you, isn't it," she joked, and he gave her a mock scowl. "But seriously, Del: I know you're anxious to fight the Qapira, but we have to make sure we're not risking our most important assets needlessly."

"First of all, I'm not anxious to fight the Qapira. If I could cast a spell that would make them disappear, I'd do it. I'm just trying to find a way to end this war before it has a chance of costing us something we can't afford to lose. Our most important assets. Because without Finnlay—"

"Finnlay?" she asked, giving him a curious smile. "I meant you, Del. You and Searsha are the core of this school. If we lost you, I don't think the students would recover." She looked into his eyes, and he felt his heart stop. "I don't think I would recover..."

He didn't know what was happening, but in that moment, the whole world stopped. All he could see was her, and all he could feel was the wind through the grass all around them, and all he could hear was—

Screaming, said Searsha, urgently, from afar.

Del blinked, pulled out of the spell he'd been under. "W-what?"

There is screaming at the school, Searsha said. *Something is wrong.*

CHAPTER 21

B y the time they made it down to the school, a crowd had already gathered, circled around someone or something near the entrance to the library. Del and Etenia pushed through, hurrying past the stunned and silenced students until they finally came to the center, and found Lathan and Bettine huddled over Safrin, one of the youngest dragon riding trainees. Her face was covered in tears as she doubled over, crying soundlessly.

"What is it?" asked Etenia, kneeling down to check on the girl. "What happened?"

Safrin came from a working-class family, and many of the people crowded around were the children of richer merchants, so Del's first thoughts went to bullying. He glared at them all. "What did you do to her?"

"Not them," said Lathan, touching Del's arm to snap him out of whatever rage was building. "It's her brother."

"H-he's gone..." cried Safrin.

Bettine was reading a crumpled-up paper soaked with tears, her face ashen. "The Qapira have attacked Pothenian merchant ships," she said. "Inside the ring."

"Her brother was first mate aboard one of the vessels," said Lathan, rubbing poor Safrin's back. "All hands were lost. No survivors."

Del felt his chest tighten. All this time, waiting for the Qapira to attack, he'd started to think maybe the day would never come. And now that it was here, he didn't feel any more prepared than at the start. In fact, he felt even worse, because now he knew what they were up against.

"They're coming," he said, grim and distant.

"Why merchant ships?" asked Etenia, with a tremble to her voice. Her family's ships might be in danger, too, and even if her father had pulled his support of the school, Del knew she couldn't help but care for him. "But why? Why now? Pothena doesn't deal in dragon eggs, and the average citizen doesn't use magic. What could the Qapira possibly have been after on that ship?"

"Do they have to have a reason?" Del asked. "Besides wanting to defeat us?

"Does it say what they were transporting?" Del asked Bettine.

She read both sides of the paper, skimming up and down. "Something about an exhibition. It doesn't—"

"The 'Ancient Ties' exhibition," said Tommen, one of the newer recruits, a young man with a nice silk tunic and a worried expression dashed across his face. "My father is helping organize it. It's...it's meant to remind Pothena how our greatness comes from our belief in science, and the alliances we've forged, and not...uh...fairy-tale creatures in the sky."

The other students glared at him like he was a traitor. He shrugged to show his innocence. "It's not like I came up with it! The Council just wants to show off how much influence they have around the world. They made deals with other kingdoms to temporarily repatriate a bunch of ancient Pothenian artifacts, to prove we've always been—"

Etenia and Del looked up at the same time, mouths hanging open. "Ancient artifacts!" gasped Etenia.

"They're magic," said Del. "They must be. The Council sent out ships to collect artifacts, except they had no idea the things were soaked in magic. And the Qapira noticed. The Council bundled them all together and made it impossible to resist."

Bettine finished reading the letter. "The Council is claiming it was a storm, and the loss was due to inexperienced crews on all three ships."

"My brother was not inexperienced," said Safrin angrily. "There's no storm he could not brave."

Del's anger was back, but aimed in a different direction now: the Council, and their willful blindness. "I can't believe they're lying to people to avoid admitting the Qapira are real."

"We have to warn them," said Etenia. "If they don't dismantle this exhibit, they'll be drawing the Qapira straight to them." She looked to Tommen. "Can your father introduce me to the ones in charge? Maybe I can make them see reason."

Tommen gaped at her. "You...you mean you don't know?"

Etenia didn't, clearly, but the second Del saw Tommen's expression, he knew: awkward and reluctant to make eye contact? Wondering how Etenia didn't already know? It could mean only one thing: "Your father's running the exhibition," he said to Etenia. "Probably to get back on the Council's good side."

Tommen nodded, eyes downcast like he felt horrible to be the one to tell her. "He's been raked over the coals these last weeks, and this was his only way out. I'm sorry. I thought you knew."

Etenia took the letter from Bettine, doing a poor job of hiding how unhappy she was with everything that was going on. Del felt awful for her, too. He knew Arretal wasn't as good and noble as he pretended to be, but Del hadn't expected he'd be betraying them quite so directly. Arretal was running an exhibit dedicated to undercutting his own daughter's dragon rider school—how was she supposed to respond to that? Go to war with her own father? Or do what he always expected her to do, and bow her head and say nothing?

He knew she would have to face this obstacle herself, but unlike Cliff-port, she wasn't going alone. Knockabout friends stuck together.

"Where is the exhibit taking place?" asked Bettine. "If it's too close to the shoreline, it will be practically indefensible against the Qapira."

Tommen's expression got even more dire, if that was possible. "It...it's not," he said. "They're holding it up the hill in Seaport. At the Browder estate."

Etenia gasped, and Del reached for her, but realized she wasn't listening to Tommen at all. She'd been reading the letter, and the color had drained from her face.

"What is it?" he asked. "What's wrong?"

"One of the ships that went down," she said, voice trembling. "It was the *Pacimae...*"

Del didn't know what that meant, and based on the expressions on the others' faces, no one else did, either. Whatever it was, it deeply affected Etenia. She covered her mouth with her hand, clutching the letter tightly, and pushed herself out of the crowd, and across the courtyard.

"Etenia!" called Del, struggling to follow. "Etenia, wait!"

She was headed for the dormitories. Del's heart sank, because he realized that if Etenia needed to be alone, something truly terrible must have happened. It made him run even faster to catch up.

A group of student mages got in his way, laughing and jostling each other as they headed off for their afternoon break. Del tried to break past, but they were blissfully unaware he was there, somehow, even when he shoved them aside. Etenia turned the corner into the laneway near their dorm rooms, just as he got free and started sprinting again.

He skidded to a stop outside her room, knocking urgently while trying to think of the words to say. "Etenia?" he called. "Whatever it is, let me help you. I...I want to help you." There was no answer, so he knocked again. "Etenia? It's..." He was tired of standing there, so he took the handle and called out: "I'm coming in!"

Her room was empty. And silent. She wasn't there.

And then he heard her sobbing, back outside. He exited, following the sound of her voice until he came to Finnlay's room, where the door was still open. Inside, Finnlay was in bed, one arm in a sling, and the other wrapped around Etenia and she lay next to him, weeping. His face was stricken, too, eyes full of tears that Del could tell he was trying to stop from falling.

Seeing them there together, in each other's arms, hurt him more than he could have predicted. It wasn't a romantic moment at all, but that wasn't the issue, Del realized. It was the fact that when something hurt Etenia so much she fell apart, she ran to Finnlay for comfort. Not to Del, to Finnlay. As much as she claimed to want to be independent, to not just be Mrs. Etenia Braitman, she really did seem to belong with him. It was like Isham had always told him: your reflexes are always right. Whatever you do without thinking, that's the truth of the matter. Her truth was Finnlay, not Del. And it stung.

Etenia didn't notice that Del had arrived, but Finnlay did. He put on his bravest face, but when he spoke, his voice was cracking with emotion. "Th-the *Pacimae* went down," he said.

Del stepped into the room. "I don't..."

210

"It was Yena's—" said Finnlay, and then his voice broke, and he took a moment to get back his composure. "Yena was her best friend," he said. "S-she was in command of the *Pacimae*, and now she's—"

Etenia sobbed even louder, and Finnlay broke down, too, cradling her as Del backed away.

"I'm sorry," he said, and left.

Lathan found Del sitting at the edge of the broken lookout, sitting on a giant stone tile that was sagging toward the abyss, but not quite committed to falling yet. Del heard him coming, but made no move to greet him. This was starting to be a habit for him, getting tracked down by his friends when he really wanted to be alone. He couldn't tell if they were dense, or he was, thinking they would leave him alone.

The sun was setting, and the seas looked like they were on fire—and in a lot of ways, Del wished they would be. Burn them all away, and start over.

"Are you all right?" asked Lathan, joining Del on the sagging stone.

Del shook his head, trying to find the words. "Her friend is dead," he said.

"I heard," said Lathan. "We're arranging a memorial for this evening, after dinner. You should be there."

"Should I?" asked Del. "I mean...do I really belong here at all?"

Lathan's jaw tensed, and Del could tell he was getting upset in that self-righteous way of his. "Don't make this about you, Del."

"I didn't even know she had a best friend," he said. "Yena. Did she ever mention Yena to you? Because the first time I heard about her was from Finnlay, while they were...were..."

"She had a life before she met you, Del," said Lathan. "She had friends around her. A whole future planned out. And then the Kraken attacked, and everything changed." He stared down at his hands. "Everything changed. But it didn't erase what was there before. We're all still who we were before the island, just...different."

"You don't have to tell me that," said Del. "I used to be a nobody, and now I'm in charge of saving the place I used to hate. But I don't hide who I was from her. I thought that's what friends did: they were honest with each other."

Lathan sighed. "I don't think she lied to you, Del. There are just parts to her life that she hasn't quite figured out how to fit back together again. How to reconcile her old self with her new one." He glanced back at the library, off in the distance, and Del got the idea Lathan wasn't just talking about Etenia or Del. "Things she never would have imagined herself believing, becoming so very important to her."

Del winced as a terrible thought came rolling down to his tongue: "What if I'm not one of those things she wants to keep?"

Lathan rested a hand on Del's shoulder. "Del, I don't think—"

"Lathan!" came Bettine's voice, from the distance, and they turned to see her hurrying up to them, face red and puffing from the exertion. She looked panicked, which drew both men up to their feet. What else could go wrong?

"There you are!" she said to both of them, stopping to catch her breath. "You might've left a note or something. I've got half the school looking for you."

"What is it?" asked Del. "Did the Qapira attack again?"

"No," she said, wincing. "It's a different kind of bad this time. Come see."

As they approached the main plaza, Del and Lathan were stunned by the sight of hundreds of citizens milling about, packed shoulder-to-shoulder—with even more coming up the pathway from Pothena below. They were from all walks of life: some with servants carrying trunks and luggage, all the way down to a large number of people who clearly only had the clothes on their backs.

"What's going on?" asked Del, trying to fathom what he was seeing. It was like when they'd put out the call for the academy and returned to find the square filled with applicants. Except this time, they were here. "Even with the Pothenian dragons, we don't have even close to enough for this many people."

"They're not here for training," said Bettine. "They're here because they're scared. Because of the attacks on the ships."

Tommen and Safrin came racing across the cobblestones, nodding respectfully to Del and Lathan when they arrived. "It's nearing a thousand, all told," said Tommen. "We're trying to get them organized."

"Organized for what?" asked Del. "We don't have enough rooms for this many people..."

"Actually, sir," said Safrin, "Tommen and I have been doing the math, and if we move the recruits into the practice hall, and the newcomers go four to a room, we might just make it."

Del blinked in confusion. "The practice hall has no roof, you know. You'd be sleeping in the open." He made sure Tommen, the rich man's son, understood: "It's cold out there with no shelter."

Tommen nodded sternly. "We're dragon riders, sir. We can take it. That's why we're here, after all. To protect Pothena, and keep her people safe."

Safrin gestured back toward the dorm rooms and spoke to Tommen. "I'll get the move started. Meet you back here in ten?"

"You got it," said Tommen, and then nodded to Del, Lathan and Bettine. "Sir. General. Professor. We'll handle this, don't worry."

They ran off together, joining other recruits in the plaza as they started organizing the newcomers into lines and helping the young and elderly to safer spots, away from the more dangerous edges.

Lathan smiled proudly at the scene before them. "Makes you think we did something right, doesn't it?"

"Yeah," said Del. He just hoped it would be enough.

CHAPTER 22

I n his dream, Del was back underwater, in a place that looked like Pothena, if Pothena had been sunk to the bottom of the ocean, very suddenly. He was walking through the market, with its stalls all stocked as they normally were, except instead of customers and merchants, there were fish swimming to and fro. The fountain was spraying coins instead of water, and through the main street, a ruined boat slid past, its torn sails dragging behind it. The *Pacimae*. Its crew were all dead, staring out into the distance like they were still trying to reach home. To be safe again.

Then he saw her: Etenia was standing at the crest of the hill, looking down at the harbor below—except there was no harbor anymore. It was a giant gaping hole beneath them, filled with darkness and dread.

"What are you doing?" he asked her, though he wasn't sure how he was able to talk underwater.

"They're so beautiful," she said, not turning to greet him.

He didn't understand what she meant. Who was beautiful? He tried to see what she saw, peering into the darkness...

He gasped. It wasn't darkness at all he was seeing, it was a massive army—the Qapira—packed so tight they seemed like a single, evil swarm. He could hear their battle cry growing louder and louder until he had to cover his ears to stop them from splitting. Etenia didn't react, though. She just stared out at them, her expression devoid of emotion.

"Etenia..." he pleaded. "Etenia, please..."

She turned to him, a smile spreading across her face—except it wasn't Etenia at all. It was the Qapiran soldier from his vision. And he was holding a long, curved dagger, aimed straight for Del's heart.

"Aren't we beautiful?" he cackled, and stabbed, and he—

Del jerked awake and hit his head on the underside of the library table. He let out a groan and rolled out into the open, careful not to disturb the others who had decided to shelter there for the night. They'd all given up their rooms for the refugees, and the floors were so incredibly uncomfortable that if they were able to sleep at all, they deserved the rest.

He snuck out the door as quietly as he could, then went for a walk to calm his racing heart. Had that been another vision? It didn't feel the same, but the idea that that kind of dream came from his own subconscious was a terrifying notion. At least he could stop the visions by defeating the Qapira. How would he stop himself from conjuring up nightmares like that?

He was just starting to calm down when he noticed, out by the steps down the mountain, a figure sitting by herself, like she was lost in thought. Etenia.

"You're up late," he said, approaching carefully so as to not spook her. "Or early."

For a moment, she looked annoyed at his question, and he regretted bothering her at all. But then that expression melted away, and she just looked upset, and so very tired. "We have a full house," she said.

Del winced. "They didn't bother you, did they? I told them to leave you two—"

"They left us alone," she said. "But Finnlay refused to take up a whole room while everyone else shared."

"Yeah, figures," sighed Del.

"He seems to like his new roommates," she said. "They'll keep him distracted, I hope."

"But how are you?" he asked. "D-do you want to talk about—"

"No, I'm fine," she said. "There's no time to worry about the past right now, when there are so many calamities yet to come." She looked down the mountain, to the city below, slumbering peacefully. "They're in the crosshairs."

"Your father, you mean," said Del.

She nodded. "I knew he was upset with me for not apologizing to the Council. When they started fining us, he begged me to stop. I told him we wouldn't—we couldn't—and I think that's when he decided..." She wiped her eyes. "He decided he didn't want me anymore."

Del wanted to tell her it wasn't true, that a father would never abandon his child—but he knew very well a father might. It was really just a question of how far a father would go before he couldn't take it anymore, and cut those ties for good. Del's parents had done it quick; Arretal had lasted a lot longer, but even so, he had his limits.

"What will you do?" he asked her. "If he's collecting those artifacts, he's in serious danger."

"I know," she said, sitting taller as she regained her composure. "But they're all so against us helping. What happens if we go down there and they refuse to listen?"

"That's the question, I guess," said Del. "How do you help someone who doesn't want your help?"

She looked at him a moment. "I don't know," she said with a smile. "How do you help someone who doesn't want your help?"

He shrugged. "You help anyway. Even if you end up getting yelled at."

Before she could say anything in return, they spotted Lathan coming down the walkway, blowing into his hands to keep them warm. It was pretty cold out, but Del had stopped noticing the temperature up in the mountains. He guessed that Lathan, with his old, creaky bones, was having more trouble.

"Can't sleep?" Del called, when Lathan was close enough.

"I do my best worrying at night," was the reply, and from the expression on his face, it was clear he really was worrying. He sat on Del's other side, joining them in staring out at Pothena below, and the ocean beyond.

"They're coming," he said, after a minute of silence.

"We'll be ready," said Etenia.

"No," said Lathan. "I mean they're coming soon. In the next day or so."

"How do you know?" asked Del. "Did Professor Staaf find something in the books that—"

"The same thing happened in Sivarna," said Lathan, nodding out at the ocean. "It didn't register at the time, but this is exactly the same as how they attacked us there. They picked off ships in the sea nearby, seemingly at random. We lost five or six in the lead-up to the attack. We deployed rescue ships to search for survivors, and dispatched our navy to protect the bay around the city. Which was exactly what they wanted."

"They were drawing you out," said Etenia. "Splitting up your forces so they'd be easier to fight."

Lathan nodded. "Exactly. When the main assault finally came, there were so few ships left, we never really stood a chance. They knew where we'd go, and how we'd get there. They'd boxed us in."

Del looked at the harbor, full of ships, with no one around to protect them. "If they're doing the same thing here..."

"They are," said Lathan, so certain.

Etenia looked panic-stricken. "We have to warn them. They're not prepared at all. We need to—"

"We've tried that," said Del. "They didn't care."

"That was a threat we couldn't prove," said Etenia. "But this, this is—"

"It's still a threat we can't prove."

Etenia wasn't ready to give up. "We have to try. We have to go down there, the two of us, with Cember and Searsha, and plead our case to the Council before—"

"Hold on a second," said Del. "Don't forget: we're all technically breaking the law up here. They were happy to deliver fines when we were a mountain away, but if we show up in person, they might decide to do something a whole lot less friendly."

"Del, we've seen what this enemy can do. What they did to Cliffport. To Sivarna. To the *Pacimae*. What do you think they're going to do to a city like Pothena without our help?"

"They'll be heading straight for her father, too," reminded Lathan. "With no one to stop them."

Del could see the desperation in Etenia's eyes, and realized this was another one of those situations where he didn't quite understand the reality she was living in, but he knew he had to play along. To him, Arretal had broken her trust too many times—if he wanted to side with the head-in-the-sand Council over his own daughter, let him suffer the consequences. But Del could tell that wasn't what she wanted to hear. Even though Arretal was being stupid and stubborn, she wanted to save him from himself. Even if it put her in a worse position, too.

"Please, Del," she said. "I can't show him he's wrong if he's dead."

Finally, she made an argument that he could appreciate.

"Your whole plan is stupid," he said, shaking his head. "It's not going to work."

"But—"

"If the Qapira are about to attack, we're going to need a lot more than just two dragons." He glanced back at the school, where the dragons and their riders were sleeping soundly, unaware of what was coming. "If we're going to save Pothena, we're going to have to fight."

CHAPTER 23

The students were moving before they were fully awake, rushing this way and that, trying to get themselves fed, dressed and equipped before the first wave took flight. Most had worn armor for at least a portion of their training—bits and pieces rescued from the Old City storerooms, fixed up and enhanced thanks to Etenia's dowry—but now the students were fully equipped, and suddenly looked like a proper fighting force. The dragons seemed anxious and skittish, like they were excited at the prospect of battle, but unsure of themselves and what they could do.

They had a grand total of fifty-five dragons, but not everyone was ready for battle. Del and Lathan had made a clear cutoff for participation: the dragons had to have flown at least three practice runs with their riders, and they had to have full control over their fire. That immediately disqualified all of the youngest dragons—much to their riders' chagrin—but also removed some of the Pothenian dragons from the roster, too. Ragir had done her part by choosing a human "worthy of the honor" fairly early in the process—a brash young woman named Vira whose main qualification seemed to be that she annoyed Lathan—but the rest had been slow to choose riders. The biggest issue was that the dragons seemed uneasy about having humans on their backs at all. They wanted to fly free.

"We can't allow it," said Lathan, quietly, to Del—though of course any of the dragons could hear them easily. "Dragons without riders are unpredictable."

"Is that an actual issue, or just one of your made-up Sivarnan rules?" Del asked with a teasing grin.

"It's a fact," said Lathan. "The bond between dragon and rider creates a shared consciousness, but also a shared conscience. Dragons who go into battle without that human element tend to..." He hesitated, like he was trying to find the right way to phrase something extremely sensitive. "They forget who their allies are," he said. "They focus on winning at all costs."

"We'll probably need that, won't we?" asked Del.

"No, we won't," said Lathan. "What will we do if these riderless dragons decide the easiest way to clear the beach is to set fire to anything they see, including our people?"

Del gave the Pothenian dragons a sideways glance. There was no doubt they could hear Lathan, but they were giving no indication his words bothered them. Was that because they were too far above his silly human concerns, or because he'd hit the nail right on the head?

"Is this because they're not Sivarnan?" Del asked Lathan, still under his breath.

Lathan shook his head. "I've seen it happen," he said. "And believe me, it's not easy to stop. We can't be fighting a battle against two opponents at the same time. For all our sakes, the unbonded dragons need to stay here."

Del still wasn't convinced, but he couldn't quite bring himself to overrule Lathan. After all, he'd taught Del everything he knew about being a dragon rider. He was right far more often than he was wrong, so ignoring his advice seemed like it might be a bad idea. He passed along the message to the Pothenian dragons—that only bonded and practiced pairs would be allowed—and continued on with his preparations.

They had forty dragons ready to fight. A far better number than just Searsha and Cember, but still nowhere near enough to hold off the entire Qapiran army. Ragir's emissaries to Chamenos still weren't back, but the odds of them succeeding were such a long shot to begin with, it was better to assume there was no help coming. It was forty dragons against a force that had dominated the ancient world with its military might.

This would be a long day.

The mages were getting ready to deploy, gathering by the path to begin the march back down. It would be a long and taxing journey for them, but there was no good alternative that wouldn't exhaust the dragons, or risk wiping out the mages' magical stamina before they even saw battle. Lathan's rules for magic-users were far more relaxed than his edicts for dragons, but even so, the mages behavior didn't seem to be too much of a concern, because his trainees were all extremely capable, and highly focused. It made Del feel a bit ashamed that his fighting force had a ragtag sensibility, and were prone to arguing with each other instead of working as a unit.

Still, at least they had a unit at all.

Del was about to find Etenia for their departure when he saw something he didn't like the look of: it was Garra, out by the library, getting ready to ride with Finnlay on her back. Del rushed over, waving his arms to make them stop, when he noticed Etenia was already there, and from her body language, she was saying the same thing.

"Hold on!" said Del. "You're not coming, Finnlay!"

As he turned to look at Del, Finnlay's sling fell off his shoulder, and he winced in pain as his arm came free. "I'm not staying here," he said. "You need me—"

"To look bruised and broken? No thanks. We're good."

"I'm fine," said Finnlay, though he really didn't seem fine at all.

"Please, Finnlay," said Etenia. "If you end up getting hurt, or worse, I don't think I could—"

"It's not safe," said Del, curtly. "You go out there like this, you're putting all your fellow riders at risk. If you lose your grip on the way down, someone's going to have to come save you—"

"I can do it," said Finnlay. "I won't make a mistake like that again, I swear. Please, Del. I need to do this. For Yena."

Etenia reached for him, her face stricken. "Yena wouldn't want you risking your life even more, Finnlay, fighting when you're not at full strength. You know she wouldn't."

He looked like he was going to cry. His head sagged, and he let out a mournful sigh, and gently slipped off Garra's back, then collapsed to his knees. Etenia knelt beside him, comforting him. Del turned away to give them some privacy. Or something like that.

Searsha found him as he made his way back to the staging grounds, landing gracefully in his path. He could feel the confidence on her. Any other day, it might have been infectious. Just not today.

Do I look ready for war? she asked.

"Yeah, stunning," he grumbled, and tried to get around her. She slapped her tail in his path, stopping him.

Do not behave like this, she warned him.

"Listen, I know you're enjoying yourself, but I'm not in the mood to—"

It is not for me, she said. *The others are looking to you for reassurance. If you walk around looking as if you have eaten rancid meat, their courage will falter, and we will all die.*

Del was suddenly aware of how many students of his were all around, watching his every move out of the corners of their eyes. Searsha was right. He didn't have the luxury of projecting unhappiness anymore. He had to be brave and in control at all times. A frown on his face could break his students' resolve, even if the frown had nothing at all to do with fighting the Qapira, and everything to do with Etenia and Finnlay.

His students were depending on him. He owed it to them to put his own worries aside and focus on winning.

"All right, I suppose we can put off dying for another day," he said.

Excellent, she replied. *Because I look too magnificent to die.*

He laughed and climbed onto her back, and together they flew to the front of the dragon force, out at the edge of the plaza, overlooking the city below. All around, he saw the Sivarnan dragons who had, it seemed, only hatched yesterday, though they were older and stronger now than Searsha had been when they'd fought the Kraken. And the Pothenian dragons, led by Ragir, were twice the size of the hatchlings, and a thousand times more prepared—but with allegiances of their own. And then there were the riders who had come to them with nothing more than hopes and ambition, and were now steady and capable fighters, ready to face off with a force that had been terrorizing humanity for millennia. He saw Kinto and Safrin, Tommen and Lufien and dozens more, focused and determined. They were the last hope for Pothena. The only hope.

Cember landed next to Searsha, and Etenia, in her armor, gave Del a confident nod. This was it. The moment they'd been training for all this time. If they failed now, it was all for nothing.

She didn't say it, but he could see she was terrified. And he was, too.

He cleared his throat and called out to the other riders and their dragons: "I know you're scared, and you have every right to be. We may not be the greatest fighting force Pothena has ever seen, but no matter what happens today, remember that you are all—"

Someone far down the line shouted something that Del couldn't quite make out. There were just enough of them now that their voices didn't carry as well as they needed to. Del replied with a: "Say again?" which was passed down the line until it came back as: "We can't hear you."

Etenia frowned at Del, and he could see her mind trying to come up with a solution that they could design and implement quickly. "We need to come up with some sort of—"

"Can we just give it a try, though?" came a voice into Del's head, which he immediately recognized as Safrin's. It was like how Searsha talked to him, but different. Safrin wasn't talking to Del, exactly, but he could still hear her in his mind.

"What the..." he gasped.

Your students are cleverer than you are, said Searsha, and he could feel her pride growing by the second. *She is using her bond with Toro to send her words to the rest of the team.*

"Can anyone hear me?" asked Safrin, through Toro, cautiously but hopefully.

"Loud and clear," said Del waving back so she could see. He tried aiming his own words back through his bond, too. He wasn't sure he was getting it right, but he had to know; it was like whispering loudly, so that every word he spoke appeared in dozens of ears at once. He felt Searsha take hold of his thoughts and carry his voice along. "Good thinking, Safrin," he said, and waited to see if it had worked.

226

"Thank you, sir."

Del grinned. "Anyone else want to try it?" he asked into his bond, without his voice at all.

"Can you hear me?" asked Tommen.

"How about me?" asked Kinto.

"I doubt this will work," said Lufien, though something in the transmission carried his emotions, too, and Del could tell he was giddy at being able to communicate telepathically.

After the full team had checked in, Del gave them a curt nod and said: "Don't talk like this unless it's important. It'll be distracting if we're all yelling at once."

Forty riders all said: "Yes, sir," at once, proving his point. They all laughed.

Safrin spoke again, through the bond, to the team: "Sir, would you mind repeating what you were saying earlier?"

He'd been talking about how they were all scared, and how they weren't the greatest fighting force Pothena had ever seen, and—

Del grinned. "You know what? It doesn't apply. We are the greatest fighting force Pothena has seen. So let's go down there and show those gill-faced fish-lovers what happens when you try to crawl up our beaches uninvited!"

The cheer of approvals in his mind was only slightly outdone by the actual roars from the dragons themselves. Del took hold of Searsha's back and gave a slight nod, and she kicked off into the air, and led the new Old City fighting force into battle for the first time.

Down the mountainside they went, weaving in and around clouds, riding air currents in a winding path toward the city below. Del could see people in the streets, on rooftops, leaning out windows, looking up in awe at the sight of a fleet of dragons soaring far above. He wondered if there was another version of him down there, amazed at what he was witnessing. He hoped there wasn't. He hoped those other Dels would have been smart enough to evacuate to the mountains by now.

Searsha and Cember led the force down toward the beaches at Seafall —the closest point to the Browder estate, where all the remaining magical artifacts were being stored, making it the prime target for when the Qapira began their attack—and picked their spots to land. One dragon, two, three, four and more and more and more until the whole beach was lined with them, some standing tall, and some with their heads low and bellies full of fire, ready to blast the first thing that peeked its head out of the ocean.

It was an awesome sight, and filled Del with more than a little pride that he'd been a part of making it happen. He wanted to hold on to this memory for the rest of his life. He swore to himself in that moment that he wouldn't use it for a spell and risk losing it forever. He wanted to remember his friends as they were. Before fate did its worst, and ruined it all.

"You there!" came a voice from behind, and Del and Etenia turned to see a small contingent of Pothenian security rushing down to the beach with their modified Snappers—deadly weapons made even more treacherous—ready to fire. "You are all under arrest!" shouted their captain, and took aim right at Searsha.

He is adorable, she said. *May I swat him?*

"No," muttered Del, then shouted down to the guards: "We're not here to fight you. We're here to save you."

"Save us?" came a different voice, and one Del recognized from their first days in Pothena: it was Mirra, from Council. He looked just as cranky and decrepit as ever as he hurried down the hill to meet them. "From what? Rumors? Made-up tales?"

"From the Qapira," said Del, pointing to the water.

"Oh, the Qapira!" laughed Mirra. "Is this a different threat than the Epyrians you were talking about, or can you just not keep your own stories straight?"

Etenia interjected, obviously aware that Del would tear Mirra to shreds, verbally, if she didn't. She was still determined to negotiate a peace treaty with people who didn't like or respect her. It was both adorable and infuriating, all at once.

"Councilman," she said, "despite our disagreements, we can't just sit back and—"

"We have no disagreements, Ms. Browder. You have broken the law by bringing a fighting force into our city. Added to your considerable outstanding fines, I'm afraid I have no recourse but to put you all under arrest at once. Captain?"

The captain stood forward, rechecking his aim, as his guards trained their Snappers at the other dragons. "Don't make us hurt you," he said in a way that suggested he really wanted to hurt them anyway.

Now may I swat him? asked Searsha.

"I'm sorry, Councilman," said Del. "It's like I said. We're not here for you. The Qapira will come whether you believe in them or not, which is why we have so many refugees from Pothena, Cliffport and beyond..." He gestured to his fellow dragon riders, who were from so many places, with so many backgrounds, it was truly astounding they could all work together so seamlessly. "They turned to us for protection because they knew you weren't up to the task."

"Not up to the task?" snarled Mirra. "You foolish boy. Pothena is more than able to take care of runts like—"

The rest of his sentence was cut short when a spear, which seemed to come out of nowhere, arched through the air and impaled him straight through the chest. He died instantly, collapsing in a heap—just as the beach was pounded by more and more spears. Del turned back to the water to see the spears bursting out of the surf, aimed straight for them.

"Go!" he shouted through his bond. "Up up up!"

The dragons took to the air, as fast as they could. Del saw two take hits to their legs, and one to a wing, but they all made it high enough to avoid the worst of it. The Pothenian guards, though, were not so lucky. The bulk of their force fell one by one, with the stragglers running for cover and fumbling with their Snappers, trying to aim at an enemy that didn't yet exist.

And then, very gradually, their foe emerged from the waves.

That moment, that horrible moment, was just like in Del's visions, but far more terrifying to see in the flesh. They looked human-like, but with discolored skin and pitch-black eyes. They were lean and muscular, with armor that shone like black crystal, and their weapons—those same deadly spears—caught the light like a thin shard of a blazing sun. There were so many of them, marching in perfect order. Maybe fifty for each one of their dragons, or more.

They weren't racing into Pothena, killing at random, like Del had always assumed they would. In his mind, he had imagined there would be a pitched battle with desperate acts of heroism, like when he and Etenia had fought the Kraken. But the Qapira were moving with a careful, deliberate pace, destroying anything in their path. Now he saw the truth: It would be a calculated massacre.

"We're not ready for this," he said to Searsha as horror filled his heart. "We're not going to make it."

We will, she said, as her throat filled with fire. *Because there is no other choice.*

CHAPTER 24

The surviving Pothenian guards let loose with their Snappers from where they hid at the edge of the city, firing blinding blasts at the Qapiran soldiers who were marching their way up the beach. The shots were brighter than Del remembered—evidently the Council's boast about being able to make the weapons even more deadly was not just empty posturing. The force of firing the modified Snappers knocked the guards off their feet, and they scrambled back as the puffs of smoke cleared from their victims—

But the Qapira were still coming. From up above, Del could see what was happening: the energy blasts from the Snappers were fizzling into nothingness when they got too close to the Qapira. It was like they turned to smoke and blew away, scattering in the wind. Pothenian science was no match for magic from the deep—so the guards were no better than any other civilian.

Del could feel Searsha itching to let loose, but he had a feeling that whatever was protecting the Qapira would probably stop their dragon-fire, too. So instead, he pointed down at the enemy and shouted into his bond: "Quick bursts! Keep it low!"

The riders and dragons had practiced it enough in training, and knew exactly what he meant: they angled themselves perfectly, shooting quick fireballs at a low angle, right at the soldiers' feet. Even if the Qapiran magic neutralized the dragonfire, at least the force of the impact would make the sand explode up and out. Sure enough, when the first dragonfire blast hit, it sent the first row of the invading force flying back into the sea, where they crashed messily, some getting impaled on their comrades' spears.

But it was just the first row, and there were so many more behind them.

"Odds and evens," he said. "Ten seconds between shots. Go!"

This was the kind of thing they'd practiced more than anything: every second dragon fired off a quick burst at the same time, hitting the Qapiran line in a dozen spots all down the beach. Soldiers were blown off their feet, tumbling into the ocean as the sand turned to glass from the heat—just as the other half of the dragon force let loose, wreaking havoc all over again. The Qapirans kept coming, but they couldn't make any real progress—and as Del knew from training, his team could keep this up for hours without tiring.

But Del's confident grin faded away when he noticed something ominous down below: the Qapiran line was inching forward despite the attacks. After a few seconds, he understood why: the sand, turned to molten glass by the dragonfire, was allowing the soldiers to embed their magic shields deep enough to block the blasts. The more they fired, the more sand they were losing, and the farther the Qapira could advance. Del glanced across the sky toward Cember, and saw Etenia's worried expression, and knew it was time to act.

"Change it up!" Del called over his bond. "Crosswise, up and down!"

Again, his students knew exactly what to do: starting at the far left of their line, the dragons fired at a sharp angle, hitting the middle of the Qapiran force from the side. The soldiers were blown into one another, causing a ripple that got even more pronounced as the rest of the dragons took their turns, until the first three lines of Qapirans were dead or dying, in flaming ruins.

But they kept coming.

Worse, the next round of shots didn't work, because the Qapirans turned their magic shields to match. They quickly got back into position and pushed the battle line a little bit closer to the city. Spears were soaring through the sky toward the dragons, thankfully without any serious injuries. That was one of the skills they'd practiced relentlessly: targeting small moving objects in midair, and hitting them with incinerating blasts. It had been a challenge, but it was paying off now: only a few spears managed to hit anyone, and only resulted in the most minor of scrapes.

Del checked to make sure Etenia was still safe—doing his best not to show it, of course. He could feel all his students' eyes watching him. If he wavered, they'd fall.

They adapt quickly, said Searsha, as she let off another blast.

"Their shields only cover one angle at a time," said Del. "We just need to be less predictable." He spoke through his bond—which was becoming more and more natural to him—to say: "Fire by dorm group! On my mark. Block A! Crosswise! Now!"

It wasn't something they had prepared for, but each student knew what he meant: before the refugees had arrived, they had all been assigned to one of six dormitory blocks. Their order in the line had nothing to do with where they slept, so the Block A riders were scattered randomly—and when they let loose with their blasts, it created a chaotic crossfire that the Qapira couldn't anticipate. Del waited until he was sure they had done enough damage, then called out: "Block B! Go!"

Again and again, the dragons fired, and the Qapirans were blasted away. But once they looped back to Block A, Del noticed fewer of the shots were working: the Qapira were ready. He tried mixing up the order, but soon realized that not only were the attacks not working, but the line was creeping farther up the beach, giving them more opportunities to strike the dragons with their spears. Del and the students were losing ground.

"We need something else," Del said to Searsha. "There's got to be something else."

They either learn exceptionally quickly, or—

"Sir!" came Safrin's voice across the bond. "Their shields don't have backs, right?"

"Yeah, but—"

"Permission to be daring, sir," she said, and Del could tell by the sound of it that if he said no, she wasn't going to listen anyway. Before he could say a thing, she and Toro broke formation and flew toward the Qapiran force.

The second her intention was clear, the Qapirans let loose with a half dozen spears, all soaring with deadly accuracy for Safrin and Toro. Del gasped in horror—

Until a mighty burst of dragonfire shot out and incinerated the spears in midair, turning them to ash. Del looked over to see Ragir finish her blast with a satisfied look on her face.

We have you covered, daring one, she said.

Del could feel—like he felt with Searsha—Safrin grin at that as Toro spun around and fired a long, constant stream of fire down at the backs of the Qapirans, setting them afire instantly. Their shields were aimed in the wrong direction, and provided no protection whatsoever! Toro finished a pass of the Qapiran line, then looped back around, out over the ocean, for another pass.

"Sir!" she called to Del. "If we split our force and attack from both sides at once, we can—"

It happened so fast, no one saw it coming. A giant shimmering net burst out of the water like it was made of water itself, wrapping around Safrin and Toro like a serpent's mouth snapping up its prey. Toro's wings were tangled so completely, there was no way for Safrin to get free.

Del felt her panic, a thousand times as strong as her pride had been, as she let out an audible scream—and the net pulled her down into the water with a mighty splash.

"No!" shouted Tommen, and raced forward to the spot she'd gone under. Del tried to yell for him to hold back, but there was no stopping it. The second he broke ranks, the whole of the dragon line started to panic, resorting to instincts instead of training. Some fired indiscriminately at the Qapiran soldiers, some flew to new positions for better angles, and some landed on the beach like they were going to physically charge at the enemy.

All the while, Ragir fired blasts to neutralize the spears being thrown at Tommen until he was too close to the water to protect, firing dragonfire at the ocean like he thought he could burn it away to save his friend.

Del focused his voice, trying not to sound as panicked as he was: "Tommen, get back here before—"

A spear shot out of the water, and Tommen's dragon, Iyfen, barely had time to react. She spun to the side, trying to avoid a fatal blow, but the blade embedded in her side. She let out a thunderous scream and twisted in agony—and Tommen slipped off her back, barely holding on to her wing by one hand.

Del looked to Etenia, and she shook her head. "Don't," she cried, as if she had read Del's mind and knew what he aimed to do.

"I'll be back," he said, as if it were a promise he could keep, and Searsha raced forward, over the Qapiran line, through the explosions and flaming debris from his students' attacks, straight out over the water.

He reached into his memories, pulling to the fore that image he'd wanted to keep—that of his students ready to launch into battle—and Safrin having the idea to use their bonds to communicate—and even though it was bittersweet and tragic, his desire to actually save his students, not just the memory of them, filled his body with so much power, it was almost impossible to contain it all.

Tommen was about to fall. Iyfen was struggling. The battle was raging all around them. And Del closed his eyes and reached out with both hands and felt the space around them, shaping it into a bubble so large and so powerful that when more Qapiran spears shot out of the water to finish the job, they bounced off harmlessly.

Tommen fell, but landed safely inside the shield, then looked to Del in shock and surprise. Del would have told him not to worry, but he couldn't afford the distractions. With every last bit of concentration, he moved the bubble off to the side, back over the shoreline, until the edges of it were knocking into the Seafall roofs. When he let it go, Tommen and Iyfen settled down, safely out of harm's way.

That was when Del noticed the heat coming from below, and was able to focus on the world he'd been filtering out. The heat was from dragonfire—Ragir's dragonfire—as she kept the Qapirans from hitting Searsha the same way they'd hit Tommen.

Hurry, Pothenians, Ragir said, and he could feel the strain in her voice. If she stopped, even for a second, they would be dead. She and Vira were working incredibly hard, as one, to keep him alive.

Del looked down at the water, at where Safrin had been taken, and felt his anger swell. She was one of his people. Not just a street kid, but a dragon rider. And they took care of their own.

He called back the same magic he'd used to create the bubble, but this time made it tighter, stronger, more powerful. He was tearing through that memory, tearing it to pieces, but he didn't care. When he felt the bubble was as deadly as it could be, he wound back and threw it down into the ocean, right where Safrin and Toro had disappeared.

It was exactly as he thought—just like throwing a rock into the fountain to uncover the coins. Except instead of finding coins—or even Safrin and her dragon—Del saw something else entirely. A lone Qapiran soldier stood there, looking up at Del. He was different than the rest—his armor was golden, and his features sharper, more severe—and suddenly Del realized he'd seen him before, in a vision. This was the one who'd been surveying the troops, and had realized the dragon eggs were hidden in Pothena. This was the leader of their army...

Before he could react, the water rushed back in again, obscuring his enemy.

"Del!" screamed Etenia, her voice ringing out across the battlefield, not just in his mind, and he remembered he was in danger. Searsha raced upward—straight up—as spears shot past, nearly slicing her. The air got colder and colder, but Del barely noticed for all his anger.

"Everyone off the beach," he said through his bond. "Let them come."

"But Del," said Etenia. "If we don't—"

"Let them come," he said, and closed his eyes. His skin was prickly from the cold, and all his ears heard was the sound of the wind howling around him, but he could see through Searsha's eyes, hear through her ears, and sense through the network of other dragons down below. The Qapira were coming.

They were coming up the beach, past the bodies of their fallen comrades, up past the blasted glass of their farthest win. They were marching in perfect order, closing in on the edge of the city. Only another minute, and Pothena would be truly invaded. A minute after that, and it might be too late.

Just as the beach was as full as it could be, Del felt Searsha give him a nod, and he smiled.

Del pulled at the memories all around him, tying his magic with Searsha's and bundling them tightly until the strands of energy formed one last bubble that was so brilliant and so powerful that it almost hurt him to hold on to it. It crackled with awesome potential like it was desperate to be put to use. He had to be sure he could maintain it, but he knew if he didn't act now, he'd lose it forever. Steadying himself with Searsha's spirit, he gave her the signal, and she dove down as fast as she could.

The clouds parted and they saw the beach ahead of them, filled with Qapiran soldiers, the waves lapping at their heels as they surged forward. He saw the dragons in the air, blasting little shots of fire to fend off spears, but obeying his orders to stay clear. And then he tightened his focus on his shield and forced it onward, faster and faster until—

They hit the beach so hard, it created a shockwave that blasted all the soldiers away in all directions. They smashed into each other, impaling themselves on their own weapons, their armor buckling under the incredible force unleashed upon them. Even the dragons recoiled at the force of it, as the wind became suddenly violent and shrapnel burst through the air.

Sand swirled like a stormcloud all around them, leaving only a ragged crater, and in its center, Searsha and Del, facing the enemy and ready for more.

The Qapiran force on the beach was decimated—the few survivors got to their feet unsteadily, only to be taken out by the other dragons above.

And then, out from the water, came another line of soldiers, led by their pale-faced commander in the golden armor.

A voice came into Del's head, like Searsha's or the other dragon riders', but somehow different. More oppressive. Cruel.

"You cannot stop us," said the Qapiran. "Our victory is foretold."

Searsha let out a fearsome growl.

"Yeah?" said Del. "Come tell me to my face."

The Qapiran's eyes narrowed. "I will enjoy killing you."

"You know, that's exactly what the Kraken said. Before we lit it on fire and watched it die."

That got the Qapiran's attention. His eyes widened and he bared his teeth savagely. "You! Oh, I have been waiting for this moment. Your treachery will be punished more severely and you will be—"

Suddenly, a gem at the center of his necklace started to pulse red, over and over again. The other soldiers wore the same gems, and theirs were all red, too. The Qapiran leader glanced down at it, and then looked back up at Del with a scowl.

"Luck is on your side, land-dweller. I will see you again."

And with that, the Qapirans began moving back, retreating into the sea. The commander, though, paused, standing, half-submerged in the waves, staring straight into Del's soul.

Neither of them said a thing, but the message was clear: there would be a reckoning between them, and they both knew, deep down, which one of them would prevail. And Del wasn't it.

CHAPTER 25

The students were rattled and anxious, so much so that Del could feel their fear through their bonds. They were circling the battlefield from the air, afraid to get too close. What had happened to Safrin and Toro had shattered their confidence—and Del's, too—and as the threat subsided, their panic was setting in stronger than ever. He could feel Tommen's grief, thick in the air like a fog, weighing the rest of them down until it was almost hard to breathe. It wasn't just that Safrin and Toro were well-loved and respected, it was that suddenly, the war was real, with real consequences they couldn't just shrug off. There was an undercurrent of doubt flowing through their bonds, threatening to break the whole force to pieces.

Del had experience with these things: when one of your fellow street kids was taken by the authorities, there was a tendency to feel as though the whole world was ending. That was a dangerous mindset to be in, because it made you forget about the consequences of your actions and do things you wouldn't normally do. For poor kids in the slums, that might get you arrested, too. For young dragon riders on magical beasts —that might get a lot of people killed.

"I need a damage report," he said over his bond. "Survey the city, make sure there's no one they left behind."

A handful of riders gave sharp: "Yes, sir!"s and took off up the hill.

"Kinto, go fetch General Phrac from the Old City. Tommen needs healing."

Kinto gave him a nod and left without a word.

There were only a handful of dragons left, including Ragir, who was down on the beach, moving Qapiran corpses around with her mighty claws. She glanced over her shoulder toward Del. *You should see this.*

Searsha and Cember landed nearby, and by the time Del and Etenia arrived at the scene—made more difficult by all the dead bodies around—Ragir had snapped the necklace off the soldier. The gem in the middle of the necklace was glowing red, but gradually fading.

"What is it?" asked Del. "Is it some sort of signal? They were all wearing them, and then when it turned red, they retreated."

It is magic, said Ragir. *Potent and specific. It has the feeling of...waves to it.*

Water, corrected Searsha. *It channels the essence of water, even out of the sea.*

"So they can breathe on land..." said Etenia. "They can't survive out here after all."

Del took the necklace from Ragir, studying the gem. "It turns red to warn them when they're running out of 'air'. Which means it can't last forever." He looked back up toward the Old City in the mountains. "That explains why the ancient Pothenians built their home so far from the water."

"Maybe if we can find some way to disrupt their magic," said Etenia. "If we disable their necklaces all at once, we might—"

Qapiran magic is too strong for that, said Ragir. *They do not use it often, but the spells they do cast are always impenetrable.*

"All right, then let's use it against them," said Del. "Can we modify the spell to let us breathe underwater? We should be able to find enough necklaces to—"

That would be a terrible idea, said Ragir. *Even if it were possible, all you would accomplish is to give us the ability to be killed in the sea instead of on land. Remember: the water is the Qapira's turf. Your people will not be able to withstand their attacks while trying to swim.*

"Maybe not humans, but dragons might—"

Ragir laughed like she'd heard the funniest joke in history. *Your Sivarnan drones may be willing to die like that, but I assure you the Pothenian dragons will never follow. The only way to defeat the Qapira is to wear them out on land. It worked before, and it will work again.*

"But how many lives will be lost in the meantime?" asked Etenia. "If we keep fighting like this, losing ground a few inches at a time, Pothena will be overrun in a matter of days."

Ragir looked up toward the Old City. *As you said: there is a reason your ancestors built their home so far from the water.*

Searsha growled at that. *We will not run from the fight.*

A Sivarnan trait, perhaps, snorted Ragir. *No wonder your people are decimated and homeland is in ruins.*

Del just barely got between Ragir and Searsha and Cember in time. The two Sivarnan dragons were moving in for blood, but together they were barely half Ragir's size, though that hardly mattered when they were so offended. Del held out his hands to calm them. "We can't fight amongst ourselves," he said. "We have to get ready for the next assault."

And we shall, said Ragir. *From up there.*

"And what about all the people stuck down here in the city?" asked Etenia, anger rising in her voice. "You'd just abandon them?"

Their fates cannot be our concern.

"But we can help them evacuate before—"

And exhaust our forces even further? Foolishness. They had their chance to flee, and they squandered it.

Del wanted to argue, to take Etenia's side, but Ragir wasn't entirely wrong. They'd been warning the Council for months about the dangers the Qapira posed to Pothena, but again and again they had resisted taking action. The last round of refugees were already putting a huge strain on the Old City's ability to function—if they added even more, how would they survive? Why should the ones who'd made wise decisions suffer because of the fools who'd come to their senses too late? Why should the Old City suffer because of the bad planning of the—

Del stopped himself when he realized what he was thinking. 'Why should the merchants be forced to pay higher taxes to protect the poorer citizens?' It was what Council said—it was what Pothena said—to absolve themselves of responsibility for taking care of those less fortunate. Like Del. And Womp. And Safrin, who had died defending those same fools.

Del could see in Etenia's eyes that she was terrified for her father. Arretal had betrayed them, yes, and sided with Council—but he was still her family, and he was still in danger. If they didn't find another way, he would die, too.

"Start the evacuation," he said, and Ragir rolled her eyes.

The mages have still not descended all the way down the mountain. How do you expect the untrained civilians to make the ascent?

"They won't," said Del. "We won't send them all at once. But if we do it in stages, we might stand a chance. We don't need to give up the city all at once, so let's evacuate the lower levels, nearest the water, first, and—"

"I should think not!" came a voice from toward the city, and they saw another councilman storming their way, flanked by a dozen guards with Snappers ready to fire. "You will do no such thing!"

Del was having a very hard time controlling his anger. "Are you seriously going to claim the Qapira aren't a threat?" he asked. "After what just happened?"

"Of course not, don't be absurd," said the councilman. "But your plan is simply unacceptable. The evacuation to the safety zone—"

"The safety zone?" said Etenia. "You mean the Old City you tried to starve out of existence?"

The councilman ignored her. "The first to be evacuated must be the ones situated closest to the mountain," he said. "It's only logical."

Del grit his teeth. "The areas closest to the mountain are the villas. Where the richest Pothenians live."

The councilman gave Del a sour face, like he found the sight of him distasteful. "Our good choices in housing should not count against us. And it's not as if all villas are safe, anyway." He gave Etenia a mean glare. "I mean, your home certainly wasn't."

Del and Etenia froze. "What do you mean?" asked Del, and when the councilman didn't answer fast enough, Del leapt at him, grabbing him by the collar and shaking him violently. "What are you talking about?"

The councilman's guards took aim at Del, only to drop their Snappers and back away when Searsha and Cember filled their mouths with fire.

The councilman cowered, whimpering: "I...I don't know what happened, but the walls were broken in and—"

Del dropped the councilman and ran for Searsha. Etenia and Cember were already in the air, racing up the hillside, toward a spot marked by a long trail of black smoke. As Searsha kicked off, Del whispered to her: "We have to get there before Etenia."

I will do my best, she said, and moved swiftly.

But however fast Del wanted Searsha to fly, Cember was feeling a thousand times the urgency from Etenia. He was cruising so near the rooftops it was a wonder he didn't tear apart the shingles with his wake. His wings were beating harder than Del had ever seen, so when he finally reached the spot where the Browder villa was, he had to pivot in midair and crash into a tree to slow down. By the time Searsha caught up, Cember was resting, and Etenia was nowhere to be seen.

"Etenia!" shouted Del, dropping to his feet and racing toward the house. "Etenia, wait!"

What was he afraid of? That the Qapira would still be there? That she might fall into some sort of trap? Or that she would be all alone when tragedy struck?

The place was in ruins. It had been converted into an exhibition, but all that remained of that effort were marble pedestals that were broken and burned, toppled over with their riches stolen. Long tables set up to display smaller trinkets were smashed apart, with a handful of dead guards lying amongst the wreckage.

Del looked everywhere for Etenia—she wasn't in her room, not in his, or her father's, or anywhere inside. He came out the front door which led out to the city and saw the broken wall the councilman had been talking about. More dead guards lay there, stabbed by spears or crushed by debris. The beach had been a diversionary tactic, Del understood in a flash. They'd been so focused on keeping the main Qapiran army from reaching the Browder estate and the magical artifacts that they'd completely missed the fact that a smaller force had somehow snuck past and raided Etenia's home.

And somewhere nearby, she heard the sound of Etenia crying.

He ran, following the sound of her voice, until he came around a corner to find her kneeling beside her father, who was lying in a pool of his own blood. Del knew the instant he saw Arretal, from the way his breathing rattled in his chest, that he was moments from death.

Del stopped by Etenia's side. Arretal reached up with a trembling hand and touched his daughter's face.

"I'm sorry..." he whispered.

She shook her head, tears streaming down her face. "You have to hold on," she said. "Lathan can save you if you just hold on."

Arretal smiled weakly. "It's...it's all right, Etenia," he said. "I can't...I..."

"No," she said. "No, you have to live. You have to live."

He seemed to snap back to attention, like maybe he wasn't bleeding to death after all. "I wanted to build a legacy," he said, his lips slowly turning blue. "To have the Browder family take its place in the history books, like all the oldest families in Pothena. I wanted to make something I could be proud of. And...and when you defied Council, I saw that slipping away. I thought we could lose it all, so I—"

"No, shh," she said. "We don't need to—"

"But I was wrong," he gasped, that horrible rattling breath again. "The Browder name isn't what matters at all." He wiped her tears away with his bloodied thumb. "And I've already left the legacy I'm most proud of."

And then his gaze shifted slightly, and his hand fell from Etenia's cheek, and Del's breath caught in his throat—because Arretal Browder was dead.

CHAPTER 26

The wind swept across the valley between the two mountain peaks, rustling the grass and flowers that grew there. The sky was gray, and darkening quickly, as they all stood there in silence, trying to think of what to say.

The graves were dug in the middle of the field, like the centerpiece of a majestic vista. Etenia stood at the foot of her father's mound, hands clasped together, tears staining her dress, as Finnlay supported her, arm holding her tight. Next to them was Tommen, stone-faced as he tried to come to terms with the events of the day. Safrin and Toro's graves were just empty mounds, but they hurt just as much.

Del, Lathan and Bettine waited a short distance away. Lathan looked as grim as ever, but Bettine was weeping openly. Nearby, Searsha, Cember and Garra watched in silence. Del could feel Cember's fury. His need for revenge. It was so strong, and so unrestrained, that it was impossible to ignore. Del could only imagine how overpowering it must have been for Etenia.

Or what was her emotion he was feeling, through the bond?

After the ceremony—led by Lathan, who sang a Sivarnan funeral hymn that only seemed to make the hurt feel worse—Searsha, Cember and Garra flew the others down to the Old City. Finnlay said a quiet goodbye before excusing himself, too. He looked even more ragged than before, and not just because of his arm. The gravity of their situation was weighing heavily on him, too.

Soon, the last of them were gone, leaving Del and Etenia alone in the dwindling daylight.

"Etenia," said Del, gently. "Are you—"

"They got past us," she said, staring out into the ocean like it was all she could bear to see.

Del nodded. "The beach was a distraction," he said. "They were keeping us busy while the rest of their force went after the artifacts."

"We should have seen it coming," she said. "We should have known—"

"There was no way we could have guessed—"

"I could have guessed!" she shouted, voice cracking. "That's what I do, Del! I figure out every angle of every action, so nothing gets left to chance. I knew they were coming, and I knew why they were coming, and I left the villa undefended."

"You didn't leave it undefended, you—"

"You say that, but they still got past us. They knew how to beat us."

"How many times have you fought the Qapira?" asked Del, and Etenia frowned, looked at him unhappily.

"What do you—"

"Is this your second time fighting them? Fifth? Tenth?"

"You know I haven't—"

"Then stop acting like you had any hope of knowing this would happen. We stationed ourselves to protect the villa. We defended the beaches, and somehow they still got past. We can't change the past, Etenia. And believe me, I wish we could. I really do. But it won't help anyone if you sit up here beating yourself up over what went wrong, instead of using that brain of yours to figure out how to prevent it from getting even worse!"

He wasn't sure if he'd gotten through to her. He knew she came from a different world, where tragedy was something you dealt with once or twice in a lifetime, if at all. To him, tragedy was so commonplace, it was like the seasons changing. You took the shock and the pain, and you turned it into something useful. Wallowing in it only put you at greater risk.

But at the same time, he knew she was hurting, and he wanted more than anything to take that pain away. He just wasn't sure he could do it —or even how to start. Maybe that's why Etenia was always turning to Finnlay for comfort—because Del was useless at it. Still, he had to try.

Just as he was about to reach out to touch her, Etenia's expression shifted slightly, and her brow furrowed. "The sewers," she said.

"Pardon?"

"The sewers in Pothena all feed into a handful of underground streams that run straight into the ocean. There's a major drain tube near my home. The Qapira must have used it to sneak past us."

Del's eyes opened wide. He knew the sewer system—every street kid in Pothena did out of necessity—and he knew just how vast it was. Their defenses were even less defensible than he thought. They couldn't plug the streams—odds were, the Qapira were still there, guarding the exits at the waterfront. The only way to keep the Qapira from using those streams again was to collapse them all—but the instant Del thought that he realized it was hopeless. Collapsing the streams would depend on knowing exactly where they lay, and to do that they would need to get the assistance of city planners. They would need surveys and maps—and Council was unlikely to help them once they found out what the plan was.

If the Qapira could get past them that easily, there was no way to stage an orderly retreat in segments, up from the waterfront. They would be fighting a battle on many fronts at once—possibly as far back as the base of the mountain.

There was no way they could evacuate the city fast enough. The mages were already trying, but even after what they'd seen on the beach, people refused to drop everything and leave. They packed. They moved slowly, carried too many belongings, and crowded the narrow pathway so recklessly that they'd only barely emptied a small portion of the population.

When the Qapira came back, they would be everywhere at once. And there was no way a handful of dragons could stop them. No way at all.

"They're going to overrun us," he said, voice hollow as the full realization sank in. "They're going to keep coming at us, chipping away until we have no one left to lose."

"We can prepare," said Etenia. "Block off the sewers, fortify the coastline and—"

"And wait for them to find another way to sneak someone past our defenses," said Del, bitterly, and then froze. "Sneak someone past..."

Etenia didn't understand, and knew him well enough not to bother hiding it. "What? What is it?"

"Remember their necklaces? With the gems? How it let them breathe outside the water?"

"I do, Del, and I have to agree with Ragir on this: the Qapira are clearly good at walking on land, but there's no way our dragons will be able to swim well enough to withstand an underwater assault. We had enough trouble avoiding their spears in the air—just imagine what will happen if we go charging in in an unfamiliar environment."

"That's why we won't charge in," said Del. "We'll sneak in. Just the two of us."

Etenia laughed, but not a happy one. A you've lost your mind one. "And just how are the two of us going to defeat the entire Qapiran army by ourselves?"

"We're not," he said. "We're going to go in, steal their magic stone, and get out."

She laughed again, but when Del didn't join in, her smile faded. "Wait, you're serious?"

"Think about it: everything we've read and heard tells us that stone is the weapon that gives them their power. It's so important to them that they came all this way to feed it more magic—"

"Exactly. Which is why they stole all the artifacts from my father's—" Etenia's face crumpled at the mention of her father, but somehow she fought back the tears that threatened and pressed on. "Why do you think their stone is even nearby? How do you know they haven't left it at home, where it's safe?"

"Would you send your whole army to a distant land and leave your most treasured object undefended at home? Because if something went wrong, all your best warriors would be too far away to stop it."

Etenia seemed uncertain. "If you're wrong..."

"If I'm wrong, we swim down there, realize there's no stone, and head back to the surface. But if I'm right..."

"If you're right, they're going to come after it, Del," she said. "And we're going to have an even bigger problem on our hands."

"You're assuming we're going to bring it back here," he said. "But what if we don't? What if we fly it as far away as we can, and leave it at the top of the tallest mountain in the world? Or in the middle of a massive desert? Someplace they'll spend a lifetime trying to reach, and forget all about us?"

"Or you could just destroy it."

"Even if we could destroy it—and we have no way to know that's even possible—that still leaves them camped out in Pothena's harbor. We need them gone, Etenia. This might be our best chance to make them leave."

Just then, Cember and Searsha returned from their trip down to the Old City, landing nearby, but keeping a respectful distance from their riders. They had probably been listening to the conversation, and knew not to interrupt.

Etenia watched Cember, then her eye caught on the sight of her father's grave, and she paused a moment. When she looked back to Del, her face was solemn again.

"We need to concentrate on certainties," she said. "We know the Qapira will attack again, and we know they'll use the sewers to do it. We need to find a way to evacuate the city, and to fend off the assault when it happens."

"But—"

"We can't risk it, Del," she said. "We can't risk you."

She walked to Cember, climbing onto his back, and looked to Del. "I'll tell Lathan and Bettine what we figured out. Can you go make sure there's no one left near the shoreline?"

He sighed and nodded, and she smiled. "And yes, I am."

"You are what?" he asked.

"I'll be all right. You were asking if I was all right, and I didn't..." She shrugged. "I lost my father, but I still have a family." She gave him a long look, like she was trying to tell him something, and Del had a pretty good idea what it was. She'd told him to stay away from her before, after all.

And with that, Cember took off, back to the Old City.

Del watched them go, his stomach twisting, slowly, in a way he couldn't quite describe. She still had a family: Finnlay. For a minute, Del had forgotten about their engagement, and all that came with it. But now that he remembered, he felt a bit foolish, trying to comfort her like he had, after her fiancé had left. He really needed to remember his place before he made a fool of himself.

He and Searsha flew down the mountain, making multiple passes over the land closest to the water in both Pothena and Seafall. The only time they spoke was when Searsha would report: *I do not hear a thing,* and Del said: "Good."

Finally, they landed on the beach, not far from where the battle had taken place. The bodies of the Qapiran soldiers were all gone, and Del was fairly certain the Pothenians weren't responsible—which meant the Qapirans had once again snuck past them, emptying an entire battle-field of corpses without being noticed. That didn't bode well for their chances at all.

Del saw one of the necklaces lying in the sand and picked it up, turning it over in his hand.

"How does it work, I wonder?" he asked.

It is saturated with the ocean's essence, said Searsha. *Like a sponge full of water.*

"So when they wear it, they're soaking up the water?"

In a sense, yes. There is a similar spell used by dragons, to protect their nests. We call it the lead foot: anyone who steps inside finds their feet weighed down until only the very strongest can move, but only at the very slowest pace. Easy targets. It deters poachers, and keeps our young from escaping, as well.

Del thought back to the Pethnian dragons' nests, and the dead warrior stuck inside. Was that why they hadn't escaped? But if so...why was Del able to walk around freely?

"How long does it last?" he asked.

Searsha gave him a warning look. *I know what you are thinking. Do not.*

"Too late for that. How long does it last? How much saturation can I pack into a single object?"

You will need something bigger than a tiny gem, she said. *And as for using the spell for air, I cannot say how effective it may be. I would suggest you perform some trials first, but that would require thinking, and you—*

"Got it!" said Del, fishing a decent-sized seashell out of the sand. "How would this work?"

I appreciate the irony, at least.

Del took the shell in both hands and focused all his thoughts onto it. He felt in the air around himself, tried to imagine breathing that air, and how it felt in his lungs. He pulled at that essence, separating it from the world and forcing it into the shell. There was some resistance, like the shell was already full of something else that didn't want to be displaced, but Del was relentless: he squeezed his eyes shut, feeling the air's essence flow past his fingertips and into the shell. More and more flooded past, until the shell felt altogether different—heavier, in a way, but also lighter. Like it was a slice of cloud shaped like a seashell.

When he was done, he opened his eyes and smiled at his handiwork.

"Did it work?" he asked.

There is only one way to know for sure, said Searsha. *Attempt to drown yourself. I will watch.*

Del ran to the water's edge, clutching the seashell against his chest, and knelt down in the glass-and-sand until the waves were lapping against his knees. There might be Qapirans lurking just beneath the surface, waiting to snatch him whole. This might end in disaster in many ways at once—but he had to know.

"Here goes nothing..." he said, and plunged his face into the water.

He was holding his breath, he realized, but had the hardest time letting go of that reflex. He opened his mouth a little, then a little more, and let the air flow out of his mouth. For a second, he didn't move at all—he just knelt there, waiting for something to feel different. But eventually panic overcame him, and he felt himself take a deep breath—

And didn't drown. There was air in his lungs. He could breathe in and out, as usual. Somehow, against all logic, the water never made it into his mouth. He was breathing underwater!

He got back to his feet, hurrying back across the beach toward Searsha.

I have the terrible feeling you were successful, she said, as he scooped up another shell from the sand. She frowned at him. *What is that for?*

He closed his eyes and focused his magic once more, pausing only to say: "You're going to love drowning, I promise."

CHAPTER 27

The water was cold, but Del was used to the cold. What he wasn't used to was the darkness, and the way, no matter which way he looked, he felt like he was lost in a heavy, crushing void. He held on to Searsha tightly, letting her do most of the swimming for him. The last thing he needed was to be stranded with no way of knowing which way was up. Or worse, to fall straight into a Qapiran trap.

Can you not see? she asked him.

He shook his head.

She grinned. *I assume you know you can still speak telepathically, even if your voice does not work.* He rolled his eyes at that, and she laughed. *Oh, this will be fun. I can feel it already. Here, let us return to the surface—*

He told her no, without words. He knew she could tell he was terrified of his blindness, and of being in the Qapirans' domain, but he did his best to communicate something else entirely: determination. Determination to protect Etenia and the others from harm, even if it was a desperate gambit.

Should we not test the magic further before—

He shook his head again, and he felt her tense as she realized he wasn't going to be swayed. Even the memory of Etenia saying, "we can't risk you" couldn't stop him, because as important as he was to her, she was far more important to him. His idea to steal the stone might be flawed and foolish, but it was the closest thing they had to a solution—so he had to try it.

He could feel Searsha's reluctant acceptance, as her senses sharpened to pick out the dangers around them.

Very well, she said, and swam deeper into the sea.

Down they went, deeper and deeper, until Del could sense Searsha's pace slowing. She didn't seem anxious, so it probably wasn't because of a threat—though really, would they even see a trap coming before it was sprung—but it unnerved him all the same. He had to know what was going on. He closed his eyes and saw through her vision instead, and understood why she was pausing: there, off in the distance, was their destination. The Qapiran camp.

Except it wasn't a camp, exactly. It wasn't a temporary structure, thrown together by an invading army as it prepared to launch an assault. It was made of stone and metal, weathered and covered in seaweed like it had been there for centuries. Millennia, even. And it had, Del realized: the ancient Qapirans had launched attacks on Pothena from close by. This was where they'd done it from. They had returned to their old camp—which looked more like a city to Del—and were settling in for the siege of a lifetime.

Searsha had slowed because there were guards by the front gates. They carried the same shimmering spears as the soldiers on the beach, but they also had swords hanging from their belts—and more ominously, sounding horns. There was a good distance between them and the gates —a space littered with stones and the spine of an ancient shipwreck overgrown with plants and corals—but Searsha wasn't exactly a subtle creature. She was doing her best to stay out of sight, but if the guards noticed her, there was no way Del would be able to get to the stone. Or even get back to the surface alive.

I cannot kill them both quickly enough, she said. *We will have to go around.*

Del wanted to argue, but she was right: there really was no other way. Even if she were able to blast dragonfire underwater, the force it would take to get both guards at once would be its own kind of alarm. He held tight as Searsha swam far around the camp, just close enough to see it in the distance, without looking like anything more than a passing whale.

Del worried, though, that his spell might not last forever. He had no way to judge how much air essence he had left—since their shells didn't turn red at the end—and he wondered if they'd even notice until it was too late. They had to move quickly. More quickly than was wise.

Yes, yes, I will do my best, said Searsha, turning and swimming directly for the camp again. She kept close to the ground, leaving a slight wake of stirred-up sand behind her, but keeping herself as obscured as possible.

They were approaching the camp again, with a few small buildings dotting the horizon ahead of them. There were no lights anywhere—when Del opened his eyes to see, all he perceived was blackness—and they saw no movement anywhere. That only made it more unnerving. Where was everyone?

Del had a terrible thought: maybe the Qapirans were, at the same time he was sneaking up on them, sneaking up on Pothena. If he was inadvertently abandoning his friends at a critical moment, he would never forgive himself. The only way to ensure it was worth it was to find the stone and get it as far away from Pothena as possible. If that didn't draw the Qapira away, there was no hope at all.

As they approached, the buildings came into clearer view, and Del could see right inside. They had big arched doorways like at the Browder villa, so from the right angles, it was clear there were people inside—and they were sleeping. Their eyes were closed, and they were tucked into a kind of silken net that kept them from floating away. Like an underwater bed. He counted three in one building, and six in another. None were children, and none were especially old. They were all in peak fighting form. Probably soldiers.

The farther they went, the more and more buildings they passed, and it became increasingly clear that, with the exception of the guards at the gate, all the Qapirans were sleeping. It made no sense to Del. Yes, they were a fearsome fighting force, but wasn't this taking an incredible risk? If Ragir hadn't vetoed his original plan, he could have led a dragon force straight into this place and gotten the jump on them without much resistance. For a race of legendary warriors, it seemed like an odd choice. The only explanation was that the Qapira simply didn't think anyone else could wield the kind of spells they could.

Over there, said Searsha, and Del immediately saw what she meant: half a mile away was a domed structure in the center of the camp, and it was ever so slightly glowing through the seams in its stonework.

Del held tight as Searsha moved faster, faster toward their goal.

There were no guards outside. No watchtowers keeping an eye on what was almost certainly the most important thing in Qapiran society. Suddenly Del worried that Etenia might be right: maybe they had left the magic stone in their capital city, and whatever this was, it was a decoy. Maybe the whole reason the city was "asleep" was to lure Del and Searsha in? What if the Qapirans could still see through his eyes after all?

He might have led them straight into a trap.

He wanted to tell Searsha to run, to swim for the surface, but he could feel her mood in that moment, and she already knew what he was thinking, and had soundly rejected it. *We have come this far,* she was saying. *It would be rude not to let them try.*

Finally, they were there, at the doorway to the dome. One, two, three heartbeats later, Searsha came into the room—

Where there were three Qapiran guards waiting for them.

Their spears raised as one, as Del tried to think of what to do. Why hadn't he come up with a plan before he actually needed it, he wondered frantically. And then Searsha blasted them with three quick bursts of dragonfire. Two were killed instantly, but the third managed to get his shield activated in time to merely be knocked backward into the wall. He shook out his head, reached for his spear again—

And Searsha swatted him with her tail, flattening him into the floor.

We will have to hurry now, she said.

Del looked up, atop a tall pedestal, where he saw what they'd come for: the magic stone. There was a fine glowing blue crack running down the middle of it, and Del felt like the more he breathed, the stronger the glow became. He swam up to it as Searsha peered out the door.

They are awakening, she said. *Tell me when you have it.*

Del arrived at the top of the pedestal, and observed the stone for the first time outside a vision. It was weathered and imperfect, and almost warm to the touch. The glow was definitely growing more incandescent every time he took a breath, and as his hands touched it, it almost seemed to vibrate.

Del? asked Searsha. *There are spears. Many spears.*

"Got it," he said back.

Excellent, she said. *Shield yourself.*

Del was about to ask her. from what. when she turned her head around and blasted the roof of the dome clear off. He created a quick shield above himself, which just barely blocked the biggest chunks of rock as they fell down around him. One piece, though, got through his spell, and knocked his arm hard enough that he dropped the stone.

"Wait!" he called, and swam down to get it.

Searsha was firing blasts out the front door now. He could feel her urgency. Whatever was coming, it was not good news. The stone had fallen between a pair of large pieces of rubble, but was easy to spot because of the blue glow. Del braced himself and pulled on the left-most rock, lifting, lifting, lifting until it started to shift and he could see the stone beneath.

He reached down, grabbing hold and pulling the stone free. He couldn't help but notice the crack was smaller now, and glowing ever stronger. It was like it was reacting to his presence.

It is time to go, said Searsha, and rushed to his side long enough for him to hold on, and then she launched herself up through the broken roof, rushing for the surface.

Behind them, spears were slicing through the water as the Qapirans tried and failed to stop them. But their path was too straightforward, too easy to predict. It would only be a matter of time. Del turned enough to see, then created another shield below them—just in time to deflect a shot that would have killed Searsha on contact.

"Swim faster," he urged her.

I am trying, she said, and he could feel the oddest sensation from her, like she was somehow fading from him, growing less distinct. He tried to reach out in his mind and figure out why—was he using too much magic? Was their connection somehow fraying? He was so preoccupied, he didn't notice a spear puncture straight through his shield and slice Searsha's right leg.

She roared in pain, and Del felt it, too. He gasped at the shock of it, and then discovered that he couldn't gasp. There was no more air to breathe. He looked down at the shell that he had tucked into his shirt, and could feel—in a way he couldn't explain, even to himself—that it was nearly empty.

"My shell is empty," he said, feeling woozy.

Not...the...shells... said Searsha, her pace slowing. *Magic...draining....*

It took Del a moment to understand, and then to fully appreciate what it meant: the Qapira had been stealing magical objects and creatures to feed their stone, and Del was carrying it with him. That was why the shells had lost their power, and why his shields had failed in the dome and just now. And why Searsha was fading fast, too—she was being killed by it.

They weren't going to be able to steal it. They wouldn't be able to hide it. They wouldn't be able to draw the Qapira away.

There was only one thing left to do.

"Searsha?" he asked.

We can try, she said.

Del used whatever magic he had left in his soul to create another bubble around the stone, and then with a desperate effort, shove it out ahead of them, toward the surface. It took off so fast, it created a violent wake that nearly knocked Searsha sideways. But as she recovered—and the draining effects of the stone lessened—she filled her belly with fire and blasted a white-hot beam of dragonfire straight at the stone—

And it exploded in a dazzling shockwave of blue and black fragments.

He hadn't known what to expect, but he hadn't expected this. Even Searsha seemed surprised her fire had worked so well. But soon their collective excitement gave way to another feeling that was quickly saturating the water around them: horror.

All around him, he could hear the screams. The Qapirans, whether awake or asleep, felt the destruction of their sacred artifact. They felt it so deeply that even after the initial sounds of their crying died away, he could still sense the trauma. They were horrified, terrified, confused and furious.

Just like Tommen had been at the loss of Safrin.

Just like Etenia had been at the loss of her father.

Del felt nothing but grim satisfaction as Searsha finally got back the last bit of speed she needed to burst through the water and into the sky above. They both took big, desperate breaths as they soared into the moonlight, twisting around and coming to a hover a few hundred feet above the water.

A second later, the Qapiran military commander's head emerged from the water, and he looked up toward Del with hatred in his eyes.

"You wretched fool," he said. "You have made a most grievous mistake."

"The only mistakes I see are you not learning when to quit," said Del. "First the Kraken, now your rock. Take a hint. Leave us in peace."

The Qapiran laughed a bitter laugh. "Leave you in peace?" he shouted. "There can be no peace now! You took that option away from us when you destroyed our sacred stone!"

"No, you took that option away when you attacked our city for no reason!" yelled Del. "Leave now, and nobody else needs to get hurt. But if you try to—"

"Try? Oh, my dear boy, the days of trying are over. We will breach your defenses, storm your lands, steal every ounce of magic you possess and kill anyone that stands in our way. We will leave your precious city a smoking ruin, with no survivors left to tell the tale. We bring death, Pothenian. We bring suffering and death, and nothing will stop us from having our revenge."

And with that, the Qapiran slipped beneath the waves.

"What have I done..." gasped Del. "I just made everything so much worse. If I'd just listened to—"

You can feel sorry for yourself later, said Searsha. *We need to prepare for what comes next.*

CHAPTER 28

D el hadn't said exactly where to go, and Searsha hadn't asked, but as they approached the Old City, he began to notice she wasn't coming in to land near the library or the main square. She was heading for the valley, up above. He didn't ask her to do otherwise, either, because he needed a moment to think, too.

When they landed, Del took a moment before climbing off Searsha's back. When he did, he still didn't go far, because his mind was too busy going over the events that had just transpired, trying to figure out exactly when it had all gone wrong, and how he could explain it to Etenia.

"What are we going to do?" he asked Searsha, running his hands through his hair. "What do we tell them?"

I suspect only the truth will do, she said. *Anything else is sure to make matters worse.*

"But they are worse!" shouted Del. "You heard him! He as good as said they might have left us alone if we hadn't destroyed the stone!"

Which was an easy thing for him to say once it was destroyed, said Searsha. *I suspect he would not have left regardless. All that has changed is how angry he is about it.*

"That doesn't make it any better," said Del. "The only thing worse than a ruthless enemy is a ruthless enemy who hates you. The last time they came at us, they used the beach as a distraction and only attacked the Browder villa in the city. Our only casualties were the people who actively fought them."

And now you suspect the result will be less favorable, said Searsha.

"Yes I do! And it's all my fault!"

I have two counter-arguments for you. First: the results would be less favorable no matter what we did, because the next time the Qapira attack, they will not be looking for a selection of magical artifacts conveniently located in one place. They will be hunting to kill, and that will, by necessity, result in a much more chaotic assault.

"You can't know that for sure," said Del.

I can, and I know you know it, too. The second assault was never going to be pleasant. Their commander already told you he would punish you severely. Will it be worse now that we've made them angry? Perhaps. But whether it is a rainstorm or a hurricane, we were always destined to get wet.

Del sat down, then tipped backward onto his back, staring up at the sky. The stars were bright against the pitch-black heavens, twinkling peacefully like they didn't have a care in the world. He envied them.

"What's the second thing?" he asked. "You had two counter-arguments. Your first one was stupid, but maybe the second one is better."

Searsha rested her head near him, looking down at him with her amber eyes that seemed to glow in the darkness. *This is not your fault.*

"Ha!" he said. "Two for two."

You put yourself in peril to go into the heart of the enemy camp and steal the weapon they would use to hurt your friends. You could not have foreseen the complications, or that we would be forced to destroy the stone to save our own lives.

"But Etenia told me not to," sighed Del. "You know what she's going to say, too. 'I thought we discussed this, Del! I thought we agreed not to go after the stone, and worry about defending the city instead!'"

Searsha paused a moment. *You have captured her perfectly.*

"And the worst part is, she's not wrong. If I'd just listened to her, we might have stood a chance. I could have helped prepare Pothena for an assault that might not have come for days, or weeks, or who knows how long? But now that I've made them angry, they'll show no mercy."

I am confused, said Searsha. *In this conversation, do you want me to offer you support, or make you feel badly about yourself?*

"I want you to be honest and tell me what to do to fix this."

I cannot tell you what to do, because I do not think it can be fixed, she said. *But while you moan about your culpability, I would ask you to examine why you disobeyed Etenia in the first place.*

"Because I'm stubborn and stupid?"

No, said Searsha. *Think back. You were standing right here when it happened. What prompted you to action?*

Del tried to remember, but so much had happened in the last few hours that had burned his memory raw. Whenever he tried to cast his thoughts back to that conversation where Etenia had warned him against chasing foolish ideas, he got stuck on two images: Finnlay, with his arm wrapped around her, and the sight of the two graves in the fading light.

He tried to focus, tried to sharpen his attention and remember what Searsha was referring to, but no matter how hard he tried, all he could see was the funeral, and Etenia weeping, and the feeling of grief and anger tearing him apart as he realized there would only be more suffering to come. He hadn't been able to protect her from pain, and it was the worst feeling he could imagine, and—

"Oh," he said.

Yes, said Searsha. *You are stupid, and you* are *stubborn, but you are stupid and stubborn for noble reasons. You wanted to save her from any more suffering.*

"She's been through enough," said Del. "I mean, we all have, but I...I just can't stand to see her cry."

It is hard to see those we love suffer, she said.

"Love?" said Del, his memory sticking on that image of Finnlay with his arm around Etenia. The closeness. The intimacy. The connection he would never have with her. Why did it bother him so much? Why couldn't he get that image out of his head?

Surely you see it, said Searsha.

"I...I don't. Etenia and I are friends. We've been through a lot, sure, but we're not—"

Finnlay, said Searsha, and Del felt a jolt of discomfort in his gut, like anger and hurt rolled into one. *Aha,* she said. *See? I felt that. Jealousy.*

"I'm not jealous of Finnlay," he said, and could tell, as he said it, that he was lying to himself. "I mean, just because I don't like him doesn't mean I have feelings for Etenia."

Do you know that Cember and I have an ongoing wager as to which one of you will admit your feelings first?

"Wait, 'which one of us'?" said Del. "You mean she—"

269

You are excited by the idea, said Searsha.

"What does it matter? She's engaged. To Finnlay."

Please just admit it. Soon, if at all possible.

Del refused to believe it, but every time he tried to move on from what Searsha was saying, his mind came crashing back to a whole new image: Etenia, lying in the grass beside him, looking at him with an expression on her face that seemed curious, hopeful, and just...waiting. Like she was expecting him to admit his feelings for her. He couldn't tell if this was an actual memory, or just a fantasy he had created out of thin air...

"But it's Finnlay she always goes to, when she needs comforting," he said.

Searsha just looked at him.

But it didn't change the underlying fact: he did love her. And he didn't know what to do about it. She was engaged, and Finnlay was—despite all Del's best efforts to prove otherwise—a pretty great guy. Even his worst characteristics were all in service of helping Etenia, which made him...

Which made him a lot like Del.

Del had gone into enemy territory to find a way to end the war and save Etenia any more suffering...and made it almost impossible for her to escape it anymore.

"So back to my first question," said Del, hands over his face. "What are we going to do? What are we going to tell them?"

There is only one way forward, said Searsha. *Work with Etenia and find a way to win the day. Together, you are unstoppable. But first, you must tell her the truth, and trust that she will understand.*

CHAPTER 29

"You what?" gasped Etenia, seconds after Del broke the bad news to her, Lathan and Bettine. "I thought we agreed that was a bad idea! What happened to defending the city?"

Del glared at Searsha. "I told you," he said, telepathically.

Tell her how you feel, said Searsha, to him alone. *That will distract her.*

He ignored her and said, to Etenia: "I'm sorry. I thought I could save Pothena from any more suffering. I just didn't expect that the stupid stone would be so dangerous. And now that it's gone..."

"Now that it's gone, the Qapira will be angrier than ever," said Etenia, then sighed. "But in the end, they'd be coming for us anyway. The only thing that's changed is that they don't have their weapon anymore. So I guess, all things considered, you actually helped a little."

Del couldn't hide his smile. "You mean you're not angry?"

"Oh, I'm furious, but we'll save that for later," she said.

"If we survive," said Lathan. "Which at this moment seems dubious at best."

"How are the mages faring?" asked Etenia, returning their attention to the maps spread out on the table next to them. Del looked at the topmost map for the first time: a sketch of the city below, with the underground streams and sewer pipes drawn in—or rough approximations, based on ancient sources Bettine had scrounged together.

Lathan traced a finger along the ridge of Pothena, dividing the lower-lying area from the higher-class villas above. "They've taken up position down this line," he said. "It gives a good enough vantage point over the city below, though the houses still make it difficult to see every angle."

"We'll have dragons for that," said Etenia. "Circling from above. It should give us more than enough time."

"Enough time for what?" asked Del.

"To evacuate the last of the refugees," said Bettine. "They've been moving all night, but there are still a few hundred left to go."

"And what happens when they're out?" asked Del. "What do we do then? I thought we decided we couldn't afford to lose the city. We'll run out of food eventually you know."

Etenia cut in: "And if we focus on the city at the expense of the people, what good will that do?"

"So we don't lose the people, or the city," said Del, and stormed out of the library. "Come on! Let's go!"

"Go where?" called Etenia, unhappily, chasing after.

"To remind the Qapira who they're dealing with!"

He came to the training grounds, where the dragon riders were sitting by assorted campfires, finishing their breakfasts. They looked a lot less confident than the day before—tired, wary, and terrified, after having lost one of their own. When they saw Del and Etenia come in, they stood to attention, but some seemed downright scared that they might be asked to fly into battle again.

"All right, everyone!" shouted Del. "Gather 'round!" He looked off to the side, where the youngest dragon riders—the ones with the dragons who were only just old enough to fly—were clustered, and whistled to get their attention. "Everyone, I said!"

The young ones—including, Del realized, Womp!—hurried over, until he and Etenia were surrounded by a circle of their students, and through them, the minds of all the dragons. They were all waiting anxiously for their orders. Some more eagerly than others.

"I'm not going to lie to you," said Del. "Yesterday was hard, but today will be harder. Last night, I snuck into their camp and destroyed their secret weapon—"

The students gasped and started to cheer, but Del waved them quiet.

"Don't get excited. It didn't stop them. They're still coming, and this time they're out for revenge. Mistakes will be deadly. Now more than ever."

The students' faces turned even grimmer at that. Some looked ready to run. Finnlay looked ill, but determined.

"I can't promise you everything will turn out all right," said Del. "I can't promise you that you and your friends will make it back in one piece. That a Qapiran net won't catch you, or a Qapiran spear won't find you. Anyone who promises you more is lying, and you deserve better than lies."

Some of the newer recruits were starting to look ill. Their eyes were downcast as they started to doubt their decision to join in the first place.

"But what I can promise you is this," said Del. "You are the best chance —the only chance—Pothena has of surviving what's coming. Because as fearsome as the Qapira may be, they are no match for the fighting force you have become. Yesterday, we held them at bay on that beach by using our training, our discipline, and our smarts. Today may be harder, with so many places for them to hide, but we will turn their advantages against them. We know this city, better than they ever could and we will send them back to the ocean where they belong!"

The students cheered, getting louder and louder until it was a deafening sound. Del could hear their dragons, all nearby, roaring their agreement, too. It was an incredible sound, and filled Del with pride. Because no matter what he said, they all knew they were badly outnumbered, badly outgunned, and fighting in terrain ill-suited for dragons, with all the narrow streets and alleyways. They were facing a difficult and dangerous battle, and they weren't going to back down. Knockabout brothers, to the end.

"Sir, one question," said Kinto, pushing her way through the crowd to stand at the front. Her face was scratched and bruised from her fall yesterday, but she showed no signs of backing down. "After a while, the Qapira seemed to know what we were doing before we did it."

Del nodded. "They watched us and learned our tactics."

"Not just that," said Kinto. "It was like they were...in our heads."

She wasn't wrong. There had been moments on the beach when the Qapira simply couldn't have guessed what was coming next. When he'd been calling out dorm blocks at random, they'd somehow managed to turn their shields to block the blasts. But Del hadn't said those instructions aloud, which meant—

"They're eavesdropping," he said.

Etenia gasped. "It's like with your visions. They're hijacking our tele-pathic bonds to hear what we're going to do next. This is terrible...the city is too big. We'll be too spread out to use our voices."

Del felt the same dread that she did until he happened to see Womp's expression: a devious smile. Irrepressible.

"What?" he asked. "What are you thinking?"

Womp gave him a shrug. "Say, not do."

Del burst out laughing. "Oh, yes! That's perfect!"

"What is?" asked Etenia. "What do you mean?"

Del grinned at her. "Trust me, you'll like it."

"I do trust you, Del. I'd just also like to know what's so perfect."

And so he told her—and the rest of them—and they got down to figuring out how to defeat the Qapira once and for all.

Two hours later, Del, Etenia, and Lathan headed for the launching zone as all around them, riders were mounting their dragons and fixing their armor, giving nervous glances down the mountainside at the city below. Del's pride was tempered by the fact that half these students were so new to flying, they were potentially putting their lives in danger just taking flight at all, let alone engaging a dangerous enemy. And there just weren't enough of them: if the Qapirans sent another force the same size as yesterday's, that might be enough to overwhelm Pothena's defenses. The last thing Del wanted was for the mages—students themselves—to be caught in the middle of that deadly chaos, with no way to escape.

There was no way they could win this day. But they could inflict such heavy losses on the Qapira that they would think twice about trying again.

Del saw Finnlay coming before Etenia did, and tried his best not to react negatively, for all their sakes. Yes, they both loved the same woman, but on a day like this, that was a distraction none of them could afford. And anyway, whatever Searsha thought, it didn't matter. Etenia had made her choice. There was nothing Del could do about that.

"I'm coming with you!" said Finnlay, shaking the sling off his arm.

"You're still hurt," said Etenia, sternly.

"I can't just do nothing, Tenny," he countered. He put a hand on her shoulder and looked her in the eye. "For Yena."

She sighed and nodded. "For Yena."

He hurried off without another word. Del said nothing, out of respect for Etenia's friend. He wanted to say it made no sense for Etenia to lose someone else close to her, but truly, if Finnlay wanted to make this sacrifice for his fiancée, Del was in no position to argue. And, he suspected, arguing wouldn't stop Finnlay from trying anyway. Maybe he'd end up dying and—

Del stopped himself, shocked at the cruelty of his own thoughts. Finnlay wasn't a friend, but he was an ally, and right now, those were in short supply. He deserved better. At least until the battle was won.

Lathan and Etenia climbed onto Cember's back, and Del onto Searsha's. They stood at the edge of the cliff, looking down at Pothena and the ocean beyond. They could see the pinpricks of color as more refugees hurried up the mountain, heading for a salvation that would only save them if the dragons fulfilled their promise.

Tell her, Searsha said.

"Etenia," said Del, voice cracking as he tried to work up the courage to say what he needed to say. "If this doesn't work, I just need you to know—"

"It will work," she said with a smile. "It has to."

"But—"

276

"See you down there!" she called, and Cember leapt off the edge and soared his way down. Del watched them go, feeling the words left unspoken drifting away in the wind, never to be caught again.

Now you have a good excuse to survive, said Searsha, and followed Cember into the fray.

CHAPTER 30

Del sat on a red-brick roof looking out over the bay, where the abandoned ships bobbed and shook in the white-capped waves. The city was silent, like a ghost town in the making. Laundry fluttered in the wind, waiting to be collected by a family that might never return. Dogs wandered the alleys, delighted to have their freedom, but wary of what it meant.

Del's feet hung off the edge of the roof, swinging back and forth, impatiently waiting for the nightmare he wished wouldn't happen. All around him, the Old City forces were settling into place: mages at choke points, Sivarnan dragons along the rooftops, Pothenian dragons waiting in the wings. They would be wildly outnumbered, but they would at least be using every last ounce of their numbers to their advantage.

Del let out a ragged breath and lay back on the roof, pressing his hands to his eyes as he tried to steady his nerves.

"Ragir?" he asked through his bond.

A moment later, she replied: *Be careful, dragon rider.*

"It's time," he said. "Let them through."

Ragir had been working hard to keep the Qapira out of Del's mind. It hadn't always worked, especially as more and more dragons joined the school and made filtering the psychic energy busier and less controlled —but for what came next, Del needed the channels opened wide. He'd been mostly saved the burden of those awful visions for so long, he was afraid of what might happen when they came at him again, but there was just no other way. He needed to talk to the Qapira, to deliver one last message, to maybe avert a disaster.

He felt the edges of Ragir's mental block slipping away, and then suddenly, he wasn't out on the rooftop with a warm breeze coming in from the east—he was underwater again, bathed in darkness and an oppressive cold, looking out at the emptied-out courtyard that had once held a thousand Qapiran troops. He felt a burning anger, made even more furious when the person whose eyes he was seeing through realized he was there. He saw his hands—Lomasi's hands, he realized—the Qapiran Empress'—grip a table as she doubled over, trying to steady herself in her grief. She turned to face the spot the magic stone had been, and the anger spiked even more, until it was all Del could feel. She wanted vengeance.

"This is your last chance," Del said, in a voice he couldn't hear himself, but knew for certain she would. "Call back your troops, and this can be over."

He felt her going into a rage, her fury burning hotter and hotter until it was all he could fathom anymore, and his mind started to crackle from the intensity of it, and he felt his body coming apart from the violence she was inflicting upon him, and he—

He sat up on the roof, catching his breath. He felt like he'd sprinted ten miles in the blazing sun, but none of that mattered in the face of what was coming next. He'd tried diplomacy, as unlikely as it had been to succeed. Now all that was left was the fight.

"Everyone ready?" he asked through his bond.

The Old City forces all answered as one—humans and dragons alike—with a resounding cheer that echoed off the buildings and right out to sea. Del hoped the Qapira heard it.

And then he saw it: down in the harbor, the ships all began to shift and bob more violently, and the waves got rougher and rougher despite the relatively calm seas beyond. There was a stillness in the air one second, and then the spears cut through the surf, and the invaders began marching onto the shore.

It wasn't just that there were more of them this time—it was that there were so many it seemed unreal. The emptiness of the harbor had thrown off Del's sense of scale, but as row after row of soldiers marched toward the city, it became clear this was a far bigger invading force than the one they'd met on the beach. That had been a formidable foe; this was an army. The ground began to shudder as they moved forward in perfect unison. Del could feel, through his bond, the other dragon riders' uncertainty growing.

The Qapira were an ancient fighting force that had dominated the ancient world and driven their ancestors into the mountains to avoid their wrath—and now they were back to terrorize Pothena again. This wasn't just a historic battle, it had the very real potential to be the final battle Pothena would ever fight. If they failed here, the refugees in the Old City would be stranded and helpless, doomed to starvation and certain death.

As the shoreline filled with enemy soldiers, Del looked back at his fighting force, spread out across the city, and hoped they would be up to the task...because there was really no other option. Across the rooftops, he saw Cember and Etenia watching like it didn't scare them at all. Maybe it didn't. All Del knew for sure was that he was terrified.

He walked back to where Searsha was waiting for him, and climbed up onto her back, holding tight with both hands. "Let's hope this works," he said.

So long as we can keep them from passing the midpoint, we stand a chance.

Del checked how much territory that would be: the Qapira were already filling the first fifth of the city with troops, with more arriving every second. The midpoint of the city, the heart of the market, would be overrun in a matter of minutes if they weren't careful. Finnlay and Garra were positioned there, perched right above what would soon be the most dangerous place in the world.

"All right, everyone," he said through his bond. "Let them have it!"

Suddenly, and without warning, bursts of dragonfire shot out from between the warehouses near the waterfront. They were short but powerful shots, careening crosswise at the Qapirans, and blowing huge swaths of soldiers off their feet and across the landscape without mercy. Again and again they fired as the Qapirans struggled to anticipate which way the assault would come from next.

Del saw spears being thrown, and soldiers breaking ranks to charge, and knew the battle had now truly begun.

"Second wave!" he called, and in from the hilltops in the east and the west came Pothenian dragons, racing down toward the shore and unleashing the most magnificent fire Del had ever seen. The Qapirans' shields were no match for the intensity of the flames, and soon the beach was again a mess of glassy wreckage and charred remains.

And yet still, more soldiers came.

The barrage of spears became too much, and the Pothenian dragons looped back toward the city to draw the projectiles away, as the dragons hiding amongst the warehouses took flight.

A spear hit one in the side, and it screamed, tumbling down and crashing into a house with a sickening crunch. Del couldn't feel a thing from the dragon or its rider, and tried not to let his anguish spread to the students.

The Qapira were moving in closer now, splitting up as they came ashore and heading for the multitude of roads and alleyways on either side of the main boulevard.

"Can anyone see where they're going?" Del called. "Anyone?"

"No, sir!" called Kinto. "Can't get a clear shot!"

Del sighed angrily. "They're using the buildings as cover."

"They know we can't fit dragons down there," said Etenia, arcing back toward the back of the city. "They'll sneak right past us."

"Permission to firebomb them, sir," said Lufien.

"No," said Del. "You do that, you'll end up burning down half the city by mistake. No, we need to force them back into the open. We need some way to box them in..."

As he said it, he felt half the dragon riders all come to the same realization at the same time, and look toward the wall separating Pothena from Seafall. And then he felt them all grin as one.

Searsha and Del took off in an instant, flying toward the wall with a throat full of fire. Del could feel her muscles flex as she powered onward, moving so fast the wind nearly whipped him off her back. When she got close enough, she fired a few quick bursts at the base of the wall, blowing it apart. She swept in, low, pulling the swirling dust away in her wake.

The wall had been reduced to large chunks of rock and mortar—not too big for a dragon to carry, but big enough to create an impression. "Dragon riders!" called Del. "Let's make some obstacles."

282

Searsha landed on one of the bigger pieces of rock and latched her claws into it, then with a mighty heave, she took off, back into the air, heading for the western side of the city. Spears flew at her, only to be deflected by magic—the mages were working furiously to keep the skies safe—or by quick shots of dragonfire.

Del could see, from above, how the battle was going thus far: two-fifths of Pothena were now solidly under Qapiran control, and he could see the glint off their spears as they hurried through the narrow alleyways, racing to overtake the rest of the city.

Up ahead, he saw a six-way intersection with a pretty little fountain sprinkling water like today was any other day. The Qapira were headed straight for it, and when they got there, they would have easy access to far too much of the city's outer edges. Del didn't say a word, but he knew Searsha could tell what he was thinking. She banked to the left, doing a broad circle back toward the mountainside, coming back at the intersection lower and faster than before.

The Qapira were just coming into the square, about to pass the fountain, when Searsha let go of the rock and sent it careening into them. The fountain was obliterated on contact, and the Qapira didn't fare any better. Del saw quick sparks as their magic shields collapsed under the sudden impact and their bodies were flattened with ruthless efficiency. The rock wedged itself between two of the buildings, making an impassable blockage that the rest of the Qapira would never be able to move. They would have to go back and find another way.

And, as he looked back across the city, he knew those options were dwindling by the second. One by one, dragons were tossing giant chunks of the old wall into the alleyways, creating a funnel the Qapira would have no choice but to follow.

As the enemy became more desperate, more spears started flying up toward the dragons—some nearly hitting their marks. Worse, he could see Qapiran soldiers climbing up the sides of buildings and engaging in close-quarters combat with the mages. The mages were skilled, well-schooled by Lathan and Taria and Wen, but as more and more enemy surrounded them, there was nowhere for them to run. They were being cut down without mercy.

"Clear the rooftops!" he called into his bond. "Riders, snatch and go! Snatch and go!"

The dragons knew what it meant, and how to do it. They each pinpointed a mage on a rooftop and swooped down for them, snatching them and lifting them to safety, while a second dragon made a follow-up pass to torch whatever Qapira had made it up the walls.

Searsha raced higher and higher to get a clearer view of the battlefield. When she finally came to an altitude out of range of their spears, Del could see how far the Qapira had come. Their trick had worked, and kept the invaders from sneaking past around the sides, but now all those soldiers were streaming back into the main boulevard.

"They're going to take the market," he said.

"We can't let that happen," said Etenia. "We'll never stop them if they get that far."

"We can make another barrier," said Finnlay. "Block off the middle."

"No," said Del. "That won't stop them. They'll just keep coming."

"So what can we do?" asked Etenia. "We can't just do nothing!"

Del took a bracing breath and made sure his next words reached every one of the riders at once, so there would be no misunderstandings: "We hold the market. Make our stand. They are not getting any deeper into the city until every last one of us is dead."

He could feel Searsha's confidence battling her uncertainty, but she pushed it all aside and dove down toward the heart of the market, landing heavily between the emptied stalls that Del had spent so much of his life stealing from. It was like a homecoming of sorts. The closing of a chapter. And maybe the whole book.

Behind him, Cember swooped in and landed, and then Garra, and more and more dragons until the whole boulevard was thick with them, teeth bared and ready to kill.

"If this doesn't work..." said Etenia.

"It will," said Del, and hoped he was right.

The ground started to shake. Loose pebbles on the roadway trembled from the vibrations of thousands of feet marching in unison up the hill from the harbor. Del heard the faint crashes of pots and plates falling off shelves as the monster-made earthquake rattled the city to its core. And then, finally, he could see the tips of the spears from just below the rise, and the Qapira emerged like a terrifying wave ready to wash them all away.

"Hold..." he said, feeling his troops' nerves fraying under the strain of waiting.

And then he saw, at the head of the invasion, the telltale golden armor of the Qapiran commander, a wicked grin spread across his face as he saw who he was facing, and what it meant.

"Hold..." said Del, rubbing Searsha's neck reassuringly to keep her from taking a potshot too soon.

The Qapira were nearly there. They were so close, Del could smell the stench of seaweed on them, taste the salt in the air. It made him sick, but he pushed that aside. He couldn't give them the satisfaction.

Finally, the soldiers stopped, and only the leader strode forward, stopping halfway between his men and Del's forces. He leaned to the side to see what he was up against, and didn't seem bothered at all.

"I will make you this deal, Pothenian," he said. "Surrender your drag-ons, your riders and mages, and all other magic you possess—and we will leave your wretched little city in peace."

"Wow, that's quite the deal," said Del. "I don't know what to say."

The Qapiran bared his jagged, vicious teeth. "We can harvest your magic from your corpses just as easily, land-dweller. But if you cross me one more time, we will raze your city—"

"No one's razing Pothena but me," said Del. "You don't even have a good reason to hate this place. Get in line."

"You mock me at your peril," snarled the commander.

"The only peril I see comes from you taking one step closer," said Del. "This is the line in the sand, right here. You want to take Pothena, you have to go through us."

The Qapiran grinned even wider now. "Oh, you poor, stupid human," he said. "You were so occupied watching what was happening above-ground, you ignored the most important factor of all...."

Del held his breath, kept his face blank as he reached out through his bond and said: "Kinto, do you have the shot?"

"Yes, sir," said Kinto.

"Do it."

From off to the side, a quick burst of dragonfire tore between the build-ings, straight for the commander, and—

He had his shield in place just in time to block it. His feet shifted slightly from the force of it, but he was unscathed. He laughed menac-ingly and tapped his temple with a long and jagged finger.

"You have no secrets from me, Pothenian," he said. "And thanks to your hubris, you are surrounded."

Del looked down at the ground, his mouth falling open. "The sewers..." he gasped.

The Qapiran sneered triumphantly.

Until Del said: "Yeah, we knew about those. And your eavesdropping trick. It's funny, it reminded us of this saying we used to have, right here in the market, actually. 'Say, not do— When we knew we were being tailed, we'd say, 'Oof! I'm beat! I'm gonna go take a little nap!' and head off into a secluded alley..." His face went dead serious. "And beat the crap out of whoever followed."

The Qapiran's face tensed with anger as he tried to understand what was happening.

Del winked at him. "Hey, Womp," he said into his bond. "Show them just how surrounded we are."

CHAPTER 31

D el couldn't see it, but he could feel it in action. Along the back edge of the city, where the landscape met the mountainside, were five intake pipes leading down to the underground streams that acted as the sewer system for Pothena. And gathered around those pipes in groups of three were the biggest, strongest, meanest of the Pothenian dragons, with their bellies full of fire, and wiry little Womp as their commander.

The second after Del gave the signal, nothing happened.

The dragons in the market grew restless, worried something was wrong, but they trusted Del, and waited.

The Qapira stood taller, emboldened by the error.

And then the ground began to shake. Not like a mild earthquake, as before, but something so big and so violent, cracks formed in the walls of nearby buildings, and—

The explosions happened so suddenly, even Del jumped in surprise. Behind them, five pillars of flame shot up into the sky as the Pothenian dragons' fire roared down the underground stream and burst up through the sewer pipes. Then another explosion, a few blocks closer to the water, as they reached another output. And again, and again, and—

The commander only realized his mistake at the last second. He turned to see he had stopped a large portion of his troops right on top of a large sewer grate, which suddenly turned white-hot and exploded up and out, obliterating the soldiers who had been standing there. The commander was thrown against a nearby building, battered but alive as the fire continued its way down the city to the shore, and then with one last mighty boom, shot fire and death and carnage into the bay.

The commander staggered to his feet, looking back at the wreckage of his army, and let out a furious cry. "You are dead, land-dweller! I will tear you apart with my bare hands!"

Searsha swatted him with her tail so hard, he was knocked out cold.

He complains even more than you do, she sighed.

Del laughed and gestured down toward the unconscious commander. "Someone lock him up," he said. "He's important to them, so he might be useful for us."

Searsha leapt into the air, firing a stream of fire down at the Qapiran troops who'd survived the explosion. Some tried to block the attack, only to find themselves being knocked off their feet by invisible shields being thrown at them from the sides—the mages, hidden in the surrounding buildings, doing their part to keep the enemy boxed in. The more the Qapira tried to run for the side streets, the easier it was to pick them off as the dragons took turns racing on through, catching them while their attention was split in too many directions at once.

By the time Del reached the edge of the harbor, the entire central boulevard, up the hill, was a smouldering ruin of dead Qapira. The dragons landed next to him, all in a row, overlooking the last dip down to the waterfront, and let out a collective roar that was both terrifying, and empowering.

And then, out of the water, came even more soldiers. Hundreds of them. Thousands. The force they'd already stopped was just a tiny sliver of the full Qapiran army. They'd had a victory, yes, but they would need to keep having victories to stand a chance.

All the Qapira had to do was continue marching on. Eventually, their tenacity would win out.

He had to make that tenacity as painful as possible.

"Dorm B! Up and out, on my mark!" he shouted through his bond, and then: "Go!"

The dragons from Dorm B all hunched low and then jerked upward—just as a flurry of spears flew through the air, right where they dragons would have been—if they'd actually taken to the sky. But they hadn't, because of one important factor: Del hadn't raised his hand when he'd given the order.

"Still listening, huh?" he said to the Qapira, with a grin. "Then let's make this interesting."

Using the hand signals the riders had devised ahead of time, Del set things into motion. The Dorm B dragons torched the front lines of the Qapiran forces with a powerful wave of fire, giving the Dorm E dragons the cover they needed to take to the air. With another gesture, the mages created troughs of energy that split the beach into pieces, throwing the enemy off-balance long enough for dragonfire to catch them without their shields.

And then Del said one word that launched the rest into motion: "Charge!"

The dragons on the beach raced forward, teeth and claws tearing at their opponents, and throwing the whole battlespace into absolute chaos. Searsha spun around, swatting a dozen Qapiran troops across the sand with her tail, then caught the rest with a fire shot that cut their legs out from under them.

Nearby, Cember was being swarmed by soldiers, all trying to stab him with their spears. Etenia was working hard, casting a spell to keep them away, but more and more Qapirans kept coming, sensing an easy victory in the making. Del was proud of her technique, at how clever and capable she was, but the more the Qapirans flooded in toward her, the more his heart filled with dread: if her magic failed her now, there was nothing Del would be able to do but watch her die. He didn't think he could bear that. Soon the enemy was climbing up the shield itself, savagely hacking away at the force field again and again until—

Etenia had been waiting for the right moment. As soon as the bubble was fully covered by the enemy, she pulled it in, and then out so suddenly, it blasted the soldiers out in all directions, sending them crashing down onto their comrades—and their comrades' spears.

Cember shook himself out, happy to be free, and cut down a dozen more Qapirans with a blast of dragonfire.

Any happiness Del might have felt was quickly dampened when he saw the bigger picture all around him: while his students were fighting valiantly, they were badly outnumbered, and already showing signs of being overwhelmed. The ones in the air weren't firing with any kind of strategy anymore, they were just trying to keep from being shot out of the sky. And the ones who'd stayed on the beach were flailing so desperately, they were very nearly hitting each other as much as the enemy.

And still, the Qapira kept coming.

A spear hit one of the land-based dragons, and its rider fell into a crowd of soldiers. Her screams were cut short almost instantly. One of the airborne dragons flew a bit too far out to sea, and before Del could warn them, a net shot out of the water and snagged them, pulling them under.

To his left, five mages were trapped inside a force bubble that was getting smaller and smaller the more the Qapira pushed down on it.

To his right, a dragon had its tail cut off by a spear's sharp edge.

There were screams. So many screams.

They had trusted him to bring them victory. They had trusted him to keep them safe.

"Fall back!" he shouted through his bond. "Everyone fall back!"

He saw Etenia turn and look at him. He could feel the worry like it was his own. "Are you sure?" she asked.

"We need cover," he said. "It's our only hope."

She nodded, and called out to all the other riders: "Defend the mages! Hurry!"

The nearby dragons sprang into action, swatting and biting at the soldiers who stood between the mages and safety. A spear sliced one of the dragons' backs, and it turned with two of its classmates and burned the offending Qapiran to ashes.

The retreat was slow and disorderly, but it was going as well as could be—

"Help!" came a desperate cry from ahead—an audible, actual voice—and Del realized it was Finnlay. It took him a second to pinpoint where, but then he saw, down near the water, Garra being attacked from all sides by Qapiran soldiers, and Finnlay desperately trying to stay out of the fray. He wasn't trained as a mage, so he had no magic to save himself with. All he could do was be Garra's second set of eyes and ears and try not to get killed.

"Hold on!" called Del, as Searsha bounded through the fray. She shot fire and whipped her tail this way and that, keeping her path clear, but there was so much ground to cover—

In a gut-twisting moment, Del saw a spear arcing down toward Garra, right toward her back, and he tried to cast a spell to shield her—but it was too late. The blade cut through her skin and she screamed and lurched onto her hind legs, throwing Finnlay off.

"Save her," said Del to Searsha, and rolled off her back and onto the sand. Searsha continued on at full speed, careening into the soldiers around Garra and snapping one in half with her jaws.

Del, meanwhile, scrambled for Finnlay, who was dazed and alone in a field full of enemies. He shook out his head, standing, dizzy, trying to figure out which way was up. Del shot magical fire left and right, clearing a path to Finnlay, who was still too dazed to run.

Just then, a Qapiran tackled Del, and he hit the ground so hard his breath left him. He rolled onto his back, casting a shield just in time to stop the soldier's spear from stabbing him through the eye. The Qapiran looked surprised to have been stopped, which gave Del the opening he needed to wrap the shield around the enemy's head and twist, snapping his neck.

When he got back to his feet, he gasped in horror at the sight of another soldier charging straight for Finnlay, spear ready to kill. He shouted at the top of his lungs: "Finnlay!" but there was just no time to—

The Qapiran was bathed in a bright yellow light for a fraction of a second before something hit him so hard, he tumbled violently across the beach, colliding with his comrades so hard, they were scattered in all directions. Del didn't understand what had happened—that wasn't dragonfire, and it wasn't magic. It almost seemed like—

"Yena!" cried Finnlay, and Del looked into the water to see a badly damaged Pothenian ship there, sails tattered and ruined, its massive

Snapper-like cannons aimed onto the shore. He could just barely read the word written on the hull: "*Pacimae*." Etenia's friend's ship!

There was a young woman with bright red hair and half-burned armor, standing behind one of the guns, giving an affectionate salute to Finnlay, who was so overjoyed, it was all Del could feel from him.

"Etenia," said Finnlay. "It's Yena! She's alive! She's—"

But Qapirans grabbed hold of the ship and started climbing out of the water, clawing their way up to meet the crew for a battle mere humans would never win. Finnlay was so horrified by what he saw that he didn't notice the soldiers closing in on him again. Searsha and the struggling Garra were still too far from the city, and when he looked back, Del saw Etenia and the others fighting a pitched battle against an unbelievable horde of enemies.

They were going to lose. They were going to lose badly.

Del spoke to Searsha, and Searsha alone: *Will she make it?* he asked.

Searsha was practically dragging Garra across the beach, pausing only long enough to clear away any Qapira who dared get too close. *I cannot tell,* she said, and he felt her bitter regret.

He saw the *Pacimae* struggling, saw Finnlay in mortal danger, felt the fear and anguish of his students behind him, and Del knew what he had to do.

Get Finnlay out of here, he said. *And then stay back.*

Searsha glared at him. He could feel it. *What do you hope to accomplish?*

Del started drawing on his most potent memory, channeling it into fire and shielding and force and fear. He would lose his memory of Etenia in the valley, smiling at him as he outlined yet another foolish plan. He would lose every memory of her that mattered. But if he did this right, she'd have a chance to live.

If he did this right, the Qapira would know never to cross Pothena again.

Del, said Searsha urgently. *What are you going to do?*

He looked out at the water's edge, where the soldiers kept marching out of the surf like there was simply no end to them, and he toughened his resolve. "I'm going to throw a rock into the fountain," he said. "And turn all the coins to ash."

CHAPTER 32

D el knew they were telling him to stop, but he blocked them all
out. He crafted a sphere around himself so thick, the spears
came nowhere near him. What he was going to do was like nothing
he'd ever tried before—and nothing Lathan had ever conceived of.
Keeping the sphere intact with one hand, he raised it up with a second
shield, up into the air.

It was unsteady at first, and for a terrifying second he thought he might
lose control and tumble down into the crowd of Qapirans below. But
then he found his rhythm, and moved the sphere higher and higher,
faster and faster, until he was up though the clouds and the only sounds
from the battle were the ones he heard through his bond.

The plan was simple: he would launch himself downward, straight into
the ocean above the Qapiran troops. In the last seconds before impact,
he would fill the sphere with the most potent magical fire he could
create, packing it so tightly that when he hit, it would go off like a
bomb, incinerating the enemy in all directions.

It wasn't the best plan, but it was the only plan.

"Mages at the front line," he said, even his telepathic voice wavering. "Full shields on my mark."

"Del, wait—" said Etenia.

"I'm sorry," he said, and closed his mind to her to keep her from changing his mind. He connected with Searsha directly: "Are you clear?"

You have to stop, said Searsha. *Do not—*

"Just get clear," he said, and used all the magic he could muster to throw the sphere downward.

The inertia flattened him against the top of the bubble, and all he could do was watch as he raced through the clouds until they parted, and he could see the ocean beneath him, and the beach, and—

He did a double take when he saw: the beach was alight with huge explosions of dragonfire, cutting through the Qapiran soldiers over and over again with ruthless efficiency. And it didn't stop there: the water itself was under attack, with flames being blown so forcefully that the sea itself was boiling away and the monsters below were being cooked alive.

And then Del saw them: massive dragons, bigger than even Ragir and the Pothenians, arriving in waves from over the mountains. Unlike Del's trainees, these ones flew in a perfect grid, and moved with such calculation, it was like they were parts in a machine. One set dive-bombed the beach while the next set up to follow, and a third group swooped down at the water, torching any fools who dared stick their heads out to see.

The Qapira were being overwhelmed by the assault. They were losing, and Del—

Del realized he was still about to commit suicide. He urgently snapped the sphere out of existence, and tried to think of another spell to slow his fall, but everything that came to mind seemed like it might leave him just as dead as before, and he wished he hadn't sent—

Searsha slipped in right under him, breaking his fall and carrying him to safety.

Next time, when someone tells you to stop, perhaps you should listen, she said.

"What's going on?" he asked. "Who are these dragons?"

I am not sure, said Searsha. *Perhaps you should ask him....*

Del looked off to the right as one of the massive dragons pulled alongside. Its rider, a slightly older man in heavy battle armor, gave Del a friendly salute, and called out something that made absolutely no sense to Del at all.

"I'm sorry?" said Del, loudly. "I dont...I can't..."

The rider slapped his shoulder, where there was a ceremonial crest emblazoned on his armor. "Chamenos!" he said. "Chamenos, yes?"

Del understood! The dragons from Chamenos! Ragir's emissaries had found them after all, and somehow convinced them to come to save their ancient allies! As Del looked down, he saw the Qapira retreating back into the water, even as the Chamenan dragons kept firing relentlessly.

"Yes?" repeated the other rider.

"Yes!" laughed Del. "Chamenos, yes! Chamenos yes!"

You sound foolish now, said Searsha. *Stop before you scare them away.*

CHAPTER 33

P othena still stood. Yes, there was serious damage to a great many of its buildings—and especially to the wall that separated it from Seafall—but it was in far better shape than the Old City had been when they'd first found it. As Searsha closed in on the market, Del could see his students, their dragons, and the mages all working together to clear the road, to clear debris, and search for casualties amongst the wreckage.

Del dismounted and was immediately mobbed by his student riders, who were both amazed he'd survived, and eager to tell him all the things they'd accomplished in the day's battles. Del knew there was trauma and grief waiting in the wings, ready to hit them full-force, but for now their adrenaline was helping them focus on the glorious parts of the day. They were making so much noise at once, he had trouble hearing even half of it, so he just smiled and said: "That's incredible!" whenever it seemed appropriate—and kept an eye open for Etenia.

The more he moved through the crowds, the more he climbed the hill toward the mountain, the more urgent he became. Where was Etenia? Had she not made it back? There were so many missing faces, and he knew some dragons had been lost, but if she'd been lost, someone would have told him by now, wouldn't they?

He hurried, faster and faster, until he was forced to stop by the oddest sight, off to his right: there, wedged between a pair of buildings near the boulevard, was a boat. A large boat, in fact. The *Pacimae*. He'd forgotten all about it, but apparently the Chamenan dragons had carried it inland to safety. Maybe that was where Etenia was—tending to her friend! He rushed over, smile growing by the second until he came into the clearing and saw Finnlay sitting there, on a bench, covered in blood.

"Finnlay..." said Del, coming to a stop and speaking quietly. "Are...are you..."

Finnlay seemed dazed. He looked up toward Del, but not at him, with tears in his eyes. "You made it," he said. "I wasn't sure—"

"Where's Garra?" asked Del, remembering the horrific scene on the beach before he'd taken off into the sky. "She's not..."

"General Phrac is tending to her," he said, like he was stuck in a dream. "He says there's a chance...there's a—" He winced, and suddenly Del understood: he was feeling Garra's pain, through their bond. Whatever surgery Lathan was performing, Finnlay was experiencing it, too. Del knelt down next to him and held his hand in sympathy.

"Garra's in good hands," he said gently. "Have you—do you know where Etenia is?"

Finnlay shook his head blankly. "I...I lost track of her."

"But you've seen her? Since the battle?"

Finnlay blinked at Del. "Yes. She was helping with...with the wounded. She said she'd be right back, and she—" He winced suddenly, and Del wondered just how much pain Garra was going through. Finnlay was so pale, he looked like he might pass out.

300

"You did good today, Finnlay," said Del. "I know it doesn't feel that way, but it's true. We were lucky to have you. And when you and Garra are both healed, I hope you'll come back to the academy, help us train the next generation of riders."

Finnlay nodded like he'd heard the words, but they hadn't quite sunk in.

Then he said: "We won, didn't we?"

Del looked back toward the ocean and sighed. "I hope so. I really hope so."

Just then, Womp came skidding to a stop at the entrance to the alleyway, panting and out of breath. He nodded to Del and wheezed: "Sir, he's awake. The prisoner's awake."

Del remembered their captive, and his heart started racing once more. He needed to find Etenia, but he needed to deal with the Qapira first, or none of them would ever be safe again. He turned back to Finnlay to say goodbye, but something in his mind caught him, kept him there.

"Finnlay," he said, trying to find the words to go with the emotions he was feeling. "Make her happy, okay? Make Etenia happy."

Before Finnlay could answer, Del hurried off with Womp, and back through the crowds. They wove up, higher through the city, and then east toward the broken Seafall wall, down through a series of twisty, convoluted side streets, and into a run-down building. Del recognized it instantly: the hangout for the street kids, when they were hiding from the law. In normal times, it wasn't an especially safe place to be, but since the city was evacuated and the scarier criminals all gone, it was a brilliant place to hide a prisoner of war.

Womp led Del into a back room where four mages stood guard around the Qapiran commander. His wrists were bound with glowing magic shackles, and he was encased in a sphere that crackled with red energy —it looked painful to touch, so Del kept a safe distance.

"Thank you," he said to Womp, and then to the mages: "I'll be fine."

They ended the spells and filed out of the room, leaving Del alone with his prisoner, and more questions than he could possibly ever ask.

He noticed the commander's necklace was glowing white, and not red, which was a curious sight. He'd been out of the water for a long time now, so why wasn't it running out of power? Del gestured toward it.

"Got enough essence in there to last?" he asked, with a smirk.

The Qapiran sneered at him. "You do not scare me, human."

"Ah, true, I guess you were unconscious for the part where we sent your army scurrying back into the sea. Trust me, though, even if I don't scare you, your countrymen are plenty scared."

That earned him a hiss that sounded like a massive snake about to strike.

"Let's do this properly," said Del. "What's your name and rank?"

"You are not worthy of the answers you seek."

"All right, suit yourself. I'll call you Fish Face instead." This clearly irked the Qapiran, so Del leaned into it: "So tell me, Fish Face, does it make you sad to be beaten by a bunch of kids and baby dragons?"

Another hiss. "You are a disgrace, land-dweller!"

"I'll put that down as a 'yes'. Next question, Fish Face—"

Another hiss, louder this time. "That is not my name!"

"It is until you give me something better to say," said Del. "Or maybe I should just call you Puffer—"

"Asanu!" roared the Qapiran. "I am Asanu, first and only son of Empress Lomasi, long may she reign!"

Lomasi? The Empress of the Qapira? And this was her son? That changed the equation so completely, Del nearly gasped. On the one hand, Lomasi would probably want her son back very desperately, and Del knew full well that desperate people made very dangerous moves to get what they wanted. But at the same time, they suddenly went from having a decent bargaining chip to having as their prisoner one of the most important people in the Qapiran kingdom!

Del gathered his composure and said: "All right, Fish Face, let's—"

"Asanu!"

"What?"

"Asanu! My name is Prince Asanu! You said you would greet me by my proper name if I—"

"Actually, what I said was I wanted you to give me something better to say. And quite honestly, Fish Face versus Asanu? Fish Face wins."

Asanu leapt to his feet and bared his teeth at Del, only to be faced by two handfuls of magical flame. That quieted him down quickly.

"I wouldn't get too feisty," Del warned him. "I have a really bad habit of lighting you Qapirans on fire."

Asanu eased back, but didn't stop his furious glare. "You spend it so recklessly, he seethed. "You foolish child!"

"Spend what so recklessly?" asked Del, then noticed the flames in his hands and realized what Asanu was saying. "What, magic? We spend magic? Is that why you're here?"

Asanu sneered. "We never wished for this. We only wanted to slumber. But you took that option away when you attacked us."

"Attacked you?" said Del, anger rising. "You sent the Kraken to destroy Sivarna! You invaded Pothena with thousands of soldiers! If anyone's responsible for this, it's you!"

"When you fractured the stone, you made this conflict unavoidable. Without the stone, we cannot sleep. Without the stone, we will die."

"I don't understand," said Del. "How does a stone help you sleep? Or survive? Or anything?"

Asanu laughed, bitterly. "You do not understand because you cannot understand the mistakes you are making, even now in this moment. You still think your magic is endless. Ubiquitous. Everlasting."

"And it's not, for you?" asked Del. "So that's why you're trying to steal the dragon eggs? To replace the magic you lost?"

"No, it is too late for that now," said Asanu. "We were hunting for enough magic to repair our stone and return to our slumber. You could have given us what we needed, and we would have left you in peace. But now there is no choice for us, no other way forward but to seize all we can find, and use it to survive."

He took hold of the necklace, cradling the gem in his hand as it glowed softly. "For the first time in my lifetime, we have filled these things with enough essence to survive weeks out of water. We are no longer fighting for our peace, land-dweller. We are fighting for our lives."

He sat back down, interlacing his long, spindly fingers like he was preparing to meditate. "We will have the magic you take for granted. It is a certainty. And when we are done, this land—and all land—will be nothing but ashes and dust."

And then Prince Asanu, first and only son of Lomasi, Empress of the Qapira, closed his eyes, and spoke no more.

CHAPTER 34

The Old City was alive in a way it never had been before. The mages had created magical lanterns that were floating in the air, and there was music and dancing, and whatever food they could find. The citizens of Pothena, rich and poor alike, were cheering and singing and carrying on like there was no tomorrow—because there very nearly hadn't been one, after all.

Del still hadn't managed to find Etenia, but he was, by default, a guest of honor—so he spent a lot of his time fielding well-wishes and thank yous from just about everyone he saw. A councilman even stopped him to offer him a seat once they made it back down the mountain again. Del politely declined, on account of having an actual job to do.

The newest recruits were telling each other stories of the exploits they all knew were lies, but they laughed and cheered anyway. Womp was recounting how he single-handedly thwarted a massive Qapiran warrior with nothing but his wits—even though he'd spent the whole battle safely in the rear. Even Tommen was laughing, which made Del's heart hurt as much as it brought him joy.

As Del approached, Lufien stood atop a table and raised a glass in the air and called out: "In honor of the proud defenders of Pothena! May their memories never die!" Del was so afraid of what he'd say next, given the arrogance he'd shown the last time Del had seen him. "To Safrin!" shouted Lufien, and Tommen broke down crying. Then, to everyone's surprise, Lufien jumped off the table and wrapped his arms around Tommen to comfort him. "She was the bravest there was," he said, his voice breaking. "She was the best of all of us. To Safrin!" and the students all cheered.

"To Calder!" shouted someone else, and another cheer erupted.

"To Massoro!" and on and on until they were cheering and crying as one, and Del found himself shouting his voice into oblivion just to keep up.

He'd hoped to find Etenia there, but the crowd was too thick to see that far. It seemed everyone he asked had talked to her already, and all he could do was chase the rumors of her existence.

Later, as they all found their own indulgences to chase, Del found himself deep in a conversation with Kinto, Taria and Wen, the mages from Mykos who had both taken quite the beating out on the beaches, but still looked alive with enthusiasm.

"No, I am saying next time, strike for the necklaces!" said Wen. "Without necklaces, they will die, yes?"

Kinto was refusing to budge on her stance: "Yeah, but what I'm saying is we can't reach the necklaces without taking out the shields, at which point—"

"Chamenos!" came a booming voice, and before Del knew it, they were surrounded by a handful of very big and very drunk Chamenan riders, including the one Del had met earlier, in the sky above Pothena. The big one patted Del on the back so hard, it felt like an assault, and laughed a booming laugh. "Chamenos, yes! Chamenos, yes!"

"Oh man..." sighed Del, as the other riders began bellowing "Chamenos yes! Chamenos yes!" over and over again.

When Kinto, Taria and Wen joined in, he took it as his cue to leave.

The party was just as loud out by the library, much to Del's chagrin. He was getting burned out by all social interaction—he needed some time alone. But as he approached, any thought of solitude melted away when he saw Lathan and Bettine holding hands. His smile was irrepressible.

"Well now, what have we here?" he laughed, giving them both a big hug, to all of their surprise. "We couldn't have done this without you two. You should be out there celebrating, too."

"This isn't our moment," said Lathan. "It's theirs. And yours." He patted Del's back. "You did a fine job teaching them. It's because of you that Pothena still stands at all."

"Yes," said Bettine. "And I'll be sure the history books properly record it, too. 'The Incredible Exploits of Searsha the Dragon and Her Brave Rider, Bel'."

Del glared at her. "You're hilarious."

"I agree." She grinned.

"You'll have to find a good name for Etenia, too," said Lathan, pondering options. "Egreria?"

Bettine swatted him. "That sounds rude!"

Lathan was about to try again when Del interrupted: "Have you seen Etenia anywhere? I haven't seen her since—"

His voice trailed off when he saw something move off to the side of the library—Etenia? But no—in the candlelight, he could see the contours of an arm in a sling. And a flash of red hair. Del gasped as he recognized Finnlay, and Yena in her half-burned armor—just as Finnlay wrapped his good arm around her, and she lifted her face up to—

Del stormed toward Finnlay, fists tightening at his sides, ears burning with anger as he watched Finnlay kiss the girl in his arms—and not just anyone, but Etenia's best friend! "Hey!" he shouted, as he barreled down at the pair, and before Finnlay could react, Del punched him in the face so hard, he fell right over.

The girl yelped and leapt away.

"I asked you one thing!" Del snarled at Finnlay. "To make Etenia happy! And now you do this?"

Finnlay held up his hands to defend himself. "Del, wait, it's not what you think!"

"Not what I think?" laughed Del, looking over at the woman Finnlay had been kissing. "I just caught you making out with...with..." He frowned when the face connected with a memory. "Yena? Y-you're both betraying her?"

Finnlay used the moment of confusion to get back to his feet. "I suppose this means she never told you."

Del took a step back. "Told me what?"

"Yena and I are in love. We're getting married."

"But you're marrying Etenia. You're engaged and—"

"It was an arranged marriage," said Finnlay, as if that explained everything. "We never wanted it, either of us, but our fathers insisted."

"So you cheated on her with her best friend?"

"No," said Yena, more gently than Del had expected, given the last time he'd seen her, she was firing Snapper cannons at Qapiran soldiers. "We never cheated. Etenia knew from the start. She was the only reason I was able to see Finnlay at all, by arranging secret meetings so our parents wouldn't suspect—"

"So wait," said Del, trying to wrap his mind around everything he was hearing. Trying to figure out what exactly the endgame for Etenia had been in all this. Forever be married to a man who was in love with her best friend? Forever be alone? "So you're saying that all this time, you and Etenia were never actually in love? That it was all an act? But—"

Finnlay looked so apologetic, it was painful to see. "I thought you knew," he said. "It was all just so we could convince her father to release her dowry."

Del took a step back, and then another. "I have to go," he said, suddenly realizing where Etenia must be, the only place he hadn't looked. "I have to go."

He raced for the main square, cutting through the crowds of revelers, heading for the edge of the Old City and the cliffside below. "Searsha!" he called out, audibly and through his bond. "I need a lift!"

Certainly, said Searsha, and Del leapt off the edge, into the open air. *Give me a few minutes to say goodbye.*

Del was falling at an incredible speed, watching the pointed peaks of the mountain below racing up toward him, and he closed his eyes and—

I kid, of course, she said, and swept in under him to carry him up, high above the Old City, to the valley between the two peaks.

She landed and he climbed off her back, giving her a quiet pat in thanks. Just before she left him there in the dwindling light of the longest day of his life, Searsha said. *If you don't tell her, I'll....*

But he didn't hear what else Searsha said, because only a few yards away Etenia was lying in the grass, watching the clouds float by.

Del made his way over, then lay down next to her with his hands on his chest, and didn't say a word. He wasn't entirely sure what he wanted to say. Or rather, he knew exactly what he wanted to say, but wasn't sure if he really should. Or even if he could. Every time he thought he'd built up the courage to try, his body made him pause, made him doubt himself, and stuck him back in silence again.

"Del," she said softly, without turning to look at him at all. "Can I ask you something?"

He swallowed slowly. "Y-yes?" he croaked.

"Are you..." she said, then took a pause that lasted a lifetime. "Are you insane?"

He frowned. "Wait, what?"

"I've been trying to figure out what you had planned with that spell of yours. You made a spherical field around yourself, and you somehow levitated into the air—"

"I made some shifting shields that let me—"

"I don't care how you did it, actually," she said. "See, what I'm trying to figure out is what you thought you were going to accomplish by doing it. You'd get way up high and then...what? Fall on them?"

"There was going to be fire," he said. "I was going to fill the sphere with fire and—"

"Ah, so you were going to incinerate yourself. That's great."

"No, I was going to hit the water hard enough to displace the water, and then the fire would explode out and it would be like a bomb and—" She smacked him on the forehead. "Hey!"

"Sometimes I really wonder about you," she said. "If you hit the water in a sphere, how is the fire going to get out, hmm? Ah, but it doesn't really matter, because once you burned yourself to death, both your spells would end and you'd basically just be a crispy corpse falling from the sky."

"It made sense at the time," grumbled Del.

"Next time you have a great idea, maybe tell me first."

"Oh, you're one to talk!" he said. "I can't believe I only just found out about Finnlay and Yena."

She quieted at that. "Oh. Yes. I was...I was trying to think of a way to—"

"But what I don't understand is: can you really just break off your engagement like that? I thought there were legacies or dynasties or something to protect."

Etenia shrugged, looking back at the sky. "Truthfully, Finnlay's family was never really keen on it to begin with," she said. "They thought we were social climbing to earn more respect in Seafall. But they wanted the Browder money, so, you know"—she shrugged. "They went along with the idea. We always thought if we had to go through with the wedding, we'd just... figure something out. So we could all be happy."

"I forget sometimes how much I love Seafall."

"Once my father...once he passed," she said, "I inherited the Browder estate myself, and finally had the freedom to do as I wanted. I honestly wasn't sure what that looked like, until Yena showed up in the battle— but then I knew for sure." She glanced at Del then, her expression both searching and somehow inscrutable. "I found Finnlay a little while ago and told him the wedding was off. That he would have to find someone new, like maybe a sea captain or something."

Del grinned. "And how did he take it?"

"There was a lot of cheering, as I recall." She laughed, and Del did, too. "But in truth, I couldn't have married Finnlay anyway. When it came right down to it, I'd have given up everything for—"

She turned her head, and he turned his, and they stared into each other's eyes so unexpectedly, Del's breath left him altogether. He had so many things he wanted to say, so many things he needed to say, but all that came to his lips was the question:

"For what?"

Etenia seemed stuck on a word, too. She started to say a thousand different things, and Del watched her mouth make every subtle change until she took a quick little breath and:

"The school."

He tried not to let his heartbreak show.

"Yeah, the school," he said, looking back at the sky. At the stars peeking through the nighttime sky.

"I never thought this would be my life," she said, and every word cut him like tiny blades he couldn't explain. "I never thought I would be living amongst dragons and mages and riders from far-off places, and—"

She reached over and took his hand in hers, lacing their fingers together and squeezing tight. Despite everything, despite the fact that it was the school Etenia loved, Del thought his heart might explode.

"We made this, Del," she said. "We took these ruins and we made a school. A community. A—"

"Family," said Del, and their eyes met again, and they both smiled.

"Family," she nodded. "Exactly." She leaned a little closer, her hair falling in front of her face as her eyes sought his. For a moment, he didn't quite understand what was happening—he was so mesmerized by her face, her eyes, her lips that it was all he could see—and then she kissed him.

It was tentative at first, like she was asking something, or testing, afraid he might say no. But when he kissed her back it unleashed all the passion they'd both been harboring all these months, overpowering them both. Del's senses were flooded—with the softness of her lips, the fragrance she was wearing, how close she was, her hand touching his chest, and so much more, he didn't know when he'd last taken a breath. He hadn't known what he'd wanted before this moment, and now that it was here, it was so surprising and familiar and it felt so right, he wished it would never end.

When it did, Etenia smiled at him and said: "I'd have given up every-thing for you."

Del's voice was barely more than a whisper. "Same here."

"Good," she said, and rested her head on his shoulder as they lay there together in the grass beneath the darkening sky, sharing a dream of what might come next.

EPILOGUE

Kosan had drawn the short straw. When the recruits had been preparing for the night of revelries, someone had mentioned how they should probably have a patrol of the beaches overnight, in case the Qapira tried to sneak back into the empty city again. It was a miserable job, and nobody wanted it, but Kosan had drawn the short straw and so here he was, walking up and down the beach with his dragon, Aggior, trying not to slip on the glassy parts, or stumble into the high tide.

"How much longer?" he asked, looking off toward the east.

Any second now, said Aggior.

"And you're sure they said we could leave once the sun came up?"

Ragir promised to relieve us come morn, he said. *She will be here.*

"Good, because I'm so tired, I can't even tell if I'm still walking or not." He sighed and looked up the mountain, to the place where the academy was nestled. "I wish I were tired from partying."

It did sound like they had an exciting evening, said Aggior.

Kosan stopped dead in his tracks. "You told me you couldn't hear them! You said we were too far away for the bond to work!"

Aggior looked sheepish. *I did not want to upset you further.*

"Great," grumbled Kosan, continuing on. "Makes me wonder what else you don't tell me. Like maybe Ragir isn't really punctual after all."

Aggior paused a moment. *I never specifically said she was punctual....*

Kosan dragged his hands down his face in frustration. "I just want to sleep. Please let me sleep."

Any second now, said Aggior, and then suddenly, from out on the water—

The sun came over the horizon.

"Yes!" cheered Kosan, jumping up and landing on the edge of some glassy beach—and then tumbling onto his backside with a crash. It hurt, but he didn't care. His shift was over! He was free! He could go home and—

The net came out of the water so fast, neither of them had a chance to react. The shimmering strands wrapped around them both, tightening on contact, and in a heartbeat Kosan felt his body go numb, even as he tried to escape. He reached out toward the mountain, far off in the distance—to his friends, to his teachers, to anyone who could save him—

And then the net was pulled into the surf, and they were both lost in the darkness.

END OF DRAGON REVIVAL
QAPIRA AWAKENING BOOK TWO

Dragon Ally, 29 December 2021

Dragon Revival, 26 January 2022

Dragon Peril, 23 February 2022

PS: Keep reading for an exclusive extract from the next book in the series, **Dragon Peril**. Also get a sneak peak into my next series, and an exclusive extract of **Dragon God (First Dragon Rider Trilogy Book One)**.

THANK YOU!

I hope you enjoyed **Dragon Revival**. Please don't forget to leave a review.

Receive free books, exclusive excerpts and be kept up to date on all of my new releases, when you sign up to my mailing list at AvaRichardsonBooks.com/mailing-list.

ABOUT AVA

Ava Richardson writes epic page-turning Young Adult Fantasy books with lovable characters and intricate worlds that are barely contained within your eReader.

She grew up on a steady diet of fantasy and science fiction books handed down from her two big brothers – and despite being dog-eared and missing pages, she loved escaping into the magical worlds that authors created. Her favorites were the ones about dragons, where they'd swoop, dive and soar through the skies of these enchanted lands

Stay in touch! You can contact Ava at:

f facebook.com/AvaRichardsonBooks
a amazon.com/author/avarichardson
g goodreads.com/avarichardson
BB bookbub.com/authors/ava-richardson

AVA RICHARDSON

DRAGON PERIL

QAPIRA AWAKENING BOOK THREE
DRACWYN PART III

BLURB

Del and his dragon riders must stop the Qapira to save their people…

The disastrous battle Del led has forced the Qapira to create a new magic stone, but at a deadly cost. With time running out, the only chance for Del and his dragon riders to save their home is to head the Qapira off before they can retrieve the raw materials needed. But he'll have to do it without help. With Etenia focused on protecting SeaFall,

Del alone will have to explore every possibility to save the human world from certain doom.

But the Qapira are relentless in their pursuit of survival, and stopping them for good will surely bring about even more destruction. Is violence the only answer to violence, and is Del ready to pay that price? Or can a street rat who's risen to be a protector of his people find a different way to save everything he holds dear?

Grab your copy of
Dragon Peril
Available February 23 2022
Available for pre-order now!
www.AvaRichardsonBooks.com

EXCERPT

Chapter One

The sea was so beautiful, it was a shame it wanted Del dead.

He sat there on the wind-worn roof of the Old City's meeting hall, staring out at the boundless horizon, trying to see the ocean for what it was, and not what it hid. It was such a mesmerizing sight—with the sun leaving a trail of yellow along it like a burst of fire—it was all the more tragic that he couldn't shake the memories of silver spears slicing through the surf to cut down his friends.

It was nearly four months later, and he could still hear their screams so clearly.

He wondered if he ever would learn to forget that day.

He wondered if he should.

Down below, far down the mountain and along the sandy shores, was Pothena, the city he'd grown up in, learned to hate, and tried to escape. But it was also home of the people who had rallied around him, had put their trust in him, and now depended on him to keep them safe. He'd grown up without anyone on his side, a bad day's begging away from dying in the streets. Now he couldn't find a moment's peace for all the people who sought him out every second of every day. The only way to catch his breath was to hide in the places no one thought to look, like the roof of the Old City meeting hall.

It was cold up here in the mountains. A brisk wind blew his dark hair this way and that, and made him hunch over, trying to conserve body heat that his lean, muscular body desperately needed to stay functional. For most of his life, his whole existence had been about finding a cool place to rest in the blazing sun. Now it was about holding on to those memories to keep himself warm at night.

Have you found it yet? came a voice straight into his head. It was Searsha, his dragon. When she had first hatched, Del had been shocked at the psychic bond they shared. A year and a half later, it was the most natural thing in the world for him, like breathing. It didn't bother him at all that he couldn't see her, because he could *feel* she was nearby.

"Just give me a minute, will you?" he sighed, lying back on the stone tiles.

I have, as a matter of fact, she replied. *Ten minutes, on top of the two you requested. But I fail to see how any amount of time will help you find your notebook if you are not actually looking for it.*

"I'm just—"

Perhaps it is a metaphorical search you are on—

"I need a few minutes to—"

—which would make sense, since I am certain you do not actually own a notebook.

"Searsha!" he snapped.

Del! she returned in kind. *You cannot hide forever. At some point you will have to face them.*

Del pressed his hands into his eyes in frustration. "They're giving me a headache."

Yes, well, at least you cannot hear them fighting from six miles away like I can. Now get up and resolve this before someone gets hurt.

Del sighed and set back up. The sea was ominous, but inside the meeting hall was dangerous. He begrudgingly paced his way to the edge of the roof, where the broken rain trough led back down to the ground at a funny, disjointed angle. He made one last check to be sure no one was watching, and then stepped onto the trough and slid down sideways. He took a few quick hops along the way to avoid the spots where the stone had crumbled apart, but landed on the cobblestone below with practiced grace. He couldn't help but smile. Riding that trough was one of the few joys he had left anymore—a reminder of the free spirit he used to be.

The closer he got to the front door of the meeting hall, the clearer the voices became, and the more he realized his ten minutes away had made things worse, not better.

"All right, I'm back," he said, waving a little hello as he came into the main room. The arguing stopped, briefly, which was like an instant relief for him—until he realized they were only taking a moment to present their arguments to him anew.

"Tell her she's being obstinate," said the silver-haired gentleman by the wall, face tense and eye twitching as he tried and failed to keep his composure. Lathan Phrac had been a powerful figure in his native

326

Sivarna, as a dragon trainer and general in their army. He still wore Sivarnan-style robes, which marked him as a distinguished figure deserving of respect. Here in Pothena's Old City, he was a senior magic instructor and a font of sage advice to any who sought him out. He was admired far and wide, except by—

"Obstinate?" shouted Bettine Staaf, already red-faced and on her way to a whole new shade of purple. "Please say you didn't just call me obstinate, you frumpy old mental sarcophagus!" Bettine was a professor of mythology from Pothena University, and one of the first supporters of their Old City dragon academy. She was a little younger than Lathan, and nowhere near as distinguished-looking, but she was absolutely impossible to ignore. She'd spent a lifetime being teased by her colleagues for her belief in dragons, and now that she was surrounded by the creatures, she was determined to never be talked down to again.

Unfortunately for everyone involved, Lathan had a knack for talking down to people.

"It's a matter of efficiency," said Lathan. "The students' schedules are already busy enough, without teaching them to speak a whole new language!"

"It's not a new language, you dry twig, it's—"

"Yes, yes, an ancient tongue pulled from the recesses of ancient Pothenian 'wisdom'."

Bettine scowled at him. "Don't think I didn't notice that."

Del's headache was getting worse by the second. Lathan and Bettine had been adversaries from the start, but ever since they'd become romantically involved, the intensity of their disagreements had esca-lated wildly. Rare was a morning that didn't start with them arguing about the breakfast menu, and how much better or worse things had been done in Sivarna.

"Guys, let's take a breath," said Del, trying his best to calm things down. "We can come back to this another time. There's no rush—"

"No rush?" said Lathan. "Del, this is of the utmost importance. If we don't act now—"

"There you go again," said Bettine. "Quantity over quality."

Lathan pointed out the door angrily. "We had four accidents last week! Four! Each one caused by a lack of communication, because we have too many students from too many places, and they don't understand what each other is saying!"

Bettine threw her hands up. "Hence the need for a common tongue!"

"Or a spell that bridges the gap with magic," said Lathan, turning to Del again. "We need to make a choice, and start rolling it out as soon as possible. We either waste countless hours teaching our students a dead language that is foreign to everyone—"

"Ha!" snapped Bettine. "Or we force our students to waste their magical resources on something as simple as saying hello. Which, in the heat of battle, will be a top priority, I'm sure."

The heat of battle. The spears slicing through the air. The screams. Again, the screams. Four months later, and it was still all anyone could think about. When the dragons practiced spinning in midair, it was because of memory of that day. When they worked out hand signals to communicate from a distance, it was because of that day. When they said their solemn prayer to the fallen before heading out on a mission, it was because of the horrors they had seen that day.

The Qapira had come from the depths of the ocean to ravage Pothena. A massive force of silver-speared soldiers had marched out of the water, fought and killed mercilessly, and would have decimated the whole city if Del and the dragon riders hadn't—

328

It had been four months of living on edge. A year waiting for a lookout to scream: "They're back! The Qapira are back!" and then they'd be back in the nightmare all over again.

The heat of the battle. It was all that mattered, really. Everything else was a distraction.

Lathan looked ready to snap. "It's up to you, Del," he said, in a decent approximation of calmness. "We have one vote for magic, and one for mythology. You're the tiebreaker."

Del frowned at that. "What about Etenia? Doesn't she get a vote?"

"She said it's up to you," said Bettine, staring at him so intensely he thought her eyes might pop out of her head. "She said she trusts you to choose my—"

"Yours?" sneered Lathan.

They started bickering again, as Del turned and headed for the door. Etenia wasn't going to saddle him with this mess alone. The two of them had started the dragon academy together, but over the last six months, she'd been less and less involved in the big decisions—much to his chagrin. She tried to frame it as giving him more authority over the issues he most cared about as chief dragon trainer, but sometimes it just felt like she was trying to avoid getting bogged down in petty squabbles.

Where are you going? asked Searsha, before he even made it to the door.

"I'm going to get Etenia and force her to pick a side," he said. "I'm not doing this alone."

I am afraid you are, said Searsha. *Etenia left for Seafall hours ago.*

Del stopped dead in his tracks. "What, again?"

An unexpected council meeting, it seems. You will need to make this choice by yourself.

"What would you choose?" he asked her. "If it were up to you, what would you prefer?"

It is a curious notion for dragons, she said. *Both sides have merit. We already communicate via magic bond, as Lathan suggests—but we do so in our own shared language, as Professor Staaf suggests. But I imagine hoping humans could be as magnificent as dragons is a fool's errand.*

Del was about to deliver a wisecrack back at her when he stuck on something she'd said: "You speak a common language?"

Yes, she said. *We think in dragon, but we speak in human. When I talk to Cember about you, I have a richer vocabulary to draw on. Did you know dragons have over eighty words to describe disappointment?*

Del ignored the taunt and turned back to Lathan and Bettine, calling out: "I've made my decision!"

They both stopped arguing and stared at him with hope and dread in their eyes. "Well? Who did you choose?" asked Lathan.

"Let him down easy," said Bettine.

"Neither," said Del, and waved them onward. "And both! Come on, I'll show you!"

Dragon's Mage (Ragond's Witch Hunter Book One)

BLURB

At sixteen, Yanna Gray is part of her family's witch hunting enterprise, helping rid the world of anything—and anyone—magic. But her militant life goes south when an enchanted amulet goes missing. Before Yanna can reclaim the artifact, the thief opens an interdimensional portal flinging Yanna into a frightening magical world.

Ragond is straight out of the forbidden fairy tales Yanna once read. Mythical creatures, witches, and mages live in harmony with humans. Here, all she's grown up believing is turned on its head—especially when she discovers her own magical abilities.

Without access to a portal to Earth, Yanna is invited to shelter at Stonehaven—the training ground for witches, mages, and dragon riders—where she discovers true friendship, camaraderie, and a surprising bond with an ancient dragon. But all too quickly, Yanna's magic-hunting past catches up to her.

Now, to save her friends and the dragon who partnered with her, Yanna must decide what she believes and who to trust.

Or her past might become Ragond's downfall.

Queen of the Dragons' Ava Richardson invites you to immerse yourself in a dragon-filled world with epic magic, fearless heroes, and the deep bond between dragon and rider.

Grab your copy of
Dragon's Mage
Publishing April 27 2022
Available for pre-order soon
www.AvaRichardsonBooks.com

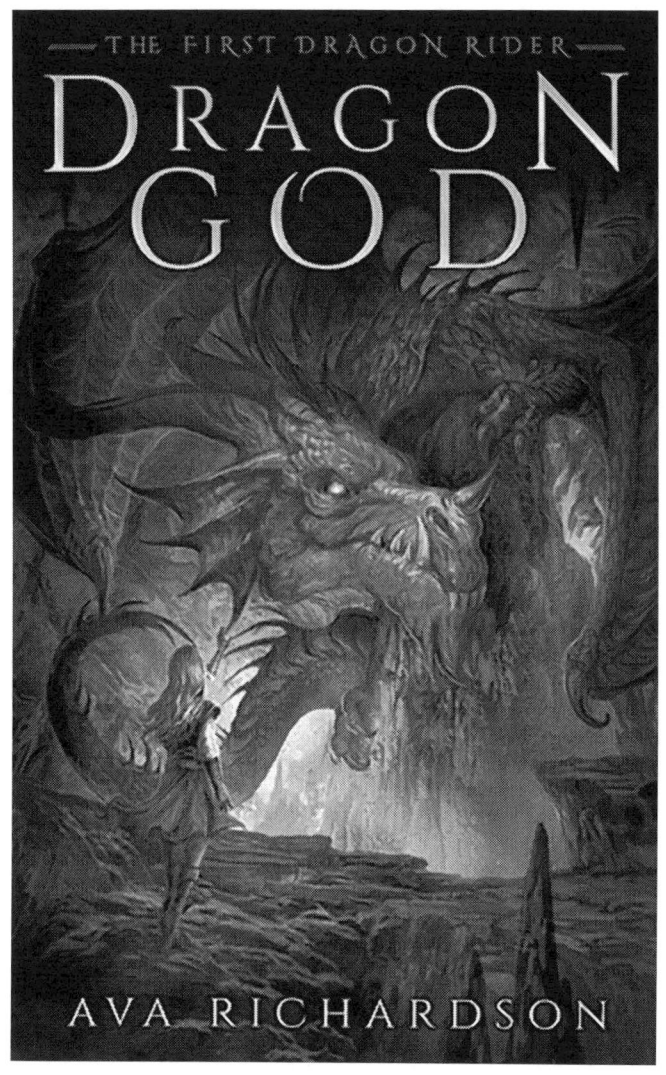

BLURB

The new world is calling...

Neill Torvald is desperate to prove himself—his father's warlord kingdom depends on him. When a vicious attack on the way to the Draconis Order monastery nearly kills him, it becomes clear that grave trials await him on this path. Jodreth, the wise monk who saves his life, advises caution upon entering the sacred halls. His mission is to learn arcane magic from the monks that will help to cement his father's power, but Neill will need more than magical arts alone to navigate the challenges before him.

Among the monks' students, Neill meets the lovely and mysterious Char, who senses evil deep within the ranks of the Draconis Order's members. She takes him to a dragon she has raised, Paxala, and the three of them become fast friends. Neill soon grows in strength as he and his fellow students gain ancient knowledge, and his closeness to Char blossoms into something more.

But when Neill 's brothers grow impatient and attack the monastery in a bid to seize power, he will have to decide where his loyalties lie: with his warlord father's domain, or the new friends he has made in the wider world.

Get your copy of ***Dragon God*** at
AvaRichardsonBooks.com

EXCERPT

Chapter One

Mired

The monastery hadn't *looked* that far away on the map, but now, my boots thick with mud and my pony refusing to take a step further, it felt like it might as well be half the world away.

"You'd need a blinking dragon just to get up there," I found myself muttering to the rangy, stubborn steed that my older brother Rik had sworn was the best of the bunch, and would take me all the way to the Draconis Monastery without slipping a shoe. This, like most of the other things that fell from out of my older brother's mouth, I knew to be a lie, but something in me had felt sympathy for the tough little pony.

You and me both are pretty unwanted, huh? I had thought at the time, and in return for my compassion, so far, the small mountain pony had kicked, bucked, bit, and balked at every boulder and hill and river on the week-long journey between the fortifications of the Torvald Clan and Mount Hammal. That was where the Draconis Monastery sat, and where I had been sent by my father, Clan Chief Malos Torvald.

But at least every movement I coaxed out of this pony got me nearer to my goal—not just the monastery itself, but to finding the information my father had supposedly sent me here to gather. That's what I kept telling myself, anyway, as I pulled at the pony's reins, and it took a halting step forward before stopping yet again. In all likelihood, my father had sent me here just to get me out of the way—the unlucky, unloved, illegitimate son that I was. The valley that I was laboring through was little more than a mountain ravine, tall rocky walls on either side, dripping with ferns and the constant rivulets of ice-melt from the mountain above. Why on earth had I ever decided to come this way? But I knew why. Ravines meant water, and I'd hoped to find a pleasant stream with low banks—an easy fjord to cross. Instead, on either side of the fast-flowing water was just heavy silt and mud. The light was green-tinged and shadowed by the overhanging vines and trees above, but through a gap in the undergrowth I could make out the slopes of Mount Hammal rising higher and higher, the trees thinning and being replaced with scattered patches of frost and snow   and there, sticking out from the top, the dark stone walls of the Draconis Monastery itself, impossibly small and toy-like.

Like the wooden forts and soldiers that my brothers were always playing with, I thought. It was hard to imagine that up there, on top of the world and so close to the cold and clear sky anyone could make a life, and certainly not monks in robes.

"And certainly not me, either!"

The Draconis Monastery was the last place I wanted to be. I should be at my father's side, like his other sons, learning how to be a warlord, learning how to lead our clan. But no. I was being sent to the middle of nowhere on a fool's errand, to be locked away and forgotten, most likely. I kicked at the mud in frustration, but with a sucking schloop all that I succeeded in achieving was removing my boot from my cotton leggings, and sending it sploshing across the gully.

"Great. Absolutely *great!*" I wanted to shout, but instead I kept my voice low. I'd already made enough noise and to be honest, I was slightly concerned about the fact that there were supposed to be dragons up on the mountain somewhere. Right now, I couldn't decide just what was worse: being eaten by a dragon in the middle of nowhere or spending the next few years of my life freezing my fingers off as a ward of the Draconis Monastery. At least a dragon might be more interested in my pony than in me?

Crack.

The sound that traveled over the watery glops and gloops all around me was sharp-edged and sudden.

It must just be a branch falling somewhere, I thought as I retrieved my dripping wet boot and bending to put it back on. It was freezing, and I knew that I would be lucky if I didn't end up getting a cold from this.

"We should never have come this way at all," I muttered to the pony, that had now stopped moving and was instead standing almost stock still but for a faint tremor running through his body.

"What have you seen, girl?" I whispered, turning my head to follow the direction of her pointing ears and flaring nostrils.

Thump-crack. This time, the sound was heavier as well as sharp, like something dragging itself across a rock, or claw or a scaled body...

"Easy now, easy there." The hairs on the back of my neck stood up as I slowly straightened. Dragons weren't supposed to eat people anymore. Not the dragons of the Middle Kingdom anyway, were they? The Old Queen negotiated with them to stop doing that, and my father had said it was rumored the Draconis Monks could control dragons. But so far, every market and crossroads inn between here and the Torvald Clan lands had been filled with stories of people who had lost sheep, cows, or goats, of distant farmhouses seen burnt out on the edge of the wilds. What was to stop a hungry dragon from eating a solitary sixteen-year-old boy and his horse if it was hungry, no matter what some dead queen or some bookish monk had said? I bit my lip in worry (a habit that my dad said made me look weak), my hand moving to my belt for the sword that should be there.

Oh no. I'd left it still wrapped and tied beside my saddle, along with the shield, helmet, and anything else that I could possibly use to help defend myself.

"Pssst! Stamper, Stamper come here!" I hissed at the rangy pony using the name that I had optimistically given it when we had set out (aside from 'you mule' and 'no, please don't do that!').

Crack-thump!

Stamper's eyes rolled white and he leapt and spun, yanking the reins from my hand as he bolted away from the sound, clattering up the shallower side of the mountain gulley as if he hadn't been stuck at all. "Stamper, no!" I shouted, but it was no good. The pony was gone, carrying my saddle, blankets, warm clothes, food, and most important of all – all of my armaments. If whatever was making that noise was as terrifying as Stamper seemed to think it was, I was going to need my weapons. My heart was hammering in my chest as I crouched, bunching my hands in front of me as if to do...*what? What was I going to do to a dragon, or a bear, or whatever was up there?*

337

"Just keep it together, Torvald…" I tried to tell myself, breathing out through my nose. "You are a son of Torvald. You are strong." After not hearing anything for several long moments (including any sign of Stamper) my heart slowed, and I turned to splosh out of the mud, scraping and climbing up the bank behind the pony. *At least I'm only a little way away,* I grumbled to myself. *I might be able to make it up to the monastery above me without that stupid horse…* I had only just got my fingers to the top of the wooded incline when the source of the previous scraping, thumping, and snapping noise became abundantly clear.

Four men were creeping and climbing their way up the stony bank by the side of the river gulley, and from the look on their faces and the weapons in their fists they had clearly only one intention in mind, and it didn't look good for me.

Oh no… My heart hammered in my chest. I thought that I had managed to make it all the way to Mount Hammal without encountering any bandits or rogues on the road. It looked like I had been wrong.

Before I had time to recall the many contingency plans I'd brain-stormed in the event I encountered trouble on my journey, the nearest man jumped at me, bringing his hatchet downwards in a terrible blow.

Get your copy of ***Dragon God*** at
AvaRichardsonBooks.com

Made in United States
Orlando, FL
25 January 2022

14061923R00193